The Winds of God

ANNE M. BRADY

CENTURY PUBLISHING
LONDON

First published in Great Britain in 1985 by
Century Publishing Co. Ltd,
Portland House, 12–13 Greek Street,
London W1V 5LE

ISBN 0 7126 0440 5

Printed in Great Britain by
St Edmundsbury Press, Bury St Edmunds, Suffolk
Bound by Butler & Tanner Ltd, Frome, Somerset

'I sent my ships to fight against men, and not against the winds and waves of God.'

Philip II of Spain

PROLOGUE

HE HEARD the footsteps outside the door of the bed-chamber and sat up, almost breathless for a moment with excitement. He had come! He was here at last! The Irish boy! The door creaked open on its unoiled hinges, and Alice whispered, 'Master Ralph! Master Ralph! Be thee awake still?'

He pulled back the bed-curtains and saw that she was alone. Lay down again, watching her come near the bed, candlelight spilling over her pale green bodice, softening the red of her cheeks.

'Oh Alice, when will he come? I've been waiting all day long!'

'Poor little mommet. 'Tis time thee wor asleep.'

'But –'

'He'll come. Soon.'

Smelling faintly of sweat and beeswax she bent and kissed Ralph on the forehead. In some ways it was like being kissed by his mother. But in other ways it was entirely different, and as Alice reached out her red, chapped hand to tuck in his covers his eyes were on the shadow of her mouth. Her hand touched the warm, smooth skin of his neck and she straightened up and whispered, somewhere between a laugh and a sigh, 'Thee'll soon be too big for me to tuck in!' He said nothing, but when she made to pull across his bed-curtains, he stopped her, watching every movement of her body until she blew out the candle.

'Goodnight to 'ee, Master Ralph,' she said softly from the doorway.

1

'Goodnight, Alice! And – and thank you!'

The door closed quietly.

I shall never, *never* sleep, he thought. And slept, and woke to the airless darkness of his curtained bed, a trickle of sweat between his shoulder-blades. Remembered the boy, the waiting. The son of Cormac O'Boyle, an Irish chief, brought here to Somerset as a hostage for his father's good behaviour. An Irish savage, in fact! Or so Lady Jane thought, anyway. 'Likely verminous', she had said at suppertime. 'The child must have a sulphur bath as soon as he arrives – and his hair clipped, of course!'

Would he even speak English? But the effort of staying awake was too much, and Ralph was drifting into sleep again, away from his bedroom, away from Tascombe, away from being the unwanted poor relation, the unwanted orphan, the 'little papist wretch' as Lady Jane called him. He was at home again in Bunsery. His mother still alive, his father happy. So that he opened his eyes reluctantly, to see Alice standing in the open doorway of his bed-chamber, a lighted candle held high in her hand.

'Alice?' He sat up, rubbing his eyes. 'What – ' His voice was blurred with sleep, with remembered happiness.

She turned to look over her shoulder, and beckoned someone behind her, hidden for the moment by her full skirt. The Irish boy! Ralph knew it before he was even properly awake, before he saw him. And he swung his long, thin legs over the side of the bed and almost ran to the doorway, jerking to a stop there as if he had run a race.

The boy tried to hide himself again, shrinking back behind Alice.

How small he is, Ralph thought, with a kind of anger, as if somehow the boy had deceived him. He looks to be only eight or nine – and I'm eleven! But – but perhaps Irish boys are smaller than we are?

The boy stared back at him; dark pools of eyes, black with the intensity of his thoughts or fears, or perhaps just with tiredness; his mouth pinched, in a white, exhausted face. He wore strange breeches and even stranger chequered hose, and a bright yellow shirt of a kind Ralph had never seen before.

2

But he certainly did not seem to be a savage. Trim and clean. And something about the set of the small head with its thick brown curls that Ralph half recognized without being able to put a name to it. Was it pride? Could savages be proud?

How young he was! He would be useless for anything. Did he not even know how to shake hands? But just as he was about to withdraw his own hand the boy put out his, small and cold and dry, like a claw.

Alice put the candle on the window ledge and opened the oak chest that stood between the two beds. She took out a nightshirt many times too big, and handed it to the boy.

'Off wi' thy cloas an' put this on 'ee do!' She made to take off his yellow linen shirt, but the child drew back and the fear in his eyes made Ralph feel somehow ashamed. With a shrug of her plump shoulders Alice said, 'Do it thyself then, if that's the way o' it!' She held out the ridiculously oversized nightshirt and the child took it slowly from her, looking down at it with an expressionless face. He is terrified, Ralph thought. Like a bird in a snare. And part of his mind longed to shake him, to punish him for being so small and stupid.

'Goo'night to 'ee both then!' Alice said. The door closed behind her and the boy turned away and sat down on the side of his bed clutching the nightshirt to his thin chest with both hands.

Ralph made a brief pantomine of undressing and pulling on the shirt, and suddenly too sleepy to try to do any more for the boy, he went over to his own bed and lay down. How long would it take him to learn English? And what did it matter anyway? The disappointment was like the taste of the wormwood powder Alice had sprinkled in his bed against the fleas. He was almost asleep, his eyes closing, closed. Was asleep. And in the moment before he let go and dropped into the darkness, he remembered something – tried to remember. The candle! Alice always saying not to let it burn out for fear of fire. He sat up, the darkness falling away, and looked across at the other bed, and the circle of candlelight. And was shocked into complete wakefulness.

'No! Oh, no!' he breathed. How *could* God do such a thing to him? To pretend to give him a friend and then –

3

'You're just – just a GIRL!' Ralph shouted, and she turned her head to stare at him, without lowering her arms, the nightshirt held above her naked, girl's body, her mouth opened slightly, her eyes huge with new fear.

CHAPTER 1

NEXT MORNING, when Alice came in to wake him, Ralph told her he would have no girl sharing his bed-chamber with him, and Alice's mouth had fallen open in astonishment.

'He – he be a – *girl*, Master Ralph?'

'Yes,' Ralph said shortly. 'A girl.' He put all the contempt he could into the word.

Alice looked across at the child, still fast asleep, curled up under the bedcovers. 'Well, I never did hear o' such a thing!'

'She'll not sleep with *me*, that's certain!' To Ralph's annoyance Alice started to laugh, until he thought she'd never stop.

'Some day – some day, Master Ralph, I'll remind 'ee – ' she gasped, but when at last to his great relief she grew serious again she agreed to move the girl to another room and he went down to breakfast in the great hall in slightly better humour.

For the next few days he scarcely saw the Irish girl at all, and when he did she was either crying in some dark corner or hiding behind Alice's skirts, peering round them from time to time and still wearing her outlandish clothes. But then, to his acute embarrassment she began to follow him around like a lost puppy. He would glare at her, make signs at her to go away but it made no difference. She would retreat a few yards, and as soon as he had turned his back she would follow him again. Alice had found her a kind of white shift which like the nightshirt was far too big for her, and now, in the most unlikely places, he would find the girl trailing

5

along behind him in this absurd garment, tripping over the hem and pulling it up with her small hands. It was really quite infuriating. He shouted at her, even cursed her, using all the oaths he knew, but of course she didn't understand a word he said and just stood where she was, looking at him with her finger in her mouth. Yet Alice had told him that she had already picked up a few words of English, so she was not simple-minded, and anyway, surely she could have guessed his meaning from his tone of voice? No, she was just being silly, like all girls.

Then one morning Alice brought her into the classroom to Parson Dagge and she was put to sit at the very back of the room, behind the three youngest boys. She sat there quietly all morning, not daring even to make a mark on her slate, and when they had finished lessons for the day and were saying their final prayers, Parson Dagge looked down at her and intoned through his long nose, 'Let us pray that our divine Father who in His – ah – wisdom has sent this young – ah – creature to us – let us pray that He will show us how to save her papist soul from damnation, and open her mind to our teaching. Amen.'

'Amen,' muttered the children between sniggers, and their teacher lifted his cane threateningly.

That afternoon the girl actually followed Ralph down to the stables. She stood in the busy yard watching him mount, her dark eyes full of silent entreaty. It was a hot, sultry day and he was longing to get away up into the hills.

'What do you want?' he said crossly, but of course she didn't or couldn't answer, and he rode out of the yard in a fine temper, leaving her still standing there.

Not a leaf stirred in the elms that lined the avenue as he rode past, and he slowed to a walk for it was really stiflingly hot. But chancing to look back at the house he saw to his horror a small figure trotting after him. The girl.

'Pox on you anyway!' he shouted as he'd heard Sir Edward do so often, digging his heels once more into the mare's sides. He galloped on down the avenue, not looking back until he was on the track that led up into the hills. There was no sign of the girl now, thank heaven, and he slowed to a walk, hearing the first rumbles of thunder in the distance and soon forgetting all about her.

Gradually, like a stalking beast the thunder came closer, and the smell of furze was thick and heavy in the still air. The mare plodded on, sweat glistening on her satiny neck, and he stopped to rest her, looking back the way he had come. And then, far back along the track he saw something move. A sheep? But it wasn't the right size. It was – God in heaven! – it was that wretched girl again! She must have taken a short cut. Little fool, he thought angrily. Serve her right if she got lost! He kicked the mare into a gallop again, and when he next looked he could see no sign of her. She must have turned back – but he'd really have to do something about it.She was becoming an absolute *pest*! Just then there was a blinding flash of lightning and a crash of thunder that sounded like Tascombe House toppling, and suddenly the rain came. The first drops gathered momentum, turned into a torrent and he thought of the girl. She couldn't possibly have got back to the house or even near it in time. Poor little wretch! She'd be terrified of the storm. All girls were. Even Alice was very silly about it, throwing her apron over her head and hiding in closets at the first rumble of thunder. Curse it anyway, he'd have to go back and look for her – he'd probably find her hiding under a bush paralysed with terror – if he could find her at all. At that thought he turned the mare's head uneasily and galloped back the way he had come, peering through the scuds of rain, his hair plastered to his head, his shirt and breeches clinging to his body like a second skin. Damn all girls to hell, anyway! And then he saw her. Saw the little, straight back of her as she ran down the track towards Tascombe, slipping and sliding in the mud, the hem of her shift trailing behind her like the train of some grand lady's dress.

She heard him coming, and stopped to wait, and when he reined in she pushed the wet curls off her face and looked up at him. Her face was pinched and white as it had been on the night of her arrival, but her eyes were steady enough. He reached down his hand to her and for the first time since she had come to Tascombe she smiled, a smile of pure delight, and then taking his hand she was up behind him in a flash, as if she had done it many times before. 'Hold tight!' he shouted, and her matchstick arms tightened round his waist with surprising strength as though she guessed what he was saying. Then they were off and away through the driving rain while the lightning split the sullen sky and thunder rolled and crashed above their heads. But even as they galloped up the avenue the worst of the storm was over, and as they turned into the yard the rain stopped as suddenly as it had begun.

Ralph threw the reins to a stable-boy and led the girl by the hand into the kitchen where he found a still ashen-faced Alice. She looked down at the pair of them, at the water running off them and forming small pools on the flagstones.

'Mercy me!' she gasped. 'You were out in all o' that? Oh, Master Ralph! And the little 'un too? She must ha' been frightened sick!'

'She wasn't afraid at all,' Ralph said slowly, 'but she's wet through.'

'I'll dry the poor lamb down in front o' the fire now,' Alice said, 'but do 'ee go and change afore 'ee catches cold.'

'Yes, I'll change,' Ralph said impatiently, 'but Alice, find her some decent clothes to put on – a dress – a *real* dress – '

The new note of authority in his voice surprised himself and Alice's eyes widened, while the girl looked gravely from one to the other of them.

'Yes, Master Ralph. Surely.'

He didn't see the girl until next morning in class, and he scarcely recognized her at first. But she was the only girl child in the house, Sir Edward to his delight siring only males – even his bastards were said to be all boys – so he knew it must be she. Somewhere Alice had found her a blue, tight-waisted dress with a long, full skirt and her curls, which in daylight were the colour of pale chestnuts, were tied back with a ribbon of the same colour. But not only the dress and ribbon gave her new status that morning. Parson Dagge with his teacher's eye had seen that she recognized the odd word of Latin. ''Tis a strange thing indeed,' he said weightily, 'that – this – ah – young – person – from the most barbarous part of a most barbarous country – should be familiar with even one word of the noble language of the Aeneid – ' And before the morning was out, with his slight knowledge of the celtic races and the few words of English the girl had picked up, he actually elicited her name. Una. Ralph had never heard anyone called that before, but it had a not unpleasant sound to it he thought, and it was mercifully short.

Una came down to the stables that afternoon too, and this time, instead of trying to send her away he told the stable-boy to bring him a small pony usually ridden by the younger children. He intended to teach her to ride, feeling that in some way he owed her that much. But he soon discovered she could ride as well if not better than himself, and with her skirt tucked up above her small, bony knees they cantered up into the hills together.

But although she could ride, and soon could speak more than a few words of English, she couldn't swim, so he brought her down to the river which bordered the estate and gave her her first swimming lesson. She was very nervous, but after a few lessons she lost her fear and soon could swim well enough. When she was swimming she used to wear an old pair of breeches, as he did, and she would pull off her dress and plunge into the water with little shrieks of joy. But on the very hot days they would not bother to wear anything and jumped in mother naked, frolicking in the water like the seals Parson Dagge had told them about but which Ralph for one had never seen. And now Ralph wanted her to stay in Tascombe – this girl who had been sent across the sea by her father to fool the queen's men. Sent to save her brother from being held hostage. Ralph knew that God had after all sent him a friend, and he kept hoping that no one would come to bring her home, that Sir Edward would not want to send her back. But no word came from Ireland and for all the notice Sir Edward, or Lady Jane for that matter, took of her, she might indeed have been a lost puppy.

So time passed, and Ralph and Una became inseparable, drawn together not only by friendship but by their common fate. Two prisoners in a largely hostile place. There to learn to conceal their thoughts, their religion. 'Dirty papists', the

9

other children called them sometimes, jealous of their closeness. 'Rattling their beads together!' – which in fact was a foolish taunt, for Una certainly seemed to have had no formal teaching in her religion before she came to Tascombe. Indeed, all her memories of her home were now so hazy as to border on fantasy. The towering, towering mountains that shut out the world. The miles upon miles of sandy seashore. Her father's vast herds of cattle. His endless fights with neighbouring chiefs. The only gentle memory she had was of her mother, and nothing of real substance remained of that save the memory of love.

When she reckoned she was about thirteen however, Una began to change. In the summer when they went swimming she not only insisted on wearing breeches, she wore an old shirt as well, and there was a new constraint between herself and Ralph. She began to take offence easily, walking haughtily away from him for no apparent reason, and coming back the following day to make amends. He found it all very puzzling, but he himself was changing too. Games they used to play together bored him – not that he was bored by her. He still wanted to be with her – but – He could not put into words what he felt, what he wanted of her. It was Lady Jane, however, who really put an end to their childhood idyll.

For Lady Jane suddenly decided to take notice of Una. The mistress of Tascombe, Sir Edward's third wife, had found a new toy to play with. From now on, instead of being with Ralph, Una had to sit with her for long hours in the withdrawing room, head bent over an embroidery frame or, worse still, walk slowly up and down the rose garden, while Lady Jane sickened her with stories about her young men, simpering at jokes that Una couldn't understand. She told Ralph that she had even begun to pity old Sir Edward, with his sagging jowls and his heavy paunch and the gout that plagued him night and day. Her only escape was when one of the young men came to call. She would go and look for Ralph then and if she could find him they would have a little time together. For his part, he missed Una as much as she did him, but at least he could be glad it was not Sir Edward who had taken a fancy to her.

10

And then, one day when he was complaining to Alice that he missed Una and she was laughing at him, her broad, strong face good-humoured and yet malicious at the same time, reminding him of his indignant rejection of 'that pest' when Una first arrived, Lady Jane overheard Ralph, and said, with her insolent, affected drawl, 'Why boy, here's a lovesick whine if ever I heard it!'

He had felt his cheeks burn with shame and anger, and would have flung away from her if the necessity of respect for her had not kept him facing her. And as he stood there, crimson cheeked, as tall now as Lady Jane herself – and she was a tall woman – her eyes looked into his as if they were seeing him for the first time. A slow, peculiar change came into her smile. From arrogance and condescending scorn for a stupid boy – it became – became what? He did not know, but he was not able to meet those eyes that seemed to be prying into his very soul.

'Why boy –' she drawled. 'Why so flushed?' She touched his cheek with her long, thin fingers, letting the tips rest beside the corner of his mouth. 'If you miss your friend so much, come walk with her – and me – in the rose garden this afternoon. It's time you began to learn the courtier's arts, if you are to make your way in the world.'

He had mumbled something sullen and incomprehensible, intending to convey that he had no wish in the world to be a courtier, or to make his way, or do any civilized, grown-up thing that involved walking in rose gardens with someone like Lady Jane. But all that was audible was a wordless mutter that could have been 'Thank you ma'am' or anything else, and Lady Jane smiled again.

'After dinner then, and you shall begin to learn how to please a lady.'

'Ye've begun that already, seems like!' Alice said, but only when Lady Jane was safely out of earshot.

'What do you mean?' Ralph whispered, suddenly and inexplicably angry with her.

'Why nowt, nowt at all, Master Ralph. What 'ud a foolish servant woman think o' meaning when her betters take it into their heads to play games?' And she went off, laughing again before he could think of an answer.

He had sworn to himself that he would not go – had found himself impatient for dinner to be over so that he could say he would not go – and had followed obediently as Lady Jane beckoned Una to follow her out of the great hall, broadening her somewhat insolent summons to include him. As for her current *cavaliere servente* as she called him, he was at the door already, bowing and showing a padded leg and a self-satisfied smile, a roll of paper thrust into his doublet advertising the fact that he was a poet. He was a neighbour's son who had been a year in London seeking his fortune, and had instead lost most of his inheritance at play and among poets and play-actors – and worse folk still according to gossip in the servants' hall. A fair-haired young man who might have made a reasonable imitation of a human being if London had not turned his head and ruined his constitution. Now he even spat poetically, and coughed into a scented handkerchief when he met any country people, as if to say. 'La, how their stink chokes me!'

But if Ralph had hoped that the poet would absorb Lady Jane's attention and leave him free to whisper to Una as they walked two or three paces behind their elders, he was very much disappointed. Lady Jane required attention from everyone who accompanied her – not simple attendance, but attention, constant and devout. She had dropped her nosegay. She desired a flower plucked to augment it or replace it. She requested to know what he had just whispered to Una, or what Una's silence might conceal. They were to listen to the poet. The poet was to consult their opinion of his verses. They were all to compose new verses as a round game – la, what subject? Aurora? Aphrodite? They did not know who Aphrodite was? Why, children – 'tis Venus, writ in Greek, is it not so master Poet? As for Venus – and she looked at Una as if desiring Una to ask for more explanations. But Una said nothing, giving Lady Jane that grave, considering look of hers with which Ralph had become familiar and which meant she had retreated into her own private world into which no one, least of all Lady Jane, could intrude.

12

It was not an hour that Ralph enjoyed. Yet the next day and the next, he returned as bidden, until it became the recognized habit for all of that summer and Sunday could have followed Monday sooner than he could have been absent from Lady Jane's promenade. To all appearances so innocent a promenade that Venus, or indeed any reference to her, might well have seemed out of place there. Master Poet's flings at Venus-worship were obviously confined to his verses. Even if he had wished to do otherwise there were too many watchers, too many gossips ready to make two and two into five for Lady Jane to grant him more than a smile and her fingertips, or for him to aspire to more than sighing adoration.

As for Ralph and Una, they were content to be together, or Ralph at times was content, and Una said neither that she was contented nor discontented, but seemed now his dear co-conspirator, stifling laughter at the poet, and now suddenly remote. Were her thoughts with her distant Ireland, he wondered, where she said children were turned into swans, and fairy people lived in green mounds into which they drove their cattle at night, for all the world like human beings –

But for Lady Jane it would have been an enchanting pastime, walking in that scented garden – even the poet was not too offensive. As time passed his unrequited, un-requitable passion for his lady became almost a part of the season, like the long evening shadows, and his poetry was food for secret jokes between Ralph and Una, providing them with a new, secret language.

'How doth my lady's shoe bedeck her foot!' That was Ralph's.

'A sonnet to my lady's eyebrow!' Una was delighted with her contribution – her English was now fluent. 'But Ralph, how *can* grown people talk so foolishly?'

'It's only poetry – and I've thought of another one –'

There were indeed good things about that summer, and to any stranger who might have seen them all together, they made a handsome quartet, even a beautiful one: tall Lady Jane with her black hair and milk-white skin, her languid affectation of being the Queen of Tascombe, the Helen, the Aphrodite of Somerset – attended by her acolytes and courtiers; Master Poet the very looking-glass of a London gentleman born and bred, or anyway manufactured; behind them Una, she too growing tall, her hair catching the sunlight, faint freckling giving her face a look half childish still, while her downcast eyes and sweeping eyelashes seemed to say – I am almost a woman now. Her eyes indeed said that more than her figure, for she had no more bosom than a boy, as Lady Jane liked to point out, casting her glance sideways at Ralph. And Ralph himself half a man, black-haired like Lady Jane, his grey eyes unrevealing, the boyish softness of his features quite gone and yet still a boy. Blushing easily and not really able to suppress laughter at the poet. And they were an innocent group too, as even Sir Edward would have had to swear if anyone had ever dared suggest differently to him.

Now the quartet would be joined by Parson Dagge, murmuring lines from his beloved Virgil and now by Lady Jane's cousin, Mistress Perkins, and now and then by any of a dozen other young or youngish women and men from the neighbouring parishes. So that Lady Jane's rose garden seemed a centre of civilization in a wild and remote part of England. A Court of Love, where all the muses were at home. More than one young man sang love songs accompanied by a lute and there was even a painter who captured a likeness of Lady Jane on a piece of ivory no larger than the palm of her hand.

All in all, a summer, an atmosphere, a garden, in which Ralph's feeling for Una might have grown into love without the least shadow cast on it, the least distortion. But in some way beyond understanding or explaining Lady Jane cast a dark shadow on it, managing to distort it almost beyond recognition as love. Not by anything she did. Not even by anything obvious that she said. But by a glance, a tone, a gesture, a hidden smile – an air of ... connivance. Of conspiracy. A mute suggestion in all her bearing that there was something to conceal in what they did – or – or – Ralph did not know what it was. She seemed to manipulate them,

14

to delve, to want to delve into their thoughts, to pick at their budding feelings as she plucked at rose buds, pulling them to pieces and scattering the petals on the gravel, only to tread on them as she passed on, laughing her cold, brittle, unfeeling laughter.

He knew he was too young to understand her. He was at least old enough to know that – and he guessed that Alice was too simple to understand her. Lady Jane did not want him in her bed, even if that had been possible – instead it was as if she wanted not his body but his – and at that point his thoughts refused to complete the sentence and he was afraid to go on. One day he cried out to Una in a savagery of hatred, 'She is wicked! Wicked!'

'Yes,' Una said. 'You are right. I've thought so for a long time.'

Yet Lady Jane did nothing evil. Nor even bad. She merely *was*. Like someone with the plague, whose very clothes convey the poison to all who come near them. As if she was corrupt and her corruption tainted the garden, the roses, the people who walked there with her, corrupted Ralph's dreams. He would wake sweating from love dreams in which he lay not with Una but with Lady Jane. With Lady Jane in grotesque ways in which no couple should lie together. Love dreams that were nightmares, that tainted his mind for hours after, so that he felt guilty when he greeted Una, and wanted to hide his face from her.

But Lady Jane's was not the only dark shadow that lay on that summer. For the certainty had come to Ralph that he must one day leave Tascombe to avenge his father's death. How he would do that he did not yet know, but Una for her own protection could play no part in it.

And an hour later he was shocked to find he had forgotten all such gravities as he taught a reluctant Una to play chess.

Sometimes they escaped from Lady Jane not only to play chess but to leave Tascombe itself for a few hours, and twice they escaped for a whole magic day, riding across the hills to Bunsery, Ralph's old home, Sir Edward's absentminded nod of consent their passport to freedom and another world. The first time was fine enough. Early summer. Ralph on his

15

mare. Una riding knee to knee with him. The sun climbing from the eastern horizon. And Tascombe growing toy-like beneath them – the outbuildings and stable yard, and then the tall, long, many-chimneyed house and gatehouse that Sir Edward's father had built sixty years ago of yellowish Ham stone. Tascombe had been built when it became clear even here in the west country that the Plantagenet wars were over for ever and the new young king Henry VIII was safely on his throne for a splendid lifetime.

Behind the house with its grey slate roof and high chimneys still lay the outlines of the old castle, its stone walls now reduced to guarding dovecots and rabbit hutches and kitchen quarters, the square shape of the old tower brought down from its Norman majesty to no more than twenty feet high and given a low-angled slate roof, so that its summit would not break the line of the new building's roofs when seen from the front or even from the rose garden.

It had always seemed a shame to Ralph that the old building and especially that tower had been almost destroyed for the sake of the new one. In some ways it seemed to him to symbolize the turning away from what some of the country people already called 'the old religion' – the religion of the Mass and of Mary the Virgin, of the Rosary and Confession and the far – away Pope in magical, unimaginable Rome, of the monks and friars who had cared for their tenants, and the nuns in the convents who had had bread and milk and soup to spare for poor men and women. Now a poor man or woman could be seized and put in the stocks, or whipped for vagrancy.

But such thoughts could not survive too long on such a day, and as Tascombe disappeared and they rode over the ridge into the next steep valley which separated them from the moor, it was as if everything in the world vanished except themselves and their horses, and the golden day. A hawk drifting overhead in the blue enamel of the morning sky. A few sheep. The sharp bark of a fox. A cuckoo calling. Wild pigeon in a copse with their bubbling love song. A stream where the horses could drink. And a feeling that neither of them expressed, perhaps could not express, that this was

16

how all days should be – that this was one day out of a lost paradise, granted to them as a gift by whatever power has such gifts in its keeping. And that they, as they rode gently up towards the moor were how all people should be. Young, and beautiful, and growing aware of love. Yet not aware. As Adam and Eve had been in Paradise before the Serpent came. How had Adam seemed to Eve? And Eve to Adam? Who can tell? Surely no more beautiful than Ralph to Una or Una to Ralph. And yet neither of them thought of beauty. Neither of them thought of love. As if the last traces of childhood still rode with them, like the last mists of morning hanging by the stream, below in the little valley, before the power of the sun reached down into it and struck fire from the stream.

Una rode astride, as easy as a boy, not needing to think of her horse, one with it. Not as Lady Jane rode, with constant little nervous cries, for support, for someone to control her mount which would surely bolt, which was born vicious, which Sir Edward had given her out of malice to make her fall. Not as the farm women rode, heavy as sacks, riding only to get from farm to market, and only on horseback because the cart was needed elsewhere.

Not as anyone else rides, Ralph thought, looking sideways at her from under down-drawn eyebrows, half consciously assuming a man's severity of expression when judging horsemanship in anyone. As if – as if – and he thought of the Centaurs in Parson Dagge's dreary exposition of the legend – those creatures half man, half horse who rode and fought in the Greek Arcadia long, long ago.

No! Not like a Centaur! An Amazon? The fierce women warriors of another legend which he had found in a book, and of which Parson Dagge disapproved so thoroughly that Ralph had earned a fine caning for mentioning it in class.

No. Not an Amazon either. There was nothing fierce about the way she rode. And yet there was no passive gentleness, no submission there either. She rode like – like one of the fairy people of Ireland! Whom she'd described to him so often. Fairy people who were like human beings, only more splendid, the air of the Other World like a nimbus round them, a halo, a magic. *That* was how she rode. Slim and arrow-straight under her small, green huntsman's hat with its long cock pheasant's feather. Hair now red-gold, now chestnut-auburn, as the mounting sun caught and burnished it. Her back bent slightly forward as her horse scrambled up the last few yards of hillside to the moor, then arching to rein him in before he could shy at a rabbit bolting suddenly from under his hooves.

A girl out of a fairy tale, a princess? But the word princess carried too much grandeur, too many ideas of royalty and attendants, of ceremony. What had been that story she had told him of the two lovers who escaped to live in the woods and love one another while the king's men hunted them? Dermot and Grainne? Were those their names?

He reached across and touched her arm in its tight green sleeve. Worn green cloth, a trifle threadbare. Worn leather gauntlets, a finger carefully mended by Old Solomon with a leather needle and stout thread, for Lady Jane, although she might give her the odd trinket, took care to see that she was not too well dressed. Now, when he touched her arm she looked at him half in surprise, as if she had been a thousand miles away and had forgotten he was there. Perhaps she had. Perhaps she had been in Ireland, that magic land of hers – and for an instant he was both jealous and angry. She at least had somewhere to escape to in her thoughts. A place where her father was still a great man. 'He is really a king!' she used to say when she was much younger. 'He is! He is!'

'A king?' Ralph would repeat, laughing. 'Of what? A herd of cows and a tribe of savages!'

'They are *not* savages!'

'They cannot speak English!'

'We have our own language! And great poets. And harpers. My father has his own harper to play for him at meal-times. And poets come from all over Ireland to praise him. When they do he gives them sackfuls of gold coins. He has his own army even – and my mother is dressed in silk and pearls – she is the most beautiful woman in the world. That's why your old Queen Elizabeth hates my family so much. She's jealous of my mother!'

'What rubbish you do talk!' Ralph had laughed scornfully. 'A king! Poets! Soldiers! Do they even have clothes to wear?'

And she had tried to hit him, half in tears, half angry until he had said he was sorry and stopped teasing her. Over the years her stories had become less assertive and less often told, and perhaps for that reason had begun to carry more conviction with Ralph, who had nothing to set against them but the humdrum truth of Bunsery, his own family's small estate twelve miles across the moor – far too close in time and place to be a satisfactory counterbalance to the Ireland of Una's stories. Although she almost never spoke of 'Ireland' but rather of Donegal, that part of it where according to her, her father was a mixture of pope and emperor.

It was Parson Dagge who spoke of Ireland, drawing a map of it on the blackboard and insisting that Ralph and Una, turn and turn about, should place Dublin and Donegal and Waterford and Galway on it. 'A savage land,' he called it, 'never, alas, blessed with the benefits of Roman law and civilization, until our own good king Henry II dispatched holy bishops there to bring the people to a sense of their Christian duty.'

'But was not Henry II a Roman Catholic?' Ralph had asked innocently, earning himself another caning.

'Our English Church has always been the true Church,' Parson Dagge had explained between applications of his rod. 'It is Rome and her damnable superstitions that have deviated from Our Saviour's teaching.'

'What is it, Ralph?' Una was saying now, the surprise growing in her eyes at his prolonged silence.

He let go of her arm, conscious that he was blushing for no reason at all, could scarcely remember himself what he had meant to say. 'Oh – I was just thinking that we've no school today! Nor tomorrow! Blessed Sunday! I'll race you to that furze bush!'

They had reached Bunsery well before mid-morning, to be greeted by the old couple who looked after the house as if they had ridden not twelve miles from Tascombe, but from the far side of the moon.

'Master Ralph! 'Tis you! And the young lady! Such a ride

19

for you both! And how you've grown!' Old Mrs Kydner bobbing curtseys, wiping her hands on her black apron before she dared take Una's in greeting. Fat and breathless and quivering like a jelly with excitement, her thick ankles under the woollen skirt splashed with mud from the farmyard where she must have been feeding the hens, her feet thrust into a pair of her husband Samuel's worn shoes, mud-splashed too and scarcely big enough to contain her bunions and swollen, rheumatic toes. 'If we'd ha' knowed thee was comin'! There's nowt ready, not a morsel to eat fit to set before 'ee both! Sam! – where's thy senses? A cup o' warm milk from the dairy – run, man! Can't 'ee see her ladyship is fair swooning wi' the heat?'

'Mother Kydner!' Ralph cried, 'leave us be, I beg you. Una could ride twice as far and not lose her breath. We are not made of glass! Let Samuel take our horses, and you can show us your hens and all that you have been doing these three years since I was here last.'

But Mrs Kydner was not to be robbed so easily of drama and he had to have a cup of wine and Una hot milk spiced with nutmeg and cinnamon in the dark parlour, and a hundred exclamations made at his height, and the adventure of riding 'all t' way from Tascombe, all alone by they two selves!' While Samuel nodded and smiled his toothless smile, his white hair straggling to his shoulders, his face brown and wrinkled and full of joy. And under his wife's clatter of words and his own joy there was a deeper excitement – the hope that this visit was different, the beginning of new things, or rather a restoration of old ones. They did not have to say it – Ralph *knew*. Because the last time he had come he had been a child, riding a pony and trailing behind Sir Edward and the steward who saw to Bunsery along with Sir Edward's own much greater and grander estate.

Ralph's father, Christopher Paulet, had died a poor man, all his money taken from him in fines for recusancy, but ever since his death Tascombe labourers had come to Bunsery to plough and sow, to reap and thresh. They had come for the lambing and the shearing. The Tascombe steward had bought and sold stock, had built up a small herd of sturdy red cattle, had trebled the number of ewes – and Sir Edward had paid for all of it. It had been the one kindness he had shown Ralph. Or had it been only family pride? Shame at a kinsman's estate going into ruin? Even a papist kinsman?

On that earlier visit Ralph had been allowed to come to his own home as a special favour granted by Sir Edward, and the Kydners had not dared make a fuss of him in their awe of all that Tascombe stood for. The whole visit had underlined the fact that the old days were gone, that Ralph's father was dead and dead a 'traitor' – that Bunsery was in effect now no more than an appendage to Tascombe, an outfarm to be managed efficiently but soullessly by the steward. All that remained in the Kydners' care was the house itself, growing damper and colder as winter succeeded winter, the rooms full of furniture of Quantock oak, covered now in dust sheets that were themselves beginning to rot. In addition to the house itself the Kydners looked after the hens in the yard and the few doves that still remained in the dovecot – the two cows were Samuel's own property as were the ducks on the duck pond.

But now, here today the Kydners' old eyes were saying – here now was Master Ralph grown almost into a man, and come without Sir Edward or his steward – and a young lady with him – a *beautiful* young lady. Maybe he was come back for ever? Or would soon? With a bride? Her ladyship, maybe? And there would be babies and – and – and –

It was too much for Mrs Kydner. She burst into sobs suddenly, flinging her apron over her head to hide her shame, and running into the big stone kitchen to fall onto the bench and bleat like a lost sheep. 'Oh, Sam, I cannot abide it – the happiness – I'll die o' it –'

At which point Ralph had come running to comfort her but her happiness had grown so much more unendurable that she truly seemed in danger of a seizure and had to be restored with a mug of wine. But it was Una who had really quietened her, sending Ralph away and bidding Samuel fetch the makings of the dinner Mrs Kydner had promised them before her happiness had become too much for her. Ralph never learned what Una had done, but five minutes later there were cheerful voices, and the sounds of the kitchen being put to rights, and he had looked at Una with new eyes, seeing her as the mistress of a house, arranging all things as if she had been born to it and needed to learn nothing. The pullets on their spits, the ducklings, a leg of lamb, the oven giving off delicious smells of rabbit pie, flakes of pastry swept from the big pinewood kitchen table, and the places set.

'Lord save us! 'Ee don't mean to dine here in the kitchen?'

'Why not, Mother Kydner?' Una had said, falling as easily into calling the old woman 'Mother' as if she had done it for years. 'Are we not your guests? And do you think we would be comfortable in that bare dining room? Are you not Ralph's friends?'

There had been a huge jug of cider and another of old ale and when he tried to stand Ralph had found his legs bending under him like willow wands, and he had sat down again and laughed as if that was the greatest joke in the world. Samuel had fallen asleep and his wife too, and Ralph and Una had sat on for an hour, looking at one another, smiling at jokes they did not need to make aloud, and at memories they did not need to express in words. To any observer they must have seemed a strange sight, a little tipsy with the rough cider, flushed with good food and the heat of the kitchen fire, young and handsome and unaware of their own handsomeness. Like two flowers opening on a flowering bush, as unaffected by their beauty as sunlight is, as flowers are.

Until at last Ralph bent his head, black wings of hair falling either side of his flushed face, grey eyes hidden. 'We'd best be going soon.'

As he said it he seemed to become sober all of a sudden – and more than sober. Older. As if in that instant, or during that joyous, tipsy dinner-time, he had grown up altogether, had arrived a boy and would ride back a man. It could not have been so and yet it seemed so, even to him. But he stood up again, and perhaps to balance himself adopted a man's stance, a trifle straddle-legged, like a horseman more used to riding than walking. A soldier's stance. And of a sudden the joyousness was gone, the atmosphere of the house lay heavy on him, and the darkness of the kitchen with its narrow deep-set windows as the fire died in the great hearth became a prison. Even the snoring of the old couple was a kind of dying.

In his father's time there had been six and seven servants here, although he could only remember some of them. Thomas. Betty, who had been simple from birth but had a wonderful way with hens and all small, living things; Samuel, who had been old even then, who had chopped wood and minded the cows and slept with them until fat, kindly Meg had come to work in Bunsery. She had come when Ralph was still a toddler but he could not remember her coming. She seemed to have been there always, always married to Samuel, just as his mother seemed never to have been well, nor able to get about, so that there was never again a toddler or even a baby in the house. Even so, in those far-off days it had been a happy, loving home.

'We'd best go,' he said again, his eyebrows dark and thick as a man's drawn down over his fine, hooked nose – his father's nose, his father's eyebrows but his mother's eyes – although he did not think of that. Una stood up, she too a shade unsteadily.

'My legs!'

And Mrs Kydner woke and cried out at seeing them standing, sensing they were about to go. 'No, Master Ralph! Not yet!'

Old Samuel woke then, struggling to his feet and grunting at the pain of the rheumatism in his joints. ''Tis not time yet!' he protested.

But Ralph insisted, almost as if he was flying from the house. As if the memory of the soldiers coming for his father and dragging him away had overwhelmed him again. It was a silent, sombre ride homewards for the first hour. Until the sun of the late afternoon drove all sullen thoughts away, and he could be happy just to have Una there, alone with him. Mrs Kydner had made them up more provisions for the homeward journey, enough for a journey to Scotland or Wales, let alone Tascombe, and just before they left the moorland for the last village before Tascombe Ralph stopped and said, 'Let's eat something here. It'd be a shame to waste Mother Kydner's cold rabbit pie, and her mince tarts.'

They laid out the food on the turf, and being young felt hungry as soon as they saw it, although that had not been Ralph's reason for stopping there. It had been – what had it been? To prolong the day? No. More, much more than that. It was to tell Una that he loved her. To kiss her. To kiss her not as they had kissed before, as a boy kisses a girl, but as a man kisses the woman he loves. He was not sure how that was – but he felt that as soon as his arms were round her he would know what to do.

The trouble had been to reach that point of mastery. And that day he never reached it. He found himself unable to move, even to look at her. She too seemed to have grown up during the day. And to have grown, not away from him – but *above* him? So that he was afraid even to touch her, and when in handing her a mince tart and again in taking the leather jack of cider from her to set it down safely on the grass their fingers touched, the contact seemed to burn him. They finished the ride home as silently as they had left Bunsery, and moment by moment the weight of the homecoming seemed to increase, until half the magic of the day was lost. It was only in the following week, suffering again under Parson Dagge's petulant tyranny, that the magic restored itself and he was able to whisper to Una that one day they would escape to Bunsery again. He had wanted to add 'For always, perhaps?' and had not dared.

But late that summer they had escaped once more. And that time, riding home, and stopping in the predestined place, he had kissed Una. Yet not in any way as he had imagined it might be. All his real kissing until then – if one could call it real – had been with Alice, and it had only happened once. Warm, moist lips, soft as fruit. Big breasts against his bony chest as she hugged him close. Strange stirrings low down in his body. Strange excitement.

But with Una, none of that. Not even the excitement. Her lips cool as water. Smooth as ivory. Her hands resting lightly in his, and then hanging limply at her sides as he dropped

24

them to put his own hands behind her shoulders. He meant to press her close as Alice pressed him, to open his lips on hers as Alice had done, pushing his lips apart with her tongue. He had meant – God alone knew what he had meant, what he had confusedly dreamed of doing night after night and all that day's ride to Bunsery and back. None of it came true. Only her lips lightly, coolly, passionately against his. Not even a mother's kiss – a fairy's kiss. And like a fairy's kiss, stealing his strength, his courage. His hands fell away from her shoulders and he drew back, his face burning.

'I – I'm sorry.' Not for what he had done, but for what he had thought of doing. Yet was what he had thought of so very wrong? To kiss her properly?

She looked at him gently, not reproachfully, yet not forgivingly. A girl of another people. Of another world. Once a travelling actors' company had come to Tascombe, and one of the company's attractions had been an 'Irish dancer' – a strange, lithe dark creature, surely more gypsy than Irish. She had danced on a stage made of empty barrels and planks, while her companions squatted beside her, playing a peculiar kind of drum, open at one end.

'I am of Ireland, out of the holy land of Ireland,' the woman had sung in her husky, throaty, not very musical voice. 'Come dance with me,' she had invited and beckoned. And the watching labourers had winked and nudged one another forward, making coarse jokes. But none of them had dared accept the invitation. And next day the company had vanished, afraid of Parson Dagge's puritanical threats against such lascivious shows.

Out of the holy land of Ireland. Ralph remembered the phrase now, although it was ten years since he had heard it sung, and before Una had arrived in Tascombe. He had always thought of Ireland as an extension of that company, rags and braggadocio and a lithe dark woman, until Una had told him that indeed it was a land of milk and honey, of gold and pearls and silks and warriors more splendid than Queen Elizabeth's own soldiers. A land where her father was a king and her mother a queen and she herself had had nurses and attendants who served her on their knees.

25

Out of the holy land of Ireland. Una.

'I'm sorry.'

Una had put one of her hands up to touch her lips where he had kissed, and then she looked at her fingertips. 'Why should you be sorry, Ralph?'

And her use of his name was like a blow of a cane across his face. He wanted to kneel down and kiss her hand – not her hand, her foot, in its patched leather boot. But he dare not.

'Let's go home,' he had said roughly. And against his will, on the way home he had found himself thinking of Alice, and her kiss, and that pulse of excitement in his body. And again his face had burned with shame and he had not dared glance even sideways at Una.

CHAPTER 2

IT IS 1586. A sunny, spring afternoon. A boy and girl watching a family of brown cygnets as they follow their stately parents across the swan pool at Tascombe. From a distance a stranger might have taken them for brother and sister, they stood so quietly there, not even their hands touching. The girl was tall, delicately made, beautiful. Something un-English about her that showed itself subtly, in the texture of her skin, the near-redness of her hair. The boy was a head taller, broad across the shoulders but lean. Even his face was lean, aquiline, under the helmet of straight, black hair. But he had a fair, lightly tanned, unmistakably English skin and his hair was not truly black. And if the stranger had come closer he would have realized that neither the boy nor the girl was at all interested in the swan pool.

'Do you know it's a whole month since we've been alone together?' Ralph's voice was bitter.

'I know. They watch us. They do not want us to be friends any longer.' She spoke like an Englishwoman, but the cadences of her voice were still Irish.

'They cannot stop us!' Ralph said angrily. 'We're no longer children!'

'That's the whole point. It did not matter when we were younger.' She said it not bitterly but with a depth of resignation that was too old for her years, or her face. But not for her eyes.

Ralph went on looking at the family of swans, his hands

clenching. He knew as well as she did that there was a conspiracy to keep them apart, but he did not want to have it put into words, for he was not ready yet. Not ready to tell her what he had imagined telling her a thousand times, this girl who long ago had been sent across the sea by her father and then forgotten.

Later, when he had paid his debt to his own father, was free of guilt, then he could tell her. And he made himself look at her, almost hoping that she could see without needing to be told. Surely she must see – must know.

A thrush began to sing in the bushes behind them, and the clear sound seemed to deepen the silence. Una's eyes had been searching his, but now they were remote, withdrawn, and already he was half afraid that she had seen too much.

'It's time to go back,' she said, moving away from him, the apple-green silk of her skirt brushing the faded summer grass. Rustling. Disturbing.

'Already?'

'Yes.' Her voice so cold he could not believe it was hers. He wanted to put out his hand and touch her, touch her dress, and at the thought of it had to force his arms against his sides.

'Sir Edward is looking for a wife for you – did you know that, Ralph?' Her voice without expression, turning to face him again.

'What?' He did touch her then, not even thinking about it. Catching hold of her arm as if they were still children, pulling her round towards him.

'Una,' he breathed. 'Una.' And kissed her then as he had dreamed of kissing her ever since he could remember. Her own mouth softening, warm, until she started back in terror. Not in anger, only in terror of what they had done. And he could not say anything, was not even sure of what they had done. Joy certainly, but a kind of terror too. Not of being seen, or of what would happen, but of what had happened. As if they were at Mass and there was that moment again when the priest bent down and laid the Host on his tongue and God was there. And the thought was so blasphemous and yet so exact that he wanted to cross himself and dared not.

He held out his hands to her, without knowing what he was asking for, and she stared at him with her eyes wide and dark and frightened, her lips still parted. Then she turned and ran, and it was a long moment before he could run after her, catch up with her.

'Una, please! I didn't mean –' The words an echo, he could not think of what, or of when they had been said before. 'Please –' But she would not turn her head, would not speak to him, and they walked in silence towards the gardens, and the great wall of the inner garden.

He could hear voices, a man's voice, and Lady Jane's, and wanted to run in the opposite direction. Be alone. Think. Or not alone. With her. Telling her, explaining – But she had pushed open the wooden door, almost running again, as if even Lady Jane was protection, better than the terror she had felt with him. There was a young man lying on the grass, holding a paper, reading from it in his high, affected, poet's voice. Thomas Barnaby the current favourite, reading one of his sonnets to Lady Jane.

Since that summer when Lady Jane had first invited, summoned Ralph to accompany them in the rose garden Sir Edward had kept him so busy about the estate that there had been no time for such frivolities. But Una had not escaped so easily, although even she was sometimes not invited and it was common gossip that Lady Jane had recently grown less discreet and preferred to be alone with her young men. She was looking at Ralph and Una now, her plucked eyebrows raised in affected pleasure, surprise, her eyes failing to conceal dislike. And more than dislike. Settling her yellow taffeta skirts into more handsome folds over the stiffness of her farthingale.

'You are just in time to hear a masterpiece.' Her eyes under their drooping, kohl-stained lids taking in their expressions. Master Barnaby lying determinedly at his ease, but flushed, as if he had not expected to be disturbed and was not pleased, his half-cloak carelessly draped, his lute lying on the grass beside his elegant, silk-stockinged legs. The long grass pressed down – and Ralph knew that a moment earlier Lady Jane herself had been sitting there close beside Master

29

Barnaby, lying back against the apple tree, and he felt a shock of distaste, of contempt for her.

'Read, Thomas, now that we have an audience,' she said now, her voice light and cold and full of malice. And they had to sit down and listen. There was no escaping.

That night, the old dream, the nightmare, came back to torment Ralph. He had thought it was gone for ever, that he had outgrown it but once again he was riding down into the hollow where Bunsery stood, riding towards his own old home, to warn his father. And no matter how he spurred his horse he seemed to make no progress, to come no nearer to his father waiting for him on the porch steps with outstretched arms. Ralph tried to dismount, but his feet were caught in the stirrups and as he dragged and pulled at them there was the sound of shouting, men running, his father crying, 'Ralph, boy! Ralph! Save yourself! Run, lad!' And he could not reach him, could not move. His father's voice fading, and then – then the screaming, and he himself falling from the saddle. Crawling on his hands and knees towards that screaming that died into whimpers, lifted again in a shriek of agony and died at last into nothing.

'Father! Father!' And there was no more sound, nothing to guide him but the ravens as they lighted on his father's body and bent their sleek black heads to peck.

'Father!'

He woke screaming.

''Tis on'y a dream! Wake up, Master Ralph! Wake up!' Alice was bending over him, her face strangely naked in the candlelight. She touched his forehead. 'Tell Alice,' she whispered, her black hair loose, falling forward as she bent. The familiar childhood smell of her body, of sweat, and starch, and comfort and kindliness and warmth.

'The same dream,' he whispered. 'I wasn't in time. If I had –'

'For the Lord's sake, thee were on'y eleven – how could 'ee have helped him if 'ee reached him? Come what might, they were going to arrest him for hiding a priest!' Her hands smoothing his own hair. 'Thee's grown a handsome lad,' she whispered. 'Too handsome to be dreaming about old, terrible things. Thee should be dreaming o' new things. Young lasses, eh, Master Ralph?'

He could not answer her. Only look into the dark, liquid softness of her eyes that seemed to hold all his childhood in them. It was becoming difficult to breathe, and she was bending closer, her hair touching his face. Thick, warm hair, very strong. It had its own scent about it, half of cleanness, half of –

'Thee's too handsome for a maid's good,' she breathed. 'But I'm no maid – not this long, long while.' She kissed his mouth, her mouth soft and burning, covering his. Open. Her breath in his mouth, sweet and warm. He felt drunk with it, wrapped his arms round her, found himself pulling her down towards him, onto the bed beside him, his hands at the neck of her gown, at her breast. And for a second she gave way, half fell, half yielded, was lying on top of him, her mouth still on his, and he thought he would die of it, his heart hammering, near to bursting. But she was sitting up suddenly, laughing, pushing him back onto the pillow, her hair tumbled, the buttons of her gown half undone, her breast showing.

'Master Ralph! Thee's too grown for that! Or not enough! Oh, there's lasses'll suffer for thee!' And she had stood up, lifting the candlestick, fumbling to close the front of her gown with her other hand. 'Goo to sleep now. An' no dreams mind, bad or good!' She went slowly to the door, put her fingers to her mouth to blow him a kiss, and left him. Left him lying awake, sure that he would never sleep again.

The next morning he decided to ride over to Bunsery, even though it was too soon for his usual fortnightly visit, and he left immediately after breakfast, riding alone, in no mood to have even a manservant with him. Returning that afternoon, he rode down over the rim of the hollow in which Tascombe lay sheltered. An hour ago he had stripped off his doublet, and the sun beat against his fine linen shirt, which like all his shirts had become too tight across his shoulders. Perhaps – perhaps – It could be a better year for Bunsery. The harvest had been good. If he sold well –

High above his head a buzzard hung in the pale blue sky,

and as he looked up the big bird began to glide downwards, wings taut and tail extended. Had it seen a dead lamb? A dying one? Ralph slowed the mare to a walk. All round him was the sickly smell of furze in bloom and some of the heat had left the sun, taking with it his small spurt of optimism, so that he was almost on top of her before he saw the red of her skirt, the black hair under the faded green kerchief.

'Alice! You're far afield!'

She smiled up at him, shielding her eyes against the sun with her hand. 'Aye, to the cottage.'

'How is your father?'

'Well enough.'

He slid down from the saddle, and began walking beside her, leading the mare, the reins loose over his arm. Walking in silence as she plucked a long grass, and bit the head off it with her strong, white teeth, her throat white under the line of the broad, strong chin, and then brown where the sun had caught it, the skin darker still down to the edge of her lace bodice, where it was rimmed with white as she moved, breathed, her breast lifting.

Full, soft breast. That last night – It was suddenly very hard to breathe, even to walk, his heart was beating so hard, his legs were so weak. He stood still and she turned to look at him, surprised at his expression, and then her own expression changing, growing unlike the Alice he had always known, becoming someone else.

'Thee've turned faint?' she whispered. 'Thee've rode too far in the sun – an' wi'out ought to eat, mebbe?'

'Yes,' he said, his mouth dry, his hand going out to her shoulder, to her neck, touching. He had not known he was doing it, and stood in front of her without willpower, his hand moving down her breast. She was close against him, her mouth lifted, reaching up towards his, her hands urgent.

'I know a spot,' she whispered. 'Over there.'

A clump of furze, covered with yellow blossom, thick and tall. Tethering the mare.

There was a narrow, trodden path into the furze brake, the spines of the bushes harsh against his stockings, his waist, the backs of his hands as he tried to guard his face. Her broad,

32

smooth-shaped back in front of him, full rounded shoulders, sturdy hips under the loose red skirt, the back of the red bodice stained with sweat, a dark ridge down the valley of her spine, sweat glistening at the nape of her neck. That smell of sweat and womanhood, and something else now that gripped his mind and body, drew him like a stallion after a mare in season, beyond resisting, beyond thought or conscience. Now she had come to the centre of the brake, a small clearing among the bushes that arched overhead to become almost a roof of green and yellow, a cave of sunlight and earth smell, and the musty hay that lay in pressed-down armfuls in a thick, golden carpet. He followed her slowly, knelt down as she turned towards him, no longer the hunter, but the prey, the victim. She seemed to have grown much taller than he was. As if he had grown small, was a child again in that dark, curtained bed where she had been his mother, and his nurse and all his comfort.

'My Ralph,' she whispered, kneeling to face him. Loosening the tightly tied laces of her bodice, the red sheath of faded wool opening, like a great flower. White linen under it, creased and scented from her breasts. And her breasts freed and naked, so full that they seemed to lift, strain towards him. 'Lie thy head against me,' she breathed, and he felt the softness of flesh against his mouth. Her bodice unlaced, her red skirt unfastened, fallen round her broad, white lap in a canoe of scarlet. Pressing his mouth against white breast, and throat and mouth, while she guided him, drew his hands, guided his body until it lay on hers and moved, and lay still, and moved like a horseman in a race, in a wild race in darkness, and he thought that he was dying. That no one could endure such joy and live. Let me die of this, his mind whispered, but his body cried out in a huge spasm of joy, No! Live! Live for ever! Conquer!

And was conquered, and lay dying. Dead. Lay on her body, sacrificed and lifeless. Her arms holding him, her mouth against his eyelids, against his cheeks, her hand fondling his hair, his shoulders under the linen shirt.

'My lad,' she breathed. 'My fine, brave lad.'

He lay still, listening to her heart beating. Or was it his?

Heard the sounds of small creatures in the furze brake. Bees murmuring, gathering. Creatures rustling. The whole of life enclosed in that cave of green and golden light. He would have lain there for ever, lost in summer until winter came. But she moved under him, made him move, roll aside from her. Sitting up, watching him, her breasts still naked, but her hands already feeling for her linen shift, pulling it up round her waist, fastening her bodice. Her fingers blunt and swift and businesslike, as if – as if she had often – The thought came unwanted, would not leave him.

He knelt up himself, suddenly uneasy, all the witchcraft gone, nothing left but the smell of crushed hay, and that time of a summer's evening when there is death in the light, however far away the darkness is.

'If anyone sees my mare –' he whispered.

'Aye,' she said, even her voice businesslike. Or sated. He could see images in his mind that he tried to drive away. Images of cattle in the fields, coupled and then quietly grazing a moment afterwards. 'Aye. We'd best separate an' goo back quick, different ways.'

Standing up, touching his hair. 'I do ha' wanted that from thee a long whiles, Ralph lad. And now I ha' had it.' Her voice no longer businesslike but sad and lost, as if she had not gained something but lost it irretrievably. 'Goo on wi' thee lad, goo home.'

The words hanging in his mind as he rode away. Go home. Go home. Not here. Not Tascombe. And not Bunsery either, he thought, a dart of savagery in the name as he thought of it. And he wished for that second that he could have gone on riding for ever, leave Tascombe and Bunsery behind him. Leave Alice. And was shocked at what he had thought, and then more shocked still as he thought of what he had really done. Like cattle in a field, two animals behind a bush. He felt his face grow crimson, burn with the realization of it, the loss of – what? Of what had not been his to give. Which belonged – belonged to Una. Had belonged to her since – since the night he had seen her girl child's body, white and naked in the candlelight, the great, foolish nightshirt gathered in her thin arms above her head.

'What have I done,' he whispered, and saw Una as he thought it. Saw her step out from the orchard trees, her face alight at seeing him, lifting a hand to catch the bridle. She was saying something, perhaps only how fine the evening was, or the day had been, or asking how he had found Bunsery. But he could not hear, could not answer. Broke away from her, made the mare canter, gallop as if he had gone mad, among the apple trees and the pears and medlars and plum trees, bending low to avoid the whiplash of the branches. Heard her cry out in astonishment. And could not stop. Would have ridden beyond the stables, have ridden until the mare died under him if one of the stable-men had not been there and caught the reins.

'Whooa hard, Master Ralph! Whooa hup there! Has she been stung, or what, running away wi' ye?' Gentling the horse, until Ralph must slide down from the saddle, leave the man to look to breathing the mare and rubbing her down before she was fed and watered. He himself having to go through the kitchens – stone vaults and a hurrying of scullions, maids and serving boys and cooks, firelight and smells of roasting, yelp of spit dogs turning the roasting jacks, as the fat spurted from a side of beef and burned their haunches. Like a vision from the Inferno.

He flung himself into the quiet of the house itself, praying he would not meet anyone. Not Lady Jane, Mother of mercy not her! Nor Sir Edward. Nor – Let him meet no one. He reached his room, went on his knees by his bed, whispering prayers for forgiveness. Most loving father – Mother of mercy – turn thine eyes – Until the prayers grew slow in his mind, grew still. And he was seeing that cave of gold and green light again. His face pressed against the cold wool cover of his bed as it had been against her body. Smelled her smell from the coarseness of the cloth. His hands spreading out, gathering, gripping the coverlid.

What have I done?

And the sweetness returning, very softly, gently, like a spy at night, testing the darkness for enemies, for danger. 'Alice,' he whispered, 'What have I done?' And the wool seemed to breathe an answer. 'Everything. And nothing. 'Tis the way we're made, lad, the way flesh is.' A thing cannot be a sin if you do not want it, nor plan for it, he told himself. Like – like an apple falling into one's hand from a tree. What sin could there be in that? And no man *was* a man until – He touched his chin where the fine down of hairs was already thickening, resisting his fingertips as he rubbed them gently along the line of his jaw. So long as Una never knew of it – And at that thought, fresh terror came and he began to ready himself for supper in a frenzy of impatience. Ran down the broad staircase to the great hall where already half the household was gathering for the meal. Ran so fast he was almost knocking Alice down before he saw her.

She caught his wrist, her hand hard and familiar, no longer a servant's hand but a lover's, claiming him. Her eyes saying, 'Not all o' thee, I don't claim all – but what I've had, that's mine. Don't forget me, Ralph lad, don't forget our moment. I want to think on thee remembering it – and maybe – maybe sometime – ?'

All that in the moment of catching hold of him, smiling up into his eyes.

'What is it?' he asked, his voice breaking on the question, half proud, half terrified. Was she going to – ?

'There be a Mass at Murleys' farm,' she breathed. 'Tomorrow. Three o'clock.' She let go of him, turned away to the kitchens, her broad, red back still sweat-stained, a wisp of hay sticking to her skirt. When she was almost at the doors of the kitchen and out of sight of everyone she turned and beckoned him. He went slowly towards her, all the triumph gone and only the terror remaining. What did she want? And he thought, she wants to kiss me, she wants me to kiss her – here, with everyone – He felt his heart beating, his mouth dry, and then a new terror as she beckoned him more urgently. Tonight. She meant to come to him tonight, and he thought he could not walk so far as the dark alcove where she was waiting for him. And yet –

'Hurry,' she whispered. 'We mus'na be seen togethering more nor usual – can thee be there? To Murleys'?'

'Aye. Yes. Of course. Although –' He could not go to Communion. Not after – what had just happened. No matter

36

how he glossed it over. And a priest on the run would have no time to hear Confessions –

A scullion went by, carrying a great tureen of hare soup, the smell thick and sweet and in that moment sickening, as if it was the smell of corruption.

'The priest do want to see thee privately. After the Mass. Can thee be surely there?'

'Me? He wants –'

He gaped at her, his mouth open, his eyes stupid with shock. Another scullion, hurrying with a silver dish of cutlets.

'Is it – is it Father Parsons?' His father's priest. His father's friend. And his father's death. Death for hiding him, for refusing to betray him.

'I dunna know his name – a young lad of a priest, farmer Murley's boy do ha' said. Young an' foreign-sounding, altho' he's Somerset bred, he do say. But thee'd best take care.' Her face suddenly old with worry for him.

'I'll be careful,' he promised.

'Goo then – goo back to sup wi' 'em – hurry –'

She turned away, and he stayed in the shadows, leaning against the stone wall, remembering. Hard, strong hands gripping his boy's shoulders, the priest's voice gruff and soldierly, as he spoke above Ralph's head to his father.

'A fine lad, Christopher. A fine lad for Christ, if you'll give him to us. What do you say, lad? Have you thought to be a priest, boy? To follow your Master along that road?'

And his father saying, 'Nay, Robert, nay. His mother, God rest her soul, she begged me on her death-bed – that's why he's page at Tascombe, and not here with me except these few holidays. Don't put such thoughts into his head, I beg you, Robert!'

'Such a promise is not binding, Kit man, and well you know it. She had no right – No, the boy shall decide for himself when the time comes. Although leaving him at Tascombe among that Reformation crew –'

'Robert! I pray you, not in front of the boy!'

They had sent him to bed then. Ten years old. It was almost all he had ever seen of Father Parsons. That night and the next day. A stocky, powerful figure walking away from Bunsery. A wide-brimmed hat on his big, grizzled head, a staff in his hand, and his Mass gear in a narrow parcel.

He had thought then, and for weeks afterwards, I'll follow him. One day I'll follow him.

Until the day the boy came to him and whispered that Father Parsons was home again, and was at Bunsery and in grave danger. Someone knew where he was and had run to tell the magistrate, Sir William Fettle.

'If you could get to him, Ralphy.' Farmer Murley's boy. Probably the same one who had come just now. Daring to tell Robert, but not daring to ride all the way to Bunsery. No one had dared to do that, and how could Ralph go? Eleven years old, under Sir Edward's eye. And yet he had gone. Taken one of the ponies from the stables and ridden until his eyes were blind with sweat and he could hardly stand when he reached the house. Slid down from the pony's back and caught his foot in the stirrups. Fell. To be picked up by old Samuel Kydner and old Meg, both weeping. And no one else there. Not his father. Not the priest. Only the silence of an empty house, the scars of the search still there. A smashed panel in the wall of the little dining parlour where they had sounded for hollow places, and broken in. The heavy oak dining chair which they had used for a battering ram lying on its side, its legs splintered. The silver robbed from a cupboard, its door hanging on one hinge.

Nothing else.

Except the echoes. The echos of his father's voice, screaming. They had knotted a rope round his head and tightened it, and tightened it again, to make him tell them where the priest was. And he had not told. Sam's voice had been hoarse with pride as well as tears as he said it. The priest's hole had been empty, and Father Parsons had got clear away, but the men had taken his father with them.

The strange thing was that in Ralph's dreams he had reached the house while his father was still there, had heard him screaming. Until now he had almost thought that it was true. For a second it seemed that Father Parsons stood there with him in the dark alcove – broad-brimmed hat, heavy staff, thin satchel – and said in a voice grown suddenly mellow, 'Come, lad. 'Tis time now. 'Tis your turn to carry our burden. Just a mile or so.' And there was another shadow, a child's shadow on the priest's broad shoulder, clinging to the shaggy, soldier's head with small, childish hands.

'I cannot!' Ralph whispered. 'I cannot!'

And both shadows were gone and Anna, one of the serving maids, was staring at him in amazement. 'Master Ralph! Be thee ill? Thee looks mortal sickly.'

'No, no Anna – it's nothing – just a faintness – I'll – tell Mistress Kyte to tell her ladyship that I'm – I'm not well –'

She went away from him, into the kitchens again where Mistress Kyte the housekeeper would be at this hour, still looking back at him doubtfully. He made himself move, up the stairs again, supper forgotten, the thought of company horrible, the loud laughter, the clatter and talk from the great hall – and Una –

'The boy shall decide for himself when the time comes.' Had that time come? Now? Of all days, this one?

He knelt down by the window-sill and made the Sign of the Cross.

'Oh my Lord,' he prayed, 'show me the way I must go.'

CHAPTER 3

THE BARN was already full of a murmuring of voices, of knees moving on the earth floor. Farmer Murley's son stood at the crooked, leaning doorway, watching for latecomers. Nodding to them as they came up to him.

'He's here a'ready. Hurry!' he whispered. His face twitching with nerves. Whatever the worshippers risked – fines, a whipping, a day in the stocks – the Murleys risked everything. Their farm, even their lives. For sheltering the priest, for treason against the queen, against her religion and her law.

Ralph crossed himself and went into the crowded, straw-smelling twilight of the barn. They had made an altar out of a rough plank laid across a couple of cider kegs, only partially covered by Mrs Murley's best white cloth, and the flame from the two thick candles steadied as Una went ahead of him, not speaking to him, not even looking his way, going swiftly to where the women knelt. He saw Alice then, her red skirt like a splash of blood in the shadows, and now Una was kneeling beside her. He clenched both hands against his chest – the two of them kneeling together. Was it a sign that he must give up both kinds of love? Even the purest of earthly loves as well as – as whatever that other had been –

'Oh Father,' he prayed as he knelt himself, 'show me the way. Let me make this a true offering of myself to You.' And a feeling of great peace came over him, like tiredness dissolving, or hunger satisfied, and for the next few minutes he was scarcely aware of anything but that inner quietness, and the knowledge that he had taken a decision, although he did not yet know what that decision was. He listened to the prayers, the half-familiar words of the Mass and heard nothing except the one great phrase of joy. Kyrie Eleison. Kyrie Eleison. Christ is risen.

'Oh, my Lord and my God,' he prayed silently. 'Let me bear my burden. Let me share Your suffering.' The young priest lifted the Host on high, offering God to God Himself, the Son to the Father.

And would I hold myself back from Him? Ralph asked himself. And even as he did the door of the barn was flung open, and there was the brightness of sunlight like a desecration of the dark – like waking out of joy, and a voice shouted, 'Run! Run! They're comin', run for your lives!'

For a moment, a poised, still moment, no one moved. Then the scrambling began, the whispered prayers, curses, a woman screaming, everyone pushing towards the open door. And the priest, with the Host still lifted, began to lower it, turning now towards the door, his face so young it was like a boy's, a boy in terror.

'Run!' Ralph shouted at him. 'I've a horse! Quick!' Thinking of Una, reaching out to pull her free of the crowd, but she was swept past him, Alice still beside her, the pair of them forced out through the doorway. Outside there were sounds of shouting, running, like a pack of hounds on the scent, and a hundred foxes. Inside the priest was kneeling, slowly kneeling, lifting the Host towards his mouth. Ralph, caught in the surge of fugitives, dragged with them to the door, shouted again to the priest over his shoulder, 'Run Father, run!' But he himself was running, one of a scatter of running figures, and there was a hoarse voice shouting commands.

'Let them go, damn you! Make sure of the priest!' Half a dozen men racing for the barn like hounds called back to the scent. He saw Una stumbling, falling, Alice vanished. Saw a man leap over Una's sprawled body. Ralph ran and lifted her, half carried her towards the withered tree where the horses were. One of the armed men turned aside to intercept him shouting, 'Halt there! In the queen's name!'

41

Ralph hit him in the face, and the man fell to one side, still shouting, trying to catch at Ralph's ankle, holding it. Ralph kicked himself free, was at the horses' heads, tearing the reins loose, a branch breaking. He lifted Una into the saddle, almost flinging her clear across it to fall the other side, but she steadied herself and he was up, both horses already moving, cantering, galloping, down one of the hidden lanes, a man flinging himself aside to let them pass. The furze and the heather of the steep bank closed overhead, so that they must bend low down as they rode or else be knocked from their saddles, or blinded by thorns.

'The priest!' Ralph called to Una. 'I must go back for him!'

But there was no way of turning, no way of going back. And if there was, what could he do against half a dozen men with swords and pistols? Letting the horses take them, have their heads, until they were out of all danger of being seen, identified.

'What will happen to him?' Una said, her face white except for a smear of farmyard mud where she had fallen, her gown stained with it. She turned her horse's head slightly, so that she came close again. 'Fifty men there,' she said, not looking at him. 'And they let him be taken.' She still did not look at Ralph, her face unnaturally white, the mud like a dark bruise.

'I wanted – I wanted to help him,' he whispered. 'But I saw you fall – '

'I am grateful,' she said, her voice cold.

'There was nothing any man could have done.'

She did not answer that, and they rode apart, taking the long path skirting the wood, and approaching Tascombe and the village from the south, so that they would not be seen with the other fugitives, or seen by them. His caution that, not hers, and it was past five o'clock before they rode into the village, past the market cross and the stocks and the bowling green. And as they rode up the gentle rise at the far end towards Tascombe and the south gates of the park, they saw a group of men coming towards them. Half a dozen, two by two, one man marching ahead, carrying a drawn sword. One man walking, staggering rather, between the two brief lines of soldiers. Bare-headed. His face a dark mass of blood and filth, his shirt torn to rags, his hands bound. The priest.

They had to rein their horses aside to let the soldiers pass. The priest did not look up at them, or seem to notice that they were there, only stumbled forward towards his Calvary – the long journey to London, and the Tower, and torture. And the last, brief journey on the hurdle that would be the longest journey of all.

CHAPTER 4

LIKE WAITING for a storm to break, the air hot and still and heavy, the thunderhead building. Nothing talked of in the whole vast house but the priest caught, and the Murleys to be taken next, the constables sent up for them, and half the parish shivering behind closed doors for fear of a sword hilt knocking on an informer's word. The maids whispering, eyeing one another with suspicion, fear, malice. The scullions boasting of their true faith, their hatred of the papists – dogs – vermin – Pope rats – traitors. Although in the dark they crossed themselves and prayed to the Queen of Heaven to forgive them. Only they had not dared to go to the Mass, and now thanked God for their saving grace of cowardice. Mistress Kyte truly Protestant, congratulating Parson Dagge on the victory of the queen's law and religion over Romish infamy. 'I wish they'd try him here in Tascombe, Master Parson! I have a woman's heart as tender as another's, but I'd see his traitor's head on a spike without a tremor! Aye, and the disembowelling too, and I'd bless my Saviour that it should be witnessed by all the parish as a testimony of bible truth. So perish all of them, root and branch!'

The talk at supper was less bloody, but not much. Lady Jane crying death to all the villagers who had been at such a wicked ceremony. Sir Edward glaring at everyone who came near him, maid or page or serving girl or one of his own family, so that his ferocious looks towards Ralph, sitting far down the long table, might mean anything, or nothing.

44

There was no longer the old custom at Tascombe of the middling servants eating with the family – that had fallen away almost the first year Ralph had been there, and he could barely remember it. Lady Jane had put a stop to such antique nonsense as she called it – so that Alice was not there, nor serving, and Una had gone to bed, pleading a headache from the afternoon's ride in the sun. If Sir Edward meant the storm to break tonight, it must break on Ralph's head alone. It was a bleak, unpleasant meal. No laughter. No music. Even the younger children quieter than usual. After a while almost no talk, no sound except the scrape and clash of knife and spoon on platter, the splash of wine being poured for those at the top table and of ale for the others. Silence falling like a dull mist on the moors, a grey swathe of nothingness hiding the bog holes, pitfalls for man and beast.

After supper, prayers. Longer than usual. Parson Dagge more unctuous than ever. Like a sick sheep.

'God in His infinite wisdom ... God in His righteous wrath ...' As though God needed Parson Dagge's approval and would be glad to learn that He possessed it.

Ten minutes, Ralph told himself, and then he could slip away. He was almost at the door when Sir Edward called him.

'Come to my study, lad. I'll have a word wi' you if you please.'

Ralph's heart seemed to grow still. Very still and cold. It was as if he had been waiting for this moment, not just for a few hours, but for years. Since that first Sunday here, when Parson Dagge had told him that everything he had ever learned belonged to the devil and the pit of hell, and that he must become, as it were, reborn. As if he had known even then that a moment would come when he must tell them to their faces that he would not be reborn in their image, but would keep his own. And this was the moment. No matter what Sir Edward had found out, or who had told him, no matter what Sir Edward said, he himself must say it. I belong to what my father taught me, and not to you.

He followed Sir Edward through the long sequence of rooms, one opening from another, until they came to the end of the north wing, and what Sir Edward was pleased to call his study. Here he received his rents, and drank in private with his dogs for company, and kept his books of accounts, and half a dozen other books he had never opened in his life. There was a table, and half a dozen big chairs, and a vast stone hearth with the Tascombe coat of arms carved above it. There were dog leashes and hawking gear; a pair of antique rapiers; a crossbow and a claymore which Sir Edward's father had brought home from Flodden. In this room Sir Edward dealt out justice to tenants, servants, children, womenfolk, according to his whim and humour and a vague acquaintance with the law and ethics.

As Ralph followed him into the room Sir Edward took up his stance before the empty hearth, spreading his legs wide, tucking his thumbs into the broad leather belt of his old-fashioned breeches, and blowing out his dark mauve cheeks to make himself look more terrible.

'Close the door!' he ordered. And as Ralph closed it, he shouted, 'Now, come here to me. Tell me! Are you gone mad! Blood an' hounds! Ten years in this house! Ten years o' rearing, of good care and good religion and the love of her majesty taught you like – like – and – and –' His face had swelled so much he looked as if he was choking inside his narrow ruff, and he tore at the starched linen with brutal fingers. 'Lucky for you you weren't caught and taken along wi' that damned traitor of a priestling. I'd not have stirred a hand to save you, I'll tell you that. A Mass at Murley's farm! That beggarly vermin! I'll have that stew of rascals hanged to the last one of 'em! But you! Ralph Paulet! My cousin's son, my own blood an' kin! *You* to go! And to take her with you! Were ye stark mad, an' longing for the rack? As for her –'

'Sir! I did not take her, but I beg you – she had no –'

'Don't lie to me, boy! Ye think I don't know her after all these years? A sly, Irish slut with –'

'Sir, I cannot let you speak –'

'Don't "sir" me, damn you! You unlicked puppy! You milksop Judas! D'you know what you ha' done to me? To this house? This family that took you in an' sheltered you, kept you even after your father did what he did, an' died as he

46

died – a damned traitor and a rascal – Nay, don't answer me
or I swear I'll ha' you chained and led like a dancing bear to
Taunton gaol and let the law take its course with you. Ye
should be down on your knees to me for forgiveness, not
hoity-toitying and looking arrogant. Ye've come near to
ruining me and all here, blast and curse you! Bringing
suspicion on me! With two papists sheltered here. One of
'em a daughter of an Irish rebel – Aye, did you not hear that
the war has started again in Ireland? And the other of 'em a
traitor's son and following the traitor's path already, you,
you ungrateful spawn of satan! And I'm your kin. I gave you
shelter, both of you. What does that make me? If old Fettle
hears of it he'll send word to London. D'ye fancy to see my
head on Traitors' Gate along wi' your own?'

He had fallen into one of the great oak chairs as his
shouting died into a venomous whisper. He stopped for
breath, tearing at his ruff again and there was a knock at the
door. Sir Edward ignored it and was about to speak again
when the door opened and Parson Dagge's long, grey nose
poked round it.

'Sir Edward –' the parson began, but before he could say
any more Lady Jane swept past him.

'What do ye want?' Sir Edward barked, getting heavily to
his feet as the parson carefully shut the door behind him.
'Can a man not have a quiet word in his own house?'

'Quiet?' Lady Jane's thin lips curved unpleasantly. 'Why,
I swear you could be heard down in the servant's hall!'

Sir Edward muttered an oath, spreading his hands on the
desk, the liver-coloured spots on the backs of them dark
against the yellowing skin. 'This ain't women's business,' he
growled, looking at his wife and then including the parson
in his glance so that Ralph had an insane desire to laugh.

'Oh, but it is, Edward dear!' Lady Jane said with
dangerous sweetness. 'It is the business of everyone in
Tascombe, in fact. That is why I have brought Parson Dagge
with me.' She looked then at Ralph for the first time and he
recoiled before the hatred in her eyes. 'This – this papist brat
has brought disgrace on us all. Going to a Mass! A Roman
Mass! Every house in the county will be closed to us, Edward!

D'you realize that? And if her majesty comes to hear of it – I shudder to think what *that* could mean!'

'Yes, yes I know,' Sir Edward said testily. 'That's just what I've been saying –'

They faced each other across the desk. Old man and young wife, their dislike for each other a palpable thing in the small, stuffy room. Did they lie together still, Ralph wondered for a fleeting second in the middle of all his troubles. Did those yellow, spotted hands – ? He looked at Lady Jane almost with sympathy – and then all the sympathy was gone as she spoke again.

'You were a fool to have taken him in the first place, Edward. Just because he was a Paulet! Because his mad traitor of a father was a relation!'

'How dare you –' Ralph began, and the parson stared at him shocked, but Lady Jane and Sir Edward ignored him completely, as if they had forgotten he was there.

'That wasn't the only reason.' Sir Edward's colour was rising again as he glared at his wife. 'You wanted to take him too because his mother was a Luttrell. You thought her family would come visiting out of gratitude!'

'Just because *my* father was only a merchant you think – you think –' Lady Jane's voice was growing shrill. 'But you were glad enough to get his money, weren't you? And the Luttrells *did* visit here – once anyway –'

Parson Dagge lifted one long, ink-stained hand. 'Sir Edward – Lady Jane – forgive me but are we not – ah – getting away from the point? The boy –'

'And the girl!' Lady Jane snapped, looking directly at Ralph, acknowledging his presence again. 'She was at the Mass too!'

'She only went because – because –'

But the parson cut across Ralph. 'The girl is a bad influence,' he intoned. 'And there has always been an unhealthy reserve in her demeanour. A typically *Romish* reserve I would call it. She is quite uninterested moreover in learning about the true religion. One day' – he gave his foolish, nervous laugh – 'one day I found her reading the holy bible, and of course I was very pleased. I thought, at last,

48

at last she is beginning to see the light. But when I told her so, do you know what she said?' He paused for effect.

'Well, what did she say?' Lady Jane asked impatiently while Sir Edward merely grunted and Ralph held his breath.

'She said –' He stopped speaking as though in pain and then went on hoarsely. 'She said she was only reading it because there was such beautiful English in it!'

Lady Jane nodded sympathetically, but Sir Edward, who was almost illiterate, only grunted again, and then seeing the beginning of a smile on Ralph's face straightened suddenly and said roughly, 'We've talked enough. You, boy –' stabbing a thick, black-nailed finger at Ralph, 'I want you out o' here by morning. The girl too.'

'Out of – both?' Ralph felt as if he had received a physical blow. 'You mean – ?'

'Aye, three weeks, a month'll see this blown over, or the worst of it. You go to Honiton, to my other place. Make a dawn start. Take John Bowden wi' you. He can bring back the Honiton rents and ought else as needs bringing. And when ye come back here it'll be to talk of your future. Which 'll not lie in this house, I can tell you that, so think on it. And now, get away from me before I repent o' my leniency and turn you over to the law as my duty calls me to do. Go on, damn you! I want to wake tomorrow knowing ye're ten safe miles from here a'ready.'

'But – I tell you – Una –' Ralph stammered.

'Damn your soul, boy!' Sir Edward looked as if he might have a fit. 'D'you mean to hang? Are ye determined on it? Get out o' my sight!'

Without looking at any of them again, Ralph walked out of the study. There was no sense in staying or arguing. He went up to his bed-chamber to pack and write a letter to Una, since there was no chance of seeing her. He wrote and rewrote the letter in his mind a hundred times with burning eloquence, but on paper it turned into a few lame sentences of regret. Until he tore up the last scrawled and crossed-out draft, and abandoned all thought of writing anything. He'd see Alice surely, and get her to tell his farewells to Una, and his promise of a swift return. And then! What thoughts he'd have worked out to tell her! Three weeks were not a lifetime. And she'd have had the same three weeks in which to – miss him? Think of her injustice to him? Or – and the rememberance of Alice came back like an ugly wound re-opening. Was he truly mad? Even to think of sending Alice to her with what amounted to a declaration of love?

And he sat until near dawn holding the broken goose quill in his hand, the ink pot open and the ink drying, the torn scraps of ill-drafted letters at his feet, his clothes not yet packed. He pushed in clean shirts and stockings, his Sunday doublet, the few books he had, and went down the stairs in the still-silent house, his mind half dazed with sleeplessness and his eyes burning. It would have to be John Bowden who would take his message to her when he rode back from Honiton tomorrow. But – she might be – would be gone by them. He'd have to find some way of passing the message on – Where would she be sent? To the Maltbys? Surely not. Maybe Wyvern, and the Oundles? They were Sir Edward's cousins and had been kind to Una more than once. It would be there, without a doubt, and John could find an excuse to ride there after he got back. That would be best. And he himself would have more time to think.

The first light of morning. John waiting, the horses already saddled. Munching bread and cheese, wiping his mouth as Ralph came out to him. 'I ha' a parcel o' bread an' summat an' a bottle o' ale fer ye, Master Ralph. Alice towd me to gi' it ye, she said ye'd not think to break your fast yourself.'

'Alice? Is she –'

'Nay, nay, back in her bed, lad. 'Tis too early for the likes o' her.'

Too early? Or too dangerous?

He turned that over in his mind as well, as he rode down the avenue. Thought, for the first time in hours of what was happening to the priest, must be happening. Or was he lying mercifully unconscious in a lock-up cell somewhere along the road to Taunton?

The priest, and Una, and Robert Parsons, and his own future, going round and round in his mind, until he found himself swaying in the saddle, half asleep as he rode, the sun already warm, and Tascombe far behind.

And found almost to his horror that it was pleasant riding, and that he was sharp set with hunger.

'I'll not eat!' he swore. And within another quarter hour was sitting by the roadside, eating a slice of game pasty, and bread and mutton that he shared with John, and drinking the bottle of ale that Alice had packed for him with the food in a linen cloth.

Three weeks were not for ever. And if he must be apart from her, well it was no wrong to her to enjoy a day's riding, and the sunlight. And then he thought of the priest again, of that shuffling, stumbling creature led between the soldiers, his face a mask of blood, his hair clotted with it, his shirt in rags. He let the last of the bread and mutton fall from his hand, into the dusty grass of the roadside. There were flowers there, yellow primroses, and small blue forget-me-nots, as if a child long ago had planted a child's garden here and then abandoned it.

Forget me not.

Robert Parsons' blunt, stocky figure, walking ahead of him down the avenue at Bunsery, turning to Ralph's father for a last handclasp, a last blessing.

The empty house. Old Sam, old Meg crying, 'Master Ralph, Master Ralph, they've taken him!'

The young priest's face, white with a boy's terror, and then calm again, as he lifted the Host in front of him like a shield. Only yesterday. Only a few hours ago. And it was already as if the picture's edge was blurred.

Oh my Lord, oh my Father in heaven, what kind of man am I?

If John Bowden had not been there he would have gone down on his knees.

'I give myself to You,' he whispered. 'I am not worthy to be Your priest. Not worthy to touch the shoes of the humblest priest who ever served You. But I will be Your servant. Let me give my life to You. For You. Let me be Your soldier. Let me fight for You. Let that priest, my father, all Your martyred servants not go unavenged.'

CHAPTER 5

THREE WEEKS. In Honiton. In the small, ancient, quiet house. Stone and timber. Scarcely lived in since the old king's time, and already ancient then. Like camping out rather than living in a house. An old woman from the next farm to clean the two rooms he used, and give him a makeshift dinner. For the rest, caring for himself. All the time in the world to think, and it did him no good. Una haunting his sleep. Haunting his days. Now untouchable, far off, like the image of the saint, coldly watching him, contemptuous.

Now very close.

To take her away from Tascombe, marry her? Bring her to – where? Live with her as his wife? How? On what? And beyond her image, Father Parsons beckoning. Let a man leave father and mother, field and house, to follow Me. But wife?

She is not your wife. And never can be. Come to Me alone.

He heard no news. Of Tascombe, of the priest who must by now lie in Taunton gaol, or be on his way to London in a cart. Or be already in the Tower.

No news of anywhere. The old woman too deaf to hear questions, too locked in her own narrow world to answer them.

A week gone by. Two weeks. Three. He did not so much as know whether he was to go back to Tascombe at the end of the third week or wait there to be sent for, or –

He began riding back that Wednesday, and met John

Bowden four miles along the road. Had to turn back with him because there were messages to give, and things to collect from the house, the nearby farm, another neighbour whose name Ralph had never so much as learned, living like a hermit there. And old John so taciturn that they had made the round of visits before Ralph could get the news of Tascombe out of him. The priest? Oh, aye. To Taunton, mebbe. Lunnon? Mebbe there too. London so far off he could not imagine anyone going there who was not there already.

Alice? Oh, aye. Well enough. What else she'd be? Sir Edward? Oh, flourishing, God be thanked. A bit humourous, mebbe. But it was the weather. And – Una? Mistress Una? You did give her my message? That I'd be gone only a few weeks, that –

John Bowden looking straight ahead, not turning.

'She be gone. Gone this three weeks.'

'I know, I know. I thought she would be. But is she not back yet? Not expected? Today maybe? Or tomorrow?'

'Expected?' The slow voice, the slow mind turning that over like a stone in the broad, weather-carved hand. 'How'd she be expected, Master Ralph? She be gone back to Ireland this past three weeks, since t' day after you come here.'

He was making a stupid mistake. Ireland? Ralph felt the sun on his back. Saw the fields around them. Felt his horse move beneath him. Ireland? It was impossible. He rode close to John and caught his bridle, pulling him to a halt.

'Ireland? You must be out of your mind! You're trying to – John!'

The old man's eyes colourless from sun and rain and age and labour. Stupid as an ox's eyes.

'What is it, Master Ralph?'

'She can't be gone! Tell me man, tell me you're lying!' Catching him by his doublet, shaking him. 'Gone back to Ireland?'

'Aye, Master Ralph. Aye.'

He let him go. Mumbled something. Turned his horse's head and rode like a fool towards the Tascombe road, John's stupid voice calling after him, and then fading. And reached

Tascombe in the summer's dusk, the house abed, a stable-man lighting a lantern, his face thick with sleep.

Into the silent kitchens.

He knew where Alice slept, in a kind of cupboard alcove beyond the sculleries, apart from the other maids – with her own door and a mousehole of a window giving onto an inner yard. He found his way by touch, pushing the door open.

The smell of sleep, stale air and warmth. Of Alice. Kneeling down for fear of stumbling on her body. Stretching out a hand to feel for her shoulder.

'Alice?' Whispering. Afraid of waking other servants. 'Alice?'

Her body stirring, turning, her arm falling sideways to touch his knee. He held it, found her shoulder, pressed his fingers into soft, sleep-warmed flesh. 'Alice! Wake up! Be quiet, it's me, Ralph. Wake up quietly.'

She sat up abruptly, began to say something, her voice too loud, and at the same time drugged with sleep. He put his hand over her mouth.

'It's me, Ralph.'

She caught his wrist, held his hand in both hers.

'What – what dost 'ee – thee's cold, lad.' One hand finding his cheek. 'Master Ralph come for warmth?' Her voice half amused, half still asleep. 'If thee's found here –'

The sound of bedclothes rustling. Her arms round his neck.

'No, Alice! Where is she? Where's she gone?'

The arms loosening. 'Mistress Una?'

'Yes! Yes!'

'Gone home to Ireland. To her own folk.'

'But she cannot be gone back! Tell me the truth! As you hope for heaven!'

'Hush, someone'll hear us! Lie down aside me an' whisper.'

'No!' Pulling himself back from her, not even a flicker of temptation on him, the smell of sweat and staleness heavy on the air. 'When? When did she go?'

'This three weeks. For mercy's sake, keep thy voice low!'

'Where – I mean, what road?'

'Road? Ireland's across the sea – by boat –'

'Damnation! What road to the boat then? Bristol? The Bristol road?' Three weeks. She could be in Ireland now.

'They didn't say –'

Out of that woman-smelling dark. Into the silent kitchens, the fires dead, a spit dog waking in its nest of rushes, whining softly in expectation of a new day's slavery. Into the stable yard.

The stable-man had gone back to his loft to sleep again, the mare no more than stabled and a cloth flung over her, not even fed or watered. Her saddle hung on the timber peg beside her, and when he had led her out into the yard he saddled her, took his sack which he had dropped on a pile of straw and began walking her, for she could not be ridden any further, after such a day's journey. He walked her down the avenue. Turned right for the village, for the road that would, if he followed it for long enough, bring him to Bristol. He walked five miles and fell asleep under a hedge, the horse cropping the grass beside him, coming now and then to blow anxiously against his face, bewildered at this treatment.

He slept until dawn, dreaming of ships. Of Ireland. Woke cold and stiff-jointed and hungry, and rode north as if he knew where he was going, and why. Rode into Bristol the second evening and knew that he had wasted his journey, that there was no more hope of finding a trace of her than of flying to the moon. Crowds. Shops. Taverns. More crowds. Men whose accents might have been a foreign language. A negro with an earring, grinning from a tavern doorway. Painted women. Beckoning. The harbour. Ships. Sailors. More painted women. Drunken men. Piles of casks. Bales. Horses. Drays. Waggons unloading and loading again. Drivers cursing, shouting, threatening porters with damnation if they did not hurry. Smell of the sea, of rotten fish and tar and cordage. Bedlam. Babel. To ask if one girl, three weeks ago – But he did ask, and the first half-dozen men he questioned only stared at him in contemptuous amazement. The seventh stole his purse, with his last testers and a crown piece in it, and he was left penniless.

Another man who had seen it happen and the thief

running, advised him not to follow. 'Unless thee wants thy throat cut. Be more careful, lad. An' mind thy horse and gear, or thee'll lose them too.'

As for a ship to Ireland, 'Aye, there were, a while back. Two or three. Dublin. Waterford. They'd sailed for Waterford likely. The north parts? Maybe. Who could tell? With the war there and the fear o' fighting no one could say for certain – best mind thy horse better than thy purse!'

Looking for a ship to Ireland. Leading the mare, as out of place here as a boat at Tascombe. Tascombe a hundred years away. In another lifetime.

'To Ireland? Nay master, we're for Rouen. For France lad, an' a load of wine.'

It was fully a minute before he understood. Rouen, France. And he stayed there like a country fool, staring at the man. Rouen. France. And knew. That this was his sign, his road.

He sold the mare for seven pounds. And the saddle for another two. Nine pounds. Would it be enough? And had no doubt of it. As if already he was in the hands of a power that would bring him where he had to go. A power that had already taken hold of everything, disposed of everything. His life. Una's.

He ate his first tranquil meal of the journey in a tavern. Roast meat and a jack of ale, sitting quietly as if he had spent half his life travelling. And under the quietness his heart beating, beating. Rouen. France. To become God's servant there, his soldier. First France. Then Spain. He scarcely needed to think of it. God would bring him there in His own time, in His own way. And he finished his ale, and paid, and went back to find the ship, and bargain for a passage.

CHAPTER 6

ROUEN. The smell of herring, and when he had left the quays, narrow, twisting streets and the interminable ringing of church bells. The fury of traffic now and the terror of being stopped, questioned. So lost for a moment that he could have wished himself in England again, in Tascombe, anywhere on earth but here. How could he find anyone who'd understand him? The few words of French that he had once learned from Parson Dagge were gone out of his head along with everything else. A carter shouted at him, the great horses crashing past, iron-shod wheels grinding on the cobbles, threatening to crush him against the wall. Still narrower streets, half-timbered houses, their yellow plaster-work breaking from the laths underneath, sordid and reeking, leaning towards one another above the narrow lane. But as he walked to the far end it opened suddenly onto a broad square. There was a stone fountain. And a church. A church so huge, so magnificent, that for half a minute he did not recognize it for what it was. A church! And all his fears vanishing. A church. Priests. What a fool he was to have been anxious. How small his faith was! Of course, a church! And he crossed the square almost running, as if he was running towards home.

So great a church he was lost inside it. Stone pillars. A mist of coloured light from huge, stained-glass windows. Candles burning. A strange, sharp, acrid smell that must be incense although he had never smelled incense in all his life. Could not remember when he had last heard or thought of it. But he

57

knew it now as though it had been his constant friend for years.

Statues. Altars. More candles burning. More windows. People kneeling, talking, walking about as though they were in a street. A priest. Two others, friars in white habits with black hoods, walking slowly, hands hidden in wide sleeves, heads bent. One young. One old. The old friar looking at Ralph. Questioning, as if he recognized a stranger.

'*Mon Père,*' Ralph whispered, searching for more words.

'You are English?' the old man said with a slow carefulness. 'An Englishman?'

'Yes, yes! Father, I –' And had no words even in English for what he needed to say. The two friars, if that was what they were, waited for him, an air about the older man as if he would wait all day, until Ralph spoke again. 'I am a Catholic,' he whispered. 'I have come to Rouen to –'

The two friars bent their heads in acknowledgement.

What could he say to them? I have come to serve God? The words sounded not only mad, but imbecile, a fool's bragging.

'To escape?' the old friar suggested. 'You are in trouble?'

'Yes – at least – if I could talk to you, Father?'

Not answering, only that bending of his head again in acknowledgement.

'I need –'

'You need somewhere to stay?'

'Yes! Yes, that too! But –'

'Come with us, my son. We will show you the way to go.'

Like another sign! The way! The way he must go to find – They were already walking on, the two friars, with a soft shuffling of leather sandals, heads bent, not looking back to see if he was following. Out into the square, the sunlight. Turning once to beckon him. Laneways. A broad street. Other lanes. Another square. And the dark, almost windowless façade of a great building that could have been a prison, it lowered so heavily on the crowds passing. A small wicket door set into a great timber one. A friar opening a grille. Closing it. Unbolting.

For a second a chill touched Ralph's mind like the heavy shadow of the building. He had not imagined barred and bolted doors, stone walls. But the old friar was beckoning again, and now there was the cold of stone. A stone corridor. Echoes. Silence. As if there was no sunlight, there had never been an open sky or the sea or moorland. As far from Murley's barn as – but he could not find an image for such an immense distance. From these friars in their quiet, ageless patience to that frightened, too-young priest.

'Wait here, my son.'

The door closed on him. A dark, stone room. Heavy table. Heavy chair. An oak bench against one wall. A great crucifix hanging above the chair. He crossed himself, wanted to kneel, and was afraid of being found kneeling. Waited. The silence so deep it was like the depths of a mine, the mines they told of, where men burrowed like moles under the ground, digging for seams of tin.

Ten minutes went by. At least that. Then half an hour. An hour? He got up from the bench where he had been sitting, and went to the door. Opened it. Only silence, broken by the door's creaking. Nothing else. What could he do? There was nothing he could do but wait. Someone must come, some time. He went back to the bench, and this time he lay down on it, his sack for a pillow, ready to spring up at the first sound of footsteps. And fell asleep as if he had not slept for nights.

He woke with a shock of fear, not knowing where he was. The ship? Tascombe? And saw the face bending over him. Thin-lipped mouth. Narrowed eyes. The shadow of the friar's hood hiding his cheeks.

'What is your name?' the friar said, standing back as Ralph jerked himself upright on the bench, fumbling for his senses.

'I – I am sorry – I was waiting so long –' Did that sound rude, impatient? 'I don't mean –'

'Your name, boy.'

Ralph flushed, the word 'boy', the tone of voice, an unpleasant echo of Sir Edward. And yet the friar was a foreigner, although his English sounded very pure. Purer than Ralph's own west-country burr. But cold. Like his face and manner. No welcome in either. Only cold enquiry, the hands hidden in the white sleeves, the face still half hidden by the black hood. What Ralph could see of it was like a carving, like the carved figure on the crucifix behind him, the flesh gouged away by suffering and discipline. A face he had never imagined for a priest's, although now –

'Ralph Paulet,' he replied slowly, his mind still dazed with sleep.

'Christopher Paulet's kin?'

'His son, Father.'

'His son? Where have you come from?'

'Bristol just now – '

The priest looked down, his eyelids white and long and waxen. So transparent they were almost blue, over the pale blue eyes. And then lifting, sudden and sharp, piercing. 'You have papers?'

'None, Father.'

'Ah.' Strangely enough he seemed pleased to hear that, if it was possible to interpret anything about his face as a show of pleasure. Only the slightest relaxation of the mouth. 'And before Bristol?'

Ralph told him. About Tascombe. His mother's death. The promise she had wrung from his father. To have him reared a – reared in a Protestant household. Substituting his own words for that long-ago promise.

'As a Protestant?' The cold, dispassionate eyes stripping away that small veil of pretence.

'Yes,' Ralph whispered.

'But you have some knowledge of the Faith?' he asked after a moment's silence.

'I have – been to Mass.'

'How often?'

'Ten, perhaps twelve times. In England – '

The priest lifted a thin, blue-veined hand. 'I know how things are. So you have learned almost nothing?'

'I – '

'It is best to confess ignorance, rather than to claim knowledge. Why are you here?' The question sharp as a knife thrust. No chance of thinking, or shaping an answer.

'To give myself - to - to the Church.'

'As a priest?'

'No, Father. As a - as a soldier.'

'Why?'

Ralph stared at him. 'My father -'

'You would fight against England?'

'Against - ?' So bluntly put. He had never thought of it in those terms, those words. 'I - yes. Yes. For the Faith. For -' He could not bring himself to say 'God'.

'For what else besides the Faith?'

'For - my father. He was a friend of - they arrested him for hiding Father Parsons.'

'I know.'

'You know him?' Suddenly there was the chance of warmth, of contact. Of all things he had hoped to find, had come here to find. That binding together in an army fighting for the Faith. 'You know Father Parsons?'

Nothing in the eyes, or the mouth. Turning the question aside as if Ralph had not spoken. 'Has he some part in your decision to come here?'

'In - in a way.' Ralph tried to tell what way, and all his thoughts, all his self-dedication seemed to lie in fragments on the stone floor of the room, like a broken cup. A boy's boasting.

'How old are you?'

'Almost twenty, Father.'

The friar lowered his eyelids as though that last answer had decided something in his mind. 'The Church will accept you,' he said. 'I leave for Spain tomorrow. You may come with me.' Then the transparent lids lifted and the cold eyes held Ralph's for a second. 'I am Father Ignatius.'

CHAPTER 7

SPAIN. The sky like a burning glass. The hills behind them like a memory of paradise, green and cool. Oak woods. Mountain torrents breaking in white foam. Deep pools. Rocks shimmering in the heat. Brown rocks. Brown road. Brown villages. Brown fields. Burned and ashen from the sun.

He sweated as he walked, Father Ignatius striding ahead of him, seeming not to notice the heat, nor the dust, nor the endless road ahead of them which vanished in dark blue shadows at the farthest southern edge of the horizon. Like walking down a long road into the fires of hell. They had not eaten since daybreak, and he had finished his flask of wine long before noon. Now it was nearing twilight, and the heat was still unendurable. Dust on his tongue, under his eyelids, clinging to his sweating body under the shirt, under his breeches, in his shoes that by now were no more than a remembrance of footwear, broken across the instep, worn through in the soles.

He wanted to call out after Father Ignatius to stop, to let them both find wine or water, food. That cluster of houses over to the left, like a wasps' nest built of mud and clinging to the hillside – surely there? Or that building – a substantial building of some sort, crowning the hill – at least, he thought it was a building, for the sun was so blinding he could not really focus on anything. And cursed aloud as he stumbled over his broken shoe.

Father Ignatius stood still, turning his head slowly as

Ralph came up to him. By some alchemy of flesh and spirit he seemed to be free of dust as far as his mouth and eyes were concerned. There were white rims to his eyes and then the mask of brown dust. And he was not sweating. 'I must warn you,' he said. 'In this country we do not tolerate blasphemy.'

'Blasphemy?' Ralph asked, bewildered, his tongue sticking to the roof of his mouth as he echoed the words.

'You have just taken the Lord's name in vain. If any servant of the Holy Office should hear you do that, you would be imprisoned. And as a heretic –' The pale, cold eyes looking to see what effect the word would have. Ralph swallowed and said nothing.

'In the eyes of the Holy Office you are nothing else. Guard your tongue, my son. Guard your thoughts.'

He walked on, leaving Ralph to follow, carrying both their satchels, neither of them heavy at the beginning of the day, but now after nearly twelve hours of walking, each alone like a sack of corn. But he would not ask for even a minute's rest. If Father Ignatius could do without it, then so would he.

Until after another mile he had to call out, 'Father, I must stop. I can't even see where I'm going.' Sweat blinding him. His legs shivering with exhaustion. He flung the satchels down and sat on a rock by the roadside. Only the ruts worn by cart wheels and the prints of oxen's hooves showed where the road lay through the brown desert of the landscape.

Father Ignatius took out his Rosary and walked slowly to and fro, from one side of the road to the other, murmuring the Pater Noster, the Aves. One decade. Two. When he had finished the second string of prayers he put away his beads and came to where Ralph sat.

'I have observed you on this journey,' the priest said. 'There is both good and bad in what I have seen. I believe your story. I believe that your motive in coming with me is what you say it is. Or almost. I know it to be revenge for your father's death, rather than the love of God and hatred for His enemies. But it will serve. Someone will make a soldier of you and you will do well enough. But God requires more from you than that. Pray that you may be able to give it to

Him when the moment comes.'

'What do you mean, Father?'

'When the time is ripe, I shall tell you. Perhaps it was truly God's will that brought us together.' Saying that last more to himself than to Ralph, turning away as a long way off a cloud of dust announced a farm cart or another traveller. Ralph rose to his feet, and picked up the satchels. What had he meant, he wondered. Both good and bad in what he had seen. God requires more – Did he still mean the priesthood? Did he think that –

Never! Whatever else this journey had taught Ralph it had taught him that. He had not the beginnings of a priest in him. Even to say the Rosary with Father Ignatius made him uneasy. He had thought it would give him piety, but it had the opposite effect, his mind wandering, pictures coming into it unbidden. Of Una. Of Tascombe. And more than once, of Alice. It had happened last night, in the wretched hovel of an inn where they had eaten bread that tasted of woodshavings and garlic, and drunk a wine like rancid oil and vinegar. The servant girl had watched him from the corners of her dark, wide-set eyes. Her hair had been blacker than Alice's, but she had the same fullness about her breast, the same walk. She had haunted his mind through supper and he had almost longed for the Rosary as a defence against his flesh. And then had let his mind wander again and thought of Alice, of – Was that what Father Ignatius meant? Ralph had made a tired, confused attempt at Confession during the long journey. Was Father Ignatius remembering what he had told him? About Alice? But I'm to be a soldier, not a priest, he thought. Can a soldier not – ? And remembered Una and was ashamed again. Una, as far away as the evening star and as near as the sunlight. Where was she now? He tried to imagine her in Ireland, to recall all the images she had conjured up for him. Her father's cattle, herds of lean beasts driven by herdsmen with bare legs and feet and hair down to their eyes. The summer pastures where the cattle were taken in summertime, her father and the whole family travelling with the herdsmen. Was that her life now? England half forgotten already?

64

Or had she reached her father at all? Was she perhaps a prisoner somewhere, in Dublin, or some other part of the north? Held by someone else as hostage? He stumbled again, thinking of that, and of how much worse a fate she was likely to come on if she was indeed a hostage. Began to curse again, a round Somerset oath that had been the small change of Tascombe talk, at least among the serving men. He saw Father Ignatius quiver into stillness.

'I'm sorry,' he muttered, but Father Ignatius did not answer, walking on ahead, his shadow grown long and dark on the road – two shadows moving slowly across the rocks alongside which seemed to have grown lighter-coloured with the coming of evening. Only another mile.

But another twelve-hour journey on the morrow, and the day after that. Mile after mile after scorched and hideous mile. Village after village. Town after town. City after city. Burgos. Valladolid. Salamanca. Coimbra. Santarem. Monasteries to stay in. Stone cells. Monks hiding their curiosity behind impassive faces, like wax masks of discipline. The atmosphere of Spain, of the Holy Office, closing round them softly, like dust settling, clogging mouths and eyes. A stifling piety. Or was it only because he was with Father Ignatius, and laughter stopped when they arrived? The girls looked as if it was in their nature to laugh, but not the men. Nor the older women who were sombre as shadows, dressed in mourning. And there were priests everywhere, like darker shadows.

The countryside no longer burned now, was green again. The hills of Portugal, woods, vineyards. A difference in the people. A softness in their eyes and voices. The river Tagus. Broad. Swift-moving. A sea coolness in the nights. And showers of summer rain.

And Lisbon at last. A vast mass of buildings. Churches, but with none of the starkness of Spanish churches. Flowers in the windows of the houses. Painted walls. Men laughing. A fortress. Soldiers drilling. A group of gentlemen in finery, watching the marching and countermarching of the men. Father Ignatius touching Ralph's arm, pointing.

'Here is our journey's end,' he said. 'I shall see you

65

established here and leave you. But we shall meet again.' He walked slowly towards the group of onlookers, his robe brushing the dust of the ground. And as he came towards them their manner changed, stiffened, all their easiness stilled. One of them bent his knee in reverence, kissing Father Ignatius' offered hand.

They talked for a moment, and then the priest turned and beckoned.

'Señor Marques,' he said, in the Aragon Spanish that Ralph had already begun to learn, 'allow me to present to you the candidate for your favour. He wished to serve God and his majesty as a soldier. May I leave him in your care?'

CHAPTER 8

A BABBLE of Gaelic rising to the thatched roof and the smell of unwashed bodies – nearly thirty people but her mother not there – Una had understood less than one word in six of what her brother Art had said, only that she was dead, and in any case he seemed indifferent as to how or why she had died, as if it had happened too long ago, or was too usual an occurrence to remember. He sat opposite her now at the long table with her father and her stepmother and the old harper. Siobhan, the young servant girl, and the other house servants, now that supper was over, squatted on the floor with her father's kerns – great, brawny men, their weapons beside them, wearing their cloaks even here indoors and watching her with bright, hard eyes through their thick fringes of hair like animals peering through undergrowth.

When she had arrived with Art from Derry a few hours earlier they had all crowded round her, the women fingering the velvet of her cloak, touching her hair, chattering at her in Gaelic. But they had drawn back soon, clearly disappointed in her. She couldn't understand them, couldn't speak to them – and worse still, maybe her own horror had shown in her face – That they should be her people – these – these – Even in her own mind she did not want to call them 'savages'. She had looked for her father in sudden terror of what she would find and Art had turned aside from the man he had been talking to as if he had read her mind, and brought her into the house.

She had not recognized her father at first. An old, fat man, bursting out of his leather jacket, fatter even than Sir Edward and with none of Sir Edward's careless kindness of expression, a harshness in his heavy face and in his voice, his short hair and beard which she remembered as fiery red like Art's, now grey as a badger. There had not been even a hint of welcome in his bloodshot eyes, nothing but a cold, calculating appraisal.

Now she sat at his table, staring into the last of her wine, ignored except as a figure of fun who could understand no more than a word or two of her own language, and her face reddened, remembering the stories she had told them in Tascombe. The gold ornaments! The silk dresses! The house that was as big, as grand as any castle! Her stepmother had indeed a gold necklet round her thick, white neck and her red dress with the hanging sleeves was made of silk. Her burnt yellow hair was coiled elegantly enough under the white kerchief and her father did wear a gold chain. There was even a harper as she'd said too, but he was an old man who could scarcely pluck the strings of his instrument and sang his own praise song – she imagined that that was what it had been – in a high, cracked, wailing voice. And the house! One room only and that like a cattle byre! The rushes on the floor seemed not to have been changed since the previous winter and were full of rotting bones which the hounds had buried there. There was no chimney and the smoke from the fire on the stone hearth in the middle of the floor found its lazy way through a hole in the roof, or filled one's lungs when the door was opened – but at least it was better than the stench of the outside privy which came with it. Surely it had not been like this when she was a child? Or did children not notice?

I should never have let them send me away from Tascombe, she thought. I should have refused to leave – promised never to go to Mass again, to be the most devoted Reformer there ever was – promising anything. For what would it have mattered? Ralph was her religion.

Later, when the last of the tapers had been extinguished and the hounds put outside she lay on a bed of straw that the girl Siobhan had put down for her beside the end wall. She was still fully dressed but she had blankets, which the girl had taken from a bag hanging from the roof, as well as her cloak to cover her. Her father, who with Art had long since finished the jug of whiskey, had had to be carried to his bed, attended by her stepmother. The bed was in a kind of wall recess, hung with a leather curtain, but the others lay round the fire wrapped in their cloaks, the men snoring drunk on a thin, sour-smelling beer – and some of the women besides.

I must sleep, Una told herself. I must sleep or I shall go mad. But she couldn't sleep, her mind, her thoughts in a turmoil. Thinking back over the long, hard ride down from Derry, to Derry itself. Seeing the straggle of huts, the steep hill and the monastery or church or whatever the stone buildings had been – much more vividly seeing the quayside and the boat moored there which had brought her from Bristol and on which she had had to wait for Art. It had taken several days to send word to her father that she had arrived and as much again for Art and five men to come for her, and it had taken the last of the money Sir Edward had given her – thrown at her would have been nearer the mark.

'I'd a mind to send you to a neighbour's,' he'd said as she picked up the leather bag from the table. 'That was my first intention. But then I – we – thought it best to send you back to your father.' We. Lady Jane and Parson Dagge. But for them she might have got round him.

She had left next day with one of the grooms, having spent an hour writing a letter to Ralph. A letter saying goodbye, and more than that – too much more – if he'd had a mind to read between the lines. And at the last minute, losing courage, thinking only of how he had ridden past her, had left no message for her, she had torn up the letter, tears streaming down her face.

The tears rolled slowly down her face now and she did not bother to wipe them away – and suddenly a shadow moved, became the silhouette of a man beside the fire. There was a hissing sound and the sharp smell of burned urine. The shadow moved back to its sleeping place. Una lay rigid. The man – the man had – had – *there*! In the fire! Too lazy, too careless, too brutish to go out to the privy. Although God knew the privy was horror enough to stop anyone using it, day or night.

She thought of her bedroom in Tascombe. The fresh linen, the dried lavender. And the kitchen – bread baking and pastries golden from the great oven. In the withdrawing room the smell of wax polish and fresh herbs, of roses from the rose garden. Oh to be there again, to be the very least of all that household instead of her father's daughter here. To be with Ralph. At night too in Tascombe she had gone to bed to think of him, hoping that next day perhaps he might kiss her – kiss her properly as he had done only once. Hoping he might – touch her, her body shivering with a strange excitement she only partly understood. But next day would come and nothing would change. She might not see him at all, or she would only see him for a few minutes and he would be as friendly as ever but with that new sternness which had come to him of late. She would look at him and remember her foolish yearnings of the night before and feel bitterly ashamed that she should have thought of such things, when clearly he never did. The evening he had rushed past her on his horse she had nearly died of hurt. And not only then, for Lady Jane liked to talk to her of their marriage plans for Ralph - marriage to an English Protestant girl, with land and money and friends at court, looking sideways at her in that way she had, each word a piercing arrow so that Una had to catch her breath with the pain of them, knowing that Lady Jane had guessed her secret long ago and delighted in tormenting her. Knowing that above all even if by some wonderful miracle Ralph did love her he could never be hers. And as she turned and twisted on the rushes she asked herself once more why he had done no more than kiss her properly that once – Was it because she had drawn back? It had been so stupid of her, so childish – as if she hadn't wanted him to kiss her – when she had wanted it more than anything else in the whole world. But she'd been almost afraid, not of him surely, but of herself, of what was happening to her, to her body. She hadn't known there could be this wonderful, terrifying excitement – this strange,

70

strange feeling – she hadn't known what to do. But Alice would have known, she thought now. Alice would have known what to do, what to say, the knowledge coming to her out of the darkness. And she remembered whispers she had overheard among the other servants in Tascombe, sly remarks which she had not always understood. There was the way too Alice sometimes looked at Ralph of late – and he at her, a fleeting expression on his face which had cut her own heart in two and made her feel childish and unwanted. She'd told herself while she was in Tascombe that she was sick, mad, to think of anything like that, to imagine that it was possible. Ralph and Alice. It was not possible. And if it was? Then she would be glad to die here. But a shred of reason told her that no one dies of evil smells, or even vermin. Or not quickly. But to lie here night after night. To live here, for ever. Why? There could not be any God, to let this happen to her.

Her tears were running, salt in her mouth, almost comforting. Why had Ralph not followed her? Why had she torn up the letter which she had written to him with such care, such love? Too much love. But he must have known – must have guessed – that she loved him. When he returned from Honiton, and found her gone – when they told him she was on her way to Bristol, to take ship for Ireland – if he had loved her he would have followed that same day, if her ship had already sailed he would have come on the next ship – if –

Her mind, half asleep, played with the idea of his following her, dreamt that it was true, that the sound outside was his horse, he was there, come to find her, marry her, fetch her back to England. But it was her horse, stamping its hooves against the cold.

Suppose, suppose she did run away from here? Back to Derry? To find a ship? It might – it must still be there. The captain had said he was waiting for a cargo of hides from one of the valleys, and a dozen wolfhounds. He might take her – surely would take her without money, against the promise of payment once she reached Bristol and could send a message to Sir Edward.

And Sir Edward – what would he say? But even more, how

could she find her way back to Derry, alone? How would she find food? Courage, courage! She could ask the way, and someone would give her bread surely, and there was water enough in the rivers. Even if she could not ask the way she would have the sun –

It was almost dawn. The window slits and the hole in the roof were grey. The horses outside were awake and moving. It was now or never. She sat up, drew her cloak into a bundle against her breast, strained her eyes to see if anyone was awake and watching her. The way they had drunk last night they should sleep until midday, but how could she tell? She remembered – she thought she remembered – her mother being up at dawn, seeing to the servant girls, and to the menservants. But had that only been her imagination, because all the household servants of Tascombe were up at dawn, cleaning and cooking and seeing to hens and cows and horses?

It was madness. She could never escape. She knew it. But she could try. She was on her feet, stepping over Siobhan. The sleepers lay like fallen trees, snoring, mouths open, arms and legs sprawling. If she trod on one she would have to say she was going out to the privy. A sleeper stirred, groaned, rolled onto a hidden face – and her hand was on the heavy wickerwork of the door. Not really a door at all, but a kind of hurdle interlaced with withers and hinged to the doorpost with leather thongs.

There was no bar, no latch. It stayed in position by its weight. She let down her rolled cloak and small bundle of possessions – there was no hope of bringing her box, or even of finding it. The hurdle was heavy, but moved easily enough. There was fresh air, like a knife blade against her face and one of the hounds came sniffing – and then left her as quietly as he had come, to raise his leg against the bawn wall.

She untethered her horse, whispering to it to be quiet, thanking God they had not brought in any cattle the night before – Nor had they so much as troubled to unsaddle it. She thought of taking a second horse but dared not. They might not bother to pursue her, please Heaven they would not, but they would surely pursue two stolen horses. Suppose – suppose they needed to catch the horses first? Before she had time to lose her courage she had slipped all the bridles loose from the wooden stakes that held them and was leading them to the main gateway of the enclosure. If there was a watchman there! But she saw him huddled asleep in his shelter beside the gate, his spear cradled in his arms like a lover, his mouth open, the smell of sour liquor wafting from him in a cloud of stench.

She unbuckled the saddles from all the horses but hers, unbridled them, slapped their round rumps, urging them to go. They needed no more than that, trotting off, shaking their heads and manes. She hid the pile of saddles and harnesses under a furze bush, mounted her own horse, clapped her heels into its sides, her skirts gathered round her hips, careless of her legs being naked to the world. The horse trotted obediently.

She must ride east, that much she knew. And north as well? She tried to calculate from the dawn light in the sky and when she looked back from the first ridge the house inside its surrounding wall lay as quiet as she had left it – like a low mound of earth and stone – several courses of dry-stone walling interlaced with turves and earth, and then the beams for the roof, sloping sharply inwards, covered over with more turves and with reed thatch. Not a soul stirring. She was free! Free!

She pressed her horse to a gallop, was down the hillside into a valley, fording a stream. She would have dearly loved to stop, to strip off her clothes and wash the night from her body, wash the memory of it out of her head in clear mountain water. But she dare not stop so close to the house, and the sun was rising ahead of her, a huge red disc which became golden as she watched. Dawn became daylight. She was clear away!

And hungry. She remembered with a sudden stomach ache of hunger that she had eaten nothing, or almost nothing since she had finished the last of the Derry oatcakes yesterday at noon. Last night she had not managed to get down more than two mouthfuls of the fat meat. She'd had none of the thick sausages nor the mutton broth, nor anything else.

She began looking for a cabin that might sell her some bread. Until she realized she had no money and, much more, dare not ask, dare not even be seen if she could avoid it. She looked back in sudden fear. But the skyline behind her was empty. How long had she ridden? Two hours at least. Hunger becoming a feeling of weakness, her head seeming light and dizzy. If she drank some water? She looked for a stream, and finding one dismounted, almost falling on the spongy, uneven ground. The water was cold as ice and she splashed it on her face, drank. On a sudden impulse, she stripped off her cloak, pulled her gown down off her shoulders and plunged her face into the stream, almost crying with the shock of cold and then glorying in the feeling of purity. Of being clean again. The sun was warm on her shoulders and she thought of stories of Red Indians in the New World, which a visitor to Tascombe had told them all. Men and women living almost naked, indifferent to heat or cold. Parson Dagge had been so shocked he had wanted to leave the table.

'How I would like that sort of life,' Ralph had whispered, his colour rather high, perhaps from wine. 'Would you?' And that brief remark had become the centre for her of a thousand dreams and fantasies, fantasies she was ashamed of owning as her real waking thoughts and which she tried to drive away, but never too far away. Of herself and Ralph as Red Indians, naked as Adam and Eve in a New Eden. They lived under the shelter of giant trees, lying on beds of leaves, and Ralph –

As she thought of the fantasy again she heard a shout behind her, looked, and became paralysed with terror. Her brother and another rider were bearing down on her from the ridge, as fast as they could gallop. She could not move, could not run, could not try to mount her horse. Could only crouch there, her shoulders bare, her wet hair clinging to her face, her neck.

Within seconds they had reached her, and her brother had flung himself out of his saddle, had raised his leather whip and hit her across her back. The cut burned like fire and she

74

screamed with the pain of it. Her brother raised his whip again but the second man said something and her brother turned away, cutting at the air in his fury.

He turned back to her. 'God's curse on you! Why did you do it? And all the horses?' gesturing at the horizon with his whip. He came close to her, poked the handle of the whip into her lap, her stomach, lifting her chin with brutal fingers.

'Pregnant? By some English devil? Is that why you ran? To get back to him?'

She understood enough to make out his meaning but she could not speak. 'You are marriage meat, do you understand that, my English sister?' He spat at the word sister. 'Get on the horse!' He lifted his whip in threat and she ran to obey, dragging her cloak with her, struggling to put it round her shoulders again.

'Are you pregnant?' her brother pursued her. 'Are you, fool?'

She shook her head, tears of rage and pain streaming down her face. They began to ride back the way she had come, the second man holding her bridle, leading her like a prisoner. Marriage meat. That was what he had said, surely, but what did he mean? She dare not ask – and knew the answer well enough.

What would her father do to her when they reached the house?

CHAPTER 9

THEY RODE out of Lisbon on a spring day which might have been July in Somerset – two officers in the service of his majesty King Philip of Spain: Captain Ralph Paulet and his friend Captain Nico Perez, who was only two years older than Ralph but seemed at times old enough to be his father; the son of a merchant's wife from Seville by an Englishman who had come to do business with her husband and then had disappeared into the unknown.

The sun was already hot on the backs of their necks whenever the road twisted towards the west and the sea. Behind them the fleet lay in the harbour. To the left an oak forest stretched into the distance, dark green and sombre. To the south the white road lay ahead of them thick with dust, the winter rains forgotten, the mud dried into ruts and deep pot-holes which could throw a rider if his horse stepped into one.

Nico's bare head blazed like white gold in the sun, and he narrowed his blue eyes against it. 'How I long for English weather!' he said. 'Clouds racing in the sky, always changing. Flowers in the hedges! And girls like buttermilk! I shall become the lieutenant governor of an English district and have all the prettiest girls brought to me to be examined for loyalty to his majesty! And as governor I shall have the English squire's right to the first night with all the newly married women! But of course if they are ugly or even plain I shall waive my rights and earn a reputation for generosity! A governor must learn to please his people.'

'The squire's right?' Ralph cried in exasperation. 'What new nonsense are you talking now? Who has been filling your stupid head with all this rubbish?'

Nico turned towards him in his high-built Spanish saddle, riding like the Spanish soldier that he was rather than as Ralph rode. Nico's legs were thrust out against the stirrups, his back exaggeratedly arched, his reins held high in one gauntleted hand close to his chest. He had already said to Ralph that he rode like a vaquero, a cow-hand. 'You must ride like a conqueror! Your horse must know who is master. Like your woman. That is what boots and whips and bridles are for.'

But with Nico it was always difficult to know when he believed what he was saying, or was making fun of it. In either case his eyes held the same look of haughty innocence. Like an Englishman turned into a hidalgo, but only an imitation of a hidalgo, of a Spanish officer and gentleman. Always behind the Spanish hauteur an un-Spanish kind of humour. It was the same now.

'Who has been filling my head with nonsense? Why, you have, my dear Señor Rafael. Your Sir Eduardo – his bastards – and everyone knows it is true. The English gentry have no morals, no chastity. They couple with the common girls like bulls with cows in a field. We are coming to set that to rights – along with everything else.' Until at the sight of Ralph's indignant expression Nico shouted with laughter. 'Rafael, *amigo*! You will hear worse than that before the priests have finished with us! They mean to turn England into a monastery, and we soldiers mean to turn it into a brothel. And between you and me I think we shall win. In Africa –'

'England is not Africa.'

Nico laughed again, clapping his free hand on Ralph's arm. 'To a soldier all conquered places are the same. First there is the boredom of the siege. Then the terror of the attack when you mess your breeches. Then – if you live – there are the women, and the looting. You take off your messed breeches and find new ones. That is a soldier's life. Get used to it, Rafael. In Africa –'

'You and your Africa! I don't believe ten words of it!'

'Before God and His Mother, *amigo* – I swear to you! I had ten negresses in one night. Negresses! Insatiable! Until you have had a fat black woman you have not lived!'

'And you told all this in Confession, of course?'

'Of course!' Nico winked at him, his narrow face with its curiously un-English mouth under the English eyes and fair hair suddenly wicked with laughter. 'I told them I taught each of the ten girls the Lord's Prayer before I took them. I was highly praised.'

'You are such a liar I never know when –'

'*Hombre*, we are on leave! Free for twelve whole days of the black beetles!'

'Are there no priests in Seville then?' Ralph asked him, his own voice grown sombre. Already Lisbon had become oppressive to him with the constant processions, the chanting of the monks, the obligatory Masses – Mass in Somerset had been a sacrifice of love accompanied by the terror of imprisonment and death, but here it had become a symbol of imprisonment only. No love. No sacrifice. Only an iron discipline, as if God was the commander in chief of the Great Armada.

'Priests in Seville?' Nico repeated. 'Oh, yes. But we shall not be seeing too many of them, I hope. We shall be in a tavern that I know of, or in my home.'

'A tavern like the one in Lisbon where you have Maria?'

'The taverns of Seville are palaces compared to that wretched drinking den. And the girls! Although little Maria –' He stopped, and then went on casually, almost too casually. 'She could hold her own with most of them – but *you* must learn to live, Rafael, *really* live!'

'I shall try. And you must stop calling me "Rafael". You must call me "Ralph", otherwise I shall be in trouble when we reach England.'

With a sudden shrewdness that made his fox mask of a face ten years older, Nico said, 'Reach England, eh? England is far away, and it will take more than the Lord's Prayer and Te Deums to get us there. But "Ralph" it is from now on –' It was as if their distance from Lisbon had lifted a weight from his shoulders. Like riding without armour – the baggage horses and the soldier servant behind them saw to the armour along with their spare clothes and provisions for the journey.

Instinctively Ralph looked back at the servant, a peasant lad from the north of Portugal who had been gathered from the vineyards above Oporto by the long arm of King Philip, and turned into some kind of an imitation of a soldier.

'Him?' Nico said, guessing at the meaning of Ralph's nervous glance. 'He cannot understand ten words of Castilian, let alone of Andalusian –' Andalusian being the variety of Spanish Nico spoke himself and was teaching Ralph. Already Ralph had found that he was falling more easily into its soft, slurring accents than into the harsh northern Spanish which Father Ignatius had taught him on their journey from Rouen.

'You need to understand us,' Nico continued. It seemed for a moment as if he was going to explain a profound secret of Spanish life which would make all things clear – the weird contrast between the puritan ferocity of the priests and of official life, and the equally ferocious debauchery of the soldiers when given an hour's freedom from priestly surveillance – between the lip-service piety and the bawdy, sensual reality of every Spaniard Ralph had met outside of the clergy and one or two elderly bigots among his fellow officers. From the tavern and a whore's bed to Confession and Communion and back again without a pause for thought or contrition.

'Well?' Ralph prompted at last as Nico remained silent. 'How am I to understand you?'

'Oh, that is easy enough,' Nico said lightly. 'It is the sun! Our souls and bodies are not sodden with rain as yours are, my poor Englishman. We are full of wine and laughter and sunshine.' But that had not been what he was going to say, Ralph knew, and they rode on with a constraint between them as if Ralph's reminder that a third pair of ears was listening to their conversation, however deaf and ignorant those ears might be, had put an end to freedom, and honesty.

But the constraint did not last long. With Nico nothing serious lasted long, or so it seemed. In ten minutes he was laughing again, boasting of his exploits during that campaign of three years before, where he had learned his trade of soldier and conquistador. Yet below the laughter and self-mocking braggadocio there was an undercurrent that was hard to define – as if Nico was two men – an openhearted, loose-tongued young soldier with not a thought in his head but wine and women and killing, and another man who stood back and judged.

'Slavery?' he was saying now carelessly. 'Why 'tis a blessing for them, heathens that they are. The priests will convert them when they reach the Americas, and their souls will be saved.' He had been describing how all the inhabitants of an African district they had conquered had been taken to the coast in chains and shipped to the Caribbean. 'They will be freed of their devils over in the New World. Do you know what happened on one of the slave ships in the harbour? Among the women there was one that was a kind of she-priestess, a witch. Five times the ship put out to sea with a favourable wind and each time as she attempted to cross the bar out of the anchorage the wind failed her and she lay helpless in the tide. Her two companion ships had stood out to sea with no trouble in the world, and lay waiting for her, day after day. Five times, I tell you. The second time the ship's master was told by a negro that as long as that woman was aboard they would never sail and never reach the islands alive. He begged the master to set her ashore so that the ship could be freed. Of course the master had him flogged for a lying scoundrel but still the wind failed a third time. After that he had the woman brought to him and ordered her to be flogged. Do you know what happened? At the third stroke of the rope's end on her back a spar fell on the gunner who was flogging her and killed him outright. A six-foot length of spar without a sign of rot in it, or a crack in the timber. It snapped off in a dead calm and fell thirty feet, crushing his skull like an eggshell.

'The master sent ashore for a priest then, a Dominican, and the priest came out in a jolly-boat breathing hell fire as to what he would have done to the woman. Burning at the stake was the least of it. By then the wind had failed them a fourth time and the crew was growing terrified of that woman. They had tied her up to the mainmast and when they passed her they crossed themselves ten times and recited Aves as if they were entering a monastery for ever.

'So out came the Dominican, and he tells the negress that unless the ship clears the bar at the next attempt he will have her beaten to death there on the deck, but that the beating will not be a quick and easy one. It will go on until the ship does clear the bar. And he will pray for her soul all the while she is dying. He was not a Dominican I would have cared for as my confessor. But the woman only smiled at him.

'"Lift your hand to strike me, Mister Priest!" she said, because she knew some Spanish.

'"It is not I who will strike you, you she-devil."

'"Then lift your hand to make your sign of the cross against me."

'And do you know, the priest could not do it? He stood there like a block of wood, his right hand paralysed.

'"Try to sail out to sea," the woman taunted the master. "The wind is fair. Call on your Jesus to help you sail away to America land."

'They tried the fifth time, and reached the bar, and the fifth time the wind failed. The priest was foaming at the mouth like a rabid dog by now, rather than the Hound of God he was supposed to be. "Kill her! Burn her!" he was screaming. And then even his voice failed and he whimpered and cried as if he was sunstruck, which indeed he was. He fell in a heap on the deck and had to be carried into the master's cabin. The master came out after half an hour and said to the woman, "Very well, you can go ashore. You can swim." And he ordered two of the sailors to untie her and fling her overboard among the sharks which hang round every ship in those waters, waiting for the offals to be tipped overboard.

'But the sailors would not touch her, no matter how the master threatened them. In the end he gave in, and six men had to row her ashore, along with three young negresses she said were her pupils and must come with her if the ship was to be freed. It was one of the six sailors who brought her ashore who told me the story. She ordered them to land her not at the settlement, but on a spit of land a mile or so to the south of it, and she and her three fellow witches walked away from the jolly-boat without so much as a backward glance. She was a splendid-looking creature, the sailor told me, and the three young witches had the look of being virgins, about twelve years old, but he said he would no more have touched any of them than he would have touched a nun. Which was a strange comparison to make, was it not, between witches and a nun?'

'What happened to the priest?' Ralph asked, wondering how much of the story to believe.

'He was brought back to Spain in a straitjacket, raving mad. I heard he was in an asylum ever since. Africa is a strange country.'

And you are a strange one too, Ralph thought, glancing sideways at Nico and thinking not only of the story itself but the fluency with which Nico had told it despite his heavy accent.

They slept that night in a wretched inn even more flea-ridden and poverty-stricken than the ones Ralph had experienced on the journey south from the Pyrenees to Lisbon. And the further south they travelled towards Seville the worse the poverty seemed. Brown fields, so burned by the sun that it seemed impossible they could ever bear a crop. Only the olive trees seemed able to survive – gnarled grey trunks, dusty grey leaves – with now and then a whitewashed hacienda nearby. The heat at midday was overpowering and there were times when Ralph began to regret the journey, the twelve days' leave and the promised visit to Nico's family, even the promised delights of Seville, free from the overbearing presence of the army of priests in Lisbon.

Until the heat went out of the sun and the visit seemed attractive once more and the journey worth while. A peasant let them pass, pulling his laden donkey aside with exaggerated respect, as they came near a small village – Ralph had noticed that the peasants hereabouts were Arab dark, small, stocky and swarthy as if they were already out of Europe and in Morocco. Any women they had seen drew the edges of their head scarves across their mouths at the approach of a man.

'They still speak Arabic among themselves,' Nico said, when Ralph remarked on this. 'Parts of the south are still more Arab than Spanish. There is a famous belly dancer in Seville whom they call the Dream-Giver. She has given more than dreams, I can tell you, to quite a few hidalgos. They say she will go only with aristocrats, whether Moorish or Spanish.'

'Moorish aristocrats?' Ralph asked in surprise. 'Are the Moors not all peasants?'

'Heaven love you,' Nico laughed. 'The Moors have older blood than ours. A Moorish family which cannot trace back its ancestry for ten centuries is considered new rich. Only the Jews in Spain have longer pedigrees.' His voice sank as he said that, and he looked round, but their soldier servant had fallen a hundred yards behind.

'I tell you, Ralph,' Nico said, growing confident again. 'You know nothing of Spain. And will learn nothing of it from the priests. A hundred years ago, two hundred maybe, all this –' his gesture indicated the desolate, olive-grey landscape, 'all this was like paradise. Gardens. Fruit trees. Arab villas. Maybe not exactly here, but all over the south. Give the Moors a desert and they will make it into a garden. And the cities, the towns! There were libraries, and schools, and hospitals, universities. There were poets and singers. My grandfather told me –' He stopped again, but their servant had fallen even further behind.

'We are barbarians compared to the people of those times, here in the south,' he went on. 'Moorish Spain was like a marvellous garden in a story book. Until the Christians from the north came on their crusade and destroyed everything, killing, burning, looting. Ferdinand the Catholic! God forgive him.'

He had said 'Christian' with a sudden, shocking tone of hatred, then his fox face had turned into a mask of laughter. 'At least, that's what the Moors say. And the Jews. You and I do not believe them, of course. You and I know that we have

83

brought God and the Faith into pagan darkness, and have taught the infidels and the Jews the only way to salvation, which is via the stake.'

'The Jews killed Christ,' Ralph said uneasily. 'I have never seen a Jew – at least – I do not know what Jews look like –'

'Oh yes, they killed Christ,' Nico said, 'only He too was a Jew. They have a lot to answer for, the Jews.' He put his brandy flask to his mouth and emptied it, then went on in the same cool, detached way. 'My grandfather, my mother's father, he was a Jew, as you know. His uncle was burned alive in Seville for spitting on the Cross when they tried to turn him into a Christian. All they had done was rack him a little. And whip him a few times. And burn his feet in a brazier. He would not be able to walk, of course, but he could always crawl to Communion on his knees. And you see, they had to be quick about converting him because he was already seventy-five years old. Oh yes, the Jews have a lot to answer for. Fancy spitting on the Cross. My grandfather said you could see the bones of my uncle's feet where they had burned away the flesh. Such an obstinate old Jew man. He must have deserved to die.'

'Nico! Nico! Stop it!'

'Of course I will stop. That is why I am a soldier. So that they won't burn me, who am a quarter Jew. Or my mother, who is a half Jewess. The other half of her is part Moorish, which makes it worse. But if her son is an officer in King Philip's holy, crusading army, if he kills pagans and infidels and Englishmen for the glory of God, then she is safe, and so is my sister – so long as my mother goes to Mass every day and Confession often enough and contributes to charity and manages to marry off my beautiful sister to a rich old Christian. God damn this world!'

There was nothing Ralph could say, and they found a tavern soon after that to give them some kind of shelter for the night, and both of them got drunk, sleeping beside the horses in the stables because they seemed cleaner than the tavern's so-called guest room. The following night's tavern was much the same, but the day after, at noon, they reached Seville, riding through the narrow cobbled streets and across one of the small plazas that like the others was surrounded with orange trees; until they came to Nico's house, and Ralph began to understand dimly what springs of passion and fear and inheritance made Nico what he was.

Nico's mother, Doña Isabel, was dressed like a nun, a rosary at her waist so large that the beads clacked together as she walked, and with a crucifix on it big enough to serve above an altar, or so it seemed to Ralph. Every room in the small, dark house was decorated with holy pictures, with statues of saints, of the Madonna, of the Child Jesus. An alcove had been turned into a small, private chapel and a lamp burned in front of a huge crucifix there, like the red eye of God watching over the house. And every second phrase spoken by Doña Isabel was a pious ejaculation until Nico said impatiently, 'Mother, do you think I would bring a spy here? For pity's sake let us have a rest from all that. Do you think we do not have enough prayers in Lisbon? And where is Anna?'

But Anna, his sister, was in a convent in the hills, twenty miles away, being prepared for marriage to the son of a merchant from Seville.

'In the name of God what does she need preparing for? And how the devil can the nuns know what preparations are needed for marriage?'

'Hush, Nico *mio!*' Doña Isabel's large black eyes slid in terror towards Ralph. She was small and stout, the traces of a fine figure still discernible under her black widow's gown as she bent to lay a dish in front of her darling son, or to fill Ralph's glass with Madeira wine. And there were more, much more than traces of beauty in her face, which was still young in spite of her almost fifty years. A smooth, oval face, framed in blue-black hair and a mouth which thirty years earlier must have driven young men to many follies. Ralph wondered how Nico's father could have left her. And how could such a woman have given birth to such a different son? Not a trace of his fox features in her face. Not a trace of her beauty in his. Except – except perhaps the mouth, Ralph thought. The same curving of the lips. And the nose. A peculiar widening of the nostrils which someone had once told him was a sign of sensuality. And she was a Jewess? Or at least – half a Jewess?

'Will you never be done staring at the two of us?' Nico said at last. 'I assure you she is my mother, and I am her son, however unlikely it seems. Or at least so she tells me. Maybe she found me in a basket, like Moses? Eh, Mama?'

'Hush, Nico, hush child!' As if any reference to religion contained hidden dangers, unless the reference was unmistakably devout.

The house was built round a sunlit patio, and against the walls a profusion of brilliantly coloured flowers filled the air with scent. It was the only place which Doña Isabel had not used as evidence of the fervour of her Catholicism and Ralph escaped to it when he could. Nico too brought him to see the Dream-Giver, but she had aged and fattened in the year since Nico had seen her last and all in all it was not a comfortable visit, even when Doña Isabel grew a shade less suspicious of Ralph. She was a woman who had lived so long with fear that she could not do without it. She almost never went out of the house during the week, Nico said, the servant woman doing all the buying in the food market, and on the Sunday she went to the Cathedral so swathed in veils she might indeed have been a nun, or an Arab woman from a harem. She was in a tremble of anxiety that her son would not go to Mass and that some neighbour would notice the failure.

'Nico, child! It is time! It is time for Mass! The neighbours –'

'God shrivel the neighbours! May a man not stay in bed of a morning on his leave?'

But Ralph had taken pity on her and had hauled Nico out of bed and gone with him to the magnificent cathedral. They had left next day, collecting their soldier servant and the horses from a nearby inn, and Ralph sensed that he was not the only one who was glad to leave.

'I hope your sister will be happy in her marriage,' he said as they crossed the plaza once more. It was difficult to think of anything more intelligent to say, and he had not the courage to ask the age of her future husband.

'Women are not meant to be happy,' Nico said quietly.

'They are meant to make men happy. But they do not even do that, not often, and not for long.'

'You don't surely believe that?' Ralph cried. 'You are trying to shock me again!'

'Of course I do,' Nico said, his blue eyes seeming almost blind as they stared at Ralph without a trace of humour or agreement. 'That is why my father stayed with my mother, and lived a long, happy life with her. That is why my mother is such a contented woman.'

'You have never heard from him?'

'No. Nor my mother. But perhaps I shall find him in England. Or perhaps he is dead. Why don't we drink the wine my mother gave us before it turns sour from the heat?'

CHAPTER 10

IT IS 25 April, 1588. St Mark's day. The *plaza major* in Lisbon. The men of the Spanish Armada kneeling in the white dust. Sweat and incense and the hot sun beating down.

Ralph knelt with his men and his fellow officers. There had been no room for them nor for hundreds upon hundreds of others inside the cathedral, and Ralph's body seemed to be melting under his tunic like a wax image placed too near a fire. If I don't get a drink soon, he thought, I shall die of thirst, for he like the rest had been on his knees for nearly two hours. The archbishop had said Mass in the cathedral, and afterwards the duke had taken the blessed standard of the expedition from there and laid it on the altar of the Dominican convent nearby – his token of personal dedication to the Crusade about to start. Now they waited for him to carry it back to the cathedral.

The Duke of Medina Sidonia, King Philip's Captain General of the Ocean Sea, had looked small and insignificant under the great banner, when he came out on the steps. But the archbishop had joined him, and the cardinal archduke, followed by the lesser clergy and the high-born officers of the Armada, and he had walked a little ahead of them all. Grown in stature. Become a leader. It was said, Ralph remembered, that he had not wanted to be King Philip's new captain general. That he had wanted to stay in his beloved Andalusia and tend his orange groves. It was even said that he had advised Philip not to sail against England. But Philip had not listened to him, and the duke

88

had accepted his unwanted responsibilities, and carried them better than more willing admirals might have done. The one hundred and thirty ships anchored in the harbour were there because of him. For months he had scoured Europe for them, had seen to it that they were as seaworthy as the Lisbon carpenters could make them. And he had done his dry, meticulous best to see that the men who sailed in them measured up to his harsh requirements. Now, on this hot, dusty April afternoon he was publicly asking God to do the rest.

'Nico, how long more?' Ralph whispered to the man kneeling beside him.

Nico turned his head briefly. 'They can't be much longer. I think I can hear –'

The sound of chanting grew louder by the minute as the procession came slowly towards them on its way back, the great banner like hammered steel in the still air. The arms of Spain and the image of Christ crucified. A gentle breeze from the hills unexpectedly stirred the folds of metal into silk, turning the banner around. And now it was the image of Christ's Holy Mother, and written beneath her feet the words 'Arise O Lord, and vindicate Thy cause'.

The dust had got into Ralph's mouth, into his throat, making it feel like old cloth, stifling as a gag. Nico touched him on the shoulder. 'The tavern afterwards, eh Ralph?'

How proud he is of his English, Ralph thought as he'd done so often before, but how truly awful his accent is! And even as he thought it, a man in the crowd turned and looked at them, his eyes narrowed and intent, as if he had caught the sound of English words and was sharply conscious of it. A familiar? From the Holy Office? Scenting heresy in a few words of English? In two men talking instead of praying?

The shadow of the offices and prison of the Inquisition seemed to fall suddenly and coldly across the square. Grey stone and shadow and once again the pungent smell of incense. Ralph had begun to hate the smell of it, as if it was something unnatural, against life and nature and everything that makes for happiness. As if it was the smell of the Holy Office, acrid and harsh and filled with suffering. He shook his head like a man shaking ill thoughts away. In a few days' time they'd be out of here and at sea, thanks be to heaven!

The procession was much nearer than he had realized. He could see the cardinal's long, white hand raised in blessing – the papal absolution, *'Absolvo, Absolvo'*, the indulgence granted to those who were to sail in the Greatest Crusade of all time; the duke, looking tired, almost ill; the archbishop; the chanting priests behind him, the shine of sweat on their faces as they looked upwards. 'My soul doth magnify the Lord.' It's as if we don't exist, Ralph thought, watching them. We're nothing to them. Ships' fodder. No more important than ammunition. If we win, they'll be certain it was these prayers that have given us victory. If we lose – Then they were past, and it was the blue-blooded sons of Spain who walked slowly by. A different kind of arrogance now. Stiff-legged. Born to wealth, and power, the red crosses on their tunics the only hint of humility, of being in any way like other men. And yet there was one of them who was different. Young and fair-skinned and handsome, looking straight ahead of him and at the same time aware. Of the crowd. The soldiers. The men who would die, who would not see their homes again. And as he passed by there was a kind of sigh among the kneeling men. Don Alonso de Leiva. The idol of Spain. And Nico turned to Ralph and whispered, 'I wish there were more like him.'

The last of the procession made its slow way through the great doorway of the cathedral, and it was over. They could go.

Nico took Ralph by the elbow when they had risen stiffly and painfully to their feet. 'Let's get that drink, *hombre!*'

But in the crowd they became separated.

It doesn't matter, Ralph told himself, searching for the fair hair, the pale, clean-shaven face. We'll meet in the tavern –

The crowd poured into the Rua Nova d'El Rei, the men of the Armada, nearly thirty thousand of them, and the others who had come to the ceremony as much out of curiosity as devotion. The ordinary people of Lisbon. Peasants in for the day. Sailors from the trading vessels in the harbour and the lodging houses on the steep hill above San Paolo.

Merchants' factors, gypsies, vagrants from all over Europe. Only the wealthy missing, gone to their country houses at Alcantara and Xabregas for the summer.

It was a good-humoured crowd. When a litter carried between two mules nearly overturned there was a roar of laughter and a rush to set the litter right, and reassure the frightened woman passenger. And yet in the crowd there were the silent, secret, hidden but always present, watchful ones. The *Familiares*. Ralph had already learned what to look for. A certain, quick turn of the head. Something about the shoulders, the careful eyes. That one there? That man in the old-fashioned *capa*? Leaning against the booth. Buying nothing. Making no pretence of even looking at the gold filigree work laid on the black velvet behind him. Better walk on, not stare, but – it does not matter to me anyway, Ralph thought. I've nothing to be afraid of. Nothing. And knew that he was afraid. For himself. For Nico. Above all, for Nico. And looked again for him and could not find him, and the clangour of the church bells which before this he had scarcely noticed seemed suddenly oppressive.

The man at the booth was far behind him now, and it was easier to walk, for many had already left the Rua Nova d'El Rei, turning down side streets to fill the taverns there, or hurrying on to their homes in the labyrinth of narrower, even dirtier streets beyond. Ralph found the turning he was looking for at last, a narrow alley between tall, old houses which looked as if they might topple inwards at any moment.

When he pushed through the door of the tavern the stale air hit him like a blow. It was as if all the men who had ever come to drink and talk had left behind their used-up energy and sweat, for there was no one in the tavern except two elderly men sitting on a bench by the wall, who stared at him from red-rimmed, hostile eyes. There was no sign of Nico.

Ralph sat down and put his bonnet on the stained wooden table and a young girl hurried from the back to serve him.

'*Buenos dias*, señor! You are alone today?'

'For the moment. I lost Captain Perez in the crowd, but he'll be coming soon.'

She looked gravely down at him, pushing back her hair which was straight and shining like black silk. 'You are most welcome, señor. And he, when he comes.'

'Thank you.' They spoke to each other as usual in a mixture of Spanish and Portuguese, and Ralph added, 'We were at the Blessing.'

'My father would not let me go.' She shrugged, made a face. 'I must work instead. But now you have come and I am glad –' She gave him a quick, almost nervous smile. 'You will drink while you wait?'

'Indeed I shall! Bring me a jack of spiced beer, please!'

'At once, señor.' There was the faintest colour under the smooth olive of her cheeks, but she did not go at once. Instead she stood looking down at him, her eyes dark and strange and so much older than her fifteen years that he felt uncomfortable. Where *had* Nico got to, he wondered irritably. She was *his* girl, damn it!

'Maria! MARIA!' Her father's hoarse voice calling her.

'Your beer, señor, I will bring it at once, but there is something –'

'MARIA!'

He watched her walk away from him. Hips moving smoothly beneath the dark skirt. Bare feet, narrow and high-arched on the dirty, uneven floor. A flower growing on a dunghill, Nico had called her, after his first visit to the tavern. He had gone there alone and not come back to camp until the small hours.

'Wait until you've seen her!' he had said to Ralph, throwing himself down on his bed in the small tent. 'The face of a Madonna! But what a body! That I should be so lucky!'

'You're always lucky with women – or so you say! Now, will you shut up and let me sleep?'

'It's not luck, Ralph.' Sitting up in his enthusiasm. 'You have to work at it – and it's worth it! Sometimes!'

'You don't "work" at it Nico. It just – happens.' He'd had to say that much.

'Oh, you're talking about – you really believe?' And Nico had roared with laughter.

Not long after they had first met Ralph had told him about Una. Afraid that he would not understand. And Nico had tried. Had done his best. But it had been no use.

'You didn't make love to this so wonderful girl, Ralph?'

'No!'

'Why not?'

'I – it wasn't like that –'

'But it's always like that!'

'For God's sake, Nico! I *loved* her! And she wasn't like your women.'

'*My* women?' The blue eyes uncomprehending, half amused, half merely bewildered. 'My dear Ralph, *all* women!'

A few nights after his first meeting with Maria, Nico brought Ralph with him to the tavern. The low-ceilinged room was crowded and Nico led the way, Ralph following more slowly, having to stoop for fear of knocking his head against the heavy, oak beams.

'Señor *Capitano!*' The young, breathless voice had seemed to be speaking to him, but when he straightened, he saw that the girl was looking up at Nico, Nico's hand touching her breast as he went to take her arm. She turned her head to look at him.

'This is Maria, Ralph,' Nico said, drawing her forward, 'and this is the friend I've told you about, the English *capitano* –' His eyes, the shape of his mouth, mocking the formality of the introduction.

'*Buenos tardes,*' Ralph had said, and tried to force a smile. So this was Nico's Madonna of the Tavern! Hardly a Madonna from the way she was looking at him, as if Nico wasn't there at all. As if no one was there but the two of them! Did she look like that at all the customers? And Nico had seen it too, and said sharply, 'Bring us two jugs of wine, and some cheese. We've no mind to wait all night.'

'*Si, si* señor –' As if a small, beautiful statue had come to life. Miraculously she found them a small table in a corner and two stools, and brought their wine, smiling at both of them now, putting down the jugs and the pewter goblets neatly and efficiently. Pouring. 'You have had a good day, señores? Yes? I am glad for you – ' Just a pretty serving girl.

And yet, when she had gone to serve the other customers Ralph had said, 'Isn't she a bit young?'

'Too young? No, *amigo*! Believe me!'

'Oh, I believe you. But – '

'Ralph, listen to me. She's a miracle! Her father is a brute, and her mother is a slut. But she – well, you have to see her! And she's mine – at least until we sail!'

'You're welcome! Honestly Nico, there are times when – '

'You envy me, Ralph? So long as it stops at envy!' His eyes sharp behind the banter.

'If you think that *I* – !' His disgust showing for a second, and for that moment they had been close to quarrelling. Over what? A tavern slut who had probably slept with a dozen men before she was twelve? Over his own disgust at Nico's folly? At Nico's risking the pox for such a creature? He had tried to laugh at his own puritanism, and had lifted his wine in an awkward, theatrical salute. 'Here's to love,' he had said, 'Both kinds, yours and mine.' And the near-quarrel had vanished almost without trace. But he had not gone back to the tavern for a full week after that night, although Nico had badgered him to come with him. He had sworn to himself that he would never go again. As if by going he would somehow be condoning – But in the end he went back. Nico spent all his evenings there and he was the only close friend Ralph had made since he left England.

And after a while it was not only because of Nico. In the tavern there was warmth. And laughter. And a sort of peace. And because she was Nico's and because he himself wanted nothing from her anyway, he did not see how much Maria had to do with it. How, almost without his noticing, he had ceased to think of her as Nico's pretty drab, and begun to think of her almost as Nico had described her. A tavern Madonna. A flower growing on a dunghill. And a Madonna, a flower, with a sense of humour, with swift, generous passions that changed her face like sunlight and clouds on a window glass, now brilliant, now dark. Quick and beautiful and passionate. He had sometimes thought that if – if he himself had found her first – And had had to drive the thoughts away.

Now, after the long, boring ceremony in the plaza he hoped she would stay and talk to him for a little while. Make him laugh. No more than that.

But there was no laughter in her today. She sat down on the stool facing him when she had brought him his beer, but she did not really sit. More like a bird lighting, ready to fly off at a sudden movement, any hint of danger.

'What's wrong, Maria?' Taking a draught of the cool liquid, putting down the jack, waiting for her to answer.

'Nothing. Nothing, I hope.'

'Is it your father? Has he – ?'

'No! No, he is quite sober. He hasn't touched me since –' Then, in a whisper, 'There was a man here this morning, asking about you, about the "tall Englishman". He named you. My father told him that you come here most nights, with your friend.'

'And then?'

'My father told me to run down to the market for some lemons. When I came back the man was gone.'

'Who was he? Did you know him?'

She shook her head. 'But he was Portuguese, I think. I have seen his kind before.' She shivered and there was no need for her to say what kind.

Staring at her without really seeing her. A man. Questioning. It was nothing – nothing! Why should it be? But fifty meaningless, small incidents came together suddenly to make a monstrous shadow in front of him, behind him. The man watching them this afternoon outside the cathedral. A few days ago – the two men whispering together as he and Nico passed by. That book missing from Nico's satchel in the tent. An English book. His father's. It meant nothing at all! A thief – or Nico had mislaid it – But who would steal an old, foreign book? And Nico had valued it above all his possessions, almost the only thing his unknown father had left behind him.

And his own baggage had been searched, he was sure of it.

95

Things subtly disarranged, handled, too carefully replaced. The priest who had heard his Confession – asking him strange questions which seemed to have nothing to do with what he had just confessed. About his friends. If he knew anyone who was not a true Catholic. If he had ever spoken to a Jew.

It was only when he was outside the church again, that he had thought, Does he mean Nico? Nico, the half-Jew? But they could not think – did they not know, if they knew that much, that his mother went to Mass every day, received Holy Communion every Sunday. Made a parade of it for fear of being accused of backsliding into Judaism? If they'd seen that house in Seville –

Maria was looking at him with her great brown eyes filled with darkness. 'Are you in bad trouble?'

He pushed back his stool, on fire with anger and impatience.

'Trouble? Of course not!' He was half-way to the door to look for Nico and warn him, before common sense brought him back to sit down again at the dirty, wine-ringed table. As sure as fate he'd miss him if he went out to look for him. Hurry, Nico! he prayed. Hurry, man!

And then?

'It's nothing,' he said, trying to sound convincing. 'Nothing. Don't worry. Just someone – '

Behind them, the heavy street door creaked open, and there was a shaft of sunlight like a sword across the floor, bright and cruel. And then the silhouette. A man's head. The bulge of his *capa*. He stood beside them. A soft, rubbery face which one would forget the moment after seeing it. And yet Ralph knew at once that he was the man he had seen earlier leaning against the booth.

'You are the Englishman, Ralph Paulet?' No attempt at courtesy in the husky, almost whispering voice, his Spanish heavily accented.

'Yes,' Ralph said shortly.

The man looked down at Maria. 'Go,' he said curtly.

Ralph said warningly, 'You'd best leave us, Maria – it's all right.'

Slowly she stood up from the table and moved to the counter against the wall, made a pretence of wiping it down.

'Well?' Ralph said to the man. 'What right have you to ask me who I am?'

The thick lips twisted. 'Right? That's good!' The laughter came out from behind the *capa* like the wheeze of a cracked bellows. 'I have the right of the Most Holy Office of the Inquisition. That's what I have. Is that not enough for you, eh? Ralph Paulet! Englishman!' Spraying the air with his spittle.

'And what does the Holy Office want with me?' Ralph asked through lips grown suddenly stiff.

'I'm to bring you for questioning. No, don't try to make a run for it,' as Ralph moved. 'There are two more of us outside.'

A heavy hand on Ralph's arm. The rubbery face very close, and the smell of garlic and rotting teeth. Ralph pulled his arm away. 'There's no need to hold me. I'll come. But it's some stupid mistake –'

'For your sake, I hope so, señor.' The man was civil, almost obsequious, now that he had his prisoner. Or was it only a refinement of his humour? A cat playing with a mouse before killing it. If Nico comes now, Ralph thought – and prayed that he would not come until he himself had left with the men. Maria looking at him, her face white with terror. And then they were walking him through the door, out into the bright glare of the sun.

CHAPTER 11

ACROSS THE *plaza major* again and a thousand, ten thousand years since the last time. The heat gone from the sun. Only two people left of all the multitude who had knelt there earlier. An old man, trundling a handcart laden with an old man's junk, secret and evil-smelling. A negro sailor. Drunk. His bare feet grey with dust, putting them carefully down as if the ground was moving beneath him. Ralph staring at him, seeing and not seeing, astonished that people were still as they had been an hour ago, that nothing in the world had changed except – except – He might never walk back this way – even that old man with his running eyes and shaking head might have longer to live – and the thought seemed so full of self-pity that he felt ashamed. Imagined escaping, breaking free from these imbeciles holding him. Running. But running where?

His two guards had refused to answer his questions, walking beside him in total silence since they left the tavern, but as they came near the massive sprawl of the prison and the cold of its shadow, he felt the sudden, urgent need to hear a human voice. Any voice. 'Please,' he said, 'tell me. Where am I being taken?' And then furious again, he shouted 'Answer me, damn you!' But they took no notice, as if they were deaf mutes, or he himself was an imbecile not worth attending to.

They brought him to a side door set in the high, monstrously high wall. Knocked. Spoke in rapid Portuguese to the voice behind the grille. The door opened and a

Dominican friar stood holding it. A lay brother? Young and quick, as young as Ralph himself and yet untouchable, beyond all camaraderie of age, Ralph knew at once. Not by anything he said, but by a kind of withdrawing of himself that showed in his eyes, in his mouth. Like a living man who looks at a dead one, and sees nothing but a corpse.

Across the yard to the inner wall, and the friar was unlocking another door, beckoning. A dark passage, the wall behind them, the slimy greyness of the prison an arm's length in front of them. Two, three storeys high. Tiny slits, holes, for windows and a rat scuttering between their feet, a dark, rushing shadow, darker than the stone. Under a low archway and another door, the oiled lock turning smoothly, like the others. Steps leading downwards. The smell of damp, of human excrement. Clang of iron and the sudden screech of giant hinges far below, as if a massive door had been opened. A scream, high-pitched, terrible. Man or woman? Endless and then ended, the heavy thud of the door shutting, the scream cut off. Or was it really cut off? Was it still – or was it only inside his head? Ralph shivered, felt sick. Wanted to stop and hold himself upright against the dark wall beside him.

'What in the name of God are they doing?' he whispered.

'Just say your prayers, señor, that you never find out,' one of the men answered grimly, taking him by the arm. 'You are to go the other way. This time. Up here.'

This time? The friar walking ahead of them, his sandals making small muffled sounds. Who had screamed? What – but the friar had not so much as turned his head, seemed not to have heard anything. Fear coming back, driving out anger, everything but itself so that Ralph wanted to soil himself, felt his stomach loosen. Until shame caught him again and he walked faster so that the men on either side had to hurry to keep up. 'Damn your souls,' he whispered, in English. And then in Spanish. One of the men bared his teeth at him in a kind of grin. As if he was saying, 'Wait. Just wait, my lad. Then we'll see who is brave.'

They brought him up a narrow, spiralling stair. Shallow steps that seemed to go on for ever, then another passage.

Closed doors on either side. No recognizable sound coming from behind them, only a constant rustling which seemed even worse than total silence. Ralph had a sudden image of himself imprisoned for months, years, behind one of those doors. Becoming old, mad, forgotten.

The friar threw open a door at the end of the passage. A small, almost empty cell, filled with grey twilight. No one in it. A mattress, blankets, and against the wall a small table with an earthenware bowl, a water jug; a bucket on the ground. Ralph turned, as if he meant to try to force his way out.

'I demand to be brought to someone in authority,' he said. 'And my colonel must be told – I am an officer in his majesty's army – you have no right –' Echoes of his voice far away down the stone tunnel of the corridor.

The friar stepping back. Leaving him to the others. 'There must be complete silence at all times in the prison.' His voice young and hard and full of authority. 'We had to punish a man for coughing, some time ago,' he added. 'Food will be sent to you later.' He signed to the men to leave, stood framed for a moment in the narrow doorway.

Ralph tried to hold the door, to prevent him from shutting it. 'Damn you! At least tell me why I've been brought here!'

'You will find that out when you go to the *Casa de Despacho*.' The door closing. The lock turning smoothly. Footsteps going away, fading altogether. And sudden panic, mindless, beyond reason, like an animal in a cage. He threw himself against the heavy timber, bruising his shoulder, again and again, until he fell back on the mattress, shaking with the futile effort, sweating. The room almost dark now that the door was shut. A grey darkness like dust, a cold grey stillness. Silence, except for his own breathing. If he could even see properly, but what was there to see? Stone walls. The bed. The table. He put both hands over his eyes, pressing his fingers into the skin of his forehead. It was a mistake. An imbecile mistake. In a few minutes – an hour or two – he'd be out again. Looking for Nico. To tell him – He lay very still, not breathing. Nico. Had they – ? Nico, half Jew. Suspect.

The hole in the wall which passed for a window was

directly above his head, but when he stood at the table and looked out through it there was nothing but the blank greyness of the prison wall a few feet away.

They came for him at last, waking him out of an uneasy sleep. Two men he had not seen before.

'Get on your feet, señor. They are waiting.'

The passage outside his door was lit by wall flares. Nothing moving. The other doors tight shut. No sound but their footsteps. Down twisting stairs, into another passage he had not seen before, which seemed to lead into an entirely different building. Well lit, dry. No hardship here, only a monastic severity. A broad oak door. One of the gaolers knocking, entering. Walking into the centre of the room. The gaolers leaving. Ralph standing alone facing a long table. Three hooded men sitting behind it. Black hoods, white robes. Dominicans. Their faces hidden by the shadows of their hoods. A scribe, a layman, sitting at a corner table, his quill poised ready. An enormous crucifix against the far wall, reaching almost to the ceiling.

'Kneel, Ralph Paulet. Swear upon the Gospels to speak the truth and to keep silent about all that shall pass in this room.' The priest in the centre, speaking Spanish with the harshness of a northerner. Lifting his head as he spoke so that his face showed. Grey features. Not young. Not old.

'I swear,' Ralph said, kneeling. What choice had he? 'Why am I here?'

'We ask the questions. You must be silent until you are told to answer. Do you understand?'

And as Ralph hesitated, the question was repeated, a shadow of emphasis in the colourless, infinitely patient voice.

'I – yes. I understand.'

'*Father*. You are to call me Father, my son. Repeat after me, "Yes, Father."'

'Yes, Father.' Against his will his voice became low, obedient. What would happen if he refused to answer? Refused obedience? The answer was so obvious he did not need to think of it. The scream he had heard came into his mind like an echo. Was cut off as that scream had been, now, by the priest's voice.

'Why have you come to Lisbon, my son?'

'Why – I have –'

'We are waiting, my son.'

'For – for the Church,' he said. It sounded not only lame but false.

'You have come to fight for our Holy Mother the Church? That is a good reason.'

'Thank you, Father.'

The old, grey ivory face, the voice kindly, almost like a father's. Perhaps – perhaps someone had suspected him wrongly, and they only wanted to see him in order to reassure themselves? Perhaps it had nothing to do with Nico at all? That must be it! Oh, thank God! Thank God!

'Then why do you not go to Confession, my son? Do you imagine you have no sins to confess to Holy Church? To God?'

'I –'

The same kindliness, the same infinite patience. The three priests, the scribe looking at him, the scribe with his quill poised, waiting, a drop of black ink gathering on the white point.

'I *have* been to Confession,' Ralph whispered. So shocked by the question, by the implications of it, that his mouth felt dry.

'You have been once to Confession. Four months ago. Have you remained in a state of Grace for four months? That would be remarkable in any young man, but especially in a soldier.'

'I – a state of Grace?'

'Father. You *must* call me "Father".'

'Father. I don't understand. A state – of Grace?'

'You do not know what that is?'

"I –'

'In these past months have you had carnal knowledge of any woman?'

The words seemed to have no meaning. He stared at the three men facing him.

102

The priest lifted his hand briefly, as if he was about to make the Sign of the Cross. 'My child, you are in grave peril, grave peril to your soul. Do you understand that?'

Soul?

'Do you understand fully what I am saying? Would you prefer that I called an interpreter to explain my questions to you in English?'

Ralph shook his head. Thought that he could see a shadow just behind him, hear breathing. There *was* someone standing behind him, just out of his vision. He found he was sweating, was ice cold and still sweating. Who was behind him? Why? Was it one of the gaolers?

'Do not look round,' the priest said. 'Answer my question. Have you had carnal knowledge of a woman during these past months in Lisbon?'

'No.' Whispering. He wanted to shout, to defy them. Instead the words came frightened and whispering. 'No!' he said again, more loudly, the loudness hanging in the air, stupidly defiant.

'You go to an inn in the sailors' quarter. There is a girl there, the innkeeper's daughter – '

He stared at the priest. 'Maria?'

'Yes, my son. Maria Fernandez. Have you seduced her?'

'No!' Shouting this time. The echoes died.

'I warn you, my son. You must not lie to us. That would be a graver sin than the one you are denying.'

'I'm not lying. She – '

'Yes. Go on, my son. She – ?'

She belongs to Nico. And as if he had said the words aloud he began to sweat again, at the thought of such folly, such treachery.

'She gives you information, you were going to say? That sailors give to her, when they are drunk?'

'Information?'

'Our concern is only with the truth. If you are here to spy for the English government that is not our affair. Others will deal with you when we are satisfied about your soul. Our concern is to discover whether you are a heretic.'

'A – heretic?' He could not go on repeating their questions.

'My son, you do yourself no service by trying to evade my questions. I assure you, we know almost all we need to know already. You were brought up in heresy, were you not?'

'I –' Staring from one face to the other. The scream echoed in his mind again, the sweat rolled down his back, his sides, his shirt clinging to his ribs, his stomach. He was beginning to feel sick and dizzy from kneeling so long, with nothing in front of him and that sense of a shadow, a presence, just behind him. He wanted to relieve himself. Why hadn't he used the bucket in the cell? He wanted to go so badly he had to clench his thighs together. It was like being burned.

'Your mother was a heretic?'

'My mother?' he said, bewildered. 'What has my mother to do with –'

'And your closest friend in Lisbon, his mother is a Jewess? Your fellow officer, Nicolas Perez.'

He opened his mouth to say something, and closed it.

'Answer me, my son.'

'I – I don't –'

'Your friend has never discussed his mother with you? His own Jewish blood?'

'I – it's not a thing that –'

'Have you discussed your own heretical upbringing with him?'

'I – he knows I was – what do you want from me? What are you getting at?' Shouting, trying to shout, swaying forward to ease the pain in his legs, swaying back. If he could not relieve himself soon he would go in his breeches. Did they want that too? Was he such a coward that he dared not so much as ask to go to the jakes? But his mind rebelled against the humiliation. Clench your thighs, he told himself. Don't think of it. But he could think of nothing else. Like needles being driven into his private parts.

'The girl, Maria. Do you know that she has Moorish blood?'

'Moorish –' Were they mad? What were they talking about? Clench your thighs harder. Bend forward slightly.

'Her grandmothers are both Moorish women. Her great-grandmother was burned as a lapsed Catholic, turning back to the Moslem faith of her ancestors. Have you discussed this with the girl?'

'No! I've discussed nothing with her! Are you mad?'

'Do not be insolent, my son. That first, that only Confession of yours in Lisbon. Was it a full and good Confession?'

'Yes.'

'Repeat it.'

'My - Confession?' Looking at them in horror.

'Repeat it, my son. Or shall I tell you what it ought to have contained?'

'I -'

'Did you inform against the priest who came to your village? Did you inform your guardian?'

'NO!'

'No wonder you shout against the accusation, my son. It is the sin of Judas. It is to crucify Our Saviour again. Kneel still. Do not move. Did you confess to the girl Maria that you had done this thing?'

'Are you insane? What are you - what do you want? Who has been telling you filthy lies about me?'

A sudden whispering of cloth beside him, a shadow kneeling.

'Confess to them, my child. I implore you. Save your soul!'

Father Ignatius. His voice. His face. Gaunt as a skull. Kneeling beside him, eyes shut, hands clasped.

'I beg you to confess, my son,' the priest was saying while Father Ignatius prayed in whispering Latin. '*Salve Regina ... ora pro nobis ...*'

'I have nothing to confess! He has lied to you! Lied!'

'Nothing to confess? That is arrogance, my son. The sin of pride, through which the archangel Lucifer fell from heaven. I implore you, look at the Pit below your feet. Reflect!'

'I have nothing to confess. Nothing!' Did they think they would get him to trap himself? Did they think that if they threatened - He had never seen an *auto-da-fé*, only heard of it, but he could smell the burning flesh now. Could see the procession of the condemned in their shameful yellow

105

sanbenitos, wearing the pointed hats like dunces' caps; could see the piled timber, the stakes, the black, oily smoke. Nico had seen an *auto-da-fé* in Madrid and had grown sick again as he talked of it. Four Jews and a lapsed Moorish convert had been burned with a dozen others, and as they died the four Jews had begun to pray in Hebrew. 'Hear me, O God of Israel ...'

'Perhaps you need time to reflect?' the priest said, his voice still kindly, still colourless, infinitely patient. 'Do not think that we wish to hurry you, even towards the salvation of your soul.'

'Reflect on what?'

'On your Confession. Sooner or later you must confess, my son. We cannot leave you in a state of mortal sin, on the very edge of damnation. You are here because we love you, we love you as we love ourselves.'

The priest made a sign with his hand and Ralph was grasped, lifted to his feet and taken away. He thought absurdly, now I can relieve myself, and when he was alone in the cell he ran to the bucket, his hand shaking as he tried to open his codpiece. He knelt, and could not urinate. As though he was paralysed. He knelt there, the pain still burning and nothing happened. It seemed like an hour before the tormented muscles of his bladder relaxed and allowed the urine to come, dark and smoking as if it was yellow fire.

When he was finished he lay down on the bed, hiding his face against the coarse grey stuff of the pillow. They were mad, mad and evil. 'Did you inform against him?' How could they think it? Did they really think it or was it only –

What would they do to him? Torture him? Burn him? Leave him where he was, to rot? They can do what they like with me, he thought. All I have is the will to refuse, and even that they can take from me in the end. Until at last he fell into an ugly twilight that was neither sleep nor waking, full of dreams that became nightmares, always ending in the same way – the dungeon steps and the sound of the door opening and that scream, high and shuddering.

Once he thought he heard footsteps and he hammered on

the massive, indifferent door. Shouted, the shouts echoing, but no one came. Nothing but twilight, and darkness and hunger. Did they mean to starve him? He began to feel light-headed and lay down. Slept at last and woke to candlelight and the two gaolers staring down at him. He wanted to go to the bucket again.

'Let me –' he said, and remembered that it was full. 'The bucket –' and one of the men kicked it. Not hard, but enough to spill an ugly stain of slops on the stone floor. The smell lifted.

'Heretic stink!' the other man said and laughed, showing blackened stumps of teeth, a yellow tongue.

'Come on, damn you,' the first man said, 'they don't like to be kept waiting.'

Echoes of their footsteps. The weight of darkness in the corridor, on the stairs, pressing against the candle flame. A man's voice crying out in his sleep. 'No-ooo! *Madre de Dios! Madre de Dios!*'

One of the gaolers kicked the door as he passed it. 'Silence, pig!'

The voice stopped.

They came to the broad, stone archway, the heavy, iron-studded door. There was the brightness of candlelight and the judges – were they judges? Inquisitors? They sat as before only now Father Ignatius had joined them, leaning forward, like someone hungry for a spectacle. The scribe sanding a page which he must have just written on. Looking up, his eyes mild with interest.

The questions beginning. Kneeling. Answering. Not answering. Tascombe. Heresy. Una. Alice. Sir Edward. The young priest. Father Parsons. And suddenly here, there, like a knife blade sliding, the questions about Nico, Maria, Nico's mother, why he had not confessed more often.

'Why did you speak English with Nico?'

'To teach him –'

'Why? So that he might read heretical books?'

'No! His father –'

'His father was a heretic also? You know that? He yearns for England, your friend? For his father's religion? And the

107

girl Maria. Did you speak to her about her ancestors? About the Moors? Did you tell her that they once ruled Spain, with their abominations of heresy, the ultimate heresy of Mahomet?'

'No! No!'

'But you seduced her?'

'NO!'

'She is your lover. She has confessed it. She has told us that she loves you.'

'You are mad! Bring me to her!'

'That will come in time. This book –'

The book Nico had lost – which had vanished out of Nico's luggage –

'These poems are full of heresy.'

'I've never so much as read them!'

'But your friend Captain Perez has read them. You explained them to him.'

'Only – only words here and there he couldn't understand! He –'

'Go on. He knows English very well, you were going to say? But not perfectly? Not perfectly enough to understand all the heretical allusions in these verses?'

There was no way to answer them. No answer they could not twist to their own purposes.

Father Ignatius leaning to one side, whispering to the priest who asked the questions. The priest nodding.

'Perhaps it is time,' he said gently, kindly. 'Would you like us to have you brought to see the girl, Maria? It may persuade you to be more open with us?'

'I – where is she?'

The same lifting of the hand, gentle, full of command. Father Ignatius stood up. 'I will go with him, Father.'

The gaolers. One on either side of him. Fastening his hands. Father Ignatius a swift shadow in the darkness. Down many stairs. There was the sense of being underground. Of wet stone. Earth. The steps slippery with wet. The hem of Father Ignatius' habit dropping from one step to the other with a soft, repulsive primness. The walls, the roof, closing in on them as they went further down. A massive door

108

grinding on its iron hinges and beyond it, a wide passage lit by wall flares, separate cells or cubicles opening off it on either side. No doors to them, just high, pointed archways, and as he stepped reluctantly forward it seemed to him that he had walked into a living, quivering rope of suffering stretched across the passage. Such desolation of spirit as he had never imagined possible. And then it was gone, but he did not want to see what might be in the cells on either side – yet could not stop himself from looking. There was no one in them, but near one archway he saw a huge, empty, iron chair, an iron halter in the wall above it, iron rings on the arms. There were stocks in front for the sitter's feet, and beside it a brazier embers still glowing, and even now an ugly smell hung about the archway, like burned meat. In the next cell there was a wooden frame on the floor, the length of a man, with ropes and wooden rollers at either end. The Rack. Which had pulled his father's bones out of their sockets in the Tower of London. His stomach began to heave, but there was nothing in it to vomit, only bile, the taste of it sour, burning his throat as he tried to swallow.

They had come to the last cell of all.

It had its own wall flares, was as brightly lit as if it was day, .and Ralph stood in the archway knowing that what he saw would remain with him for the rest of his life.

Maria hung by her arms in the centre of the cell, her hands tied behind her back, the rope which bound them running over a pulley fixed to the ceiling. She was naked. Her legs slack, her head thrust awkwardly down between her shoulders, her feet not quite touching the ground. Behind her a white-robed figure held the rope, his head completely covered in a black hood with slits for eyeholes. Father Ignatius stood to one side.

'For God's sake!' Ralph shouted, trying to run forward. The two gaolers held him as if he was a child, forcing him down onto his knees.

'Raise her,' the priest said, not so much as turning his head to look at Ralph or his gaolers.

The hooded figure pulled on his rope, Maria's feet lifted high off the ground, her legs dangling, her body turning towards them and then away, the nakedness like an insult, her body half woman's, half child's, blue shadows under the breasts. She did not seem to be conscious of what was happening, her head still lolling as if her neck had been broken long ago and carelessly mended.

'No!' Ralph shouted, trying to shout, his voice only a cracked, horror-stricken whispering. 'No! I'll – I'll – for God's sake cut her down!'

She was high up from the floor, her feet above their heads, her body arched forward by its own weight, like someone diving from a high rock into the sea below.

'Drop her,' Father Ignatius said, his own body bent forward, eagerly, like a huntsman watching a kill.

The executioner let the rope run free, the body fell, and at the last second the rope tightened, the body twisted in the air. There was a thin child's cry of agony, shrill as a bird screaming, and then nothing, nothing but a soft, whimpering silence. She hung still, her arms unnatural, far up and out behind her back, the shoulders dislocated. The blood ran out of her mouth, onto the floor below. He knelt between his gaolers, vomited bile. Could see nothing, hear nothing, only feel the cramps and spasms in his own body. 'For God's sake!' he whispered again. 'I'll do anything – anything you want – only stop! For the love of God, stop!' His voice dying.

Father Ignatius smiled, touching him, forcing him to look up. 'You will confess to us? Everything?'

'Anything. Anything.'

Father Ignatius waved his hand and the executioner let the rope run through his hands. She fell on the stone floor her head making a dull, heavy sound as it struck. She tried to move and cried out with the pain of it. He heard bone grinding against bone and retched again. Nothing came up, not even bile.

'Come,' Father Ignatius said. 'You must make your Confession now. In writing.'

'Help her,' Ralph whispered.

'She will not be drawn up again,' Father Ignatius said. 'Unless you make difficulties.' He made a sign and the executioner took a blanket and covered the girl's nakedness.

'As soon as you have confessed someone will attend to her.'

They had to carry him outside into the passage under the archway. It was not defiance. He was unable to walk. They dragged him past the rack, and the iron chair. Up the steps. He saw the body lifting, twisting. Then the fall. And the scream inside his head. The sound of her broken bones grinding as she tried to move. She will not be drawn up again. Unless you make difficulties. Again?

They sat him at the table. Someone read from a paper. Tascombe. Heresy. Priest. Informer. Nicolas Perez. Maria Fernandez. Jew. He wanted to protest. Wanted to say, 'No, it's a lie. All lies!' And saw her lying on the stone floor. Small, white shadow, nakedness. Heard her scream as if they were torturing her again outside the door.

'I, Ralph Paulet, Captain in His Most Catholic Majesty's Army, late of Tascombe in the county of Somerset in England, do solemnly swear before Almighty God, that this is my true Confession –'

Trying to say 'No'. His tongue sticking to the roof of his mouth. His lips stiff and dry and burning.

'Sign, my child. Then kneel for Absolution. Your soul is on the point of being saved, Glory be to God on High for His wondrous mercy. Sign again, here. Initial each paragraph.'

He signed. Knelt.

'In the name of God the Father, God the Son, and God the Holy Spirit, I absolve you from your sins.' And in another voice, 'Take him back to his cell, gaoler. Let him have food.'

He began to shout, half mad, not knowing what he was shouting. They carried him away. His cell, the stench of the bucket, the spilled vileness. They threw him onto the bed. He lay, not thinking of anything, only seeing, hearing. Over and over, the thin body lifted up, bent forward, arms reaching back. Falling. Screaming.

What had he done?

After an hour or so they brought him food. Stale bread with a smell of mould about it. Something that might have once been a slice of roast meat. No water. The door slamming shut. Darkness. Silence. He thought it would be impossible to eat. Unthinkable. And found he had eaten bread, meat, the last crumbs fallen on the dirty blanket. Began to feel thirst.

It was two days, two nights, before they came for him again.

CHAPTER 12

THE ROAD out of Setubal twisting and turning, baked brown by the sun. Riding alone. No gaolers, not even a soldier escort with him, but with Maria held as hostage, still a prisoner. Blue arch of sky and the sharp smell of pines. Like incense, Ralph thought, and yet quite different. Filling his lungs with it, trying to drive out the foulness of prison air which seemed still to be in them, to cleanse them as he had tried to cleanse his body that first evening in Setubal, in the monastery where they had lodged him. Bathing and bathing again, a change of clothes, his old filthy ones burnt. Three days ago and he could still smell himself, smell the prison.

I wonder if they're still alive, he thought. Two men, English sailors, seized off the coast and brought to Setubal for questioning.

'Ask them if Drake is ready to sail,' the Portuguese officer in charge of the interrogation had shouted, running stubby fingers through his greasy curls, furious that he could not speak English himself, that he must speak through someone he did not trust. 'Ask them – damn you! You know what I want! ASK THEM!'

And Ralph had asked the questions and prayed that they would not answer, or would not tell the truth.

The first sailor, a heavy, middle-aged man, had stared at him in horror when he finished speaking. 'Thee's English! Thee's from hoam!'

A west-countryman too. Ralph had had to force himself to meet his eyes. 'Best make some kind of answer,' he said quietly.

'Dirty traitor! I'll tell 'ee nothing!' Spitting. The guard twisting the man's arm behind his back, twisting and twisting until he bellowed with pain.

'Ask the other one –'

The second man was dragged forward, his face swollen and bleeding. 'Drake's in Plymouth.' Mumbling the words. 'But he ain't ready yet –'

'He knows nothing,' Ralph said. 'He's been at sea for the past month. So has the other fellow.'

'It's possible, I suppose,' the Portuguese captain growled pulling at his lower lip, looking from one sailor to the other in disgust. 'Try again. How many ships were there in Plymouth before they left?'

'How many ships in Plymouth?' Ralph asked.

'I dunno – I swear – I'm only –'

'He does not know,' Ralph said. 'He is only an ignorant fisherman. How could he know?'

A quick jerk of the black curls. The guard's boot moving. The sailor doubling up, collapsing on the floor.

'Take them away. It has been a waste of my time and yours, *Capitano*.' The Portuguese officer stood up, walked out of the room leaving Ralph to watch as the English sailors were dragged away.

Two lives. Two English lives. He could not have helped them any more than he could have refused to go to Setubal as interpreter.

But he saw them everywhere he looked. With the others. His father. The young priest. Maria. His ghosts. Beside him. Behind him. In front of him. Seeing them not clearly, not really as people. Only as shadows. Carrying their suffering on his own shoulders like a huge cross. And at the end, whose Cavalry? His or theirs?

His horse stumbling, bringing him back to reality.

'Maria is alive! Alive! At least I've saved *her*,' he said aloud, tightening the reins. She'll be all right – the nuns will look after her. They had brought him to her cell just before they let him go. A cell like his own but even smaller. Leaving him alone with her, her huddled body scarcely lifting the thin

114

blanket, her face grey with pain. She was conscious, her eyes recognizing him.

'Maria!' Going down on his knees beside her, taking her ice-cold hand in both of his.

Her lips moving but no sound coming.

'Maria, they are going to release you!'

Watching his face, not seeming able to understand.

He laid her hand down gently on the blanket, smoothing back her matted hair. Madonna of the Tavern. Nico's flower. 'I'm sorry,' he whispered again. 'So very sorry!'

Futile, useless words, but she tried to smile, the blood spurting from her cracked lips, trickling down her chin in a thin, red line.

'Enough of that!' Rough hands pulled him back, but he scarcely felt them, saw only her face transfigured with joy. Oh no, he prayed, as they jerked him to his feet, No! Dear God, don't let that be why –

The salt taste of her blood was on his lips. 'When are the nuns coming to her?' he asked hoarsely. 'A surgeon?'

'Soon.'

She had turned her head away, face to the wall and the gaoler looked down at her with less interest than he would have shown a sick animal.

'She needs them now!' Ralph could see the muscles of her throat working and knew that she was crying.

The second gaoler came into the cell, took Ralph by the arm. 'Out with you!'

They had taken him away then, locking the cell door behind them.

He rode through the night until the moon, the stars, faded. Blackness turning to grey. Bird song, and the sun like a great orange rising from the rim of the world. Cachilhas to his left and the distant gleam of water.

The roofs of Lisbon beneath him.

But he scarcely looked at them, his eyes caught and held by the town, the city beyond it, rocking gently on the blue-green water of the Tagus. Waiting. Medina Sidonia's fleet, the Great Armada. A forest of masts, tall and straight as if they were still growing on the slopes of the sierras, sails tightly furled. And almost against his will, without even thinking of it, he felt his heart caught by the vastness of it, and he pulled up his horse and bent forward to look, and look, and look again. Did it mean that the Armada was finally about to sail? Ralph felt his stomach muscles clench at the thought, that soon he might be on his way back to England. But sailing with the Spanish. Against all which was familiar, all to which he knew he still belonged. And not only as an enemy. As a spy. Hearing Father Ignatius' harsh voice as if he rode beside him. 'You must tell no one that you were brought here, nor about the girl either. And remember. Our people are everywhere. Even in England. Especially in England.'

'But what am I to tell my commanding officer?'

'He knows. Enough. That you were required for questioning. And cleared. And have since been of assistance to us in Setubal. He will ask you nothing.'

'And Nico – Captain Perez?'

'Tell him you have been in Setubal all the time since you last spoke to him. That you were needed urgently and had no time for goodbyes. That is *all* you may tell him.'

Dropping down the hill, letting the tired horse pick his own way.

If only he could pray – but he hadn't prayed since they brought him to the dungeons, since he saw Maria there – I shall never pray again, he thought bleakly.

The ringing of the church bells and the sound of iron on iron from the shipyards came up the hill to meet him as he began to gallop, not caring if the horse stumbled or not, and even before he reported back to camp he went to the prison. Stood holding his horse in its grey shadow while the crowds hurried to early Mass across the sunlit square behind him.

'What do you want?' The familiar voice behind the opened grille was like the touch of a whip.

Trying to sound confident. 'Has Maria Fernandez been released yet?'

'No.' The grille beginning to close.

'Why has she not been released?' Raising his voice, beginning to shout.

116

'I don't know why not. I'm only the porter.' The false humility suddenly infuriating.

'I want to see her *now*! At once!'

'You cannot see her. Only priests are allowed to visit prisoners.'

'Then bring me to Father Ignatius.'

Silence from behind the grille, until Ralph was afraid the man had gone. Just as he was about to knock again, the voice said curtly, 'Wait.'

This time Ralph could hear the sandalled feet cross the yard, heard the other door open.

He had to wait twenty minutes. Twenty minutes in which to wonder if after all they had tricked him. To wonder if Maria was even still alive, if he had put his own head back in a noose.

The feet returning. 'Father Ignatius cannot see you. He is in the audience chamber.'

Ralph looked up at the massive wall towering above him. I can't force my way in, he thought. All he has to do is to refuse to see me – damn his soul to hell! 'What about the girl? Did you ask him?'

'The girl will be released as soon as she is fit to go.'

'Yes – but when will that be? How is she now?'

The grille beginning to close again.

'Is she all right? Did the nuns come to her? Have you no spark of humanity?'

This time the grille closing with a sharp finality, and the slap-slap of sandals going away.

All he could do was return to camp. Talk to Nico if he was back. But tell him nothing. Lie. Lie for Nico's own protection.

It sounded easy. Was easy if he was prepared to play the spy, to twist and turn, to lead the double life with two faces.

He found the camp in a frenzy of excitement, the date of sailing not fixed but surely in the next few days. The brothels and the taverns were being searched for missing men, the roads closed to deserters, the malingerers being taken from the makeshift hospital. And Nico came back from Coimbra late that afternoon, riding in with a handful of his own men and a sorry-looking bunch of conscripts – peasants, torn from their families and their vineyards, staring blankly about them at the great, bustling army camp.

It was evening when he came to the tent he shared with Ralph. 'Good to see you, *hombre*!' Throwing himself down on the narrow mattress. Stretching. 'God, but I'm stiff and sore! Only a dozen men to show for it and not one of them who knows how to fire a musket!'

He mustn't know, Ralph thought. 'How was Coimbra?'

'Dead as a brothel during Mass! They told me you were in Setubal? What were you doing there? They said something about interpreting English sailors?'

'Yes. A rotten job.'

'I can imagine.' The blue eyes very clear, very direct as if seeing Ralph properly for the first time. 'You look terrible! What have you been up to? Besides interpreting? Drinking all night?'

'No – it's just the heat – I'm not used to it – '

Nico's teeth were very white, but was the smile as frank as it used to be? 'It may be hotter soon! You have heard the news? That we are to sail in the next few days?'

'Yes.'

'You still want to go?'

'I'm – not sure. Are we ready?'

'The duke does not think so, they say. But it's what the *Escurial* thinks that counts. By and by, why did you not tell me you were going to Setubal? I waited all evening for you in the tavern, and there was no one amusing to talk to at all. Maria's younger sister was serving instead of Maria, and *she* is definitely too young! And even their pig of a father seemed to be avoiding me – '

Careful. I must be careful, Ralph thought. 'I went to the tavern as we arranged,' he said quickly, 'but I had to leave. Did you not receive my message?' Feeling his cheeks burn. Did Nico see them darkening, guess he was lying?

But Nico was beginning to laugh, easily, naturally. 'Sorry, Ralph! I never got it. I went to help a young lady whose litter was upset – and time slipped by! You know how these things are!'

118

Ralph laughing himself. It was so typical of Nico, so likely a thing to have happened that it must be true. And he actually remembered seeing a litter upset. 'I hope she was pretty?'

'Very! And young, too!'

'And grateful?'

'That's something I've yet to find out! So I, for one, am in no hurry to sail!' Nico swung his booted legs off the bed. 'Where's that valet of ours – I smell like a drain – ' He began to untie the points of his doublet. 'You know, I thought at first that you and Maria had eloped!'

'Maria – and me?'

Nico shrugged. 'I've seen her look at you. I wish she would look at me like that.'

'Don't be a fool!' So much real anger in his voice that Nico's thin face sharpened and Ralph said hastily, 'I'll send for the valet – and maybe we'll go down to the town later – see if Maria's back?'

How can I go on lying, Ralph thought. If I could trust him. But even as he ducked his head and stepped out of the tent into the summer half-light new doubts came flooding in. Why hadn't he seen Nico near the litter? Surely he would have noticed the white-blond head even in that crowd? And had he really been at Coimbra all that time? Could he have been with Ignatius as well?

Nico's my friend, he reminded himself stubbornly. But Nico could wear two faces also, and with his quick, subtle mind more easily than Ralph himself could.

They went to the tavern late that night. Ralph, Nico and three other young officers, and Ralph had to seem surprised that Maria was not yet back, had to listen to her father's story of a sick aunt and look as if he believed it. Does he know, he wondered, trying to read the small eyes set like raisins in the yellow pudding face. Does he know where she really is, and that she's there because of me? I must talk to him alone.

It was after midnight before he had the opportunity. He had gone outside to relieve himself and was standing in the yard, in no hurry to come back into the thick air of the tavern, feeling heavy and stupid from lack of sleep, when he heard his name called.

'Here, señor.' Maria's father standing beside him in the shadows of the small yard. The smell of garlic, of sweat. The smell of fear.

'Have you any news of Maria, señor?' Whispering.

'You – you know then, Pedro?'

'Of course I know! I was here when they came for her, but if word gets out that we are in trouble with the Holy Office – we'll be ruined! No one will come to drink in my tavern – as if we had the plague! You – you understand?'

'Yes. I understand. But –'

'You must get her out, señor. It's because of you – they told me that I should not let my daughter be with Englishmen –'

'But we were not –' If only he didn't feel so tired – if he could make his mind work – 'She's to be released in a day or two –'

'Have they harmed her? Have they?' Clutching at Ralph's arm, no longer a bully. No longer a rogue. Just a fat, helpless lump of flesh.

'She's all right – they told me so. You must have patience.' God forgive me, Ralph thought.

'Thank you, señor! Thank you! She's a good girl – a good girl – and I am a poor man, señor. It's a hard world, a hard, hard world –'

'Ralph, is that you?' Nico stumbled through the open doorway. 'Where have you got to, eh?'

'I'm coming in,' Ralph said quickly, and Pedro Fernandez bowed to Nico over his fat paunch and disappeared into the shadows.

CHAPTER 13

IT IS 9 May, 1588. Such a day as Lisbon would never forget. Every man, woman and child who could walk seemed to be at the quayside, cheering until they were hoarse, drowning the sombre chanting of the one hundred and eighty priests, and the answering cheers of the men standing shoulder to shoulder on the decks, in the waists and castles of the ships – and above them all, perched on the drooping pennants the seagulls screamed derisively as if their beady eyes alone could see what lay ahead.

There was hardly a ripple in the water of the Tagus as they cast anchor, only the gentlest of breezes, giving the lie to King Philip's astrologers who had warned that May would be a month of strange happenings. Freak hailstones had indeed killed cattle in the fields of Normandy, but had He not sent this beautiful summer's day as a sign of His protection, His blessing on the greatest crusade of all time? Anyway, whether it was God's will or not, the duke was as ready as he ever would be to invade England. And ready or not, the strange one sitting in his cell-like room among the splendours of the *Escurial* could not bear to wait any longer.

All this and more the people of Lisbon had said to each other earlier that morning as they flowed down the narrow, dirty streets to the water's edge, looking over their shoulders now and then at the bare, scarred hillsides which a short time before had been covered with tents. Nearly thirty thousand men there in the end. Drilling. Sleeping. Eating. Talking round their campfires in half a dozen languages. Not even an echo of their voices up there now. Nothing left of that huge camp but the smell of the privies, nothing stirring but vagrants and cur dogs searching for food among the debris. The men had marched down the hillside, through the town, down to the waiting ships the previous day, and they had left nothing of themselves behind, except the children who would be born to the women they had smuggled into camp.

Early that morning while it was still dark, while Nico still slept, Ralph had gone to the prison, knowing it was his last day ashore, his last chance to see Maria. This time the porter had opened the door, brought him inside as if he was expected. Had taken him into the audience chamber, to the gaunt, hollow-eyed man sitting behind the long table. Father Ignatius' eyes had lifted, pale and dead, like the eyes of a blind man. And yet they saw too much. Saw Ralph's hatred, and more than that. Saw his fear.

A slow, thin smile. As if the bloodless, unhealthy lips were tasting his fear and finding it pleasant. 'You sail today, my friend?'

'Yes.'

The long, white fingers half hidden by the wide sleeve, pointing to a stool. 'A great trust is being placed in you. A great trust. I hope you will prove worthy of it.'

Ralph could not answer, could only sit, still and silent.

'I shall not be with you, I am afraid. But you will not be alone. Never fear that. Friends will watch over you. Every hour of the day and night.'

If I killed him, Ralph thought. If I rose up and took him by the throat and killed him?

The eyes watching him seemed to know what he was thinking. The smile flickered again. 'Great powers are interested in you, Ralph Paulet. Those very close to his majesty know of your existence. If you do well you will be rewarded well.'

'The girl,' Ralph whispered. 'How is she?'

'Almost recovered. The nuns have her in their keeping.'

'When can she go home?'

The hands spread out in a gesture of resignation. 'Soon. Soon. Poor child.'

'You? *You* to say that?'

The hands lay flat on the heavy table. The thin, burned-out face turned to stone, ashes. 'It was God's Will.'

'God's Will?' His voice rising, caution vanishing. 'To torture a child?' How did I ever call him 'Father' he wondered with a distant part of his mind.

The cold, level voice went on. 'Her pain will be set against her sins. And yours. Yours, Ralph Paulet. Remember that. It was you who brought her here. See that you do not bring her back.'

Ralph had half lifted himself from the stool in his burst of anger. He sat down again, slowly. 'Bring her back?'

'If you fail in your mission. We have great hopes of you. And if great hopes are disappointed –' The hands turning palm upwards for a moment, and then palm down, falling softly on the table with a cold finality.

'What mission? What do you want of me? To spy on my friends?' All his anger, all his self-disgust in his voice, impossible to hold back. Now, he thought, now he will call them in, and –

But the ashen face only smiled at him. 'Ralph! Ralph! You must learn self-control. And patience. And obedience. Words are not realities. The only reality is obedience to our Holy Mother the Church, and to Her great servant, the king. You belong to us now. You have no other reality beyond that of our will, our service. No other duty. No other loyalty. No other friendship. God has brought you to us, Ralph Paulet. Pray that He continue to show His mercy to you. The girl was an instrument in His plan for you, our plan for you. Nothing more. Nothing less. Do not think of her again. She has served her purpose. And you cannot imagine how great that purpose is.'

'What purpose, damn you!' On his feet now, close to the table, only the table between them. 'To tell you that someone has failed to say the Rosary, or has cursed the Holy Office? Let that child go and take me!'

Meaning to say that and saying none of it, only standing there, mute, shaking with anger. And with fear. Not of this man in front of him. Not even of the torturers. But of himself. His own weakness. Of breaking when they tortured him, of telling who knew what enormities to escape the pain. Of being unable to do what Maria had done. To keep silent, keep faith. 'What – purpose?' he repeated hoarsely instead.

'You will know the purpose when we are ready. Until then, obey. Do as you are told. If there are things that we should know, tell them to us. Keep your counsel. Learn secrecy. Learn to veil your thoughts. All these things will be necessary to you later. This voyage is a time of trial for you. See that you pass the test.'

'Who are you? The Holy Office? You say *us*, *we* – '

'You will know in time. Only be assured that we are very powerful. Now you may go. I wanted only to remind you of the need for secrecy. And obedience. When we next meet, do not recognize me until I tell you that you may.'

'When – ?'

'You may go now. Remember. Secrecy. Obedience. Both absolute. If you have something to tell, go to your commander. Tell him you wish to make a particular Confession before battle. He will bring you to the person who is to hear what you have to say. Now go quickly, and may God be with you.'

'Maria – the girl – '

'She is in safe, good hands. Have no further thought for her.'

He had not seen or heard any signal, but the door behind him opened and the porter was there. Had he been listening, waiting outside?

'At least let me see her. Let me say goodbye to her.'

'That would be impossible. No layman can enter the convent. Go with God.'

Already his eyes had turned to the papers in front of him, the porter had stepped forward, was waiting, arms folded, hands hidden, eyes cast down in humility. Or was it merely inhumanity? Ralph still hesitated. 'Come, señor,' the porter said. They were outside the room, the door closed.

The corridors. The courtyard. Sunlight. Outside the prison. And yet not truly outside. As if he carried chains, hidden under his clothes. The shadow of the stones with him.

The gate in the great doors softly shut behind him. Where was the convent? As if he could break into it. But they must keep their word. Must. And why not? What purpose would it serve to keep her locked away? The threat of re-arresting her was enough.

He rode down the hill, his face, his mind, as bleak as the stones in the road. As if in these last days he had aged ten years. Twenty years. There was no way of measuring how much he had aged. What had happened to him. And he knew no more of why it had happened than he had known ten days ago. Only ten?

It might have been a thousand. Who were *they*, the *we* he had spoken of? If it was not the Holy Office. Who? Why? And the answer came as clear as if a voice had spoken the words aloud in his ear. Spain's secret service, the service that sent spies into England and half Europe. Bribed, stole secrets, murdered enemies, betrayed friends. Spun its web from Madrid to Edinburgh, and far beyond. They wanted tools, obedient, silent tools who would stay obedient through fear. Who would fear their Spanish masters more than they feared the rack or the burning irons in the Tower of London, or anywhere. Who could be controlled by blackmail, by terror, by fear for others, the more innocent and helpless those others, the better. And he had walked, stumbled blindly into their grip like a moth fluttering into a spider's web, and fastening itself there more helplessly with every beat of its stupid wings. And now?

Now he had done it and it could not be undone. Unless – he sacrificed Maria. And Nico. And probably himself. To run? Where? He would not get a hundred miles before they caught him. And for every step of those miles he would be thinking of Maria and what he had done to her. Again. No. There was no answer there. No answer anywhere. Except, perhaps, a quick death in the fighting that lay ahead. Was there any other man in all that fleet who could think like that so calmly?

He rode down into the outskirts of the city, and up towards the camp. To arrive there barely in time for the Assembly call, the silver trumpets calling the pride of Spain to war. The banners, stiff with embroidery in the heavy air. The armour flashing silver, the dust clouds rising from the endless columns of marching men. Crucifixes borne on high, priests chanting, women crying as they watched their men march away from them towards the sea, and England, and the huge unknown. He saw Nico marching, hard-faced, as if already he had changed, become all soldier – and suddenly recognizing Ralph, grinning in pride and self-mockery at one and the same time, shouting, 'Hurry *amigo*, the colonel is looking for you, your men are already falling in.'

He did hurry then, and found them waiting for him, mostly new recruits, falling sullenly into line behind him, the red cross on his tunic like blood, and the roll of drums deafening. Left, right, left – left – the poor devils can't even march, he thought.

Young girls throwing flowers at them, blowing kisses. Softness and warmth. And then the quays and the body of a deserter hanging in the gallows. A small boy reaching up to touch the dangling feet. The crowds making way. His men piling into the boats that would take them to the ship. Getting in himself. And at last the ship itself, the Guipuzcoan *San Salvador*, the men going below, down into the holds that were already stifling. Nico and the other officers waiting for him on the poop. The rattle of the anchor chains running out.

Goodbye, Maria.

CHAPTER 14

IT WAS early spring again, nearly a year after Una had come back to Donegal, and a cool breeze slanted in over the bay from the south-west, carrying with it the smell of the sea and the crying of seagulls. They rode along the beach at Narin on the hard-packed sand just above the waterline. Two girls with nothing in common but their age. Even Una's cloak was different to Siobhan's. A chief's daughter wore a long cloak of fine wool but a servant girl had to make do with a half circle of rough, shaggy cloth which scarcely covered her knees.

It had taken all Una's blandishments to make Siobhan come with her for the girl was terrified of the sea and had never before been on the beach – nor indeed had Una but for a long time she had been fascinated by the distant stretch of golden sand and the curling waves.

'We must ride over to the island some day, when the tide is out,' Una said into the silence.

'Oh no!' Siobhan moaned. 'We might drown – like poor Fiacra!'

Fiacra was a fisherman who had drowned off the headland the week before. There had been no attempt made to find the body for it was believed to be unlucky to take a body back from the sea, but the women in the huts had keened for him the whole of that day and night, their wailing carrying all the way to the O'Boyles' house.

'We wouldn't drown. There would be plenty of time to go there and back before the tide turned. I promise you!'

'But I can't swim!' Siobhan was almost in tears.

Una knew that nothing would induce the girl to go into the water. Indeed to tell the truth she did not really want to swim in the sea herself. The waves were gentle enough today but looking up at the headland she remembered how the sea had looked one day in winter when she had gone too close to the edge – dark, bottomless depths further out, and at her feet, seeming to reach up for her, mountains of spume as the waves crashed against the rocks. She had been reminded then, strangely, of the picture of Dante's Inferno which Parson Dagge had once shown her during one of his sermons on sin – her thoughts running on until in spite of herself, in spite of all her resolutions not to think of him, she was with Ralph again. He was teaching her to swim in the gentle river of that other world of long ago – remembering the day she had thrown herself on the bank afterwards in her wet clothes, hoping Ralph would notice that her breasts were beginning to develop.

Siobhan's querulous voice brought her back to the present. 'It's time we went back. They'll be looking for us and my bottom is growing sore – this creature is nothing but a bag of bones! Ah, curse on you anyway!' she cried as her garron nearly went down in a soft patch of sand.

'Oh Siobhan, we've only just come here!' Una looked at her in exasperation. The girl sat hunched over her beast more like a sack of potatoes thrown across its back than anything else. Why couldn't she learn to ride properly, to swim, to read – But what was the use? Nothing would change her. Still, she was a dear, kind soul, her only friend. 'All right,' she said, relenting. 'We'll turn when we reach the sand dunes.'

Una hated going back, hated returning to the squalor, the smoke-filled house, the quarrelling women, the looming presence of her father and Art, the spiteful remarks of her stepmother, Aoife. But when they reached the dunes, higher than she had expected them to be, fringed with coarse grass, and pitted with rabbit holes, she kept her word, turning her mare's head reluctantly, while Siobhan jerked her poor beast around, kicking it into a canter now that they were heading

128

for home. Out at sea a small boat rode the waves light as a cockleshell. If only I could be out there, Una thought, with the blue sky above and nothing but emptiness for miles. Even if one drowned, weren't there worse things?

Behind the headland she could just see the place where her mother was buried. There was a small grave alongside her mother's, and sometimes in her dreams it seemed that it was she and not her baby sister who lay in that grave. Her sister had been called 'Una' too, because, Siobhan explained apologetically, 'They thought you were dead.' Two Unas. One dead. One only half alive.

But she no longer cried for Ralph at night. She no longer cried for anything, since that day they had caught her and brought her back, the terror of it with her even now – the nausea she had felt as her father screamed at her, throwing her to the ground in his rage, bitter in her throat again. She had cried then for the last time, cried until there were no more tears left in her, and some time in the night while she lay dry-eyed, her mother had come to her. She could not see her mother, could not touch her, or rather could not turn her head to look, or lift her hand. As if she herself was paralysed, but not with fear – with some other emotion she could not put a name to. She knew when her mother came and when she left, but she could not judge afterwards how long she had been there, and when her mother was gone she had fallen asleep at last – and woken next morning with new courage in her heart and a determination to survive.

She had survived, and more than that. She had become fluent once more in Gaelic. She had even grown used to her surroundings, the squalor, the filth, and the feeling of being apart, different. She supposed that given time one could grow used to anything, but she had her own sleeping recess now, with a kind of box bed hung with a cloth curtain, and this small space became her home. Her clothes hung in bags from the rafters and on a shelf alongside her bed she had her toilet things and her sewing box and the few books she had brought from Tascombe. Her father too was often away for days at a time. Once he was gone for nearly two weeks with half his men, coming back with a bloodied bandage round his head and a corpse slung across one of the horses. The fifty head of cattle the O'Gallaghers had stolen from him straggled behind. The women had started to wail for the dead man as soon as he had been lifted to the ground, and they had gone on keening all evening until Una could bear the sound of it no longer and had run out of the house with her hands clapped over her ears.

Her father had been outside and he had swung her round and pushed her back in. 'You should be with the women,' he growled. 'What do you think you are?'

It was no use arguing with him. She had knelt down at the back, pulling the hood of her cloak over her head, her mouth shut tight, until she could slip behind her curtain and bury her head under the pillow.

Another time he left taking a string of garrons laden with oats, butter and mutton, and carrying his rents for the Great O'Neill. He stayed with the O'Donnells for several days himself and all the other chiefs who had gathered there for Hugh O'Neill's spring visitation, and came back in high good humour saying that The O'Neill had promised him his protection against any more raids.

Not for the first time Una marvelled at the respect, the veneration that he had for this man who had been raised like herself in England and was said to be as English in his ways as any of Queen Elizabeth's favourites. Why then did her father hold her 'Englishness' against her, when it was none of her own doing? Was it because she was a woman, or because she had no power? And in all her father's absences she never seriously considered trying to escape for Art was always there, and she feared him as much if not more than her father. It had been a happy day when she first discovered that Art was not her mother's son, but the son of Cormac O'Boyle's first wife. She hated to think that her gentle mother could have borne such a brutish son, that he could be her own full brother.

It began to seem as if life would go on like this for ever and her greatest fear now was that she would not want to escape, but one day Siobhan told her she had heard her father talking to Art about marriage.

'Marriage? Whose marriage?'

'Yours, Una.'

'I will never marry, *never*!' Una said fiercely. They were sitting on the heather out beyond the bawn sewing, and she looked down at the blood welling from her finger where her needle had pricked it. After a moment she said more quietly, 'Did they say – who I was to marry?'

Siobhan shook her head. 'I didn't hear that – they knew I was listening and your father told me to leave the house. But – but wouldn't it be a grand thing to have your own man, and a house and children and everything?'

'You do talk a lot of rubbish sometimes, Siobhan!' Sticking her needle in the cloth Una stood abruptly. 'I'm going for a walk. By myself.'

She walked for what afterwards seemed to have been hours, aimlessly, without sense of direction or time, her thoughts beating against her mind like small birds caught in a storm. Marriage. She had known that this moment would come, that some day they would try to force a marriage on her, but the months had slipped past with no word spoken and she had put the fear from her, with all the other things she could not bear to think about if she was to keep her sanity. What a fool I was, she thought now, only vaguely conscious of the stony ground beneath her feet, the furze which caught at her skirt, the hidden rabbit holes that nearly turned her ankles. How could I think I could go free for ever? Free? She had laughed aloud at that, so harshly the sound had frightened her and she had clapped her hand over her mouth. She was a prisoner just as surely as if she was in a locked cell. She had realized that the day they had come for her.

It was Siobhan who found her, crying her name into the gathering darkness. 'Una, Una love, where are you? Oh Una, answer me!'

And at last she heard her. 'I'm here, Siobhan.'

Siobhan had taken her back to the house then with her arm round her, gently, lovingly, but it really was no different to that other time.

But in spite of what Siobhan had overheard they said nothing to her of marriage in the weeks that followed. She managed to convince herself that the girl had been mistaken, and soon afterwards they left for the summer pastures, the sun warming their faces and the mountains purple with heather; the men driving the hundreds of small, red cattle before them, Art and his father riding up and down alongside the vast, lowing herds, shouting and cursing, Una at the back with Siobhan and her stepmother Aoife, and Aoife's servant, the other women and the garrons laden with provisions behind them again. It was impossible not to become caught up in the general excitement, and the weeks that followed were like a picnic that went on and on. She shared a small hut with Siobhan and Siobhan's two young sisters and they cooked their own food and ate out in the open, and even the older women began to look young again as their skin soaked up the sun, shedding the smoke and grime of winter.

But then the long, warm days began to shorten and soon they were back in the house again. On an autumn morning when the leaves were turning and down on the beach there was an ugly sound to the roar of the waves, Una came into the house to find Aoife having her hair bleached. The woman servant lifted the jug of ashes and urine over the bent head of her mistress while the grey slime ran onto the cloth round Aoife's shoulders. In spite of herself, Una turned away from the sight and the smell, and her stepmother laughed maliciously. 'We'll be bleaching *your* hair soon, my girl!' And then to the servant, 'You stupid slut, don't pour it into my eyes – Yes, my girl, your idle times are nearly over, I promise you!'

'What do you mean?' Una asked her, trying to keep the fear out of her voice.

'I mean that your father is finding a husband for you, that's what.' Aoife made an impatient sign to the woman, bending her head again over the bowl and this time the woman poured clean water over her. Una had to wait until Aoife raised her head once more. 'One man is willing enough to take you but he wants eighty cows. A bride-price of eighty cows for *you*!'

Una watched stricken, unable to speak as her stepmother rose to her feet and sat down on a stool while the woman

132

began to dry her hair with a cloth. After a moment she pushed the woman away from her and said through her broken, blackened teeth, 'But your father will find someone, sooner or later! Though he may not be to your high and mighty taste!'

So Siobhan was right, Una thought, walking away to the other end of the hut. But perhaps – perhaps it will not happen for a while – perhaps some miracle will prevent it – Oh God, don't let it happen –

Nor did it happen, at least not right away. She heard her father and Art arguing about it, and the bargaining seemed to go on and on, until the day Siobhan came to her, bursting with importance, her round face solemn. 'He's dead!'

'Who is?'

'The man you were to marry! My aunt told me. He was killed in a fight!'

'Thank God!' Una breathed. 'Oh, thank God!' While Siobhan gaped at her in astonishment.

'But I am sure they will find someone else,' the girl added consolingly.

Poor Siobhan. She was so kind, so friendly, and so stupid that Una wanted to shake her. And yet was she really so stupid? Was it not a natural enough thing to want a man, your own house? Would it be so terrible after all to marry a man and bear his children even if she did not love him? If maybe he was young and kind and passable-looking? Would it not be better than her present mindless existence? But it was not likely that her father would care about gentleness or kindness or even looks, if the man was wealthy enough and had influence enough to bring credit to the O'Boyles – and such thoughts anyway were a betrayal of something buried deep inside her, a conviction, a certainty that she belonged to Ralph, would always belong to him. She could not, even more, she *should not* marry anyone else.

The months drifted by and this year the booleying was over earlier than usual because the weather had broken and Old Peig predicted a month of storms. They were back in the house again, when Siobhan came to her one evening, her rosy cheeks unusually pale.

'They are talking of another marriage for you,' she whispered.

'Who is it this time?' A coldness in her heart, her mind.

'Come outside with me.'

They hurried through the gate, to the level ground beyond. 'He has agreed to take sixty cows,' Siobhan said, not looking at Una, 'and he doesn't care about your English ways.'

'But who *is* he? What is he like?'

Siobhan looked directly at Una for the first time. 'He's old,' she said huskily. 'As old as your father. And – and he's sick.'

Old was bad enough. But sick? Una had taken the girl by the arm and she saw her flinch as she tightened her grip. 'Sick? What do you mean?' She was beginning to shout.

'My aunt says – she says he has the pox.'

Una released the girl slowly, feeling the blood leave her own face, seeing the girl's head become two, then one, then two again.

'Una, don't faint! Don't faint on me!' Siobhan's voice seemed to come from a great distance. 'Maybe my aunt's wrong. Maybe he's better now. And he has land and money and folk in Scotland.' Siobhan's voice was louder now. 'Maybe it's a good thing for you.'

Una found herself running, running in through the gate, into the house where her father sat behind the table, alone.

'I won't do it!' she panted. 'I won't marry him! You can't make me!'

'What loose mouth has been tattling, eh?' Her father struggled to his feet. 'But no matter, I'd have told you soon anyway. The wedding is to be in November. That's the right month for marrying, and you can count yourself lucky. A man with close kin in Scotland! Who has agreed to sixty cows as a bride-price. Only sixty! He says he does not care where you have been raised – '

'Of course he doesn't care,' she cried, her voice beginning to break. 'An old man, riddled with pox! But what do you think he will do to me, what kind of grandchildren do you think you will have? They'll be diseased like him – like I will

134

be! You – you are unnatural – sick in your own mind – '

'A curse on you!' he shouted, and he raised his hand to strike her across the face but she was too quick for him, stepping back before he could reach her.

'I'll kill myself first!' she panted. 'It's easy enough to do that!'

'Do you think I'd let you? You fool!' There was spittle at the sides of his mouth and the veins in his forehead stood out like cords.

'I'll find a way! You can't stop me!'

He came round the table to where she stood, poised for flight. 'This man can get us help from Scotland, can you not understand what that means, girl? Or are you still lovesick for some English whelp, eh?'

If she had had a knife she would have stuck it into him, and he drew back before what he saw in her eyes. 'Don't!' he muttered, putting up his arm as if to shield himself. 'Your mother used to look at me like that – '

She turned away, sick at heart, and left him staring after her.

She had until November.

CHAPTER 15

THE 958-TON *San Salvador* was in the front line of ships: two squadrons of galleons and four galleasses leading the way down the Tagus, the rest close-bunched behind and yet seeming to fill the bay; a city on the march through the greenish, silk-smooth water, as if nothing on this earth could withstand its slow, ponderous advance to the sea; the tiny figures on the quayside becoming a solid line of shadow, their cheering fading into nothingness, so that the cries of the rowers in the galleasses were now clearly audible as the whips found their naked backs.

Below the poop men stood at ease, talking, laughing, still cheerful.

'How do you fancy weeks of this?' Nico asked, coming to stand beside Ralph, his bonnet under his arm, his hair white in the sun as if he had prematurely aged.

'I don't fancy it at all.'

'Nor me.' Nico looked over his shoulder. 'I wonder when we shall see Lisbon again?'

'God knows.' I'll never come back, Ralph thought suddenly. When this is all over, I'll take another name, start again – somewhere. Let Ignatius think I'm dead. And for a moment, for just one short moment on that bright summer's morning, it really seemed possible.

Nico was talking again. 'I liked Lisbon,' he was saying thoughtfully. 'I even got to like that frowsty tavern and the terrible stuff Pedro gave us to drink!' He spun his bonnet on one finger and added cheerfully, 'Damn that aunt of Maria's!

I could have done with a laugh before we left – '

A laugh! Dear God! Ralph tried not to draw back, but the past came crowding as if it had never left him. If only Maria really had spent those few days in some dirty hovel looking after an old woman instead of –

She'll be all right, he told himself for the hundredth time. Surely a convent was a refuge for the sick? He had never spoken to a nun in his life, but he had often seen nuns in the Lisbon streets and wondered what went on behind the pale, aloof faces. It had always seemed to him a strange way for a woman to spend her life, but those faces had not been unhappy, nor unkind –

'God's wounds but I think you miss the girl yourself!' The smile not quite reaching the blue eyes.

'Don't be ridiculous!'

'What is wrong with you then? I swear you have been down in the mouth since I came back from Coimbra! You are not sorry you have joined with us?'

'Of – of course not.' Turning away so that Nico could not see his face. I shall have to come back to Lisbon, he thought, watching the swinging bonnet. I shall have to come back, after all. To kill Ignatius. That is the only real solution. I should have killed him that last time, when he was alone. It would have been easy. I had my knife – or I could have throttled him. Taken that long neck and twisted it, like killing a fowl. His hands clenching as if he was actually doing it.

Why didn't I? he asked himself. Was it because he was a priest? But he knew now that even a priest can be evil.

The bonnet had stopped swinging. 'Ralph – there is something wrong. I know. Tell me. Please.' The blue eyes were full of concern, but nothing else in them, surely?

And Ralph would have given a year, ten years of his life to have been able to tell him everything, to ask him if Ignatius was using him too. And if the answer to that had been 'yes' he would have said, 'I understand. I know what they can do to your family. Even if you have to spy on me. I understand.'

But Ignatius could always find Maria. He could not risk it. 'There's nothing wrong,' he mumbled. 'Nothing. Really.'

And Nico turned away abruptly, the moment gone, lost.

Over by the rail a stout Franciscan priest was reading his office, frowning in an effort to isolate himself from his surroundings. Was he one of Ignatius' people? Or could it be one of those hidalgos chatting together by the ladder? The blue-blooded ones. Related to God. Even better, related to the king. Elegant clothes, elegant voices, the holds cluttered with their belongings, and their useless, gossiping servants. Watching Ralph Paulet? Why, they didn't even see him! If he fell at their feet they would step over him!

The ship's bell rang for Mass and the Franciscan closed his breviary and blessed himself. Ralph caught his eye and the priest smiled, a fat, kindly smile full of such innocence that Ralph felt ashamed. I see evil where there is none, he thought. In a way I am becoming like Ignatius himself. God's curse on him anyway. Why didn't I kill him?

Later he went down to dine in the great cabin. The others were already there, waiting at the long mahogany table to say Grace. Officers and gentlemen adventurers. Velvet doublets in all the colours of the rainbow, and the black of Spain. Satin breeches. Ruffs gleaming white, every other man festooned with jewels as if, since he could not bring his lands or his houses with him, he had brought their value in precious stones instead. The walls behind them hung with sumptuous tapestries. Tall candles guttering in elaborately wrought candlesticks, but most of the light coming from a massive lantern hanging from the low ceiling.

Grace was said by the Franciscan and they sat down in front of the mounds of steaming food, Nico on Ralph's right, the priest taking the empty stool on his left, settling his heavy body with a gusty sigh, wiping the sweat off his face with his brown sleeve. Two more priests, Dominicans, hurried in to sit further down the table.

'It is very hot, is it not, señor?' the Franciscan said, his Spanish slow and careful – long after they had left the *San Salvador* Ralph discovered he was Irish.

'Yes, Father.' Why does he have to sit beside *me*, he thought. I never want to speak to a priest again. He turned his head away, began to listen to Nico talking Italian to a young dandy beyond him, seeing the youth rest his hand on Nico's stockinged thigh, and Nico move his leg away.

'I hope the good Lord will send us a calm passage to England. I am not a good traveller by sea.' Another gusty sigh beside him.

'I'm sure He will if you ask Him, Father.' The words right, but the tone of voice wrong. The soft, gentle face puzzled and the hum of talk and soft tinkle of music rising to the ceiling. Gold and silver plate – and the newfangled forks. The young Italian pouting and Nico smiling sardonically.

And beneath them the ship heaved gently as the wind began to rise.

The wind continued to rise for the rest of that day, and during the days that followed in spite of all the prayers as if, the priests said, God had decided to test His favourite children. When the Armada was still inside the bar, the signal was given to cast anchor and wait.

They had to wait for seventeen days at the mouth of the Tagus, and early in the first week a *patache* had gone from ship to ship with a list of instructions from the duke – his most recent orders to his fleet, to be given to every officer.

Ralph had read the crabbed writing with a mixture of incredulity and amusement. Gambling was prohibited, as was brawling, and to enforce this no man was to wear a dagger. To utter any oath or to take in vain the name of the Lord or Our Lady or the saints was forbidden on pain of the most severe punishments and stoppages of wine. And to take a woman aboard was most expressly forbidden, since, the duke said, it was well known that women on board a ship were an inconvenience and an offence to God.

'*I* am to enforce these rules?' he handed the paper back to Nico, still laughing.

Nico for once was serious. 'Each officer is responsible for his own men.'

'But the poor fellows will go mad with boredom! What *can* they do? I'm in favour of no brawling. Of course. But the rest –'

139

'You do not really know us yet, do you? We are used to this kind of discipline.' And for once Nico was wholly, sombrely Spanish.

As far as gambling and swearing were concerned Ralph chose not to see or hear, but on the whole he found that Nico was right. Even though boredom hung over the ship like a fog, the men huddled miserably but docilely enough in the now freezing lower decks while gale after gale roared through the mouth of the passage. The officers still changed into velvet doublets and satin breeches in the evening, and there was still a hum of talk in the great cabin as the servants scurried in and out with the broth which was no longer as good as it had been in the beginning, and the meat which was no longer as fresh as it had been in the beginning. The priests at least were kept busy, saying Mass and hearing Confessions, and every morning the ship's boys sang the morning salutation at the foot of the mainmast, and at vespers, the Ave Maria and Salve Regina. And now, every other day a man was flogged for some minor breach of discipline. But none of Ralph's men.

Towards the end of the month a favourable wind came at last, and on 28 May the duke in his flagship the *San Martin* led the fleet past Castle St Julian out to sea. There was a quietness now in the men of the *San Salvador*; none of the excitement that had been there when they pulled away from the quays at Lisbon, and below decks the sour smell of diarrhoea and vomit hung in the air. Ralph and Nico had not so far fallen ill, but the cabins, like the holds, were full of groaning men, their bowels loosened with dysentery from meat which had turned rotten, and water which was found to be green and stinking when the barrels of unseasoned wood were broached.

It took the fleet thirteen days to reach Finisterre, since it could only sail at the speed of its slowest tub of a supply ship. Thirteen days of capricious winds in hot, steamy weather, during which more food went bad, more drinking water turned green, and the brown hills of Spain drifted slowly by. And at Finisterre, although the duke waited for four days, the promised victualling ships failed to turn up. A council of

140

commanders decided that there was nothing for it but to put into Corunna, and a *patache* darted from ship to ship with the new orders.

The *San Salvador* went in with the duke's flagship and fifty others and anchored in Corunna harbour, but the rest stood out to wait beyond the headlands. It was a sultry evening, ominously still, and Ralph left the hot, airless cabin just before midnight for a breath of fresh air. He had scarcely put his foot on deck when the wind suddenly strengthened and a tempest came howling out of the south-west. He had never seen a whirlwind but it was as if he had been caught in the centre of one, and as he struggled to his feet there was the sharp crack of canvas above him and the urgent shrill of the captain's whistle.

The storm raged all through that night, and next morning there was not a sail to be seen outside the harbour. In the afternoon, when the wind dropped at last, a search was begun for the missing ships.

Up and down the coast the *pataches* darted, looking for them, going as far north as the Scilly Isles, the point chosen for rendezvous, should for any reason the fleet be scattered. The *pataches* found nine ships there, including the Duke of Florence's galleon, the *Trinidad Valencera*, the fourth-largest ship in the whole fleet, and one by one the battered, leaking strays limped back into Corunna harbour.

Soon, tents dotted the hillsides above the town like early mushrooms. An old, empty house down near the quay was turned into an emergency hospital, and the countryside was scoured for fresh food. Every day vast quantities of oil and rice and beans, fruit and meat and vegetables arrived by land and sea to feed the camp, and be loaded aboard the ships against the next sailing. Yet for many of the men it was too late. They died of dysentery and ship's fever in the camp, in the grey house by the quays and in the streets of Corunna.

And in all of that time there was no message, no sign from Father Ignatius, nothing to show that anyone at all was watching, so that there were moments when it almost seemed to Ralph that there had never been a girl called Maria nor a white-robed figure sitting behind a table whispering

141

obscenities. Moments when he played with the idea of deserting. Guards were posted on the roads out of Corunna to stop deserters, but it would be easy enough for an officer to get by them on some pretext or other – and there was the whole of Europe to hide in.

He lay awake one night thinking about it, listening to the sentry outside cough into the darkness, Nico's breathing deep and regular from the other side of the tent. Perhaps without knowing it he fell asleep himself, but it seemed to him that he was back in Lisbon, not in the prison but in the tavern with Maria, everything as it used to be, weeks, months before in that other lifetime. And he came out of his waking dream to the sound of her laughter, and knew then that it had all happened. That nothing had changed.

So he stayed. And in the evenings when the routine duties of the day were over he went drinking with Nico to the taverns, and in one of them the serving girl showed her preference for him. When he woke up beside her hours later he discovered that she was even younger than Maria, her childish breasts scarcely showing beneath her dirty shift. He had been sober enough earlier to know it was not her first time, but now in the cold greyness of early morning he hated himself. He had emptied out his pockets on the soiled, worn blanket and before he had left the bed to pull on his doublet she was gathering the coins together with thin, eager hands. He never went back to that tavern again.

Day followed day after that as if they were to be there for ever, but by the middle of July the last of the wounded ships in Corunna harbour had been made whole again. Leaking hulls had been recaulked, and spars and masts lost overboard during that night of sudden storm had been replaced. New sails flapped cleanly in the gentle breeze and the twenty-six coopers rested at last from the task of repairing the wrecked water casks. Then rumours began to circulate that the duke had received instructions from the king to sail without further delay. The immediate spiritual cleansing of every man in the Armada was ordered. The priests were taken to a small island in the port, tents and altars were put up for the occasion and long, straggling lines of men were formed for Confession.

Ralph did not join any of the queues. Instead he stood quietly among the men who had already confessed and received Communion, and as he watched he was reminded of the weekly procession from Tascombe to Sunday service in St Mary's and he wanted to run, to leave behind the whole terrible charade. He had actually turned to go when he saw him – and his first thought was that it was a trick of the sun, of the mind. But seconds later the figure in the white habit with the black hood was still there, only a few feet away, an unnatural stillness about it. Ralph felt cold, ill, and suddenly the strange, dead eyes met his directly, seemed to come alive, to accuse him as if they knew he had not taken his place with the rest. Then Father Ignatius had stepped aside. Lost himself in the crowd.

Ralph could not have moved if his life had depended on it, but the ceremony had finished and the men around him began to surge forward for the boats like children released from the classroom. They took him with them and as he felt his feet move he gathered his wits and looked about him – but he could not see a white habit anywhere.

And in the few days that were left before they sailed, Ralph did not see him again. He stayed as much as possible in camp, but even there he half expected to see Father Ignatius come out from behind a tent, or a group of men, or rise up off the ground suddenly like an ungainly bird of prey. But 22 July came, the last of the mules who would later draw the artillery was taken aboard, the ships were searched once more for women, the signal was given to cast anchor – and still there was no sign of Ignatius.

CHAPTER 16

THE SUN blazed down on the white walls and vineyards of Corunna, on the long chain of the Galician mountains behind them. The crowds cheering as they cheered in Lisbon, how long ago? And the great city of ships once more making its slow and ponderous way out to sea, leaving two thousand dead behind it. The wind holding just long enough to get them out of Corunna harbour. When they were still within sight of the coast it dropped, leaving them to drift with flapping sails.

A cannon shot cracked the stillness like a sharp, small thunderclap and men came running. The *Zuniga* was in trouble, they said. Her rudder hinges were broken and there was no way now to steer her. And as Ralph left the rail, he saw a longboat setting out towards them from the *Zuniga*. Someone was coming aboard. A priest. As it came closer he saw who it was. Father Ignatius. Coming on board because the *San Salvador* was the nearest ship? Or because he was on it?

It was as if the door of his cell had clanged shut behind him once again.

It was nearly dawn before he slept, to be wakened only minutes later by the shrill whistle to weigh anchor.

He went up on deck with Nico, and stood beside him on the poop as the *San Salvador* set sail for England on the early morning tide. A good south wind filled her sails and she was still in the forward line. Ralph could see Father Ignatius at the rail and he stared at the back of the narrow head with loathing. Two men were with the priest and every now and then they turned to search the faces behind them with their policemen's eyes. It must be from habit, Ralph thought, watching them. What could they possibly be looking for at such a time? But in the days that followed the same scene repeated itself time and again. Father Ignatius with his back turned, the men for ever on the watch, their eyes always finding Ralph, until it seemed to him that the ship began to shrink, and the shadow of prison seemed to hang round him like a shroud. Once, coming out of the great cabin he saw a grey-haired Dominican walk away from him. There was the narrow, familiar head, the stooped shoulders, the stealthy walk. And for once, for once, alone. Ralph stepped swiftly forward, grasped at the loose white sleeve. 'Wait!'

The priest turned a startled face. 'Yes?' It was not Father Ignatius.

'I'm – I'm sorry, Father. I thought – '

The thick, disapproving eyebrows climbing, the cold eyes saying 'I know you. You are the one who does not confess his sins with the rest. Who does not receive Communion – '

'I mistook you for someone else, Father.' Bowing. Walking away, thinking, I'm a fool. An utter fool. If it *had* been Ignatius what could I have said to him? Why are you watching me?

I know why.

There were four days of watching, of being watched, as they moved nearer and nearer to England, but only slowly, the whole fleet held to the pace of their clumsy supply ships, and on the fifth day, when they were nearly as high as Ushant, the wind dropped and they drifted again, becalmed under a lowering sky. The following night the wind changed, began to blow hard out of the north, then hauled round to west-north-west, started to blow a full gale. The *San Salvador* rode the heavy, driving seas easily enough, but it was rumoured that other ships were falling back. There was no sign of Father Ignatius, though his two familiars still prowled the ship below decks, and it was Carlos the Andalusian boy piper who told Ralph that the 'new' priest was sick as a dog in his cabin.

May he die of it, Ralph wished silently, but the wind dropped next day and the great hills and valleys of green water disappeared as if they had never been.

Even so, Father Ignatius did not come on deck again until after land had been sighted from the crow's nest. His face was jaundice-yellow, the cheekbones looking as if they might pierce the skin, but he stood straight enough between his two watchdogs, staring towards the dark outline of the Lizard. What was he thinking, Ralph wondered, from further down the rail. What did it mean to him to see England? And what does it mean to me, he asked himself. To be here at last. Bringing the Faith back to England. The Faith? Christ's own religion? Or a girl with broken bones and blood running out of her mouth?

Blue sky. Blue sea. Saturday morning, 30 July. This time Martin de Bertendona's squadron led the way; behind them, the royal galleons of Portugal under the duke's direct command; then Diego Flores de Valdes' Castilian squadron and after them, the supply ships with the Guipuzcoan squadron under Miguel de Oquendo and the Andalusians under Pedro de Valdes on either wing. The Biscayan squadron under Juan Martinez de Recalde brought up the rear.

No crowds to cheer now, no drums, no chanting priests. A tenseness about the waiting men, ranked shoulder to shoulder on the decks, the sun glinting off the polished steel of their guns and pikes, bringing the sweat out on their bodies under the heavy armour. As they came nearer the land Ralph saw the smoke pluming upwards from the beacons lit on headland after headland along the English coast. 'The Spanish! THE SPANISH HAVE COME!' He started to shiver and looked with horror at the red cross on his tunic.

'Think of what the English would do to *you*, señor!'

Ralph thought at first that he had imagined it, that the low-voiced Spanish was a whisper in his own mind. Then he saw the tall, white-robed figure walking away, saw the yellow face in profile.

Damn him! DAMN HIM! He must have been watching,

been so close he could have touched him. Ralph found his
hand searching for the hilt of his dagger, felt his body shake
with hatred.

And all because a girl had thought she loved him. No, that
wasn't true. It went further back, much further back than
that. To another girl whom he thought he had loved, whom
he *had* loved. Back to his father, his mother, to – where did
anything ever start? And what did it matter anyway? The
mainsail swelling in a sudden gust of wind, the huge cross
on it suspended above his head. Follow Me, He had said. But
was this a way that He would ever have gone? I bring not
peace but a sword. Was this what He had meant?

Far ahead one solitary English pinnace appeared suddenly
from nowhere, and Ralph could hear its tiny cannon firing,
and the answering roar of the Spanish guns. The pinnace
darted away unharmed.

An hour later, when the Armada had re-formed into a long
line of ships there was a shout from the lookout on the *San
Salvador*. He had seen the glint of sun on the enemy's
topsails.

Nico came running, shouldering his way through the
crowd of officers on the deck.

'Ralph! Ralph! The English fleet! Have you seen it?'

From the decks below such a cheer rising that the seagulls
lifted from their perches in the rigging. Rumours running
like fire through the crowded ships. Signals flying, men
shouting; there were a hundred English, fifty, three hundred,
a thousand. A priest kneeling on the quarter deck, arms
spread as if he was being crucified, praying for victory over
the infidel, the enemies of God and man, the servants of that
whore of Babylon, the usurper Elizabeth. Gunners sweating
by their guns.

'Sixty English ships, señor *Capitano*. Sixty!' Carlos came
over to Ralph, stood beside him, trembling with excitement.

'How do you know?'

'Everyone says so, señor. Pedro my friend heard the other
officers speaking together, the high-up ones. Only sixty
ships, señor, and such little ships! We shall take them all

prisoner tomorrow, señor, is that not right? We shall not even need to fight them, they were saying. They will all surrender.'

Sixty ships. And Drake probably leading them. But there would be more soon. Surely? Ralph realized that the boy was still there, and behaving oddly. Looking round him quickly and secretively as if he was afraid they were being watched. And then whispering, not looking at Ralph. 'Señor, that priest, the one who came from the *Zuniga*, is he your friend or your enemy?'

'What the devil do you mean?' He caught the boy by the shoulder, twisted him round to face him.

The childish face reddened, and then grew pale with fright. 'Señor, I meant no harm! Only – he was asking the men about you – if you speak to them of Our Saviour – of religion. He asked me – '

'What did he ask you?' He let go of the boy's shoulder, not even wanting to question him further. He felt as if he was ill, as if he had ship's fever coming on. And yet why? What was there new in this?

The boy mumbling, frightened at the look in Ralph's eyes. 'I – señor – if – He asked me if – if you ever – if you – ' He could not say it.

'Tell me!' Shouting. 'Tell me,' he whispered, 'don't be afraid.'

'He asked me if you ever touched my body.' The child's eyes which knew too much, had seen too much, dropping. What did the sailors, the soldiers below do with him, during the long, sleepless nights? Ralph felt sick again, wanted to throw the boy away from him.

'Damn your soul! What did you tell him?'

'I – I told him – yes. That – that you had healed my back when I – the time I was flogged in Corunna.'

'What did he say then?' His hand shaking as it held the boy, so that the boy's head trembled on the thin, girlish neck. Suddenly he realized what he was doing, how it might look – if someone – Wanted to shout 'Get away from me! Get away from me!' Wanted to clean his hand. 'What did he say then?'

148

'He said you must be a kind officer, señor. That I must be grateful to you. And I said I was, señor.'

'Did he ask you anything else?'

'No, señor. He went away then. But the men said he was a spy, and meant you harm. Is that true, señor?'

'They were talking nonsense, boy. Go along now, go to your work if you have any.' The boy turned away, like a little dog unsure of whether or not it had done wrong. 'You were right to tell me. Thank you.' The boy ran off, pleased now that he had done as he had.

Rain scudded across the deck, soaking Ralph. The wind had risen and it tore at him so that he had to hold onto the rail. There were no lights ahead of them, nothing to show that another fleet waited out there for them in the darkness. His sodden clothes were cold against his skin, but his anger held him there, and he stayed on deck until the first streaks of dawn were in the sky, and the men began to pour out from below.

Sunday morning, 31 July. The rain clearing and the sky miraculously blue again. More ships must have joined the English fleet during the brief night, for Ralph counted eighty ships astern of them now, and another eleven inshore. And soon a single shot rang out from the duke's flagship – the long awaited signal for the Armada to take up its fighting stations. He almost forgot Father Ignatius as he watched the fleet come about, like a huge, infinitely slow dance, a vast game of chess. The great ships turned, shortening sail, bringing themselves into line, until they formed a giant crescent, the *San Salvador* remaining with the rest of the Guipuzcoan squadron and the Levanters.

Seven miles of ships. A floating city. A line of fortresses. And Ralph looked at the thin straggle of the small English ships with a strange clutching at his heart. The English were in single file, one behind the other, small and trim and neat. Ships for playing games with, for chasing pirates – but not for fighting the great timber castles which any moment now would drive them down into the green, endless silence.

May God help them, Ralph thought involuntarily and

watched with the rest as the duke hoisted his sacred banner to his maintop and an English pinnace made for the *San Martin*.

'Drake has sent his challenge,' Nico said, beside Ralph. 'The fight is on, *hombre!*'

The English fired first, directing their fire at de Leiva's *Rata Coronada*, the rearmost ship in the left wing, the Spanish guns answering them, the sounds oddly small, lost in the distance, the puffs of grey smoke like scraps of wool against the dark sides of the ships, the sound of the firing coming seconds afterwards, lost in the immensity of sea and sky. Bertendona's *Regazona*, one of the biggest ships in the Armada, swung in behind de Leiva and the rest of the Levanters, the Guipuzcoans following, guns firing on the right wing now and the smoke thickening. Until slowly the darkening fleeces joined, and spread a grey curtain across the entire crescent of the fleet. Men fell on the decks of one of the Levanters, but so far away from the *San Salvador* that to Ralph they seemed like dolls knocked over at a Punch and Judy show. It was not until later, when the two ships came close together that he saw the dark liquid coming through the scuppers and realized that it was blood.

The *San Salvador*'s own guns fired, and the noise was deafening. Then there were the sounds of guns running back on gun decks after the salvo and the gunners shouting, screaming orders to the gunners' mates and the loaders, as they heaved the iron cannon balls into the smoking mouths of the guns. And far down below, like a herring boat, so low in the water it was below the level of their gun ports, an English boat slid in. Ralph could see the sailors on the English deck. So few of them. The officers. Two. Three. No soldiers at all. A narrow deck, sails filled, swift-moving. A sudden crash of firing, and the *San Salvador* shuddering, the screams of wounded men, of men dying. The English ship already away from them, turning, driving back under the *San Salvador*'s guns. She fired her other salvo, from her starboard guns and there was the same heaving of the deck, the screaming, the splintering of timbers as there had been the first time. The great guns of the *San Salvador* fired back,

150

but uselessly, the sea showing white foam where the cannon balls struck, far beyond the English ship. The great galleon turned, tried to run down her attacker, to bring her into the line of fire – like a cow chasing a hare, Ralph thought. Below him, a wounded man dragged himself across the deck, his leg trailing, leaving a long stain of blood behind him. Ralph could not force himself to look away, and the man looked up at him, half blind with pain, not really seeing him or anyone. A wounded creature dragging itself to shelter, a place to die. The group of officers, hidalgos, leaning against the poop rail near Ralph, did not so much as notice the man or his shattered leg, or the blood. They were watching the English ship race away from them, and one of them in a boyish, would-be indifferent voice was wagering whether their next salvo would hit the English ship or not.

'Ten reales, Don Luis? Do you take me at evens?'

Below them the man lay still, his face still twisted upwards, looking at the sky, but he saw nothing of it, neither light nor shadow. And from far down in the holds there was a deep groaning, cries of agony, the sudden shriek of a man gone past enduring.

Ralph found himself going slowly down the companion ladder to the main deck, to the huddled body. It lay in a pool of blood which glistened in the sun, the eyes still open, seeing nothing. The man had not shaved for days, and sweat and gunsmoke lay among the hairs like a dark slime, but the skin of his chest under the torn shirt was clean and white as a woman's. He was – he had been young. All day Ralph had been watching death, but far away, clean death. Marionettes which danced and fell and lay still. Not this.

He looked up at the rail where he himself had stood a moment ago. The hidalgos had moved away. Perhaps the sight of death offended them, or bored them. Had the young officer won his bet? Were Englishmen on that small, narrow ship lying on the deck like this? He closed the man's eyes, looking round him as he did it, half ashamed of his own action, his weakness. But he could not help himself. There was blood on his hand now, and a grey stain of gunsmoke.

He stood up like a man walking in his sleep, and went to

the hatchway leading down into the hold. A belch of smoke came up to meet him, a fury of sound, of stench, the ship heaving as the port salvo roared, the sound crashing in the narrow darkness of the hatchway. There was a solid rush of hot air, of blood smell and gun smell, sweat and agony; the ring of iron balls in the muzzles, and the dark sheen of naked, sweating shoulders as the gunners' mates rammed and wadded and the gunners swung their burning matches like ropes of fire. Powder monkeys ran and staggered, slipping in pools of blood, stumbling and crying, their blackened faces streaked with white tear tracks as their red eyes wept for the smoke and powder. A great gun crashing backwards, the ropes which held it straining, twanging like bow strings. A gunner's mate screaming curses, blaspheming God and man. 'Get out of my way, señor! Out of the way of my gun!' Clasping his ramrod like a giant phallus, his gun his bride.

'Where are the wounded?' Ralph shouted, his ears ringing, Dante's hell below him. 'The wounded men?'

The gunner stared at him as if he was mad. Then pointed downwards, and ran to his beloved, the iron maiden. Rammed his phallus into her gaping throat, the salvo crashing, thundering, the smoke so thick that Ralph could not see. He staggered forward, found the ladder leading to the deck below, slid, fell, was on his knees in a pile of bodies, as if they had been thrown down the ladder pell mell before him.

Lantern light, yellow and smoking. The smell of death and blood. Two surgeons sweating in the three-quarters dark, cutting, sewing, amputating legs and arms. A pile of legs beside the bench where they were working. A priest giving absolution to the dying. Ralph had had a vague idea of helping, of closing someone else's eyes, holding some man's hand to ease his suffering. But before this seventh circle of the damned the ideas fell away like imbecility, and he could only kneel and stare, and feel the vomit rise in his throat, spill out. He was sick until he could not see, dry spasms of retching that tore his guts in half. Words, phrases, prayers, ringing in his head like mockery. Hail Mary, full of

152

Grace. The Most Fortunate Armada. *Ego te absolvo* –

Images. Maria lying in her blood. The young priest. His father. Carlos being flogged. The man dead on the deck above, staring at nothing.

'What has God done?' He found he was saying it aloud, whispering it between spasms of retching. And then, 'What have I done?' And found one of the surgeons looking at him, raising his eyebrows at seeing a man down there who could still move himself unaided.

'I came to help,' he mouthed.

The surgeon stared at him, shrugged, pointed at a man's foot, hanging from its sinews and shattered bones. 'Hold it steady!' he shouted.

Ralph touched. Held. Gripped hard as if it was he who needed steadying. The foot was in his hand. Cut clean away.

'Throw it there, man!'

He went on helping. Blood. Rags. Lumps of flesh and bone. Lifting men off the bench to lay them against the bulwarks. Lifting other men on. The surgeon stopping once to shout at him, *'Madre mía,* you had best learn to move faster! The real fighting has not even started yet!' Hating the man for a brief moment and envying his skill – and then ashamed of himself. The ship heaving, splintering overhead, the lanterns swinging. No end to it. Amputating. Bandaging. Men crying for water.

He went to fetch some brackish, stinking water in a leather bottle. Tilted the neck into parched, gaping mouths, feeling useless. The guns had stopped firing and he went on fetching water, until the cask was empty, and still men were crying out. 'Water! For the love of God, señor!' He went up then to the gun deck to find out if there was another cask of water. The guns were silent, the crews, what was left of them, crouched round their braziers, cooking, half asleep where they crouched. A dead man lay against the timber truck of his gun, his hands crossed on his breast. When Ralph asked where the water casks were kept a man looked at him as if he was mad, and Ralph went on towards the companion ladder and up to the main deck, to where there was sunlight and clean air.

And then shadow, as someone came down the ladder from above.

Ralph knew who it was even before he saw the white habit and the sandals. He stepped back and Father Ignatius came down slowly, his narrow head bent, eyes searching the dark. Ralph pulled him swiftly, silently, behind the massive timber stairway, went for his throat, felt the thin sinews of it under his blood-stained hands. Tightened his fingers, thumbs hard under the jaw bone, against the jugular.

The pale eyes bulged, filled with something – not fear but hatred, fury, a fury like a trapped wolf, a snake whose back is broken and who cannot reach to poison. His hands clawed at Ralph's wrists and then, the fingers hooked like talons, at Ralph's eyes, his nails tearing so that for a second Ralph was blinded. He brought his knee up, but the blow was muffled in the folds of the habit and Ralph tightened his own hands until the fingers no longer clawed at him and the body went limp. He let it fall to the deck but he sensed that it was still alive, as though in these last few hours he had gained an instinct about death, and could tell its presence in skin, in breathing. He felt for his dagger, drew it, stooped down, feeling in the shadows for the throat to cut it. Touched flesh and brought the point, the edge of the blade against it – and hesitated.

Go on! his mind shouted. Strike!

And he could not. And in that second of hesitation the deck heaved under him. A flash of what seemed to be lightning turned the shadows into daylight, and such a crash of thunder came with it that he was knocked sideways by the blast, hit his head on a beam, fell stunned. But only for a second. Then he heard men shout, 'The magazine! The powder store has gone up!' He heard the crack and roar of flames, felt a wave of heat roll over him, scorching his face and his body. He came to his knees, saw the white shadow of Ignatius' habit scrambling and crawling, clutching at the timber sides of the stairway.

He's escaping me, Ralph thought. Found his dagger gone, lost in the darkness, and felt for it, stupidly. Men rushing, clambering upwards past him, the white habit gone. A wall of flame at the far end of the gun deck. Men screaming below, shouting for help, feet running on the deck above. The flames swaying, bending, a huge whiplash of crimson and yellow fire flickering towards him, driving him back behind the stairway. He lost all thought of anything but the fire and of how to save himself. Found himself on deck. Men running past, shouting, sailors with useless buckets slopping water, trying to form a chain of men to fight the fire. He saw Nico, staggering, holding his face in blackened hands, only recognizable by his hair. An officer stumbling, dazed and blinded, going over the side before he could save himself.

The sails overhead were sheets of orange fire, the rigging burning, tar smoke billowing, covering the deck in a pall of smoke. He stumbled over something and looked down. It was Carlos, his body shrivelled like a dead leaf, blackened and cindery. And his face untouched. The girl's face, the lips drawn back in a shriek of agony which death had locked there.

Nico stumbled into him and Ralph caught his hands, pulled them away from his face. 'I cannot see! Who is that?' For the first time since he had come to know him Ralph heard fear in Nico's voice.

'It's Ralph, Nico! It's all right now – I'll stay with you.'

All right? The nearly blinded eyes searching for his and then covered again with Nico's hands against the pain of even that much light. Behind them men were shouting now for the longboats to be lowered. Another explosion and another half deafened them and a great fountain of coloured fire gushed up from the foredeck, twisting and flaming in the rigging, climbing the foremast like a scarlet dragon. A spar fell, crushing men, scattering flames and the ship tilted, fire spouting, writhing, hissing, as burning timbers met the water. Ralph saw one of the officers, the hidalgo who had wagered ten reales on their salvo hitting the English ship. 'The wounded men!' he said hoarsely, catching the man by the arm. 'We must get them up from below!'

But the hidalgo shook him away, not hearing anything, not seeing him. And the hopelessness of saving anyone, saving anything, hit Ralph like a blow in the chest. He almost lost his footing as the deck heaved again and had to catch at Nico to support himself.

'Nico! Hold onto me!' Trying to pull him to the rail but the deck at such a slant it was impossible to climb it except on hands and knees, behind them the port bulwarks already close to the wave crests, the sea breaking over them and men fighting and clawing their way up the sloping deck, away from the sea and the green water.

Ralph touched the rail, the smooth mahogany hot under his hand. Below them were the open gun ports and on the other side the sea would be pouring into these same openings, filling the hold, drowning, bringing silence. There was a last explosion from far down as sea touched flame and the last barrels went up in the darkness. The foredeck opened like a crimson flower, and then there was no fo'c's'le, no foredeck, and the *San Salvador* began to fill like a stoved-in cask in the sea. Sailors flung ropes and netting, torn rigging, anything, over the bulwarks, and swarmed down, trying to encourage the soldiers to follow them. There were boats already in the water below, with sailors in them calling, 'Jump señores! Jump for the love of God! We cannot wait any longer for you.'

A sailor looked up at Ralph, seeming to be shouting directly at him, and he caught Nico round the waist, heaved him up on the bulwark rail, climbed over, and still holding Nico to him, jumped.

They hit the outward curve of the hull, slid on it for a yard or so, then fell clear, and for a second, a sickening, endless second, there was nothing and they were falling, falling into infinity. Then they hit the water, solid as rock, bone-shaking and terrifying. Were going down. Down and down. Green, choking darkness. Ralph flailed his free arm, Nico clinging to him like ivy, strangling him. And suddenly hands were pulling him up and up, over the side of a longboat, until he fell in a drowned heap in the belly of the boat, his feet up on a thwart and his head down in the scuppers, water running out of him in a thin stream, salty as blood. Nico was flung beside him.

When at last he could raise himself up and see anything,

the *San Salvador* was still burning, low on the water, its fire echoing the fires of sunset. The wind was rising again and naked, blackened bodies floated in the choppy sea and thudded gently, sickeningly against the sides of the boat. Ralph felt his stomach turn as he helped to lift them, their flesh, their limbs sometimes, falling away in his hands. Only a few were still alive, clinging desperately to whatever debris they could find, and since Ralph was the only one in the boat who could swim he stripped off and went into the water to help them aboard – and no one of them was anyone he knew. But once, when something like a white sack bobbed up on the crest of a wave he felt such a rush of ugly excitement that he cried out.

It was a Dominican habit, and the man inside it was dead, his face already swollen – but it was not Father Ignatius, and Ralph had to hide his face for fear anyone would see his disappointment.

They brought their handful of survivors to one of the hospital ships, and went on searching until darkness fell, but they found no one else alive, and when the signal was given to return to ship the longboat took Ralph and Nico and a young Portuguese sailor to the *San Juan*, for no other reason than that it was the *San Juan*'s longboat. Twenty minutes later the three of them were giving their names to the Venetian captain of the Castilian galleon – and down in that green, translucent world where the winds never blow the gods must have laughed so loudly that the fish stopped swimming, and the scuttling things that live under rocks went back into hiding.

CHAPTER 17

THE FIRST time he tried to stand he fell back, his legs like jelly, his whole body shaking like that of an old, palsied man. He lay quiet for a few minutes, his heartbeat slow and heavy, seeming to fill the cabin, and only then did he realize that the guns were silent. He forced himself to stand again, to walk to the narrow door, beginning to feel a little stronger, but the smell from the heads was like a blow in the face when he left the cabin, making him want to retch as he groped his way up the companion ladder. The ship was full of the grey light of dawn, and men lay asleep where they had fallen – but he could not find Nico among them.

The air was cold and sharp and sweet as he leant against the deck rail. Above his head torn sails hung limply from the masts, and far below the green water was smooth as a mill pond, scarcely rippling as the *San Juan* moved across it no faster than if it had been a rowing boat. Ralph could see the English fleet about two miles behind, the sun glinting on their topsails. As many as ever, it seemed to him, but behind them, far, far behind, was that the hint of coastline? The English coast? Was England safe then? The hope, the certainty of it gave him new strength. And as the sun rose higher in the sky and the *San Juan* came to life he could see more clearly what had been endured while he lay below. The ruins of ships scattered and drifting across that calm, treacherous sea, the dawn mist evaporating like the remains of his fever, as he breathed clean air, leaving behind a consciousness of difference, of being older. Ten, twenty years older in these last few days and nights.

Nico's voice, cutting across his thoughts, seemed to come from a distance, although he was actually standing beside him, he realized now. 'Ralph, you are crazy! You should be still below!'

'I'm better, Nico. I'll rot if I stay down there much longer.' He was impatient with his body's weakness. 'Where've you been?'

'I was asleep. Somewhere.'

'What day is it?'

'Saturday.'

So it was days, not hours that he had spent below. Ralph looked properly at Nico for the first time, noticed the razor thinness of his face, the greyness of the skin under the dirty stubble. 'How bad has it been?'

Nico shrugged. 'Last night we could sleep, and I could see again.'

'And now?'

Nico shrugged again. 'Who the hell knows? They talk of making for the French coast. Calais. A safe anchorage until –' He made a gesture towards the crippled ships drifting against the clear horizon. 'It will take a month to put us into shape again. If we are lucky.'

When Mass was over Ralph and Nico found some food. A hunk of salted meat, hard as timber. Two small biscuits mercifully free from weevils. A little of the rough wine. They took their meagre provisions to a quiet corner of the deck.

'We are short of food. Bullets. Powder. Cannon balls. And when we get to Calais, Justin of Nassau will be waiting for us,' Nico said, tearing off a piece of meat with his teeth and chewing grimly. 'That is the rumour which is going round. More heretics to cut our throats while we are helpless. The Great Armada! Look at it!'

'So what do we do?'

'Trust in a Spanish God. What else can we do?' Nico handed the jack to Ralph with a sudden flourish. 'Shall we drink to it?' His thin face sardonic, his eyes clear and cold as glass.

Ralph put the jack to his mouth and drank. The wine was harsh as pain and he welcomed it because it was like that.

For the rest of the day he searched the ship for Father Ignatius. The *San Juan* was half the size of the *San Salvador*, but even so, weakened as he was, it took him that long to make sure the priest was not aboard. To make physically sure, that is. All his other senses had already told Ralph that he would not find him. Yet he went from deck to deck, cabin to cabin, down the length of the enormous hold, ankle deep in water now, even though the pumps never stopped; past the rows of sick and wounded men. Searching. To see with his own eyes.

That evening the *San Juan*, with the rest of the fleet, dropped anchor east of Calais Cliffs. The English were half a mile behind, like hounds waiting for a stag to weaken enough for them to go in and finish it. And the following morning, after they had been to Mass, Ralph and Nico made for their now familiar corner of the poop. They were no longer hungry. Fresh victuals from Calais had been taken aboard at dawn, but the unaccustomed food lay heavy in their shrunken stomachs and they slumped against the deck rail, belching weakly in the August sun. Most of the time they were silent. No one spoke to them and as hour followed hour it was almost possible to believe that those quietly waiting ships behind them, lying so low and snug in the water, would do nothing; that the fighting was over and that they could lie and sleep, be clean again.

'Something is happening out there!' Nico said, waking Ralph from as near to sleep as he had come all day. The sun was going down and he shivered with cold as he rose to his feet.

'What is it? What – ?'

The decks began to fill with men as Nico was talking, those who could walk and even those who couldn't, who had to be carried or dragged along by their companions, all pouring out in terror of being trapped below, the voices harsh with fear becoming silent, the soldiers who could stand forming rank and standing stiffly to attention, staring blank-eyed in front of them.

They had to wait until after midnight, while the wind freshened and the sea broke into choppy waves. When the new day had just begun there was a shout from the lookout of the *San Juan* and Ralph could see what appeared to be lights at the edge of the English fleet. But they were not lights. They were fires, moving fires, coming rapidly towards the Spanish, growing in size and brilliance with each moment – eight ships in line, two pike lengths apart, their rigging, their sails orange sheets of flame. If they were loaded with explosives as they had been at Antwerp –

'We are done for,' Nico said heavily. 'We cannot move out of the way in time.'

His voice was drowned by the shrill of the captain's whistle and the curses of the sailors as they shoved and pushed their way through the terrified soldiers. 'We've to cut the cables, damn you! Out of the way!' Lashing out with their fists until the soldiers fell back and let them through.

There could only be minutes left, the fireships driving with the spring tide and the channel current and the wind. 'Over the side, man!' Ralph shouted to Nico and tried to drag him with him but there was a solid wall of bodies between them and the rail. He was separated from Nico, could not see him, went on shouting, 'Nico! Nico! Here!' But he could not see him anywhere, and there was a sudden roar of guns from the fireships as the powder caught in the touch holes. A monstrous wall of flame towered above them, began to fall, as the cannon balls shrieked and a man standing near the companion ladder became a bleeding mess, torn in half.

The wall of fire was so close that Ralph could feel the burning of it on his face. It was no longer possible to go over the side before the fire reached them, and he felt suddenly calm, as if he had reached a point of total acceptance – that death no longer mattered. He looked up at the bellying sails of the *San Juan* without even realizing that the galleon had drifted out of the fireships' path with only yards to spare. The mass of fire was passing them. Clear water between them, men cheering, praying, shouting with joy, frantic with relief.

'A miracle!' Nico shouted, thrusting his way to him through the crowd, and putting his arm round Ralph's shoulder. 'It is a miracle, *hombre!* Thanks be to God!'

Dawn found the *San Juan* running helplessly before a strong wind, out through the Straits and on towards the Flemish coast. Most of the fleet was making the same course, as best they could, but the *San Mateo* was drifting helplessly, the sea round her red with blood, and as the *San Juan* came abreast of her, Ralph saw that the decks were crimson. And the *Maria Juan* was sinking, men clinging to her tops and ratlines. As Ralph watched she sank like a stone, the screams of the men cut off with a terrible abruptness.

The wind grew stronger still, and the *San Juan* and her sister ships had no choice but to run for it, with the English close behind. By dawn it was raining hard, and through the scuds Ralph could see the foaming tops of enormous rollers breaking on the Banks. The sea was already brown with roiled-up sand but the *San Juan* cut her way through it almost joyfully, as if she actually wanted to be broken by the surf, as if she wished any who were lucky enough to survive to be massacred by the waiting Dutch.

On her decks her men waited in orderly queues to receive Communion – soldiers and sailors, hidalgos and peasants, white men and negros. All one now, preparing for death, oblivious of the rain that streamed off armour or plastered rags of clothing to dirty, famished bodies. Earlier they had confessed, mumbling their sins while the two weary priests looked out to sea over their bowed heads. *Absolvo te.* Were priests afraid to die, Ralph wondered. He did not think he could ever bring himself to confess again. Some force which he did not understand, however, had driven him to stand in line and receive Communion, but as the Host melted on his tongue he felt nothing, nothing at all, and he stepped aside to make room for Nico, full of a strange kind of panic.

Already the English had stood off, as though their enemy's destruction was now a certainty and needed no further effort on their part. On the *San Juan* each man strained his ears to hear what the leadsman had called. Seven fathoms. Six. A sudden gabble of voices from the lower decks was bellowed into silence from the poop. Six. Still six. And then – five.

Five fathoms. It could only be minutes, Ralph thought,

and told himself at the same time that one began to die with the certainty of it.

'The wind is changing, Ralph! It is CHANGING!' Nico was catching him by the arm in such excitement and with such strength in his thin fingers that the blood seemed to stop.

'It couldn't be!'

But Nico was right. In that moment the wind had changed to west-south-west and soon the call was six, then eight, then ten fathoms. They were saved.

Not long afterwards the *San Juan* stood away with the rest into deep water, while *pataches* scurried from ship to ship, to summon the squadron commanders to a council of war on board the duke's flagship.

It could not have been a happy meeting.

'As you perhaps already know, señores, we may sail home by the North Sea, and make round the north of Scotland to turn south again past Ireland,' the commander of the *San Juan* told his officers as they gathered round him the following morning. 'Or,' he continued, 'we may once again try to take the English Channel.' He was a short, squat man huddled inside an embroidered doublet, and his Valencian accent softened his Castilian without concealing his contempt for his audience. 'The wind will decide,' he added with a snap, his small, angry eyes going from face to face as if daring anyone to question his authority.

But no one spoke. Only Nico said quietly to Ralph, standing with him behind the others, 'Has the wind not decided from the beginning?'

One by one the other officers walked away, in total silence, and for the first time since he had left Spain Ralph felt almost sorry for them.

CHAPTER 18

AT FIRST Ralph was conscious only of an overwhelming relief that the fighting was done with, that he would not have to kill his own countrymen, or see his own legs torn off by an English cannon ball on the decks of the *San Juan*. But the old unease returned when he realized that unless they were wrecked, unless by some miracle he could leave the ship, he would find himself back in Spain in a matter of weeks. He put the possibility that Maria might need him out of his mind. By now she would have recovered, be back with her family. His presence would be more of a danger to her than a help. Or so he told himself as day followed day and the *San Juan* beat her way northwards. There was no longer any fresh food. What there was of meat and fish was mostly rotten and rationed at that. The water barrels were leaking, and to save what was left the duke had ordered all horses and mules thrown overboard. The animals' terrified neighing had come thin and high across the water to the *San Juan*, and even when they had been left far behind in an empty sea Ralph could still see the long heads bobbing as they swam to nowhere.

On the seventeenth a thick fog isolated the *San Juan* in its own small, miserable world. When at last the fog lifted the cold remained, and the men had no protection against it. Many had bartered half their clothes for food, and such clothing as they still had was sodden, like the mats they tried to sleep on at night, for the *San Juan*, and every other ship in the fleet, was leaking. And worse. The pumps worked day and night, their sound infinitely menacing, like drums heard from a distance, but still the water rose in the holds and trickled down the great, curving walls as if the ship herself was weeping for the sick and dying who lay there.

Nico had not been well for days. At first Ralph had thought it no more than his own weariness and hunger, but as they came into the last week of August it was clear that Nico was very ill. Ralph had discovered a small cabin with its door jammed, and when he kicked the door open he found the cabin empty and the single cot mercifully dry. He carried Nico in and laid him down, shocked to find how light he was. The thin body shook with fever, and Ralph took off his own ragged doublet and covered him with it. Where could he find blankets?

There were none, but in the wrecked remains of the great cabin he found velvet hangings lying behind the overturned table, and these too by some miracle were comparatively dry. He bundled them under his arm and brought them back to the cabin, afraid that someone would want to take them from him, but no one stopped him or even looked his way.

There were crimson patches on Nico's cheekbones now, and his long, thin fingers plucked at the velvet like an old man's when Ralph had covered him. 'You'll be all right, Nico,' Ralph said, wiping the sweat off the high forehead with the sleeve of his own doublet. 'I'll fetch the surgeon – it's – it's just a touch of fever – '

Nico's dry lips parted in an attempt at a smile, and he tried to say something, but even as Ralph bent down to catch the whispered words Nico's eyes closed and for a terrible moment Ralph thought that he was dead. He grasped the narrow wrist to feel the pulse but in his haste he could feel nothing, and while he was still frantically trying, Nico had moved restlessly and turned his head away.

But he could die. And soon. If the fever rose too high –

No! Ralph prayed. Don't take him, God! Please! You've taken everything else – but not him. Don't take Nico!

There was only one surgeon aboard the *San Juan* and when at last Ralph succeeded in bringing him to look at Nico he said brusquely, 'There is nothing I can do.'

'But surely – '

'Surely what, señor?' The surgeon was a middle-aged man with eyes gone far back into his skull with exhaustion. He still wore his blood-spattered apron and he carried the smell of the holds with him so that the cabin stank with it. His voice was hoarse with anger as he added, 'Do you know that there are men dying by the hour on this ship? Dying of blood poisoning, of dysentery, of ship's fever – and no medicines left. There is nothing I can do for them. Some are dying of hunger and cold and despair and I cannot even help *them*. I can still cut off a limb. I can still do that.' At the door he turned and said gruffly, 'I am sorry, señor. Truly sorry. Keep him covered, and if you can get it down his throat, give him a few drops of wine as often as possible.'

He was gone.

Ralph stayed most of the time with Nico after that, while the fever sank and grew worse again, like a tide ebbing and rising. When he shivered with cold Ralph wrapped him tightly in the heavy velvet, and when the sweat broke out on him he still kept him covered. Every few hours he forced a little wine down his throat and after that there was nothing more he could do. Some of the time he dozed on the floor beside the cot, his arm round the precious jack of wine for fear someone might come and steal it while he slept, but no one came near them. He thought a lot. 'Ye think too much,' Sir Edward had said to him, years and years ago, and perhaps he had been right. What good had all the thinking done him? It seemed to him now as he lay there in the tiny cabin, his long legs drawn up uncomfortably, that he had failed in everything he had set out to do, failed everyone he should have helped – even the English sailors at Setubal. And first of all he had failed Una. And as his legs grew cramped and he had to stand to flex the muscles he knew that what he felt for her was still part of him, as much part of him as his arm, as his mind itself, and that knowledge was like a lighted candle in the cold, dark box of a room. If only he could have told her.

He went up on deck and found that the weather had worsened. It would no longer be possible, he thought, to see the polar star at night, nor even to take astrolabe measurements at midday. How then were they to keep on course? Above his head the wind screamed through the tattered sails and it seemed to him that the *San Juan* rode the heavy, driving waves less easily, like a gallant horse which has begun to tire.

That night the squalls which had been blowing off and on for days became a storm threatening to tear the *San Juan* apart. Ralph stayed in the cabin with Nico, expecting a green sea to come flooding in at any minute, and the storm was at its height when he knew that Nico was over the worst of the fever. He woke to find Nico watching him in the grey light which came in through the half-opened door.

'Nico! Are you feeling better?'

'I feel terrible. What day is it?' His voice hoarse, but growing stronger with each word, lifting a hand from under the covering and drawing it across his forehead.

'We're into September, I think – Nico, thank God that you –'

'You were afraid I would die? Maybe I did. A little.' Laughing weakly, and sitting up. 'But I'm alive now, all right, and I want to go to the jakes.' He tried to climb out of bed and fell back. 'You will have to give me a hand, Ralph.'

'Slowly, Nico. Take it slowly. You've been ill, really ill.'

Peering up at Ralph from bloodshot eyes. 'September you said? That means I have been here for more than a week?'

'It could be. I have lost track of time.' Ralph had almost to lift him but once on his feet he steadied, could stand upright with his arm across Ralph's shoulders, but as they moved slowly to the door, the wine jack tucked under Ralph's free arm, there was a thunderous crash of waves hitting the decks. The ship bucked and reared, throwing the two of them against the door.

'Has it been like this for long?' Nico gasped.

'Since last night.'

'God save us!' Nico said quietly.

They started forward again, and this time they reached the heads, but the smell there was so terrible that as soon as Nico had relieved himself he began to retch, dry retching which bent him double, so that Ralph feared he would do himself an injury and wanted to take him back to the cabin. But Nico would not go back. 'Fresh air – I must have fresh air!'

Making their way forward. Men lying so quietly they could have been dead, or huddled together like sheep in a thunderstorm, staring dully in front of them, only their eyes moving as Ralph and Nico staggered past, and when he had at last brought Nico to the closed hatch Ralph knew it was hopeless to try to get him out on deck. So they stayed where they were, where at least there was the memory of fresh air, and when after a time the hatch opened and a wild-eyed sailor almost fell through, Ralph caught at the sodden sleeve of his canvas jacket. 'Where are we? Do you know?'

The man blinked stupidly at Ralph from under salt-rimmed eyebrows. 'What – what –?'

'Are we off Norway?' Nico asked wearily.

'Nor-way?' The sailor rolled the unfamiliar word slowly on his tongue, shook his massive head with the same terrible slowness, and Ralph realized that the man was near to dropping with exhaustion. 'We – we are off – Ire-land,' he said at last, and Ralph caught his breath.

'And the other ships?' Nico questioned. 'Where are the others?'

The great shoulders lifted in a shrug. 'I do not think that even the captain knows, and I certainly do not, señores.' The bearded mouth parted in a grin. 'Maybe God knows, señores. If you care to ask Him.' Without waiting for an answer, the sailor padded away on his bare feet – great hams of feet that could have carried two men.

They found a quiet corner and squatted there, sharing Ralph's last half-sodden biscuit, eating it slowly crumb by crumb, to make it last as long as possible and drinking a mouthful of wine from the nearly empty jack. Ralph felt closer to the storm here and not in a mood to talk, but after a while Nico said, attempting to sound off-hand, 'Thank you for staying below with me.'

'It was not much to do. For a friend,' Ralph said and knew at that moment in a curiously detached way that the time had come for him to speak, if he was ever going to. 'We may not

168

have much longer,' he added slowly.

'I know.'

'There's something we have to talk about, Nico.'

Nico looking at him sharply. His face changing. Growing wary. 'Yes, *hombre?*' And then altering again. 'I know. I know.' His eyes looking away from Ralph.

'How much do you know?' Ralph asked, afraid in his turn of meeting Nico's eyes.

And Nico drew out his dagger, and with a sudden, terrible passion drove the point of it down into the timber beside his out-thrust legs. It stood there quivering, and it took an effort for Nico to pull it out again. 'I know that I would like to kill myself. And him. Only I would like to kill him slowly.'

And they both knew he was talking of Father Ignatius.

'How did he get you to do it?' Ralph's lips felt dry, stiff. The shock of knowing as terrible as if he had not known it always.

'I am part Jew!' Nico said, his voice shrill with bitterness. 'Isn't that enough? Ralph, for God's sake try to understand. My mother, my sister! What do you think would have happened to them if I had said no?'

Ralph watched a sailor as he padded by, a big-bodied, simple man who would never face any problems except dying for his king, and God.

'I swear to you, Ralph,' Nico was whispering. 'I swear on my mother's soul that I have never harmed you, never told that devil a word he could use against you. All I ever told him was that you were a good Catholic, a loyal servant of the king, an enemy of the heretics. I swear as I hope to save my soul. Can you try to believe me, Ralph?'

'I believe you,' Ralph said tiredly. It was like swimming in a sewer. 'Can you believe the same of me?'

'Of you?' Nico breathed. 'Of *you?*'

'The same story,' Ralph said. 'He got me in the same way. You're part Jew. I'm part heretic. He could have us both burned.'

Nico staring at him. Horror in his eyes that looked suddenly child-like, no longer a man's, a child who has seen

169

the real world for the first time. 'No, Ralph! Not you! I thought – '

'You thought I was different to you?'

'I thought – I thought – ' He had begun to cry, which was strange to see, and very painful. Ralph touched his arm, not knowing what else to do.

'You thought I was a better friend than you were?'

'My mother and sister,' Nico whispered. 'If it had not been for them – if it had only been me – I swear to you, Ralph – '

'And you're thinking that I was alone? That there was no one else? No one else that he could use against me? You have forgotten Maria.'

Nico stayed very quiet for an endless moment. 'Maria?'

'They arrested her. He had her arrested. And tortured. To make her confess that I had tried to seduce her away from the True Faith. He told me that if I did not give in, did not agree to do what he wanted, he'd have them go on torturing her.'

Nico suddenly gripping him by the doublet, his face like a madman's, his eyes half out of his head with rage and hatred. 'He – what did he do to her? Tell me, damn you! What did he do to her?'

'Let go of me, Nico.' Putting him away from him like a child. So tired, so sick of all of this that he could have lain down in a quiet place and let himself die of the pain of it. All of it came back. Not Nico. Not Nico's childish spying, childish attempts at loyalty. Not his own. What could either of them have done differently? So it was not any of those things. But the rest. His own madness in running away from England, from the memory of Una. Going to Spain. This war. Religion. How could men call this religion? Torture, treachery, warfare, killing. Turning friend against friend, child against father, lover against lover. Hatred, cruelty, betrayal. In the name of God.

'What the hell does any of it matter?' he said bitterly. 'Neither of us is likely to see him again, nor Spain, nor anything else.'

'Tell me about Maria, damn you!' Nico was crying again with rage and shame and the remains of fever, his whole body shaking.

'What is there to tell?'

'I knew she loved you,' Nico whispered. 'But why did you take her away from me?'

'I never took her away from you. Never.'

'Do not lie to me, Ralph. I know you were lovers, he told me so.'

'Nico! Nico! *He* told you. How could you believe anything *he* told you? For him to say it proves it was a lie. She loved *you*.' Ralph found suddenly that he could tell the lie and meet Nico's eyes as if he was telling him the deepest truth. And who knew, perhaps it was the truth, and that small, tragic child Maria had given her little packet of child's love to him because Nico had refused it, or seemed to refuse it, or to mock it as he had pretended to mock all love. Perhaps she would have given it to anyone else who seemed kind, was kind to her for a moment. 'She loved you,' he repeated. 'She wanted to make you jealous, that was all. To make you love her.'

Nico looking at him, trying to believe, believing. Suddenly reaching out both hands to take his. 'She loved me? She really loved *me*?'

'Yes, you fool! And still does.'

'Still? You mean – she is not dead?'

'Why should she be dead? She was taken to the hospital before I left the prison. They promised that as soon as she was well they'd send her home again. She's there now, dreaming about you.'

It was absurd to talk like this, about a girl a thousand miles away, when they were both within days of death. But perhaps it was best, perhaps this was the only thing worth talking about. What else was there? But Nico was shouting at him again. Or trying to shout, his sick man's voice breaking with the effort. 'Send her home? You fool! Do you really believe – '

'Why not?' Ralph said. And found his own words of a few minutes ago like an echo in his mind. For him to say it proves it was a lie. He stared at Nico, a feeling of cold spreading through him. 'Of course they sent her home,' he whispered. But when he tried to find reasons why they

171

should have done so, he could not find any. 'I tried to kill him,' he said slowly, and put his hands over his eyes. 'God forgive me for failing.'

CHAPTER 19

THE MOON came out briefly from behind the jagged black clouds. Came out to mock the stricken ship and then withdraw, leaving the *San Juan* to meet her end in darkness. In that brief moment of light Ralph looked at the faces of the other men on the poop. Nico. A handful of officers. The captain a little apart, his useless whistle still hanging from a cord round his neck. The same greenish pallor in all the faces, the same expression in the eyes, for the single anchor cable which had held the galleon for four days off the ill-famed Irish coast had severed, and they had saved only that one anchor from the disaster in the Calais Roads.

Above their heads the wind howled and raged through the rigging and the almost useless sails, driving the *San Juan* mercilessly forward on the mountainous waves towards the beach and the rocks. The *Lavia*, the Levantine vice-flagship, was still with them and there was a third ship whose name no one seemed to know. Otherwise they were quite alone, not another sail, not another mast to be seen. Three ships. Out of the greatest fleet the world had ever seen, the mighty army which was to walk across the sea and conquer England.

Ralph had just come up from the holds three decks below where he had gone in the foolish hope that he might be able to help. There had been nothing he could do. He could scarcely tell the living from the dead. A Franciscan priest had been there, the skirt of his tattered brown habit belling round him in the slowly rising water as he knelt to say the prayers for the dying. Ralph had at least been able to pretend he was helping, supporting him each time he struggled from his knees beside a dying man. It was the same priest who had sat beside him in the *San Salvador*'s great cabin but it was only the voice which Ralph recognized, for the once-full cheeks hung in grey folds, and the whites of the sunken eyes were yellow with jaundice. He was Father MacSweeney, he'd said when they came to the last man, and No, he would not come up on deck, there were so many of them still to die, poor fellows.

In the end Ralph had to leave him. The stench of the hold, with its floating cargo of excrement and vomit and drowned rats was sickening, and there was nothing he could do down there, except die with the men and the priest.

Nico had shouted at him when he came back to the poop. 'Where the hell have you been?'

'In the holds.'

'Are you gone mad? Any minute now we can – can go down and you – you – '

Before Ralph could answer the bows sank under a solid mass of water and the ship lurched down and sideways as if she meant to plunge straight to the bottom there and then. Ralph's worn boots slid from under him and he crashed against the rail and only saved himself from falling by grabbing Nico's shoulder. The heavy leather pouch at his hip caught against Nico's dagger sheath, tangling them together for a moment. 'What the devil have you got there?' Nico said, freeing his dagger and pushing Ralph upright.

'Jewels,' Ralph said. 'An officer was packing his jewels into it when – ' He had seen him through an open doorway, frantically stuffing jewellery into a pouch from a larger sack. Ralph's eye had been caught by the gleam of gold and the colour of the jewels as he came up from the hold, and in that instant the ship had lurched and shuddered as it had done a moment ago, and the officer had run for it, pushing Ralph out of his way with terrified violence, his face panic-stricken. So terrified that he had let his jewel pouch fall on the companion way and never noticed it. 'He dropped it below,' Ralph said, 'and I picked it up. I shall have to find him.'

'Hell's teeth!' Nico shouted. 'Look!'

174

Ralph turned and saw it – a towering wall of water. A mountain of it. Greenish grey streaked with a darker green, the foaming tip of it already beginning to curl over on itself. He watched it coming, unable to move for horror. Not even able to cry out. He felt his hand moving of its own accord, grasping uselessly at the rail in front of him and Nico was beside him, shouting. 'Hold on to something, Ralph! HOLD ON!'

The wave came faster than a horse could gallop. Monstrous. Overwhelming. Unimaginable, even though he was seeing it with his own eyes. Higher and higher above their heads. Seeming to be above the mast tops, blotting out sky and light, until there was only this wall of sea above them, leaning, falling, crashing. Ralph screamed then, and felt himself lifted like a cork, a feather, nothing. A huge weight crushed him, an enormous force drove him back from the rail, tore him from it, smashing the breath out of his lungs, spinning him head down. Water in his mouth, his lungs, choking him. The world turned to a dark flood of sea, green-dark and icy.

There was a pain at the back of his knees like having both legs cut off, and he screamed again and choked, lungs and stomach filled with that icy weight of sea. Then he was hanging six feet above the deck, his legs caught in the rigging, knees hooked round a stay, hanging head down-wards, the green flood racing below him yet seeming above him, like the sky gone sea-green. The last of it washing over the side, leaving the deck cleared of everything the sea could tear away, the gratings, coils of rope. Nico.

Falling head down, saving his skull from being smashed as he fell by breaking the fall with his arms. Lying flat, rolling to the far rail and finding he was lying on top of someone, on top of Nico.

They dragged themselves upright, not sure if they were dead or alive. The sea had taken the foremast and it lay overboard now in a mass of tangled shrouds and canvas – a sailor was hacking at the shrouds with an axe like a madman. There was no one else on deck. No one. Nothing. Deck hatches ripped away. The last canvas torn from the spars, shreds rattling in the teeth of the wind, snapping like pistol shots. And another wave lifting, coming, falling, smashing.

This time they clung to a stay like leeches, arms and legs wrapped round the thick rope, and even so they were almost torn from it before the wave passed. When it had passed the mainmast itself was falling, smashing down to crush the port-side bulwarks, to tear up the deck planking as the huge heel of the mast came free of its shoe, deep down below the gun decks. As it went over it brought the hull out of the water to starboard, so that the galleon listed hideously, almost showing her keel to the waves. The deck slanted like the roof of a house, impossible to stand on without clinging to the stay.

And in that moment there was a sudden calm, the wind seeming to catch its breath, the sea hesitating before it struck again, like a huntsman choosing the place to give the *coup de grâce* to a foundering animal. They could see again, almost think. Between them and the shoreline there was nothing but wreckage. Men swimming, drowning, throwing up an arm, vanishing, sucked under by the drive and force of the currents. A few men clung to spars, gratings, smashed timbers, and beyond them all were the beach and rocks, livid in the stormlight which was neither day nor night. Black rocks streaming white foam like witches' hair. Rocks like teeth to tear the ship's hull to pieces when they struck. And beside the rocks a wide crescent of beach, men crawling up it, clawing their way forward against the backward pull and drag of the waves as they broke and ebbed.

Other figures running towards them, weird figures with cloaks like flapping wings. Men. Come to save them? And Ralph saw arms raised, what looked like clubs swinging downwards. They *were* clubs. A crawling man reared up on his knees, flung his arms over his head in supplication. The club swinging down, the man falling, the cloaked figure stooping and the club striking again.

It was the Irish, killing.

And the moment of calm was gone and the wind lifted into a shriek of rage, seeming to heave at the *San Juan*'s helpless

176

bulk, to keel her onto her side by main force so that the deck was as upright as a wall, with the sea under Ralph's feet as he hung from his arms, still clinging to the stay. He saw Nico lose his grip of the sodden rope, and begin to fall. And in the next instant his own grip was gone, and he was falling too. Losing the air in his lungs in a useless cry of shock and fear, falling like a stone straight down into the green cavern below them. Hitting water like hitting the ground, and then under it, not breathing. Lungs bursting, ribs caving inwards. Down, down to death. And then suddenly he was in the air, lifting on a wave like a hillside, a hill of green glass. Deep in the hill he could see a man, hair floating, eyes and mouth open, and knew it was Nico and could do nothing.

The hillside falling, and ten feet below him Nico coming to the surface, a white face, arms floating loosely like a corpse's, hair plastered across his forehead. 'Nico!'

He struggled towards him, gripped his arm and the two of them slid down the glass hillside into a valley which heaved its hollow up towards them. And with the heave and lift of the water, a wooden grating drove up from below. There was a man clinging to it and in the seconds before he vanished Ralph recognized him as the young man of the jewels, the terrified hidalgo. A hand lifted above the surface of the water, trying for a last grip of the grating's edge, then the hand was gone, and the grating came to Ralph as if the drowning man had sent it to them with his last strength. Ralph caught at it with his free hand, dragged Nico towards it and tried to heave him onto it. It was impossible, and instead he began to haul himself over the edge of it, force his chest and shoulders onto it while still holding fast to Nico with his right hand. It took minutes, seemed to take hours, and then he was lying flat, face down on the sodden timber, holding Nico's head above water.

'Nico! Nico! Help me! Help me to get you out of the water!'

Ralph pulled, hauled, nearly turning the grating over, nearly going over the side of it himself, and clawed his way back with one hand, never letting go of Nico's arm, feeling his muscles tear with the weight, until the body came slowly,

slowly on to the edge of the grating, water streaming out of the open mouth, and the eyes opening, staring at Ralph. Holding Nico there until he could grip the sides himself, try to save himself. The grating lifting, sinking, half under water with their double weight, the sea trying to smash them loose from it, driving them in towards the rocks, the beach away to their right and the Irish still killing men who had crawled ashore.

But the current was carrying the grating beyond the rocks. Hiding the beach from them, and them from the killers. Into a small cove, a narrow, flat, sandy beach, a mass of reeds. The grating was driven into them as if it had been thrown from a catapult, rushing into the tall, waisthigh reeds and piles of seawrack, grounding, and then beginning to slide back in the undertow. Ralph caught Nico round the waist, rolled and flung himself over the edge of the grating, and was knee deep in water, in what seemed to be the mouth of a stream, mud underfoot. Staggering forward, falling, hidden among the reeds, lying among them, Nico beside him. He began to vomit sea water, until at last he lay helpless, half alive, half dead, but breathing. And then nothing but darkness – and sleep, if it was sleep. To come out of nightmares to the sound of voices, themselves nightmarish.

The savages again. Until the voices went and he lay still. The wind had dropped and there was only the huge roar and tumble of the sea, the crash and breaking of the waves on the beaches and the rocks. Very slowly, inch by inch, he crept forward, until he was at the edge of the screen of rushes, and could peer through it.

The beach was littered with bodies. In some cases they lay across each other in small piles, and these were mostly naked, as if they had been stripped and thrown down by men working together in a group. Up near the dunes behind the beach the cloaked horrors squatted in a circle and appeared to be dividing their spoils. Ralph could see clothing being tossed from one to the other, and he caught the gleam of gold as one of them held up a chain to catch the sunlight. There was an outburst of angry shouting after that, and then it died too and a man stood up from the circle and came running and whooping down the beach towards where Ralph and Nico lay, a Spanish military bonnet held aloft on his club like a trophy. There were yelps and screams of encouragement from his companions and Ralph felt his heart stop beating. The man came running to within a few yards of the reeds before he turned and raced back again, still yelling in triumph. The other men stood up, waving their clubs and shouting encouragement and suddenly all of them turned and ran, over the crest of a sand dune, to vanish, their voices lost in the storm. And still Ralph was afraid to move.

The day died slowly and Ralph slept again. It was almost dark when he woke completely, feeling if not stronger, at least capable of moving. Very cautiously he sat up and peered round. The waves were still huge, driving sullenly against the land, and the forecastle of a galleon showed as each wave rose and fell. Beyond the galleon, or what was left of it, were what appeared to be the masts of another ship. And on the beach a few of the Irish were still hunting for treasures among the corpses.

Ralph watched as they went from body to body, hunting for rags the earlier band of Irish had not thought worth the effort of looting. He woke Nico then and they crawled inland to look for better shelter. It was bitterly cold, and towards morning Nico was taken with such a fit of shivering that Ralph knew he must get him moving again, or else he would die of exposure. They started off in the grey light of pre-dawn, crawling at first through the spiky grass, only rising to their feet when Ralph was sure that there was no one watching, not even a survivor of the killing. Keeping under cover as much as possible, going from bush to bush and tree to tree. Once Nico stumbled, fell over the naked body of a man, stiff as a board and half hidden by the grass, and lay face to face with him, almost mouth to mouth, before he threw himself sideways with a cry of horror.

It was growing lighter by the minute. Away to their right they could see a high mountain with a strange plateau-like top, but directly ahead was the same rough, uneven grassland, dotted with thorn bushes and spindly trees grown crooked with age and sea winds. They kept going for another

hour or so without meeting a living soul, but Nico's face by
now had become so pale and haggard Ralph knew they
would have to rest. Just ahead was a large rock and they
threw themselves down and leant their backs against it.

'Do you know at all where we are?' Nico asked after a long
silence.

'The talk on the ship was that we were off the coast of
Donegal, but maybe south of it.'

Nico squinted at the sun. 'We are heading north?'

'As well north as south,' Ralph said. 'If – it's only one
chance in a thousand, ten thousand, but I thought that if we
could find Una – I don't know how, but if – then maybe she
can help us. Otherwise we're finished. Maybe we are anyway.
The English will get us. Or the Irish. Those horrors on the
beach – '

'Una is Irish.'

'I'd not forgotten.'

'All right, *amigo*, for God's sake don't let us quarrel. Even
if we do find her, what about her father? What would he do to
us? Or her husband? She may have married since.'

Married. It was the one possibility which had not occurred
to Ralph in all his thinking about her. He stared at Nico.
'Yes,' he said slowly. 'She may be married, and gone away, or
she may not want to help us, or we may not be able to find her
at all. But have you anything better to suggest?' Knowing
that he was being unjust and yet unable to prevent it.

'We could try to board a ship. Sooner or later, if we stay
near the coastline we will come on a port.'

'What port? Where? We could be months trying to reach
one because we cannot travel by the roads – if there *are* any –
it'd be too dangerous. Una is our only chance.'

'And I say our only chance is to find a port. And a ship,'
Nico said stubbornly. 'I want to return to Spain. Your girl is
here, but mine is there, and everything else is there. Are you
going to throw away both our lives for the sake of a girl who
probably does not care if you are alive or dead, and for all you
know is married to a man who will cut both our throats? Or
have them cut?'

'Damn your eyes!' Ralph whispered, suddenly hating

him. Sick with hatred, and fear, and hunger, and weakness. 'For heaven's sake!' he said then. 'What's wrong with us? With me? I'm sorry, Nico! I'm – '

They did not even hear the grass rustling. The man seemed to come from nowhere, big and heavily built, wearing the familiar, shaggy cloak but grasping a long stick instead of a club, as if he might be a herdsman. He made no move to touch them, or even to come close, just stared down at them from under a thick fringe of hair. As Ralph started to rise to his feet, the man turned and ran off through some nearby trees.

'Come on,' Ralph said, pulling Nico up. 'We'd best move on fast.'

But they had gone only a few yards when the man came running back with two more men, like himself but younger. Ralph and Nico stopped and waited, holding their breath while three pairs of eyes examined them curiously from head to toe. Again, there was no move to come closer but there was menace in the way the men stood shoulder to shoulder, and Ralph's hand felt for his dagger. He drew it slowly and stepped in front of Nico, but the men still made no move, and began to talk to each other rapidly, their eyes all the while on the dagger.

'Friends,' Ralph said. 'We are friends. Not enemies.' He moved the dagger to his left hand, and with his right hand made the Sign of the Cross. 'Catholics. *Católicos.*'

The men stared at him with the same blank wonder and hint of menace, and began to gabble again in their own language. Then one of them pointed at the dagger, at himself.

'He wants you to give him the dagger,' Nico said. 'Look out.' Nico had his own dagger drawn.

'Do you think I'm mad?' Ralph said. 'If they attack I'll take the big one. You try to get the one on his left.' And raising his voice he said again, 'We are Catholics. Spanish soldiers. Not English. We are your friends.' And as an afterthought, 'Hungry.' He pointed to his mouth, mimicked a man eating. Rubbed his belly. And still the three pairs of eyes watched him. Until the thin, youngest man to the left of the others seemed to understand. He rubbed his own belly under the heavy cloak and spoke to the big man who nodded in sudden enlightenment.

The big man stepped forward, said something, waited. Pointed again to Ralph's dagger and then to his own mouth. Patted his stomach and grinned in a pantomime of satisfaction.

'You give us food? For my dagger?' Ralph said, holding the dagger up. The man nodded and grinned again, obviously understanding the gestures rather than the words. The others jabbered, growing excited.

'Not this,' Ralph said. 'But gold. We will give you gold.' His eyes still on the man he fumbled at his pouch, opened it and pulled out a gold and jewelled ring – the first thing his fingers grasped. It was a thumb ring set with an emerald, and he slipped it onto his own thumb and held it up for the light to catch it and for them to see it. 'Food?'

One of the men edged forward to look, gabbled again, tried to take the ring. But Ralph pulled his hand away in time, lifted his dagger warningly. Suddenly the three men turned and ran, calling out to one another in a strange, high-pitched shouting, as if they were half a mile from one another instead of side by side.

'Let's run,' Nico said, 'before they change their minds and come back.'

But it was impossible for Nico to run, and Ralph had to support him as they walked and trotted, staggering over the rough ground. The men had vanished behind them, hidden by a fold of hillside and the tall bushes which grew everywhere. Rabbits ran from them as they stumbled onwards – there were rabbit holes in the short, cropped turf. And there must be cattle as well as rabbits Ralph thought, for he could see the droppings. If they could find a cow and milk her – or catch a rabbit –

The idea of food had become painful, clamorous in his stomach, and ahead of them now he could see a wood. A dark mass of trees. They reached them at their last gasp, and lay against the trunks of two enormous oaks, catching their breath, the twilight of the wood round them like protection.

182

There were birds singing, familiar birds. Thrushes and a wren, and blackbirds. And after a while they walked on slowly, feeling an irrational sense of protection in being among the trees, until within a quarter mile they were at the far side of the wood, staring down into a small valley. In the valley there was a huddle of thatched huts, the thatch blackened by rain, with here and there sprouting grass, as if the rain was to turn the huts into mounds of earth and turf. Not even a dog barking.

'Wait here,' Ralph breathed, and before Nico could object he was creeping forward, hiding among bushes as he crept, until he was within a few yards of the nearest hut. Still no sound. In a few seconds he was at the door of the hut. Nothing moved. Not a shadow. Either the village was abandoned, or all the people were out gathering food, or working somewhere. Even the children.

In the hut there was nothing but the ashes of a fire, a pad of dried grass flattened down like a bed, a skin bottle hanging from the centre post. And a stench of sour dirt, stale sweat and unwashed bodies. Nor so much as a stool to sit on, or a crock to drink out of or eat from. In the ashes there were bones.

He took down the cowskin bottle and sniffed. Sour milk. Sour as vinegar, but at least milk. He took it, and in the next hut found a hunk of meat on a leg bone, half cooked and still lying in the fire which had gone out. He thought he heard voices then and slipped out of the hut like a shadow, holding the leg bone like a club, the leather bottle hanging from his other hand. He saw no one. Ran like the wind. Was in the wood beside Nico before the voices became two women and a child, the women wearing the same shaggy cloaks as the men had worn, walking towards the huts from the far side of the village – if that cluster of hovels could be called a village.

Ralph and Nico went back into the depths of the wood, and ate and drank, slashing off lumps of the half-raw, smoke-tasting meat with their daggers, sucking the sour milk from the neck of the bottle as if they were calves and it was their mother. Until they began to feel better, and could settle down to pick the leg bone clean, and scrape the marrow out of it with the points of their daggers.

'I do not think I ever tasted anything so good in all my life,' Nico said, lying back. 'Twelve hours' sleep and another meal like that, and I could walk to Spain, I think. I wonder if the sun ever shines here?'

'Neither of us is going to get anywhere if you sleep now,' Ralph said. 'If they haven't found out yet that we have stolen their food from them, they soon will. The farther we can get from here the better. Ten minutes rest at the most and we shall have to go on.'

Even the ten minutes tore at his nerve ends, and long before they were up he was urging Nico to make ready. They made a wide detour round the village, and he did not give Nico another rest until they had put a good two hours' march between it and them. But that night they found another wood, and slept huddled together for warmth like two dogs, sheltering in the hollow of an oak tree which must have been old when St Patrick came here, if he ever did come to such a sodden, desolate corner of the earth. And they woke with their bones aching and their stomachs empty again, to face another day of rain, and broken half hours of pale sunlight without any warmth in it. And twelve hours of marching, stumbling up hillsides only to find an identical valley to the one they had just left. And another and another. Furze. Heather. Grassland. Green and lush and wet and cold, the wind on the hill ridges like a knife finding its way into their stomachs, into their bones.

They came to another cluster of huts. There were three women there, and with his heart in his mouth Ralph bartered a gold chain with one of them for meat and milk and a kind of soft cheese wrapped in grass. Every instant he expected men to come running with clubs to kill them, but the women only stared, more terrified of him than he was of them or their absent men, and when the exchange was made and the woman was holding up the chain for the others to look at, he ran back to Nico, and they had food again.

For days after that they lived by stealing, or by occasional barter, making their way painfully, slowly, north and north again. Nico growing weaker by the day, so that there were days when they scarcely made an hour's full march. And it was growing colder, and the weather was still worse, if that was possible. Ralph began to ask himself if he had made the right decision in heading north in search of Una. But Nico had long since given up arguing, and the truth was that it was too late now to turn back.

They did not always have to steal, or even barter. A few times they met people who were friendly and gave them food. And one night, perhaps it was the fourteenth day they had spent walking, the night of that day, they found an old woman who had a smattering of Latin and who knew about the shipwrecks. She told them she had seen no English soldiers, and offered to sell them her dead husband's cloak in exchange for a gold brooch. She let them sleep that night at the fire in her hut, while she slept on the far side of it. Next morning she gave them porridge, and buttermilk to drink from a two-handled wooden vessel, and while Ralph chopped wood for her, she cooked a lump of mutton for them in an animal's hide slung over the fire.

She called her valley Glengesh, and when they were leaving Ralph asked her as he had asked the others, 'Do you know where Cormac O'Boyle is?'

She pointed vaguely to the north-west, as all the others had done, and he could not be sure if she understood him, or knew, or was only lying to make him happier.

'Do you know where the island of Inishkeel is?' he asked, as she wrapped up the mutton for them in a piece of cloth. He had to repeat himself half a dozen times before she understood what he was saying, and then, when he had given up all hope she nodded her head, and said matter-of-factly, in her broken, Church Latin, 'Yes. I have been to St Conaill's island. I will show you how to get there.'

It seemed like a miracle, after the days and nights of hunger and misery, of thinking themselves lost for ever in a desolate world of stone and heather; that this old woman could recognize a name, could have been to an island where Una's mother had brought her on a pilgrimage, an island that was close to Una's winter home – it was unbelievable! Even Nico's face had colour in it now as he followed Ralph

185

and the woman out of the hut.

She walked with them to the end of the valley, matching them stride for stride. 'There,' she said, when they came to level ground, 'beyond those hills, beyond that again is the island of Inishkeel.'

'How – far?'

'Two days' walk.'

'Are you sure? It seems more.'

But she nodded her head vigorously. 'Soon you will see the sea on your left, but you must go on.' Pointing again. 'Then you will see the sea again and the island.'

He could not shake her certainty, and in the end he believed her, perhaps because he so much wanted to.

They came within sight of the sea the following day, left it behind them, went on. But they had hurried too fast for Nico. He began to cough, a hard, dry sound, sitting down at first and then lying on his side, wracked by spasms of coughing until at last he lay exhausted. After a couple of minutes he dragged himself onto his knees. 'I am finished, Ralph,' he said. 'I cannot go on. I am sorry. You will have to find Una by yourself. I – I will wait here until – until – ' He started coughing again and it began to rain. Perhaps, Ralph thought, if he could find a place for Nico to shelter in, it would be best to let him rest there for a few days. If he grew ill again –

They found a cave near a small lake, no more than an overhanging rock flanked by banks of earth, but dry inside. Ralph gave Nico what was left of the mutton and a large oaten cake which the old woman in the valley had given them as well. He gave him too the cow's hide he had found pegged out to dry on a rock and a clutch of eggs they had stolen that morning. Nico had not wanted to take anything but Ralph had insisted, had gone out and collected sticks for a fire while he was still arguing. When he had the fire going there was only one more thing he had to do. He opened the leather pouch and gave half of the jewellery to Nico, and when that was done it was time to go.

CHAPTER 20

IT WAS only an island, with some kind of stone buildings on it, but Ralph looking down on it from the headland felt like Moses seeing the promised land for the first time. It lay close to the shore, so close you could walk across to it at low tide, she had said, and sure enough Ralph could see a narrow strip of sand running out to it, like the fin of an enormous fish, growing shorter by the minute as the tide crept in.

It must be Inishkeel island, and the strange stone circle he had seen earlier had to be Una's childhood 'hide'. Could it be then that the solitary, ugly house thatched with reeds, which he had cautiously reconnoitred a little while ago before climbing the headland, was her home? She had often boasted that she had three homes and that the biggest was a castle, but this house was no more than a very large hut. It was surrounded by a stone wall which could have been the bawn, as she called it, where her father's cattle were sometimes penned at night. It could not conceivably be called a 'castle' however – but then he had always suspected that Una fantasized about Ireland.

He had seen a plume of smoke coming from the roof of the house, although at the time, just after dawn, there had been no sign of life. On a lake island nearby there had been the ruins of a similar house but there had been no other inhabited dwelling of any size for miles. It *must* be Una's home, and there was nothing for it but to go back and watch the house. Sooner or later he would see her – and if he didn't? But he was too tired, too hungry to think now beyond that point.

He went back the way he had come, using whatever cover he could find, half crouching most of the time, like the wild animal he sometimes felt he had become. Until he reached the hill and the large clump of furze behind which he had hidden earlier. He could see the house now and it had come alive since he last looked at it, like a nest of ants which someone had trodden on. He watched for a while, unable to tell men from women at this distance, forcing himself to stay awake and his eyes closing in spite of himself, for he had travelled all night and finished the last of his food the day before.

He must have slept, for they were almost up the hill before he became aware of them. It was the leader's voice he heard first, loud and authoritative, speaking in Gaelic. An old man, thick-set, with short grey hair under a strange-looking, tufted hat, bearded and moustached and wearing a long leather jacket, high to the throat and coming down over his hips. On his gauntleted wrist there was a hooded falcon, and running beside his horse a young boy in a saffron-coloured, belted shirt. Behind them rode a younger, red-haired man in a shorter cloth jacket, and they all wore the same kind of close-fitting breeches and hose which Una had worn when she first came to Tascombe.

They stopped only a few feet from Ralph's hiding place and he thanked God that they had no dogs with them. He could feel the thorns prick his skin through the rags of his doublet as he pressed his body against the bush, and he thought he must surely be visible on the other side. There was a shout from the leader and Ralph drew his dagger, but the man was obviously telling the others which way to go, and they rode off, turning left, the boy running easily behind the horses, like a two-legged hound.

Who were they? And if he had shown himself, what would they have done? Killed him? Taken him prisoner? His impulse was to run. But they might come back, and there was no other cover at all apart from the furze. So he lay where he was, hoping he would not have to stay until darkness fell – and then he heard women's voices in the distance.

They too were speaking in Gaelic. Laughing. He

crouched lower, and the voices came nearer, up the slope as the men had done, as if they were following the men but on foot. Girls' voices, one low and sweet, the other more high-pitched. His heart beginning to beat fast, almost stopping as he peered through the bush. A girl, walking up the hill towards him, another behind her. A girl in a long, yellow tunic under an overdress of blue. Red-gold hair. Her head was down as she picked her way through the rock-strewn heather but he knew it was Una – Not by her walk or the colour of her hair, not even by the sound of her voice, but because she was Una. He would have known, even if he had been blind and deaf, and in his fierce joy he came near to showing himself. If only she had been alone, but the other girl was coming closer now. She wore the familiar, shaggy cloak and was about the same age as Una. A servant? They were talking again and he could see Una's face now and he wanted to jump up, to take her in his arms, to laugh, to cry – and just stopped himself in time. The look of pride she had had when she first came to Tascombe was more noticeable now. She looked older too he thought, and thinner, and her face had a sadness now that had not been there in Somerset, for all the reasons she had had for sadness. He wondered what part the man in the leather jacket had played in making her look like that, or the younger one either, and his hand clenched on his dagger.

But the girl in the cloak was walking away – only for a few yards though. She had put down the basket she had been carrying and begun to unpack it. This was his chance – before Una went over to her.

He began to whistle *Greensleeves* very softly. She turned abruptly and walked over to the other girl and he realized that she had heard him and was frightened. She stopped, came back, was staring at the bush, all colour gone from her face.

'Una! It's Ralph!' he whispered. 'Don't scream, for pity's sake. It's Ralph, from Tascombe! I'm not a ghost, I'm from a Spanish ship that was wrecked – '

She stood where she was, biting her lip, her eyes huge in the ashen pallor of her face, so still she might have been a statue. He thought she was going to faint. Then suddenly she came to life, went back to the girl. Ralph could hear her speaking, it sounded as if she was giving an order, and the girl rose to her feet and began to walk down the hill. When she was out of sight Una came running back to the furze bush.

'Ralph?' Her voice breathless. 'Ralph?'

He rose to his feet, regardless of who might see him, opened his arms and crushed her to him until she freed herself and stood back a little to look up at him.

'I never thought to see you again,' she whispered. 'I did not think it was possible.'

'Nor I you,' he said hoarsely. 'Watching the house I thought some of the time that I was mad - raving mad to hope - '

'But - what - where have you come from? Were you with the men at Loughros Bay?'

'Loughros? Where is that?'

She looked over her shoulder. 'The other side of that headland. Four, five miles away. A ship was wrecked there during the week, a Spanish ship. There are hundreds of men camped on the beach.'

'So I might have walked straight into them! Thank heaven I didn't. No, we came ashore nearly eighty miles away from here. We've been - '

But she interrupted him. 'Eighty miles! You've come so far? Oh Ralph, no wonder you look - '

'Like a scarecrow?' He laughed, and she laughed with him as if nothing mattered now that they had found one another again.

'What were you doing on a Spanish ship?' she asked then.

'I'm not sure myself, but there's no time to explain now. I have a Spanish friend who was shipwrecked with me. I had to leave him some miles back - he's half dead from ship's fever and the journey up here. He needs food and warm clothes. Can you get them for us?' As if they had parted only days, not years ago. Wanting to touch her again and not daring.

She was saying, 'Of course. I'll think of a way. And you?

190

Are you hungry? But of course you are!' She touched his face with her hand, the fingers cold, and then burning against his mouth as he kissed them, holding them pressed tightly there. 'Let me go, Ralph! If someone comes – ' Her voice trembling like her hands, her eyes looking this way and that in sudden terror. 'Let me get you some food.'

She pulled her hand free and ran to the basket, pulling at things inside it, oversetting it, running back and giving him one of the soft cheeses packed in damp grass and a couple of oaten cakes. 'Now, hide yourself again, Ralph! But where will you hide? Oh, *where* is best?' Looking round her distractedly. 'If that girl – she's such a fool she'll never keep her tongue still – ' She started to push him, to make him run with her towards a clump of bushes in a hollow, parting the branches for him with her hands, careless of tearing them. 'Here! Go in, quickly! I'll be back at dark, and I'll bring everything. Only hurry.'

A minute later he saw the servant girl coming back, carrying a cloak. She gave it to Una and then went over to pick up the basket, and while she was tucking in the cloth covering the food Una dropped the cloak in the heather beside Ralph. Another moment and they were walking away in the direction the hawking party had taken, the girl having apparently noticed nothing.

He was wolfish with hunger and it was good cheese, the cakes still hot, but he forced himself to eat slowly, to make it last. There was too little however to make much difference, and the meal was finished almost before it began. He could hear seagulls screaming and the distant rumble of sea breaking on rocks and he wrapped himself in the cloak – Una's cloak which had warmed her body – and lay down among the rough stems. To have found her! Like a hundred miracles in one. For the moment it was almost enough, was enough. When she returned – that would be the time for questions.

He must have slept for hours, for when he opened his eyes the sun was going down and the chill of evening was in the air. The bushes tore at the woollen cloth of the cloak as he tried to stretch his cramped muscles without showing himself, and he wondered at the same time if his caution was absurd. He seemed to be quite alone, but he could not be sure, could not see further than a few hundred yards in the failing light. He huddled down again inside the cloak which could no longer keep out the cold, pulling the thick fringe at the neck of it high round his ears.

It was after dark when Una came back, and he watched her run towards him in the moonlight with the same fierceness of joy he had felt when he saw her for the first time that morning. He was standing, taking her by the arm as she put down the sack she was carrying. 'Are you all right?'

'Yes!' she gasped, trying to catch her breath. 'But I was so afraid that – that you might be gone.'

'After finding you? Never!'

She was wearing some kind of soft, white shawl about her shoulders and he could feel the warmth of her arm through it. 'I – I couldn't get away,' she said more easily, 'my father – you must have seen him this morning – he was drunk, but not drunk enough, and anyway he has set the servants to watch me.'

'To watch you? Does he – suspect I'm – that anyone – is here?'

'No – no, it's not that – I tried to run away a long time ago, and – and I threatened to kill myself.'

'But – why?' His voice hoarse. 'What did they do to you?'

'I – oh, we all have to marry, I know that. But this – this man – he's – '

'Marry?' he cut in, the word sticking in his throat. He dropped her arm and stepped back from her without realizing he had done so. 'You are to *marry*?'

'Yes,' she said, her voice lifeless. 'A man nearly as old as my father. He has already put away two wives. They say he has the pox.'

Ralph was so still he might have been turned to stone, but it seemed to him that inside his body he was bleeding to death. At last he said quietly, 'And you've refused, of course?'

'Refused?' He could hear the disappointment in her voice, disappointment that he could be so lacking in under- standing. 'How can I refuse? My mother died while I was in

Tascombe – there's no one to help me.' Her voice had grown husky. 'My father has been trying to marry me off since I came back. He says only an old, diseased man would have me because I was reared in – in a Protestant whorehouse and that even this marriage will cost him sixty cows – '

'But – surely – he can't *force* you to – '

'You don't understand,' she said flatly. 'It's the way of things here. You don't know what Ireland is like.'

'No,' he said slowly, the anger dying in him, 'of course I don't. Only what you used to tell me.'

'It's not as I used to tell you. That was all dreams.'

'I'm sorry.'

'I made up dreams because I didn't belong in Tascombe.'

'And do you belong here?'

She turned her head away from him. 'I tell myself that I do,' she said quietly, and then, as if the words were being physically torn from her she added, 'I wish you had not come – had not found me.'

'You wish?' he repeated slowly. 'You wish that I had *not* found you?'

'Oh, can't you try to understand?' Her voice had broken as if she was close to tears. 'I thought I'd never see you again – I tried to make myself believe that Tascombe – that you – were all a dream – and in time I would have believed it – I know I would – '

'You want me to go then?' he said quietly. 'Go, and leave you to this – this – ' His voice no longer quiet.

'No!' she said quickly. 'Oh no! I don't want that!'

'Surely there must be someone who would stand by you?'

'There is no one,' she said. She turned her head to look briefly over her shoulder into the darkness. 'Back there in my father's house there is my father, and my stepmother, and my brother – my half-brother – Art. There are my father's kerns and the ordinary servants and there's not one of them who'd save me from this marriage – not even Siobhan, my own servant, my only friend would help me.'

'Why? *Why?*'

'She is afraid of my father and Art, and with good reason – but they all think because the man is a MacDonnell, with kin

193

in Scotland, that he'll bring allies, mercenaries from Scotland into our wars here – '

'Against the English?'

'The English? One day, perhaps, if the O'Neill demands their help – but now all they care about is their own valley and how much they hate the people in the valley over the hill – they're like – like – ' She hid her face in her hands and he took hold of them and pulled them down against his chest. It was so dark now that Una's face was only a pale blur, as if she was already taken from him and he said quickly, 'You tried to run away, had you some plan in mind?' His own mind racing ahead, considering possibilities, rejecting them, searching frantically for alternatives, trying not to feel helpless in this antique world of tribal conflict and age-old customs at which he could only guess.

'Yes, I tried to run away,' Una was saying, her voice dull and lifeless again as if she had read his thoughts and doubted his ability to help as much as he did himself. 'But I had no real plan. I just – just – '

She began to cry quietly as if something had broken inside her. 'Oh Ralph,' she whispered, 'you don't know what it's like to be with someone who – who cares – even a little. It's like coming alive after being dead for a long time. You see, there's no place I can run to. Long ago, I tried to go back to England but they caught me. I thought – I thought that if – if you were there that – that – '

He felt the softness of her body in his arms without even being aware that he had reached out for her. The feel of silk against his skin – of warmth beneath the silk. 'You can't marry him!' he whispered. 'I won't let it happen!'

At that she broke away from him, stood back. 'How can you prevent it?' Her voice husky and yet a distant, faint note of hope in it which was like music.

And the mad, crazy idea came to him full-blown. 'You can come away with me!' If he had been a man with a name, with a home he could have brought her to, he would have risked saying, You could marry me. But he was no more than a scarecrow. So, instead he said only, 'Will you come away with me?' And held his breath, waiting for her answer.

194

'You don't know what you are saying,' she whispered.

'I do! I do! We can't go back to England but we'll find somewhere - so long as it's out of this accursed country. We'll pick up my friend and make for the nearest port.'

'Lough Swilly is the nearest port but we'd never be so lucky as to find a boat there. Derry is full of English soldiers, and if you're caught - ' She stopped, and then said in a rush, her voice full of tears. 'Oh, why are you tormenting me like this, Ralph? You know it's not possible!'

'The only thing that's impossible is this marriage you've told me about.'

'Oh Ralph, even to hear you say it! But - we would need money and I have none at all. I don't have even my mother's jewellery.'

She was no longer whispering however, and he said confidently, close to believing it himself, 'I've enough for both of us, and I can work. So can Nico. We'll find somewhere - ' Taking her hands, feeling them go still, her skin warm and smooth against his.

'I don't know the way - not really - '

'We'll have the stars - '

Her face raised to his, pale in the darkness. Come with me, his mind begged her. My love, my sweet love. I will care for you with my life, my soul. I will show you what love is, what love can do. Only come with me.

His mind cried out to her, but only his mind. His lips felt stiff and awkward as if he was still the young boy who had been with her in Tascombe long, long ago, and when her hands moved in his he had to release them.

'I'll come,' she said quietly. 'Of course I'll come.'

They had been so long talking that she was in a panic to return to the house quickly, for she insisted that they must have horses and food and warm clothing for the long journey ahead, and in the end, reluctantly, he had had to agree with her. But he hated the thought of her going back, of being caught and made a prisoner. Even more he dreaded the possibility that she might change her mind about coming away with him, if she thought about it for too long and saw all the dangers that leered at him from the corners of his own

195

mind. But now, at the same time, while she was still with him, beneath her anxiety to return quickly he sensed a growing excitement, a feeling of purpose and determination, and he felt such a rush of pride in her that he almost choked with it.

'I'll be as quick as I can,' she said, pulling the shawl over her head so that all he could see was the darkness of her eyes and the shadow of her mouth. 'Don't worry. They'll all have drunk enough by this time and they sleep heavy afterwards.'

He put out his hand to stop her, but she was already gone, running away from him into the darkness, and he stood where he was without moving, while the wind that had been blowing all day across the bay beat his cloak against his starved body. But it was minutes before he became conscious of the cold, minutes before he could rouse himself even to eat the food she had brought. When at last he fumbled open the cloth he found he was no longer hungry. His teeth sank into the cold meat, he tilted the heavy wine-skin, and the sour, thin wine made him shudder as it ran down his dry throat, but he was only going through the motions of eating and drinking, so great was his anxiety for her. I should not have let her go back, he thought. How can she possibly get safely away a second time, lumbered with food and clothing? And she might have difficulties with the horses. 'My mare would come to me if she had to swim the width of the bay,' she had said, 'but it may be hard to catch the others.' And there was no one she could ask for help, no one she could trust. We should have gone on, as we were, he thought. We should have risked it. And yet he knew in his heart that she'd had to go back. That whatever hope of escape they had, and God knows it wasn't much, they must have horses under them, and some protection against the cold which every day grew that bit worse.

The long night of waiting lay ahead of him like an illness that has to be borne, and when he had bundled up the remaining food and the wine-skin he set himself the task of walking so many paces away from the thicket and back again, in an effort to pass the time and beat the cold. Eight. Ten. Twelve. The distant howling of dogs – or were they

196

wolves? Not from the direction Una had taken, thank God. And not close. Not yet. His hand tightening on his dagger. It would be a strange quirk of fate he thought grimly, if he survived the Inquisition and a shipwreck and fell to a pack of wolves. Staring into the darkness until his eyes stung and ran with tears. Would she never come?

As he started the endless pacing again he thought of Nico. Would he be in a fit condition to ride when they reached him? And was the waiting as terrible for him, alone in his cave? Would he himself be able to find the cave again? Up and down, like a prisoner in the condemned cell. She was gone two hours now, nearer three surely? Forcing his thoughts onto a new track, and seeing her father again. The thick-set body. Hearing the loud, authoritative voice. How could a man make a child, and then let her be destroyed by another man's diseased lust? And he thought then of Maria, whom he had not thought about for a long while. So different to Una and yet alike in that she too was a victim. Whose victim had she been? His own? Or was she really Nico's victim? If *he* had left her alone in the beginning – I must sleep, he told himself. I must sleep. I'll go mad if I don't sleep soon.

He sat down at last beside the thicket, huddled inside the cloak. The first streaks of dawn were in the sky. For a short time he had tried to pretend that they were not there, but now he could no longer hide from himself the knowledge that dawn had come, and it could not possibly have taken Una all that time to get away. She had either changed her mind about coming or they had caught her. His body slumped inside the cloak and his mind was numb so that the woman who rode towards him out of the early morning mist a few minutes later was almost on top of him before he looked up. A cloaked woman, riding side saddle but on the opposite side to that on which English women rode, her hair covered by a white kerchief, leading two other horses behind her own, one with a couple of sacks thrown across its back. Una. At last.

'Thank God!' Ralph said as she pulled up. 'I've been nearly out of my mind!'

'Get up quickly!' she gasped, and Ralph caught hold of

197

the high saddle, and swung himself up on the horse that was not laden, taking the reins from her. 'They were up for hours with a child sick with the flux' – she was speaking so quickly that he could scarcely make out what she was saying. 'I thought I'd never get away – '

'Are they after you?' he asked, cursing his hands which were so stiff with cold he had trouble gathering the reins, but he had thrown off the last of the stupor in which she had found him.

'No – at least, I don't think so – I can't be sure I wasn't seen leaving – but it won't be long before I am missed – ' She seemed calmer now, speaking more slowly, as if getting away from the house was for her the worst part.

'We'll make for the cave,' he said, 'as we planned last night, and lie up there for a bit.' He took the leading reins of the other horse from her in his still-wooden fingers, glorying in the feel of the animal under him after the long, weary days of walking. There were no stirrups and the horses were small, more like ponies than full horses, but there seemed nothing ridiculous in the way his long legs hung down on either side of the round belly, and he led the way out of the hollow ready for whoever or whatever might be waiting for them beyond it. But the wind had dropped, and nothing stirred, nothing came at them out of the mist which still, mercifully, shrouded the headland, and he rode on as fast as he dared, afraid above all now that he would lead them over the edge into the sea.

The mist began to thin, disappeared completely, as they came off the headland, and he could see on their left the low hill which he had skirted the previous day. Somewhere behind that hill he knew was the house, and Una's father with his men and horses and dogs, so that the distant, homely lowing of cattle waiting to be milked was not as comforting as it might have been, since it surely came from near the O'Boyles' house. But it was best not to think too long about it, better to think of Nico waiting for them, of how quickly they could reach him.

The hill was behind them now and they came to a small

lake which he remembered also, dark and still in the morning light. They were scarcely past the lake when they heard it – the shouting of men, men on horseback, coming from far behind them, but coming closer by the second.

'Someone must have seen me!' Una was very pale. 'There's a wood – come on!'

She kicked her mare to a gallop and Ralph followed her, but the ground was uneven, and he was hampered by the animal he was leading, the sacks on its back beginning to slip sideways and threatening to fall off. The thud of hooves was much closer now, although he could not yet see their pursuers – he was quite certain that that was what these men were – and when he saw the wood he thought that all was lost, for the wood was not only small, it was so dense as to seem completely impenetrable. Whatever about themselves, they could never force in the horses.

But they had both reached it, and Una was dismounting. 'I found a way in last summer,' she said. 'Hurry!'

She was pulling branches aside, holding them high, trying to lead the mare in behind her, but the animal pulled back nervously and would not follow her. She held the branches higher, coaxing, cajoling, while the thud of horses' hooves grew louder – and still her mare would not obey her. Ralph could feel sweat, cold and clammy, break out on his body. He drew his dagger and pricked the shivering animal. It jumped forward and Una dragged it into the wood, Ralph following, dragging his own two horses and steadying the sacks. In moments they were all of them inside, the thick branches fallen into place behind them, the foliage like a green wall in front of them.

Una's kerchief had come off, and her face in the twilight of the wood was milk-white against the darkness of her hair. Then they heard a man's voice speaking Gaelic. 'My father!' Una whispered. 'Listen!'

They heard it again, much nearer this time. Someone answering. 'My brother!' Una whispered again. The thud of hooves close now, slowing, stopping, seeming to be only yards away from them – and Ralph's horse lifted its head suddenly, its ears twitching. Ralph began to stroke him desperately. If it made a sound, neighed to the other horses outside the wood –

The horse dropped its head, began to nuzzle Ralph as Una's father spoke again, the loud, harsh voice which Ralph remembered. Una caught him by the arm. 'They are looking for me,' she whispered. 'And my father said I couldn't be in the wood – that it's too thick – ' There was another flood of Gaelic from behind the green wall. 'He said they're wasting time – that he thinks I might try to go to England this time! Oh, dear God! He thinks someone must be helping me because I took the two garrons.' There was a bark of Gaelic like a command, and Una's grip on Ralph's arm tightened. 'They're going back towards Narin,' she breathed, 'in case I'm making for Derry.'

'Where is Narin?'

'Near the beach.'

'So if we go south for my friend – it's about ten miles – '

'We should be safe enough, for a while anyway.'

More shouting. The whinny of a horse, and then the thud of hooves going away from them, dying into silence.

A few minutes later they fought their way out of the wood into the bright, cold daylight, and for the rest of that morning and well into the afternoon they rode south through the hills, without seeing anyone. Una led, riding astride, keeping clear of Rossbeg and the lake with its small island, on which, she said, were the ruins of an O'Boyle castle in which some of the Spanish had camped. They did not stop until they came to the small river and the wide bay away to their right which Ralph remembered from his own journey north after he had left Nico.

They let the horses drink and then Ralph led the way across the river which was scarcely more than a stream, and when he had crossed he dismounted to wait for Una without any feeling of impending danger. Her little mare had only just scrambled up the bank beside Ralph when something came out of the bushes behind him. A man. Although in the first second Ralph was not sure if it was man or beast, there was so little of his face visible, the hair on it and on his head so long, so matted, so much a part of his long, shaggy cloak. There was no mistaking the heavy axe in his hand though, or his intention as he lifted it above his head.

'Ralph!' Una screamed. 'Behind you!'

But Ralph had seen him, had struck at the man's arm with his knife and seen the axe fall even as his horse reared, knocking the man to the ground where he lay stunned. 'Come on!' Ralph shouted to Una, 'come *on*!' He waited until he was sure she was close behind, and at the same time saw another man come out of the bushes further down the bank and run to his fallen companion, lifting his shaggy head to stare after them as they galloped away.

They did not stop until they had put a couple of miles between them and the river and were well past the settlement which Ralph remembered from his own solitary journey. They ate their first meal of that day in the shelter of an old ruin which might once have been a small church.

'That man –' Una said into a silence.

'Men like him attacked us when we first came ashore,' Ralph said, half reluctant to tell her, half wanting to.

'They helped the Spanish at Rossbeg,' she said quickly. 'Even my father did. The MacSweeney sent them food and clothing too, and when my brother brought them salted meat and animal hides as well, he was told that the Blakes had sent up provisions all the way from Galway.'

The sudden flush of anger faded leaving her pale and tired-looking. She had been tying the neck of the food sack and now as she put it away she said quietly, 'I have some clothes for you. You'd best put them on.'

The trews were in two parts – one, shapeless as a bag, loosely covered his tattered breeches; the other, long and close-fitting as stockings, covered his legs, and were warmer even than his boots had been. And since the soles of these were rotted through, he buried them under a heap of stones and put on instead a pair of heavy brogues which Una had also brought. They were too big for his narrow feet, but there were thongs to tighten them and they were better than going barefoot. There was also a cumbersome shirt with a kind of pleated frill at the bottom of it, and a battered leather jacket which at some time must have been gilded here and there. These he kept for Nico, whose doublet was in an even worse state than his own. He gave Una back her cloak and took the coarser one she had been wearing, covering his own strange mixture of clothes with it, warm for the first time in weeks. And when all that was done, even though they had hurried the sun was almost gone down.

In the grey dusk, as they set off again, it was hard to tell a small bush from a crouching man, harder still for their horses to pick their way safely through the dried clumps of heather and tufts of spiky grass, and yet the failing light brought its own protection, and Ralph resolved that when they had rejoined Nico, and by the grace of God set off on the last leg of their journey, they would not travel in daylight.

He had his landmarks firmly in his mind now, and he ticked them off carefully one by one as they came nearer and nearer to the cave. Another small lake. A strange group of giant slabs of rock – two standing feet apart with one lying across them both, making a giant table, exactly like the stones they called the Giant's Grave near Bunsery. And the last landmark of all. A group of withered trees, bent sideways by wind and time, like old men struggling against a storm. The cave only yards away.

'Nico? Nico, it's Ralph!'

There were a few sticks smouldering on the floor of the cave, but there was no sound, no sign of life, and Ralph was quite sure that Nico was dead or had been taken away. But he called his name again, more loudly this time, and something moved at the back of the cave. A grey shadow in the half darkness, wolf-thin.

The shadow crept forward. Became Nico.

'Ralph!' His voice hoarse, not with illness but more as though he had forgotten how to use it. 'God above! I never thought I would see you again!' He scrambled to his feet, clutching at Ralph.

'You're all right?' Ralph asked. 'I was afraid – '

'I'm empty as a drum and gone half mad with waiting, but that is all. But what – who?' Nico added in a whisper, peering over Ralph's shoulder at Una standing quietly behind him.

'This is Una,' Ralph said quickly, drawing her forward. 'My friend.'

Nico bowed over her outstretched hand, raising it to his lips suddenly as if they were in Lisbon. It was incongruous, it was even funny, but it did not strike Ralph as being either. He was only conscious of a tremendous happiness that these two people were both alive. That they were together at last. And now all things seemed possible.

They tethered the horses behind the trees, rubbed them down and left them to graze. Brought in the sacks and built up the fire with more sticks and while Una unpacked the food Nico pulled on the shirt and jacket over his rags of clothes and wrapped the extra cloak she had brought for him round his famished body. They ate then, and Ralph told him about Una's father and the man she was to have married, and with the food and the warmth Nico lost his wolfish look, though he said little. Even when they told him about the Spaniards camped at Rossbeg he only nodded thoughtfully, glancing swiftly at Ralph and away again.

When they had finished eating Ralph asked Una to draw a map for them, and this she did, drawing it with a sharp stone on a larger, flat one, marking in where they were, where they had come from. Marking in Derry.

'And our best way to Derry?' Ralph asked, hoping he did not show his dismay at the distance they would have to travel.

'I'm trying to remember the way we came from Derry when Sir Edward sent me back – ' Her hair was loose now about her shoulders, her cloak fallen back to show the low-cut bodice laced tight across her breasts and the whiteness of her skin above it. She was frowning, staring down at the flat stone. 'We came first to Letterkenny,' she said slowly. 'It's a small village – but not what *you* would call a village – here, I think.' She marked it in. 'Then – then we went on through the mountains until – until we came to a river.' She drew a long, snaking line running south. 'We followed the river until we came to the bay. Our house is here, behind the headland – '

The two men studied the rough map in the flickering light

from the fire, and Ralph said after a moment, 'We should go north-east then, until we come to your river?'

Una nodded in agreement, and Nico spoke for the first time in a long while. 'When we reach Derry, what then?'

Ralph was reluctant to tell Nico that when they reached Derry it seemed that their troubles would only really begin, but he had to tell him and when he had finished Nico said slowly, 'The English are there, and you want to find a boat to take us – where?'

Ralph shrugged. 'Scotland. The continent. I just don't know. So long as we get away.'

Nico started to say something and instead began to cough, a harsh, racking sound which Ralph had foolishly hoped he would not hear again once Nico had had food to eat. When he could speak Nico said huskily, 'This cursed country has got into my lungs. I'll be glad to get away from it.' And Ralph looked at his grey face, the tell-tale flush high on the cheekbones, and knew that he should be in a warm, dry bed with proper medicine and hot food and someone to care for him. And that there was not the slightest possibility that he would have any of these necessary things for weeks to come. 'In Rossbeg – ' he began.

Nico shook his head. 'Not for you. Not for me, either. I've had enough of priests for a while at least. Derry it is.'

They agreed that they should travel as much as possible by night, or at least in the late evening or very early morning, sleeping during the day and taking it in turn to keep watch, but for the rest of that night they would sleep. And yet they were all reluctant to turn in and went on talking as they sat round the fire. Telling Una about Spain, about Ignatius, a little about Maria, but only a very little, as if there was an unspoken agreement between Ralph and Nico not to tell her all. Telling her about Seville and something about Doña Isabel while she looked frowningly at Nico as if she was trying without success to imagine that such a scarecrow of a man could have a home, or even a mother. And Nico's fox face had lit suddenly with his old wicked humour as though he had read her mind and they had smiled across the fire at each other like old friends. She had told him then about

Tascombe and her childhood there, but he had only wanted to know about Sir Edward, about his life as an English country gentleman. He had wanted to know if she'd been to London, and when she shook her head, Ralph having long ago admitted he had never been either, Nico was clearly disappointed. So Ralph, to make up for their lack of travelling experience, told him more about Tascombe – and heard himself mention Alice, and stopped, appalled. And knew at that moment without even looking at her, that Una had suspected something.

At the same time he knew that it no longer mattered to her. That she had left it far behind her, and he dared now to look at her and wonder how much else of her young girlhood she had left behind. Was this a Una he did not really know at all? But her quiet face told him nothing, was a challenge to the man he himself had become since those far-off boy and girl days of Tascombe. If only I could be alone with her, he thought. Just for an hour. And yet all the time of their journey to find Nico – had he been afraid to talk? Afraid of what either one of them might say? He made a show of building up the fire, and soon Nico grew drowsier and drowsier, leaning sideways against Ralph and then starting upright for a moment, blinking and smiling in the firelight, until his head nodded again, and he almost fell forward into the fire, muttering something about taking his turn watching – in a minute, a minute or two. Then he had fallen onto his side away from Ralph, as fast asleep as a dormouse in winter, snoring gently.

'I'll watch,' Ralph said to Una. 'You sleep.' But she shook her head, hunching her shoulders under her cloak.

'I wonder how they are in Tascombe,' she whispered. But if her concern in whispering was for Nico, she might as well have shouted. He lay as if the Last Trump would have failed to wake him. 'Tascombe seems so far away, so long ago. Lady Jane and Sir Edward – '

'How could they have sent you back like that?' Ralph said.

'Not they – not Sir Edward really.' She had raised her voice after glancing briefly at Nico. 'Only Lady Jane. And of course Parson Dagge. *She* was terrified. I never saw anyone

205

so sick with fear. She tried to cover it with anger, screaming at me like a gypsy woman, but she was so afraid her hands shook. And she made Sir Edward afraid. Isn't it strange? She seemed so great to us once – not good, or wise but – important – didn't she to you? And in reality she was so – so *little*. Inside herself. So full of fear. And poor Parson Dagge. I think *he* imagined the queen's men coming to Tascombe within the hour to hold him to account for us. He even spoke of it to Sir Edward – talked of the rack and the Tower.'

She seemed to realize then what she had said and reached across the dying fire to touch Ralph's hand before she put on more furze branches to build the blaze again.

'Maybe they were right to be afraid,' Ralph said. 'And all in the name of Christ! The men who killed my father would have killed anyone else just as gladly. I think – I think there must be a kind of man born only to torture other men. And religion gives them their chance.'

'I'm so sorry to have reminded you.' Her voice was very gentle. She put on more furze, and the flames leapt high, crackling like an *auto-da-fé*, like a heretic burning.

They stayed silent for a long time after that, until Una spoke again, shivering suddenly. 'Do you know,' she said, 'I had almost forgotten my own language when I finally arrived here? My father called me "the stranger".' She poked at the fire with a half-burned stick, coaxing heat from it again, while Nico slept on as if he was dead. 'How I hated everything! Not that it was really so bad – until they wanted me to marry that – that man, at least. But it was so different from what I remembered. Or imagined I remembered. You know the stories I used to tell you?'

'Indeed I do. Although even then I don't think I believed you. All the gold! And the fine horses! And the ladies in their silk gowns – so much more beautiful than Lady Jane!'

'Oh, sometimes I knew I was telling stories – downright lies, just to make you or Parson Dagge open your eyes wide. But sometimes – some things I remembered – my mother – she *was* beautiful – And to come back to – to – ' She stopped speaking, holding out her hands to the dying fire. 'My mother was dead. Had died soon after my father sent me to

206

England. And he had taken another wife, after living for years with three trollops, each claiming to be his wife. My brother was as ignorant as any hind on one of the outfarms at Tascombe – and so peacock proud in his ignorance! The stink of what my father calls his "castle". And his anger when I spoke of it. As if to long for cleanliness was to be a traitor to my people. To want decency was to have turned Protestant. Catholic? They know no more of what being Catholic means than my horse there, or yours. I who had learned only to be a Protestant know more than they. I never realized how much old Dagge taught us of our own faith in condemning it.'

'And that man – the one you were to marry?'

'Don't let's speak of him.' She bent forward, hair glinting in the light of the embers like a reflection of dark red fire, her face pale, eyes pockets of dark shadow except for two other glints of reflection, her mouth dark – no longer a child's mouth as he had remembered it, but a woman's. 'Is there anywhere on earth where one can be left alone, to be at peace, to enjoy – enjoy just being alive?'

'Utopia? Prester John's land? The new world?'

She shook her head. 'If there are men there – or women – there will be hatred and violence. What is wrong with us? When I came back here first, that first summer, I used to escape from them all, with only Siobhan my servant girl. We'd bring a pony to carry our food and our cloaks and a couple of hounds – my father always wanted two men to go with us but I was more afraid of them than of being alone. We would escape, and it seemed a *real* escape. Two or three minutes and the noise and the stink were all behind us. We would be out in the hills alone, and the whole day before us – to run and laugh and be foolish, and eat honey cakes and drink sweet milk – although we needed to strain the filth out of the milk before we drank, and it always tastes of smoke. But you grow used to it. We would tell each other stories – mine about Tascombe, and hers about Finn McCool or the Banshee, and I don't know which of us thought the other's tales the more extraordinary. There would be the distant mountains, purple with heather, the blue sky and blue sea, and islands far out beyond the bay like Hy-Brasil – or maybe they were only clouds on the horizon – and I would imagine reaching those islands in a boat, with Siobhan and the hounds and the pony, and living there for ever, among the fairy people. Never growing old. Never coming back to this wretched, wretched world of men and hatreds. Surely at least Hy-Brasil exists?' Her mouth smiling sadly in mockery of her own words.

How much she has learned, he thought. She has become a stranger.

'Would you come with me to Hy-Brasil?' she said. 'In a little boat? With Nico of course?'

'With all my heart,' he answered her, making his tone light. 'It would be a fine thing never to grow old.' He felt his breath tightening in his chest. Did she really mean what she had said – you and I – she and I – together always? But Nico had heard his name in the depths of his drowned sleep, and woke, sneezing and coughing with the smoke.

'Lord, Ralph!' he gasped. 'How long have you let me sleep? And both of you keeping watch!' And he had insisted that he would keep watch now, and though Ralph and Una both said they could never sleep, Ralph himself drifted off as soon as he lay down.

Nico did not wake them until late morning, and Ralph woke to the warmth of the fire on his back, feeling more rested than he had in weeks, glad to see the colour back in Una's face. They spent the remainder of that day in the cave, resting, talking, gathering themselves together for the journey. At dusk they set off.

CHAPTER 21

IN THE ten days it took them to reach Letterkenny there was never a chance to sleep again as they had done in Nico's cave – at the most they stopped for three or four hours at a time. Sometimes at night, when there was no moon and it was too dark to ride in safety, sometimes during the day. In a wood, behind a clump of bushes or a pile of rocks, or in a hut, empty since the summer grazing which Una called booleying. There were dark shadows under her eyes now and the bones of her face were sharply beautiful. She wore her hair plaited closely round her head like a small, red-gold crown, her kerchief long since lost, and if she was hungry or tired or cold, as she must have been all of the time, she never complained. Ralph had no chance to be alone with her, but one evening they found themselves a little ahead of Nico. She had drawn level with Ralph, and as if the question had been in her mind for a long time, she asked him why he had gone to Spain in the first place. 'There's so much I still don't understand,' she added. She had not said, There's so much you haven't told me, but he knew that was what she meant.

'I thought I wanted to serve God,' he said reluctantly, not wanting to talk even to her about it, seeing himself now as a callow, emotional youth who had remained too long a child.

'I don't understand,' she cut in, her voice cold and lifeless, and when he could think of nothing to say which would not sound even more stupid than what he had already said, she went on. 'I suppose it's not easy for me to understand. I know very little about religion. There's old Father O'Dogherty who often comes to my father's house. Father O'Dogherty has his women and his bastard children like my father, but he says Mass and hears Confessions and baptizes babies. Then there's the young Franciscan who came this summer for the first time. He's what my father calls one of the new kind. He told my father to get rid of his mistresses and that divorce was sinful, and my father told him to go and not come back again. Which kind of priest would you have been, Ralph?' She turned to look at him but he could not read her face.

'I didn't want to be a priest,' he said slowly. 'I knew I would never make any kind of priest. Although it was the priest in Murley's barn that started it all. I – wanted to pay them back for him. And for my father.'

She said slowly, 'When you reached Spain, what happened then?'

'I became a soldier, like Nico.'

'And came to Donegal,' she said, smiling.

'Yes,' his voice deepening, 'and found you.' But I haven't really found you, have I? he thought, looking at her eyes which since the excitement of their first meeting on the headland still told him nothing; at her mouth that promised nothing; at her body that seemed to withhold itself without actually drawing away from him. Only her voice sometimes seemed to hint that he was more than just a one-time friend who had found her at a desperate moment. Only her voice. Everything else hidden behind that quiet face. And in a sudden rage of frustration he wanted to pull her off her horse onto the brown, withered heather. Knew that if Nico had not been there he might have done it. Might have taken her. Damn it, Una, he whispered in his mind. Why can't you see? Don't you *want* to see?

And if Nico had not ridden up at that moment he might actually have said it to her, but Nico was there, looking from one to the other of them half apologetically, as if he knew he was intruding, and the moment was gone. They had ridden on then, all three of them together, while one half of Ralph burned with shame and the other wished for the hundredth time that he could be alone with her. But they had to stay together, while they followed the river and watched for the tell-tale gleam of English corselets until their eyes watered – for they were so far north now that their greatest fear was that they might ride into a company of English soldiers.

It was three more days and three more nights before they turned away from the river, and even at that they had to retrace their steps several times, not sure if they had left the river too soon, not sure of anything. At the mercy of the mountains which seemed to be saying, When you get round us there'll be others. We'll never let you by! And Ralph would look up at their great, stony flanks and find himself shivering.

Una had had to ask their way several times. Once, from an old man stumping along a mountain path, an Irish wolfhound as big as a donkey at his heels. He had answered her in a flood of Gaelic, staring at the three of them as if they had dropped out of the evening sky, and then had hurried on, almost falling in his haste to get away from them, the hound loping along behind him. 'He thinks we're fairy people,' Una said. 'He's never been further than this mountain in his whole life.'

Another time she'd asked a young woman drawing water from a lake, and the woman had silently pointed to the east. The last time she had asked a boy driving a herd of cattle through a deep valley. They had been travelling then for over a week, and had nothing left to eat but one small oatcake. They were within a day's ride of Letterkenny, the boy told Una. When they left the valley they were to follow the river which they would soon come to and it would bring them there.

They found the river. Wider, stronger-flowing than the previous one, and they followed it in the dusk of evening, but it had begun to rain and the wind was rising. It had often rained before and their clothes were never dry, but this rain was different. It seemed to fall in steel rods which pierced them to the skin, and there was no shelter, not a rock, not a bush, nothing but flat bogland. Until they came to the hut.

Una went into the hut, stooping low, and they followed her, the smoke from the fire in the centre of the floor so thick

211

that Ralph could only see the outline of the man standing beside it. He was a huge fellow, wild and shaggy and growling in his throat like an angry dog, but Una spoke to him and he stepped back and let them come closer to the fire. There was a woman crouched beside it, a baby in her arms and behind her several older children huddled together. Behind them there was a cow, small like all the Irish cows Ralph had seen, but here in the hut seeming massive. In a corner a few roosting hens pouted their chests and against a wall an old man, or woman – it was impossible to tell which – lay on a pile of rushes, watching Ralph with the same beady, unblinking eyes as the hens'. 'It's all right,' Una whispered. 'I've told him we mean no harm.' The man pointed to the fire, and Una prodded Ralph forward. 'Sit down, and for God's sake, *smile!*'

Ralph did as he was told, and sat down gingerly beside the woman, forcing a smile, smiling even at the baby and the other children, but they only stared at him, and the woman clutched the baby more closely to her. She was quite young, but her face was old with hardship and childbearing, and even the baby, who could not have been more than a few weeks old, had a wizened look in its tiny face.

'I've told them you are Spaniards,' Una said quietly, as he sat down beside her and the water dripped from their clothes onto the mud floor of the hut.

'You *told* them?'

'They prefer Spaniards to Englishmen.'

'But – ' Ralph stopped. 'Surely then we shouldn't be speaking English?'

'They won't know it's English.' Ralph looked at the blank, uncomprehending faces of the couple and knew that she was right. 'The man was in a village not far from here, a couple of days ago,' she went on quickly. 'While he was there three Spaniards came looking for food. There was an old man in the village who spoke Latin and the Spaniards told him that they had come from Derry – that hundreds of them had been killed near there by English soldiers – that they themselves had escaped by pretending to be dead – '

'Go on,' Ralph said grimly when Una stopped speaking,

212

as if considering how best she would put what she had to say next.

'It's not as bad as it sounds,' she said slowly. 'We have an alternative now.'

'What is it?' Nico cut in hoarsely.

'These Spaniards were on their way to Lough Swilly.' Una's voice was full of a growing excitement. 'They'd been told by a priest that they'd find a boat there to take them to Scotland.'

'And instead of going to Derry, we could go on this boat too?' Ralph glanced at Nico to see what he might be thinking, but Nico's face showed nothing but exhaustion.

'Yes,' she said. 'Why not? The priest had orders from some bishop to help get all Spaniards out of the country.'

'What do you think, Nico?' Ralph asked.

The narrow shoulders under the now-steaming cloak lifted in a shrug. 'I have no wish to be shot down by an English soldier.' Nico turned to Una. 'Can our host tell us where the boat is? How we get there?'

Una began to talk to the man again, and while Ralph and Nico listened impatiently to the flow of Gaelic the woman stared at Una, and Ralph wondered what Una had told the couple about herself, and what they might be thinking of an Irishwoman of her class travelling alone with two men.

'The boat is waiting at the mouth of the river Leannan,' Una said, cutting across Ralph's thoughts. 'I think we should be able to find our way there from what he has told me.'

'How long would it take us?'

'About two day's ride, he says. And the other Spaniards were on foot, so we might even arrive ahead of them.'

To try to find this river – or go to Derry. Which? To be killed by the English, or brought back to Spain?

'We try to find this boat, then?' Nico asked, and Ralph nodded. He reached inside his cloak then and took out a coin, held it towards the man. 'Ask him if we can have something to eat,' he said to Una, and when the man and the woman and the children had examined the coin, rubbing it until the gold shone in the firelight, and exclaiming over it

213

as if they were all children, the woman filled a bowl from the pot which hung from a hook over the fire, and gave the bowl to Una. It was a kind of soup, thick and greasy and with not much meat in it, but it was food, and it was hot. They sucked greedily at the bowl in turn, too hungry to care what else besides food they might be swallowing. Afterwards the woman put before them a large cake of the familiar oat bread and a lump of yellow, rancid butter, and another bowl of milk still warm from the cow.

They left the hut soon after, and rode across the flat, dark bogland, leaving it to the horses to pick their own way. Once Ralph looked back, but although they had not yet gone very far the hut had been swallowed up in the darkness and might never have existed.

They rested that night in a small wood, but even with a fire it was becoming too cold to sleep and they rode on until after a few hours they saw the waters of Lough Swilly and the island mountain the man had spoken of. Soon they found themselves looking down into a small valley, at a river that wound its way through it and out into the lough. There was a cluster of huts at the mouth of the river, and close to shore a few currachs rose and fell on the grey water. Beyond them was a much larger boat, a galley, its sails flapping idly. A small crowd of squat, cloaked figures had gathered at the water's edge, and as Ralph led the way down the low hill a man came out from one of the huts, followed by two others carrying sacks. These three were all big men, towering over the hut people as if they were a different race from the starved villagers. English soldiers? Ralph reined in, held up his hand to the other two to stop, and they watched as the people at the water's edge made way for the three giants, staring at them in a dull silence. One of the three shouted in Gaelic, calling to the crew out on the galley, his voice harsh and ringing, which meant that whatever or whoever he was, he was not English. Ralph tightened his reins and set his heels to the flanks of his tired horse.

'I'm going down,' he said to the other two. 'Stay behind those rocks and don't show yourselves until I give the signal.' He kicked his horse forward, rode down the hill path, and

214

they had seen him now, the sailors and the villagers. Had turned, still silent, staring as he rode towards them, his eyes searching the cluster of huts rather than the apparently harmless group of men, women and children by the water's edge. Watching for the shadow of movement, for horsemen in concealment, for any threat. But there was nothing. And as he turned to beckon the others to follow him he saw that they were already following, had almost caught up with him. 'I told you to – ' he began angrily, but Una cut across him.

'How can you ask them anything without me?' she said. She called out to the three sailors and one of them stepped towards her, broad built as his own ship, rolling forward on wide-planted legs as though even ashore he felt the deck heaving beneath his feet. A worn, grease-stained leather jerkin strained across his barrel chest and his breeches and high leather sea boots were whitened with salt. He had his hand on the pommel of his dagger as he came to a halt a yard from Una, and stared up at her, and then at Ralph and Nico, his pale eyes unsmiling, his face unreadable.

Not a pleasant face, Ralph thought, trying to guess what Una's questions meant, and the man's short, hostile-sounding answers – the eyes too wide apart, the nose too small, like a snout above a small, thin mouth set in a wide expanse of pale cheeks, astonishingly pale for a seaman. As if the skin and flesh were dead, salt-pickled like a chine of pork, gone colourless. No trace of beard, the skull seeming to be bald as ivory under the flat, misshapen leather cap. The flaps of the cap were hanging downwards, hiding his ears. But as he moved his head, shaking it in a determined 'No' that had no need of language to express it, one of the ears showed for a moment. Or where the ear had been. A small lump of gristle was all that the executioner's knife had spared him. The man had been ear-cropped.

'Watch our backs,' Ralph whispered, touching Nico's arm. And to Una, 'What is he saying "No" to?'

'He says he won't take a woman on board his ship – it means ill fortune.'

'Have you told him we can pay? In gold?'

The man had turned to Ralph. 'Gold?' he said, the English word strange in his mouth. '*Oro?*' His eyes had not changed, but something of the blank hostility had gone from his face. 'You Spain? *Castilano?*'

Ralph hesitated. But what was there to lose? At the worst they could ride for it. 'Make sure he doesn't grab your reins,' he said to Una, and then to the man in Spanish, '*Si, señor. Castilanos.* We were sent here by the bishop.'

'Ah, yes! Three people. I have been waiting for you.' The man's Spanish was slow and laboured. 'But there was no word that one is a woman.' He held up a dirty, stubby-fingered hand. Looked at Ralph and turned one finger down. At Nico, and turned down the second. Then lifted his thumb and stabbed thumb and forefinger at Una in the universal sign of warding off the Evil One. Spat carefully and noisily on the rough ground in front of Una's mare.

Ralph reached inside his cloak, felt in the pouch and drew the heaviest of the gold chains. 'Look,' he said.

There was a murmur from the crowd as the chain glittered in the morning sunlight, and the tip of the man's tongue showed palely between his blackened teeth. He stared at the chain, then at Ralph's cloak as if his pale eyes could pierce the cloth and see what else might be hidden beneath it. Looked up at Una and said grudgingly after a moment's silence, 'The woman too then. I go to Holland, but first I bring you to Scotland.'

It seemed too good to be true. Ralph said quickly, 'Can you take us to Holland? Better for us than Scotland – '

But the big head was shaken again in another determined 'No'. 'I bring you to Scotland. No further. My boat is too small for so many people.'

Ralph could hear Nico cursing softly but there was no way past that flat refusal, and even to reach Scotland – 'When do you sail?' he asked curtly.

'Now. Already I have waited too long, señor. The tide – ' He pointed towards the lough. 'I thought you must be dead.'

'We must wait,' Nico whispered. 'If there are three others – '

Ralph turned in his saddle to look at the dark line of hills

216

behind them, but nothing moved in the mass of stone and faded heather and rough grass, and the sailor had caught the sense of Nico's whispered words.

'There is no time,' he said impatiently. 'No time, señor. Give me the chain.' He held out his thick hand.

'When you land us in Scotland,' Ralph said quickly. 'Not a link of it before we set foot ashore.'

For a moment the man held his eyes, then he smiled foolishly and turned away.

'I think we'll need to keep a sharp watch on our friend,' Nico breathed against Ralph's ear as he put the chain back in the pouch. 'I would not trust him an inch!'

'Nor I,' Ralph whispered. 'But we've no choice that I can see. And as for the other three – he wasn't going to wait for them anyway.' He gave a last look round and slid down from his horse. 'Will you tell the people that we need food,' he said to Una. 'We shall have to leave them the horses in exchange.'

The crowd of villagers had edged forward while Ralph and the galley master had been talking. Now, as Una spoke to them they turned their heads away and shuffled their feet uneasily, as if astounded at being spoken to, even noticed at all by great folk, their faces dulled by hunger and hardship. But at last a man found the courage to answer, and even came near enough to touch the bridle of Ralph's horse, with a look of disbelief on his gaunt features.

'They have no bread,' Una said. 'But he says they have salt meat and fish and cheese. And sour milk.' She nodded to the man and he went off towards the huts, accompanied by half the crowd, chattering now in growing excitement.

'God help our poor horses,' Nico whispered. He began coughing, and Ralph had to support him until the fit was over. Across the water the galley yawed and swung at its anchorage and Ralph tried to imagine it out in the Atlantic, in a gale, in the kind of storms which had wrecked the Armada – and saw a cockleshell, a dot, in a vast, heaving ocean. Beside the currachs it seemed big enough, but it could not have been more than twenty-five feet long, twin-masted, with some kind of superstructure like a tent near the mainmast. A cockleshell. But how else could they get away?

217

It took nearly half an hour to exchange the horses for the food, and there were angry shouts from the galley master, waiting impatiently by one of the currachs. His name, Una said, was MacFadden, and at last they were ready. While the men on shore were still chattering and arguing over the frightened horses, Ralph helped Una and then Nico into a currach. When he had swung the sack of food and their own few possessions into the belly of the light, dancing boat the galley master cast off, cursing Spaniards and women and his own men as they bent to the narrow-bladed oars.

Ten minutes later they sat huddled together on board, Una between them, while the galley made its slow way up the lough, keeping close to shore, the wintry sun glinting wetly on the oars as they rose and fell, for there was still no wind. They spoke very little, afraid that MacFadden might know more than just a few words of English as well as Spanish. Sat mostly in silence watching the wooded shoreline slip past the backdrop of the mountains. The lough had widened, and narrowed again when they saw a square, stone castle on the left-hand shore, its window slits like sightless eyes staring blindly across the grey water.

'That's the MacSweeney's castle,' Una whispered. 'Where the English kidnapped Red Hugh O'Donnell last year – my cousin Owen O'Gallagher was taken as hostage at the same time. They got them aboard a ship by a trick, and sailed away with them.'

Nico was asleep, his head fallen forward on his chest. Ralph felt the warmth of Una's shoulder against his and without making a conscious decision to do so drew her close to him. For a second she resisted. Then he felt her body relax, lie warm and heavy against his, and he tightened his hold, with sudden, disbelieving joy. She lifted her head slowly and looked at him, her eyes questioning, shadows under them, and he bent and kissed her cold lips. A swift, stolen kiss behind the shelter of the sails. Like a boy's kiss, but with a man's knowledge that passion will follow.

In this small, crowded boat there could be only that first kiss of new beginnings, yet he kissed her again, could not have stopped himself as her mouth grew warm and soft and

218

hungry under his. Like kissing life into a marble statue. Until MacFadden shouted at his men from the stern and Ralph lifted his head slowly, the feel of her mouth still on his. Her eyes were still closed and she was smiling as she laid her head on his shoulder, just as she had done years before when they were in Tascombe. But when he put his cheek against her tangled hair which had long since come undone from its careful plaiting, it smelt of the sea and wind and was no longer silk-smooth. Soon afterwards he knew from her breathing that she had fallen asleep, and he went on holding her, afraid to sleep himself, while the back of the rower nearest to them bent forward and straightened in perfect rhythm, the muscles of the man's naked forearms like great cords, his sweat sour and acrid smelling. On Ralph's other side the pouch which he wore next to his skin and tied to his belt was still heavy and he began to think about Scotland and how best they could use the remaining jewellery when they arrived. The west coast was mostly Catholic he knew, and families like the Argylls could be counted on for help. But how to contact people of that kind? The priests in the monastery might have had contacts, surely did, but MacFadden would not have waited. He drifted into uneasy sleep then, thinking of what lay ahead.

He was the last to waken, and when he did he was immediately conscious of cold, of loss. He was no longer holding Una, she was no longer close to him. But she came to him almost at once, kneeling down beside him, not touching him and yet a new awareness between them which was closer than touching.

'You slept well?' she said softly.

'Yes. But I'm ashamed – I should not have slept.'

'Don't be foolish. You have stayed awake so often – it was our turn to keep watch.'

Shaking his head and not really listening to the words, nor, he suspected, was she. So close he could feel her breath on his face. Their eyes telling each other – not everything, not yet. Like doors opening, with the promise that some time all would open – or almost all, knowing there were selves inside both of them which neither would ever know completely. Wanting it to be that way. And Nico, who had been fumbling with the food sack, unnoticed and forgotten, said with the ghost of his old grin, 'Is it not time we ate?'

They made a great show of helping him then, unwrapping the unappetizing-looking lump of salted meat, the hard bread, the round of soft cheese. Their hands touching. Laying the food down on the sack which covered the dirty, wet boards of the boat as if it was Tascombe's best linen cloth. Eating, while in front of them MacFadden's men rowed towards the open sea as if they themselves were invisible. Laughing at small jokes while Nico looked on with affectionate exasperation. He seemed the better for the day's rest. The long, thin face under its weeks of pale golden stubble was not so gaunt, the bloodshot eyes not so sunken, and he did not seem to cough quite so often. If we have a good passage, Ralph thought, it should not be too long before he is well again.

When they had finished eating, Una took out a needle and thread from her small bundle of possessions and began to mend the torn, muddied skirt of her overdress. Ralph and Nico watched her in silence for a few moments, then Nico looked up at the evening sky and said in Spanish, as if to himself, 'The world is full of beautiful women, most of them willing, thank God. And afterwards all a man can remember of them is that they were willing. But a few times, if he's lucky, a man finds more than that in a woman, and if he is wise he will not let that woman go.'

'She – may not want to stay.'

'Then he should make her want to.' Nico turned his head away to stare in silence at the shoreline which was no longer green and woody, but black and stark with craggy rocks running out to sea. It had grown much colder and the sky was darkening, but Ralph was not sure if it was with rain clouds or the coming of evening, and it seemed to him that the improvement he thought he had seen earlier in Nico's face was already gone. He said into the silence, picking his words with care, 'Will you – go back to Spain, Nico?'

'I would like to see my mother.'

220

'And – Maria?'

Nico did not answer immediately, and then he said slowly, 'Maria is dead.'

'No!' The word burst out so violently from Ralph that Una lifted her head and stared at them both, frowning. 'She is alive! I made the deal with Ignatius – '

But Nico shook his head. 'She is dead. I know. I think I even know when she died. It was while I was waiting for you in the cave. She was so – alive, you see. It is difficult to explain.'

Ralph knew what he was trying to say. There had been so much of life in Maria, it was conceivable that Nico would know if it had left that small, passionate body. Ralph saw the prison cell again, heard her tears, saw Ignatius' yellow face and swallowed, and it was like swallowing bile. He tried to think of something to say to the sick, wasted man beside him but no words came, nothing that was not so banal as to be an insult, and it was Nico who spoke first, who said cheerfully enough after a few minutes, 'Where to after Scotland? We cannot stay there. France? The Netherlands? Although they say that Dutch women are neither willing nor beautiful!' His smile such a parody of the old grin that Ralph had to look away.

'It is a great pity that MacFadden would not take us to Holland,' he said after too long a silence. 'There's the war, I know, but – '

Nico interrupted him impatiently. 'There's war, or the threat of it, everywhere.' His bloodshot eyes held Ralph's. 'Which side would you fight for anyway?'

'Neither,' Ralph said flatly. 'God above, I have grown to hate the very words, Catholic, Protestant! They sicken me, and yet I seem to have been born with them branded on my mind.'

'I know.' Nico nodded his head. 'But what would we do if we didn't fight? Teach dancing? Mend clocks?'

'We'll find something that is not soldiering.' Ralph tried to sound confident. 'Someone told me the Low Countries are full of refugees from everywhere. Of every creed. We might

221

find a group we could join. Or maybe even go on to the new world. We have the jewels, don't forget. Would you come with us?'

'Maybe. If it were not for my mother – ' He began to cough again. The familiar, hard, dry sound. No depth to it and yet seeming to tear at him, going on and on. Ralph listened to it and wondered if it was possible that Nico could ever fight again for anyone. He looked at Una, head bent over her stitching, lost in some private woman's world. Listened to the waves slapping against the wooden sides of the galley and realized that there was a new viciousness in the sound.

Not long afterwards they cast anchor in a small bay near the mouth of the lough. The lough had widened so much at this point that the right-hand shore was no more than a dark, craggy outline and the bay itself was encircled by towering walls of rock which seemed to lean forward as if about to fall on them at any moment. MacFadden talked easily to his men as they ate from a huge pot slung over a brazier. Now and then one of them would look over his shoulder at their three passengers, looking at Una in particular, but no longer with the sly speculation they had all shown when she had first come aboard. Spaniards' whore. Ralph had not needed a knowledge of Gaelic to guess what they were saying then, or why they were laughing, and was grateful to MacFadden for having offered her, even if grudgingly, the privacy of the leather tent behind the mainmast. But when later she had emptied her slops over the side with a coldly regal disregard for whoever might be watching, the men had looked away and gradually the laughter and the sidelong glances had stopped.

MacFadden decided to spend the night in the bay, and as it had begun to rain heavily he even more grudgingly let all three of them shelter with him inside the tent. It was an anonymous togetherness in a stuffy, constricted space and Ralph was glad when dawn came and it was time to weigh anchor. By then it had stopped raining, but there was still no wind and when they came to the mouth of the lough the men had to row hard against the swell heaving in from the open sea. The lough had widened even more, must have been fully

222

three miles across, and on their left a low, rocky headland thrust itself out into the Atlantic. On their right there was a much higher promontory, and even at that distance they could see the whiteness of rollers breaking at the foot of its black, perpendicular cliffs. Behind the headlands bare, rugged hills etched themselves against the dawn-streaked sky, and in front of them clumps of high rocks mushroomed out of the grey water.

It seemed to Ralph that they would never succeed in reaching open sea but at last they were through and out, and had headed east for Scotland. Soon afterwards the wind began to rise and the oars were pulled aboard and the sails hoisted. The galley, with the wind behind it, cut its way with new swiftness through the choppy water.

But MacFadden was clearly not happy. He kept staring at the lowering sky which had the look of evening although dawn was not long gone; at the distant coastline, black and threatening, away to their right; at the faces of his silent men. He had told Una that it was too late in the year for such a long journey. Weeks too late. Hadn't the Spaniards proved that, he'd said to her, with ships a hundred times the size of his? He was a fool to have ever agreed to make such a trip – bishop or no bishop. It wasn't worth losing a boat and maybe his life for a bit of gold he'd added sourly, and Una had not liked the way his eyes had tried to pierce Ralph's cloak. She had warned Ralph to be on guard against a sudden attack, speaking now in French as they had agreed to do, but as the hours of that interminable sea journey dragged slowly past Ralph began to realize that their greatest danger lay not in MacFadden or his men, but in the sea and the wind, and the frailness of their craft.

Una was already seasick, her face greenish grey. She lay against the open side of the boat with her eyes closed, unable to bear the stuffiness of the tent, while the wind grew stronger and the swollen sea rose and fell beneath them in hills and valleys which steadily increased in size. Then they were in the lee of a long, black island, a wall of sheer black cliffs rearing menacingly out of the heaving grey of the sea. One of the sailors began rattling Gaelic, the others joined in,

223

all of them pointing at the island.

'What's the matter?' Ralph whispered. 'Do they mean we are to land there?'

Una crossed herself and shuddered. 'No, no! They are talking about the massacre. Lord Essex murdered the women and children and the old people, while the men were away. Six hundred of them. They threw the bodies over the cliffs and the sailors are afraid of the ghosts.' She began to vomit, leaning far out over the side, her body shivering and heaving. MacFadden was quarrelling with his men, insisting on something, while they still pointed at the cliffs, seeming to say no. But evidently MacFadden had his way and the men turned sullenly to obey his orders. The anchor went over the side and the men huddled together, their arms sheltering their heads against the mist of rain which seemed to feel its way into everything and cling to the naked skin under Ralph's clothes – and theirs too, presumably, although obviously the ghosts of the murdered islanders worried them more than the rain.

MacFadden did not leave the anchorage until late evening, when the wind had begun to rise again. And not long after they had left the death island behind them Ralph saw in the distance a new, dark outline which was the coast of Scotland.

But although they could see their journey's end, they had not yet reached it, and soon they could not even see it. Across the evening sky clouds were rolling and changing shape every few minutes, and it began to rain more heavily. The wind changed and the galley ran before it like a bolting horse in the pitch dark, the bottom of the boat inches deep in water. Ralph helped to bail it out but even though two of the crew worked the clumsy-looking pump, the water continued to come. So that even the great black cooking pot was awash and had to be lifted to a place of safety along with the provisions.

It was MacFadden himself who told Ralph that they were being driven back out into the Atlantic, his big, smooth face waxen in the lantern's light. 'The woman!' he had added viciously, 'the woman is to blame! She brought bad luck!'

He did not bother to wait for Ralph's reply, his thick body

224

in its streaming wet leather jerkin, his cap still miraculously in place, battling against the wind as he climbed back to the stern. Ralph stayed where he was, half deafened by the roar of the wind which was becoming louder, stronger by the minute, while the galley rose and sank, rose and sank again in the now mountainous sea. In the darkness he could see the white, curling tips of the waves as they reared up behind the stern, and the miracle was that so far none of them had broken over the galley. In a sudden frenzy of anxiety to be with Una, with Nico, he began to clamber forward, clutching at oar benches, ropes, anything that would give him a hold, while MacFadden's men struggled to lower the mainsail.

They were trying to lash it down when the galley heeled to the pressure of the wind and the man nearest to Ralph slipped. His scream, thin and high and terrified, was carried away by the wind even before the man himself went overboard, falling backwards over the side, his bare feet for one grotesque second poised in mid-air, then vanishing as if he had been plucked from beneath by a sea monster.

The galley righted itself, hovered for another second or two on the crest of a wave, rode down into the next valley while the man's two companions remained crouched over the sail as if turned to stone. Ralph crawled into the tent shivering and Una came to him and clung to him.

'I saw it,' she whispered. 'Was there nothing they could do?'

'Nothing.'

The man who had gone overboard had been younger, friendlier than the rest, and he had told Una that it was his first voyage. And while they could hear MacFadden screaming curses into the wind Una lay against Ralph without speaking, her body grown light as if she had vomited half of it away. The man must be half a mile behind them now, Ralph thought, and imagined the black, heaving water as it rushed past them, hiding everything. Was he still alive? It would be better for him, Ralph thought, if he could not swim.

'God save his soul,' Nico whispered, and yet they had not

225

known so much as the man's name. Ralph put his arm round Una, drew her close to him for whatever warmth his own half-starved body could give her – and suddenly there was a tremendous roar. An almighty crash, like a hill, a mountain, falling on them. And with no other warning a solid sheet of water engulfed the tent.

The cold of it was heart-stopping, like being encased in ice. Ralph tightened his hold on Una's body, gulped for air and took in water instead. There was a roaring in his head threatening to burst his ear drums – and then the water began to subside. He could breathe again.

They struggled to their feet, coughing, retching sea water, splashing clumsily about in the water which was still knee high. Everything floating in it – Una's sack, the animal skins which had served as sleeping mats and coverings. The small remains of their food.

They rescued what they could, the water only ankle deep now. Went outside. MacFadden himself was at the steering oar, trying to keep his boat bow on to the waves. Two men were working the pump and the others using pails to empty the water over the side. They each took what they could find. A leather bucket. A huge ladle. The cooking pot. Began to bail, the steady rhythm bringing a little warmth back into their frozen bodies, their few sodden possessions in a small pile on an oar bench. Gradually the waves grew smaller and the wind lost some of its ferocity. By the time dawn had come the gale had blown itself out and there were only a few inches of water left in the bottom of the galley. Nico had long since given up bailing, but Ralph and Una had continued, and she seemed so tired now that she could scarcely stand.

MacFadden left the stern at last, stood facing Ralph. 'We cannot go back, señor,' he said. His voice was hoarse with anger. He made a gesture that embraced the sea, the driving wind.

'To Holland?' Ralph said quickly.

'Yes, señor.' MacFadden's face was rimed with salt, his huge cheeks which had been smooth and curved like pale cheeses were sunken, and he looked at Ralph, at the other two, with hatred. 'I will not try to land again before we reach

226

Holland – A woman! I knew what would happen! Holland it must be, señores.'

But what chance did they have of ever reaching Holland in this cockleshell? As the galley master turned his back on him abruptly Ralph looked at Una and Nico, but they seemed too miserable to care now what happened to them.

Soon afterwards MacFadden had the mainsail hoisted again and the galley, with the wind behind it, ran north through a short, breaking sea. And after a while the sun appeared, cold and distant and strangely unfamiliar. Another day of it. Another night. Their bodies turned to ice inside their sodden clothing. Only the small tent giving some faint comfort, some shelter against the knifing cold, but everything in it sodden like their clothing. Past speaking. Huddled together like sick animals, so used to Nico's cough that Ralph scarcely noticed it now. Until soon after dawn they came to the channel running between the Outer Hebrides and the mainland of northern Scotland – MacFadden growling their whereabouts in answer to Ralph's questions. And for the rest of that day and the next, and the next, the little galley raced forward, sheltered from the full force of the Atlantic by the islands. There was no rain, but their clothes which had never dried lay damply against their bodies, neither keeping the heat in nor the cold out, and the frozen pallor of Una's face worried Ralph as much as the hectic patches in Nico's. Nico seemed to have no strength left at all, could not even stand, and Ralph had wrapped his own cloak round him and made him as comfortable as he could in the tent. Even MacFadden seemed to accept that Nico must remain there all the time, and had reluctantly given Una some of his wine for him. She had managed to coax Nico to drink a little of it but he could no longer eat anything, and after the galley had fought its way out into the open Atlantic and was heading north-west for the Orkneys Ralph stayed in the tent with the man who lay there, who hour by hour grew that much weaker, could scarcely talk.

What else should I have done, Ralph asked himself, watching the sweat trickle down Nico's flushed, wasted face, and wiping it away with his sleeve. And he tried to hide from himself the knowledge that soon there might be nothing at all that he could do for him.

Una however forced him to face that knowledge, talking to him in a whisper outside the tent in the early morning. 'He's dying, Ralph. Can't you see?'

He went back into the tent. Nico was conscious but his eyes were closed and his breathing shallow and very rapid. Ralph loosened the neck of his shirt as he struggled for air, and Nico began to cough again. Ralph put his arm round him, lifted him to a sitting position and as he did so bright red blood spurted from Nico's mouth. A froth of it, running down his chin into the fair stubble which had never quite become a beard, into his hair, onto his shirt. Ralph tried to stop it with the corner of his cloak but still it came, as if Nico's lungs had burst like rotten fruit. At last the blood stopped coming and Nico lay against his arm exhausted. Ralph put his hand on Nico's forehead, and his skin was cold and wet with sweat, the pupils of his eyes as he stared blankly up at Ralph strangely dilated. He was trying to say something, but there was no sound, only the bloodless lips moving. 'Just rest,' Ralph said, forcing himself to speak calmly. 'You'll be all right.' All right. The stupidity of it. Blood everywhere. Nico's long, straggling hair matted with it. Blood on Ralph's hand, on Una's cloak. He was trying to speak. 'Take back my – my jewels, Ralph.'

'No!' Ralph said. 'No, Nico!'

'I – won't need them.'

'You will! We'll get you to a doctor soon – '

Again the bloodless lips moving. 'Take – them.' The effort of speaking so terrible that the veins on Nico's high forehead stood out like cords. Ralph felt Una's hand on his arm, saw her nod her head. Reluctantly he put his own hand inside Nico's shirt, felt the hard outline of the jewels he had given Nico weeks before, and drew out the cloth bag which Nico had fashioned from the rags of his clothes.

'I'll mind them for you, Nico,' he said. 'Until you're better.'

There was the faintest of smiles on the ashen lips. The

bloodied face turned slowly towards Ralph, the narrow head rested against his shoulder, and but for the fact that Nico's eyes remained open Ralph would have thought he had fallen asleep. He went on holding him, afraid of making even the smallest movement for fear of starting the haemorrhage again, his arm, his whole body growing stiff and sore, and he never knew when Nico died. There was a moment of intense cold in the tent and perhaps it was then. Not long afterwards Una closed Nico's eyes, whispered, 'Let him lie, Ralph.'

He felt for Nico's heartbeat but there was none. He withdrew his numbed arm at last, laying Nico down, and feeling the warmth of Una's hand on his arm with surprise, as if it was strange that someone else was still alive.

'It's better for him,' Una was whispering, 'no one could have made him well again.'

An hour later MacFadden came to them and said, 'He has died, your friend?' But it was a statement more than a question. 'He must go now. Before dark.'

Ralph began to argue, but again Una laid her hand on his arm. And MacFadden said, 'If you don't put him over the side, we will. And maybe you with him.' He turned away, but moments later was back with a length of frayed rope and a stone from the ballast.

'If you touch him,' Ralph said slowly, 'I will kill you. Give me the rope. And the stone.' MacFadden put the things down and went away again. 'Nico, Nico,' Ralph whispered. 'Try to forgive me.' He began fumbling with Nico's sodden cloak, wrapped the stone and Nico in it like an awkward bundle, tied the rope round Nico's shoulders and then his legs. Una watched, saying nothing. He lifted the heavy, no longer human burden in his arms and struggled out of the tent.

He stood for a few seconds balancing himself against the movement of the boat and the wind, Una behind him, MacFadden watching from the stern. I should pray, Ralph thought, but I can't. Forgive me, Nico.

The body slid into the water, floated horribly, the cloak bellying up like a sail, then drifting further and further astern. Sinking slowly, slowly.

Ralph stayed watching until there was nothing more to

see, far, far behind the galley. He felt ice-cold, empty. Una's voice was calling him and he turned back to her and sat down beside her on an oar bench. Put his arm round her and held her close to him.

The full force of the storm hit them soon afterwards, driving them far to the north beyond Scotland, beyond the Orkneys. Until on the fourth day the wind changed, swung almost full about and drove them south-east towards the coast of Norway, and then sheer south. The long waves sweeping them forward, the wind gusting, now a gale threatening to tear the reefed mainsail from its halyards, now no more than savage flurries which turned the sea to an ugly, broken mass. Ralph had thought that he had learned the worst of seasickness on the journey from Spain, but that had been nothing to this, a pleasure trip on a summer's afternoon. The first night of it he thought he would die. The second day and night and those that followed he no longer cared whether he did or not. He tried to care about Una, but she seemed so close to dying it was difficult to imagine she could survive, and by the third day they lay in the tent as if they were already dead. Not able to speak, no longer able to crawl to the flaps in order to hang over the gunwhale as the next spasm tore and wrenched at their bodies. Occasionally MacFadden came to look at them and to fling a bucket of sea water over Ralph to bring him round for a moment.

'Fresh water,' Ralph managed to croak. 'Give us fresh water!' as he tasted the salt caked on his dry, cracked mouth.

'My men need it all, señor.'

'Sell it to us, then, curse you! Can't you see she's dying?'

There were still a few gold coins in his purse as well as the jewellery and Ralph managed to open the purse and hold one coin in his hand against MacFadden's next visit. But when the fresh water did come, in grudging cupfuls, it was almost as brackish as the sea, and both of them vomited again.

Until the fifth, or maybe the sixth, or the seventh morning – he had no idea how long that hideous voyage lasted – the wind fell away to nothing. The sea was no more than a queasy, leaden swell. There was fog, and the sky hung over them as leaden as the sea. Ralph knelt outside the tent, feeling hungry for the first time since they left Ireland, since Nico – How long had it been since he thought of Nico? Or anything else?

He went back into the tent and rummaged in the food bag for what might be still edible, and not long since ruined by salt water. Una was looking at him with huge eyes, unnaturally bright, like a dying animal's. He lifted her head, his arm behind her neck, and tried to feed her with crumbs of iron-hard cheese.

'No,' she whispered. 'Please. No.' Let her face rest against his sodden doublet, as if it gave her peace to be lying there.

'You must eat. You'll die if you don't eat something. And – and the sea is calmer – the storm is over. You must eat!'

She rolled her head so that her mouth was hidden, buried against him.

He held her closer, cold and wet and thin as a skeleton, like a half drowned skeleton. And yet his body seemed to burn as he held her. 'We'll live,' he whispered. 'We're going to live. I promise.'

A man began to shout outside the tent and a few moments later MacFadden was at the opening, his head thrust inside. 'Land, señor. We have sighted land. Come.'

Ralph went reluctantly, MacFadden grasping his arm, pulling him outside.

'There, señor. Do you see it?'

The fog was lifting and somewhere overhead there was a hint of sunlight, as the clouds drifted and broke before the gathering strength of the day. The fog wreaths parted here and there and in one of the gaps, to what must have been the south-east, a shadow did seem to lie more solidly on the horizon, flat as a sandbank but standing higher, and motionless above the slow, uneasy movement of the sea.

'The Low Countries, señor. In an hour or so we will run in with the tide – that is one of their sea dykes. And now, please. Your fare!'

Ralph put his hand on the pouch. 'When we land,' he said. 'That was the bargain.'

MacFadden reached out, his eyes hardening. 'No, señor.

231

Now. And all that is in the pouch. Not just the chain. We bargained only for a journey to Scotland. Not to the Netherlands.'

Ralph unsheathed his dagger and held it point upwards, so that the steel was no more than a few inches from the thick, white throat. The galley master stared down at it, and then at Ralph. 'If I call my men – ' he began hoarsely.

'If your men make a move towards us, you will have a hole in you before they reach me.'

'Patience, señor!' The galley master was whispering. 'I did not mean – please, señor!'

'When we land,' Ralph said, 'I will pay you. Not until then.'

MacFadden turned away to shout at his men while Ralph sheathed his dagger. He went back into the tent then and tried to lift Una in his arms, and found he was too weak. But he managed to half lift her, half drag her to the opening of the tent, and he sat there holding her, so that she could get the air and he could watch the galley master at the same time. The fog cleared and the sun came out, pale as water but still the sun. And slowly the horizons widened to landward and to seaward. He could see the long, man-made dyke, one of the sea walls built by the Netherlanders to keep out the sea from their low-lying fields, and the empty wastes of the North Sea stretching far to the west towards the invisible shores of England.

The galley hung on the tide for another half hour, the wind too slack to carry them in against the ebb and the men too weak and exhausted to row in. 'Come and row,' MacFadden called. 'I thought Spaniards were strong! Come, señor!' But Ralph ignored the taunt.

The seagulls had begun their morning search for food, sweeping in long, grey arabesques over the dunes to the northward and the shallow waters covering the banks. The dark brown sails of a fishing boat became visible a mile astern of them and a bigger ship, much bigger than their own galley, was beating south, white topsails and jibs and spritsails all spread to catch the best of the breeze which was holding the galley motionless.

232

Land seemed to form itself out of a world of water. Low islands, dunes, flattened whalebacks of sand barring the entrance to the river, fringed by white breakers. Fish broke the surface near them, there was the smell of herring and a huge silvery shoal slid by them, dorsal fins feathering the surface. The tide had slackened, was balanced between ebb and turn, and the wind freshened in the same moment, driving them forward. MacFadden heaved himself into the bows, swung the lead overboard, shouting guttural orders back to his steersman, as he hauled up the lead-line and flung it out ahead of the bows again. Sandbanks slid by them and clusters of reeds. The galley's keel touched bottom, shuddered, drove free, and they were over the bar and in the broad estuary of the river.

'Where are we?' Ralph shouted. 'What river is this?'

'How the devil can a man know that?' the galley master shouted back in his rough Spanish, and then gave more orders in Gaelic as the galley headed towards the high north bank. There was a building on it, and a lamp burning in the window, and as they went by a man came out and shouted at them in Dutch.

'Land us along here,' Ralph ordered. 'Strike the sails and pull in to the bank.'

'No chance,' MacFadden said, kneeling up in the bows and half turning to face Ralph, 'and have you run without paying? Do you think I am simple? No, no señor! We go to the nearest landing place, and you pay me there in front of witnesses – '

CHAPTER 22

THE LANDING place was a small wooden jetty. Behind and a little further back Ralph could see the roofs of houses. Not enough of them to be called a village, and yet there were people gathered to watch as MacFadden pulled close in. Ralph had succeeded in getting Una out of the tent and they sat together on one of the oar benches. She was staring at the people, at the house-tops, and there was actually the hint of colour in her face.

'Leave our sacks behind,' Ralph whispered. 'We'll have to make a run for it.'

She looked up at him and nodded, but she said nothing, and Ralph wondered grimly just how far either of them would be able to run, but now the galley was bumping against the rough timber of the jetty, and he lifted her over the side while the galley master was still tying up. Ralph felt the planks beneath his feet then and tightened his arm round Una who seemed in danger of falling. All of the quiet watchers were men – tall, heavy bodies in smocks and long trousers and high boots. Falling back a little to make way for them as Ralph began to push his way through. Staring at them curiously for a moment and then closing in behind them to watch MacFadden. Hiding them.

A woman stared down at them from one of the house doorways. The house was raised on stilts and she was high up above the level of the jetty. Her mouth opened to shout at them – a round hole in the fat redness of her face, and Ralph dragged Una past her, down into the rough, spiky grass of the fields, half carrying her. There was shouting behind them, MacFadden's voice, and Una fell, pulling Ralph with her. But the grass was not tall enough to hide them, even if they lay down in it, and waves of dizziness swept over him so that the outline of the dunes appeared to melt into the sky. He tried to lift her and almost fell again himself.

The thud of running feet was close behind them. He looked back and saw MacFadden and one of his men, Una forcing herself to run, stumbling against him, sobbing for breath. MacFadden only yards away. Something hit Ralph on the side of the head and he lay on his back, dazed, half-stunned, the galley master grinning down at him. Ralph could feel the cold evening air on the bare skin of his chest, his doublet torn open, the leather jewel pouch in MacFadden's hand.

He heard Una scream, and saw her flailing arms, the colour of her dress, one of the sailors bending over her, raising a clenched fist, throwing himself down on her. Heard Una screaming, 'Ralph! Ralph!' He had his knife in his hand and rolled sideways, cut at MacFadden's hamstring. The laugh became a yell of rage, agony, MacFadden falling on top of him like a sack, onto the upturned knife point. It went in hilt deep, into flesh, grating against bone. He heard MacFadden grunt and grunt again. Felt him roll away. It was a huge effort to pull his knife free, and he came drunkenly to his feet, saw men riding towards them, but he scarcely looked at them. Found himself dragging at a man's shoulder, saw the sailor from the galley turn from Una to stare at him. Drove his knife into his neck, under the gold earring.

The man screamed, there was a fountain of blood as he tried to move his head, to pull away, to raise his hands. But he was already falling sideways, already dead. The horsemen were round him now and Ralph gathered Una to him with his left arm, holding her close so that her naked breasts were hidden against his body.

She was so shocked she did not seem to recognize him, and the terror in her eyes was worse than her screams had been. She began to shake, a paroxysm of shaking. MacFadden's man lay where he had fallen, but the galley master himself was sitting up, cursing in a mixture of Gaelic and Spanish, holding one hand to his shoulder.

'It seems we were just in time,' one of the horsemen said in heavily accented Spanish. A young, fresh-faced man in a military coat of brownish leather and a high-crowned hat. 'Who are you, and who are these men?' He pointed at MacFadden and at the dead sailor.

'It is a long story.' Ralph was trying to think, to guess what would be safest to tell. 'If you could bring us to the authorities – this fellow has stolen the only possessions we had left – my – my wife's jewels – ' One of the horsemen-soldiers, Ralph saw, had dismounted and had already picked up the jewel pouch from where MacFadden had let it fall. He gave it to the young officer who held it up for Ralph to see. 'This belongs to you?'

'Yes!' Ralph said quickly. 'The rogue knocked me out, took the pouch and then his man tried to rape my wife – '

After a slight hesitation the young officer handed the pouch down to Ralph. 'It seems to me that you run a grave risk in carrying so many jewels on your person, without servants to protect you?'

It was more of a question than a statement and Ralph said quickly, 'You can see my wife is very distressed. Later perhaps, we can talk.'

'Of course.' The broad face under the tall hat flushed slightly, and as Ralph helped Una to adjust her cloak and rise to her feet the man lifted his hat and made her a small bow. 'I am Captain Frans Geyl, ma'am, at your service. I regret that you have had such an unfortunate experience.' And yet, behind his sympathy, his youthful embarrassment, there was clearly a growing wonder that she should have found herself in such a situation. The rest of the patrol who had, earlier watched her distress with stolid indifference seemed to have come alive as the pouch changed hands. They were much older men than their captain, in worn-looking doublets and baggy, slashed breeches, and they looked as if they did not understand Spanish. But they must have guessed that the pouch contained something valuable and he

236

wondered how much control Captain Geyl had of them. But MacFadden had begun to shout incoherently and the captain was frowning. 'Where have you come from?' he asked Ralph with sudden abruptness, and Ralph said as authoritatively as he knew how, 'My wife is exhausted, ill. She must have food and a place to rest. Then I can talk to you. But you must believe nothing that scoundrel tells you!'

The pale eyes studied Ralph's face unblinkingly from under the hat's brim. Northern eyes, cold and grey as the sea behind them. Their owner said nothing for a moment and then the Dutchman seemed to make up his mind. 'I will bring you into Lemvan,' he said with hard finality. 'You can tell your story to my commanding officer. We will take the other man with us.' A soldier succeeded in heaving MacFadden, still mouthing obscenities, to his feet. Captain Geyl walked over to the dead sailor's body, stirred it with his foot. 'We shall leave him here for the time being,' he said. 'You and your wife can ride with us to the town hall. My men will escort the other man on foot.' But MacFadden could not stand, let alone walk, and the officer ordered another of his men to dismount and heave the galley master up into the saddle. Two more of the soldiers helped Una and then Ralph up onto one of the massive Dutch horses, Ralph holding her close with his free arm as he gathered the reins. Behind them MacFadden was shouting again. 'He is a spy! A Spanish spy!' And Captain Geyl's voice was bleak as he said over his shoulder to Ralph, 'I hope for your sake that this man is not telling the truth.'

'He's a liar,' Ralph said quickly. 'The greatest rogue unhung! My wife and I are from England. From Somerset.'

'I hope you speak the truth,' the Dutchman said grimly. 'For both your sakes, I hope so. You speak good Spanish for an English gentleman.' He gave the signal to ride on and they set off at a walking pace, Ralph and Una behind the leader, three soldiers riding behind them and last of all, MacFadden, grown mercifully silent. Ralph looked at the broad shoulders of the man in front of him, the hat set uncompromisingly straight on the round head with its short, blond hair. It'll be my word against MacFadden's, he thought grimly. But surely mine will carry more weight? Or would it?

He looked down at his sorry rags which were all that was left now of his clothes. At his doublet, his Irish breeches, torn and caked with dried mud and vomit. At his Irish brogues which had been sodden almost from the beginning and had risen in great, salt-rimed ridges of leather. He had seen his face reflected in a pool on a fine day in Donegal, and had not recognized it. Bearded. Swarthy as a gypsy's. A great hook of nose between sunken black eyes, the cheeks fallen in, the bones of them high and sharp under the brown skin, the whole framed in a mane of black hair falling to his shoulders. Who would believe he was a gentleman farmer from Somerset? And Una? What would they make of *her*? – her shaggy cloak, matted and stained like the pelt of a sick animal, her hair tangled, wild-looking. She had not been able to comb it since she had lost her comb in a Donegal bog-hole.

The only evidence we have of Englishness, of gentility, is speech, Ralph thought. Pray God I use it to our best advantage.

But now they rode on in silence. Against the skyline, at the edge of the seemingly endless flatness, things moved, and moved again, like the wings of a great bird but in a circular motion. The sails of windmills. And soon, across the uniform green of meadows he could see the outline of towers, a belfry, roof-tops. As they drew nearer still to what must be Lemvan, he could see the brick walls which surrounded the town. Lemvan was of some importance then.

They came to a massive gateway, its drawbridge opening not onto a road, but a canal, and they rode beneath a great arch. Before them the town opened out pleasantly enough in the already failing light. Tall, prosperous houses on either side of the canal, a small boat disappearing silently under a humpbacked bridge. But nothing else stirred, not a cat nor a dog, as they rode along the tree-lined path which ran beside the canal. They might have been the only living creatures in Lemvan. Until the silence, the emptiness, the echoes of their hoofbeats on the roadway began to seem unnatural, and he

238

had the feeling of hidden watchers staring at them fearfully as they rode by. As if the town was afraid. Even of them. He could smell the fear, and in the half circle of his arm Una shivered suddenly. He saw something floating in the water of the canal. Greyish, bloated. It turned slowly in the scarcely moving water, and it was the body of a woman, her skirts, her body, her light-coloured hair like weeds floating round the pale oval of her face. A suicide? Or had there been fighting in the town? The Spanish? Dear God, he prayed, don't let it be a sign. When the time comes, tell me what to say, what to do!

Soon they reached a wide square, and a high, stone building. Captain Geyl held up his gloved hand, dismounted. Walked past Ralph and Una to the rear of his party and gave what seemed to be an order. He came back and said curtly to Ralph, as MacFadden was led away into a courtyard beside the building, 'Wait here until I return.'

There was a gibbet standing in the far corner of the courtyard. Mercifully there was no body hanging from it. 'What will happen to us?' Una whispered.

'I don't know. At least he's making a difference between us and MacFadden.' But was he, Ralph wondered, or would he come out in a few minutes and order them inside too? There was no point in trying to make a run for it, with the other three soldiers drawn up close behind them.

It was very quiet in the rapidly darkening square, and just as he thought he could not bear the silent waiting a second longer the Dutch captain came striding towards them. He swung himself up on his horse and said flatly, 'I am to take you and your wife to an inn where you can spend the night.'

'I am very grateful,' Ralph replied quickly but there had been nothing cordial in Captain Geyl's voice and as he urged his horse forward again Ralph was uncomfortably aware of the muzzles of the arquebuses just behind them, and the dark, secretive water so conveniently close to hand. But at last they came to a house wedged between two taller ones, a house overlooking the canal. An old, tired house, with smoke coming from its chimneys and small windows let into its steeply sloping roof and wooden walls. Some of the

239

windows, like those of other houses, were already lit by the pale flames of oil-lamps.

'Wait.' Again there was the short, hostile note of command as the captain dismounted. It had become almost as cold as it had been on the galley, and when the Dutchman pushed open the door of the inn the hint of warmth as well as the sound of men's voices and the smell of beer drifted out on the evening air, making the waiting even worse than it had been outside the town hall. But at last Captain Geyl returned, bringing with him a tall, grey woman in heavy, thick skirts. She peered up at Una and then at Ralph as if she could not believe her eyes. '*Weduwe* Koster will look after you and your wife for tonight,' the captain said. 'I have told her to give you food and a place to sleep.'

The woman's eyes went from one to the other of them, alert and for some reason frightened, but she said nothing.

'I am very grateful,' Ralph repeated, and the Dutchman turned on his heel and led the way back into the inn, into a low-ceilinged room where men sat drinking at a scatter of tables, men who had fallen silent as soon as they came through the doorway, staring curiously at them as they walked across the sanded floor. A fire burned in an enormous, open hearth and it was blessedly warm. Then there was the darkness of the passage beyond the room, only an occasional oil-lamp lighting their way, and they were stumbling down steps and up others, a few at a time, as if the house was built on different levels. Until at last they came to a door, and the woman opened it and went inside. Captain Geyl beckoned Ralph forward impatiently. A small room. One tiny, uncurtained window, black with the evening, the starless sky. Two stools, a wooden chest just inside the door, and a bed like a cupboard let into the wall. Another cupboard recess, with a pail on the floor and a bowl with a ewer beside it.

The woman left the room then, stood in the passage with the two soldiers, and Captain Geyl said from the open doorway, 'I shall come back for you in the morning and bring you to Commander Pieter Hooft. You can tell your story to him.'

The door closed, and a key turned in the heavy lock. The clump of the woman's wooden clogs and the captain's quick impatient footsteps going away from the door, into silence. Ralph put his ear to the door and heart the faint rattle of metal as the soldiers on the other side of it rested their weapons on the ground. Avoiding Una's eyes he went to the window, but he knew already that it was too small even for her to climb through, and he came slowly back to where she stood watching him.

'So we're prisoners after all,' she said quietly.

He nodded. 'But at least we are to be fed. And you can rest, maybe even sleep.'

'Sleep?' she repeated huskily. She began to laugh, a dry, harsh sound, and then stopped on a rising note of hysteria. He went to her and held her. 'Don't cry,' he begged her. 'Don't. They won't harm us. They'll believe me.'

'Believe what?' she whispered.

He held her closer to him, kissed her, until she drew back, put up her hand and drew her fingers down the side of his face, the tangle of beard. 'I love you, Ralph,' she said softly. 'I've always loved you. Am I going to – are we going to – lose each other again? Now?'

He tried to say something, and could not.

'I wanted you – to know,' she whispered. 'At least that much.'

'We'll be safe,' he said huskily, finding his voice at last. 'I know. it. I promise you. We'll be together. All our lives.'

Her body quietened. Her face. Her eyes. She was no longer crying and he kissed her again, touched her breast, passion stirring remotely in his frozen, half-starved body, like fire seen at a distance. Her mouth was soft with love, her eyes luminous with it against the dead whiteness of her skin, and they scarcely heard the footsteps this time, only the key rattling, the door opening. She was still in his arms when the Dutchwoman came into the room, a girl behind her carrying a laden tray. One of the soldiers was holding open the door while he grasped his arquebus in his free hand, and the woman stood to one side of the table as the girl put down the tray and left the room. The woman gestured to Una and

Ralph to sit and eat, then, with a quick look over her shoulder to the doorway, she whispered in rapid Spanish, 'Are you a Catholic?'

He stood very still, afraid to answer, afraid not to answer. Was it a trap, to trick him into an admission? And if it was, could he lie about it? Even to – But the woman seemed so frightened, so urgent.

'Yes, I am a Catholic,' he whispered, 'but I am English.'

'I am a Catholic too,' the woman breathed, 'and they do not trust me either. They brought you to me because I speak Spanish, and they will question me about you – ' She looked once more over her shoulder. 'I own this inn but my man is dead – I have no son – no one – do not ask too much – but I will help you if I can. Eat now. I will have a fire made soon.'

She turned to go and the giggling and talking out in the passageway stopped abruptly. Again there was the rasping sound of the key turning in the lock, and a few seconds later, the clatter of clogs on the wooden floor of the passage, fading into silence.

'Come and eat,' Una said. 'The broth is growing cold.'

She had put the steaming pewter bowls on the table with the black bread and a round of pale cheese, and a jug of beer. Ralph was ravenously hungry, so hungry that he had to force himself to sit first before he lifted the bowl to his mouth, but after the first wolfish gulps he found that it lay like a stone at the bottom of his shrunken stomach and he was afraid that he was going to vomit. Una had taken a few sips but now she too put down the bowl, said tiredly, 'I seem to have forgotten how to eat.'

Ralph forced himself to eat and drink a little more but she pushed the bowl away, and put her head down on her arms. He carried her over to the box bed and laid her down on the feather mattress, covered her with the blankets and stood looking down at her face, wondering with the objectivity of total exhaustion if they would see another night together. Then he lay down beside her, outside the covers, as if he had been washed ashore, half drowned.

The room was cold, the Dutchwoman had forgotten her promise about the fire and a chill shaft of morning light came through the small window, reaching but not entering the dark cupboard of their bed. Una lay on her side, her face turned towards the wall, so still that for a terrible second he thought that she had died during the night. But she was only asleep, so deeply asleep she never even stirred when, without warning, the door opened. The Dutchwoman came in, followed once more by the servant girl, both of them noiseless now in slippers. This time the woman carried the tray, the girl almost hidden behind a pile of clothes. With a quick glance at the bed the woman whispered, 'We must not wake your wife. She needs to sleep.' She made a sign to the girl to put the clothes down on the chest, and beckoned Ralph to the far side of the room, away from the bed and Una. 'You are to be brought for questioning this morning,' she told him. 'The commander is back.'

'What do you think will happen to us?'

'The Irishman who was with you – he is saying that you are a spy – working for the Spanish – he is turning the soldiers against you – my servants told me – '

'I am not a spy,' Ralph said urgently. 'I swear to you!'

'Do not waste time,' she said quickly, looking nervously over her shoulder at the two men waiting on either side of the open doorway. The girl had gone and they were not the two who had been there the night before. 'The Spanish are very close and there are only a few soldiers left to guard the town. That is why everyone is so afraid – they drowned a woman yesterday because they said she was pregnant by a Spaniard.'

'I saw her body in the canal.'

'I hate them!' the woman breathed. 'I love only God, and our Holy Father the Pope. And the king of course. If I help you – you will tell the Spanish when they take the town again? You will tell their commander that the Widow Koster is loyal to Holy Church and his majesty? Will you swear it to me? So I may keep my inn?'

The soldiers were peering in through the doorway, the muzzles of their arquebuses pointing into the room as if they expected Ralph to attack the widow. Or them. They were obviously suspicious of so long a conversation.

'The fire,' Ralph said, pointing at the empty grate and

making a pantomime of shivering. 'You never gave us any fire.' He repeated the word 'fire' in both English and French as well as Spanish. One of the soldiers said '*vuur*' or some such word to his companion, pleased and proud to show that he understood what the prisoner was saying. Ralph made another pantomime of striking tinder and flint, his mind racing. Was she lying? Tricking him? Her round Dutch cheese of a face seemed the last possible camouflage for trickery or any kind of subtlety. And what had he to lose? It was either trust her, or see their one hope of escape vanish.

'I swear,' he said. 'And more than that. I have some gold.'

But she looked uninterested in gold. 'In Herzenhoof,' she said, 'they killed all the women. Disembowelled them because they had abandoned the true Faith. But here they force us to listen to the heretic sermons. What can one do? But I swear to you – '

It was his turn to grow frantic at her waste of precious time. 'You say there are only a few soldiers here?'

'Yes.'

Ralph made gestures towards the clothes the maid had brought and left on the window seat. Pulled at his own ragged doublet, making faces of disgust at his own smell. Mimicked the act of shaving, of drawing a razor down each cheek. The soldiers watched him, as fascinated as if he was a mountebank in an Easter play.

'Could you get the soldiers away from the door for even a minute or two?'

The woman was rummaging among the fresh clothes. A clean doublet, tight-sleeved. Grey, woollen stockings. Baggy, old-fashioned breeches. Her dead husband's clothes? But what did it matter so long as they were clean, and Dutch? She was holding up a razor, soap, a small mirror.

'I will try,' she whispered. 'Tonight.'

She echoed his play-acting with the razor, as if they were both imbeciles who could not understand anything except gestures. The soldiers laughed. Another moment, Ralph thought, and they would have been clapping for more. And he might have – He measured the distance to the doorway, imagined seizing hold of one of the arquebuses, muzzles now harmlessly pointed at the floor. The fool's powder had probably fallen out of the pan by now. One kick – but Una. And their filthy appearance – the first patrol to spot them – the very children would shriek at the sight of them. He put away the idea regretfully and bobbed and smiled and mimicked with the widow, laughing himself as if he had no care in the world except to be shaved and clean again.

'Tonight after dark,' she whispered. 'Warn your wife to be ready.' She laid down the razor on the clothes, pointed at the fireplace, nodded, turned away and was gone. The soldiers laughed, closing the door after her, already less suspicious of the mad, harmless foreigner.

He had just finished dressing when they came to take him. Una was awake, but he had only time to kiss her and whisper as he kissed her, 'Tonight. Be dressed and ready when they bring me back. This is only a formality – a few questions. The inn woman has promised to help us. She's a Catholic. Don't be afraid.' She looked as if she was dying, would fall forward the moment he took his arm from her, but the soldiers signed to him to follow them, and when he did not move quickly enough one of them came forward and took him roughly by the arm.

He heard her cry his name just before they shut the door and locked it, and the echo of her voice rang in his ears as they forced him along the passage, down the stairs, through the now empty taproom of the inn, out through its wooden, painted door onto the tree-lined path.

The canal. The market open now, fish stalls, women in blood-stained aprons shouting their wares in guttural voices. Vegetables. Meat. Bread. Cheese. People staring at the prisoner and his escort. A church bell ringing somewhere, and carts rumbling.

Una alone in that room. And ahead of him?

They were in the courtyard of the town hall, and in the corner of it the gibbet had come out of the night's darkness, stark in the daylight. The soldiers pushed him through the great wooden doors and the crowd inside fell silent. Then a low babble of talk broke out as the soldiers brought him through the hall and through a doorway in the far wall of it, into a dark passage.

Until they came to another door, and Ralph found himself in a small room, lit even now in the daytime by an oil-lamp. The soldiers pushed him forward and left him standing in front of a large desk, while the man behind it stared silently up at him. Behind the commander Captain Geyl stood obsequiously in shadow, hat in hand. The commander spoke slowly, his English thick and guttural. 'Why have you come to Holland?' At close quarters the still fresh-looking skin was meshed with fine lines like a fractured glaze, and the flat eyes were like wet stones between wrinkled lids; the hair was short, iron-grey, and the aggressive chin above the white ruff, like the great jowls, was clean shaven. A man of power. A man who would not be easily deceived. 'Well?'

'I had intended to go to Scotland,' Ralph said carefully. 'But we – were not able to land there because of the storm. Since the galley master was making for Holland and refused to put in on the way, my wife and I had no choice but to come with him.'

The man behind the desk sat back, folding his well-kept hands across his heavy stomach. 'You are English, is that so?'

'Yes.'

'There is war too in Ireland, I believe?'

'Yes,' Ralph said. He could not make up his mind about the man, whether to regard him as an enemy, or a possible friend. 'Yes, there is constant war in Ireland.' He tried to smile winningly. 'Hence my anxiety to leave there, with my wife. We are new married.'

'A very understandable desire.' The man looked at Captain Geyl and they spoke for a moment in Dutch, as if, Ralph thought, they were debating whether or not to let him go. He felt a beginning of relief, and found that he was letting out his breath in a long, almost audible sigh. The man turned back to him. 'We regret that you have been inconvenienced, sir. I assure you of it. But you must understand – ' He lifted his hand in apology. 'We are beset

246

with spies, traitors of every kind. You would not expect us to forego vigilance.'

'Of course not,' Ralph said. 'I fully understand. But if you are satisfied – ' His heart beating with the beginnings of joy, the thought of seeing her face as he came back to her free from all threat. Free to go. To begin their lives –

'Except for a formal question or two,' the man was saying. 'For my report.' He lifted his hand again in apology, a gentleman's condescending disdain for the necessity of such bureaucratic trivia as reports. He smiled as much as to say, you are among friends. Open your heart to us and all will be well. 'Why were you in Ireland?'

'In –?' For some reason the question took Ralph by surprise, obvious as it was. 'I – my wife – is of Irish family.'

'Of course. Of course. So Captain MacFadden mentioned. But for the report, sir. Simply for the report. Can you be more precise? You were with the English garrison there, perhaps? A soldier? Captain Geyl remarked to me that you had a soldier's bearing?'

The feeling of relief, of being at ease, had vanished. And yet the man still smiled.

'Come, sir. It is not a difficult question. Why were you in Ireland?'

'I – went seeking my wife – my wife to be. Is that not explanation enough?' A sense of picking his way between pitfalls. Damn them, damn this smiling man, his mind cried. Tell him the whole truth. Fling it at him. But he could not.

'Why, a perfect explanation, perfect in all degrees. Except – except for a matter that puzzles me. Why did you wish to go from Donegal – it was Donegal, was it not, sir? From there to Scotland, and not to your home in England? Are there not packet boats that sail from Dublin to England?'

'It was not convenient for us to travel so far as Dublin by land. The state of the country – the war – '

'But Scotland is Catholic, is it not? The west coast at least?' The smile fixed now, like the smile on a mask. Captain Geyl's expression had changed too. Like a man watching a game, a cruel one, who sees the end of the game coming near.

'I am not answerable for Scotland's faith,' he said, feeling his mouth dry, knowing his voice was too loud.

'Why, no,' the man behind the desk said soothingly. 'But I must ask these questions. As a matter of form. We are at war, remember. A war of religion, unhappily, which is the worst of wars. Your wife – is she by chance a Catholic?'

Now let me lie, and lie like a man, Ralph prayed. But he could not. He stayed silent, his throat working, staring at his torturer. He could have drawn the man's portrait in the dark.

'Why are you so pale? It is no offence among us, here, to be a Catholic. I myself was born into the Romish religion. We are not responsible for the religion bequeathed to us by our parents. You too, sir. Your father would have been born a Catholic. Is that not so? What else could he have been?'

'Damn you,' Ralph whispered. 'Get this over, do what you like with me. You have the power. What has my father to do with it?'

'Why nothing, sir. Nothing at all. Did he remain a Catholic?'

'Yes!' Ralph shouted. 'Yes, he did. And died for it.' The words echoed in the dark, low-ceilinged room.

The man behind the desk nodded as if he was not at all surprised at what he had heard. 'And you too, perhaps? You too are a Catholic?'

'Yes,' Ralph said through numb lips. 'Now, do as you please with me. But my wife – '

'Do not go so fast, sir. We have not yet quite exhausted the matter of your being so strangely in Ireland – without servants and without English money, so that you must pay for your journey with a gold chain – or rather, not pay for it. And of course, speaking Spanish. And making for Catholic Scotland instead of your native England. All this does require an answer. But no doubt – '

'Damn you!' Ralph shouted. 'What do you want from me? I am a Catholic. Is that not enough for you to hang me?' They meant to hang him. Had meant to from the beginning. Let them do it and be damned to them and – The thought of Una coming again like a wave of icy water drowning his courage. His knees growing weak under him. She would be alone. She would be –

'What do I want from you, sir?' the man was saying. 'Why only the truth. Or shall I tell it to you, instead?' And the mask, the smile dropped away and he was an executioner. A Father Ignatius grown fat, and having changed his faith. But nothing else. Only the crucifix was missing. 'You are a spy. In the Spanish service. You were with the Armada, and wrecked off Donegal. You had yourself set down here in Holland, in Protestant territory, instead of farther south among your co-religionists, so that you might spy out our defences and report them to the Spanish commander in Bergen-op-zoom. What have you to say to that? Have I told the truth for you?'

'No! I –'

'You were not with the Armada?'

'I – yes. Yes, I was. But not as you think. Not for the reasons you think. My father – Damn you all! Damn all religion! Damn all the men who make religion what it is!' He found to his shame and horror that he was close to crying. Not with fear, but with rage. With the futility of everything, of all the hopes, all the dangers run, all the terrors. All the love. And now – to hang for a lie, for the lie of the great and holy Catholic Armada, the invasion of England, the overthrow of the Protestant religion. What was there that was not a lie?

'Then tell me. Tell me the truth.'

'The truth? The truth? I – The truth is that if I had been carried back to Spain I would have been burned as a heretic. I hated the Armada, but I was forced to sail with it. I hated what I saw of the Catholic Church in Spain. Women tortured –'

'Why, this is interesting,' the man said, interrupting. 'And it has a ring of truth to it. I am not so naïve that I disbelieve everything a prisoner says, simply because it may serve his purposes to say them. Sometimes even the truth may serve his purpose. Go on, sir. So you hate your one-time faith? Your one-time masters?'

Ralph felt a stillness inside himself. A deep stillness not of fear, not even of expectation. Only of waiting. And in the stillness a small, whispering voice seemed to prompt him, gently, like a dear friend. Say yes, the voice breathed.

'And if – I said – yes?'

'I should understand. As I understand your hesitation. No man cares to turn his coat in public. Or for a benefit. But have no fear, we are not moralists, nor theologians. We are practical men. And as I have told you, most of us have turned our coats, for the best of reasons. For hatred of tyranny, and corruption, and falsehood. It is never a shameful thing to accept the truth, and the true word of God. If you are sincere, and you have a look of sincerity, no man in Holland will reproach you for abandoning Spain and joining us.'

'Joining you?'

'Why, yes. We will welcome you like the prodigal son. We will kill the fatted calf for you. We are not so rich in men that we could despise a newcomer trained in the Spanish army. A Spanish officer. Knowing all you must know of Spanish military affairs. I can think of a thousand uses our hard-pressed army could put you to. Speaking Spanish. Able to pass as a Spaniard or an Englishman.'

'I – '

'No, no. Let me speak. I have had this in my mind from the beginning. To hang you would be like – throwing a sack of gold into the sea. I have been but testing you. I knew from the beginning what you were. And you stood up to me well. Do not reproach yourself. I shall be much pleased to speak on your behalf to my superiors. Only give us the pledge of your loyalty. Renounce the faith you have come to hate. Accept God's truth as Master Calvin has taught it to us. And you shall have all the honour and promotion you could ever have gained in the Spanish service. Come, your hand on it, sir.'

Ralph closed his eyes. Felt himself swaying. And again the small, whispering voice in that deep, inner silence said Say yes! Accept! What does it matter if you change one faith for another, when you believe in neither of them? In a day or two, a week or two, I – Una and I – can escape from them and – Escape to where? To the Spanish, Catholic Netherlands? To Protestant Germany? To Protestant England? Catholic France?

Or else – to keep his promise, fight for the Protestant Dutch in earnest. Why not? For freedom against tyranny. Against men like Father Ignatius. Against men who wanted to set the *auto-da-fé* burning in the streets of every town in the Netherlands? Why not?

Say yes, the voice was whispering, urgent as a loving friend. Say yes, you fool! Think of Una. Of love. Of bedding her. Of marriage. Children.

The man was reaching out across the desk to grasp Ralph's hand. And Ralph saw himself standing up at a Calvinist meeting, saying, 'I renounce the Catholic Faith and all its Romish ceremonies and falsehoods.' He saw his father as they tortured him. Saw the young, frail priest stumbling towards his Calvary. And even more clearly saw Maria, lying on the stone floor, Father Ignatius watching her.

Why not say 'yes'? Why not turn Mahomedan? Turn anything? Could God even exist if He allowed such things, and in His name?

But he could not say it. And the man holding out his hand to him across the desk saw in his eyes that he could not say it. He made a sign to Captain Geyl. 'He will not join us, I think. Am I right, sir?'

'Yes,' Ralph said, not even knowing that he was saying it. 'You are right.'

'I am sorry. I am truly sorry. You know the alternative?' Ralph nodded.

'Captain Geyl! Have this gentleman put in a safe place.'

'May I see my wife?' Ralph whispered. 'You will not punish her in any way?' And the voice within him cried, Fool! Fool! Who could punish her worse than you have just done? How can you think of facing her, telling her? Not only fool but wicked fool! For a whim, a fancy in your head, in your so-called conscience. To throw away two lives for what? A word? And you – you will only hang, but she – what will her life be? Here in Holland, without a friend – among soldiers – war – fighting – what will become of her? You are mad! Mad and wicked!

But all he could manage to say aloud was, 'May I ask you

to – protect her? She has a little – jewellery. But without me –'

The man behind the desk bent his head. 'I will have it seen to. My wife perhaps –'

He was being led away.

CHAPTER 23

ONE OF the guards unlocked the door for him. A woman
stood facing them. Crown of red-gold hair. Billowing dress
of yellow silk. Because she was Una he knew her, but she was
so different to the girl he had left a short while before that in a
crowd he might have passed her by. She was staring at him,
trying to read his face, and seeing what he had to tell her in
his eyes before he could say a word.

'No!' she whispered. 'No!' Her hand was across her
mouth, her eyes huge and dark with pain.

The door was closed and locked behind them and they
were alone. He took her in his arms, laid his cheek against
the red-gold crown and she put her own arms round him and
they held each other close, drawing from each other's
strength until they could speak. 'Tell me,' she whispered,
looking up at him. 'Tell me what happened. All of it.'

When he had finished she said only, 'When? When is – it to
be?'

'I don't know. Tomorrow, I think.'

'Oh, my God!' she moaned. 'Oh, my God!' She hid her face
against him while he stroked her hair with his free hand, and
after another moment she said piteously, 'Why did you not
agree to join them?'

'I couldn't,' he said dully. 'How could I?'

She pulled out of his arms, stood facing him. 'Why?
Who'd have cared? There's no one in the whole world who
cares about either of us!' Tears of grief and anger spilled
down her cheeks. 'God cares. Is that it?' And when he did not

253

answer she went on huskily, 'What kind of God is He to let you hang for Him?'

'Una, please! We have only a little time left. I want to talk to you about – about yourself. What you will do – afterwards.'

'I want to die with you,' she whispered. 'I don't want to go on alone. Not again.'

'You must be strong,' he said. 'You must go away and start a new life. The inn woman will help you and maybe even Geyl or the commander's wife. You have the jewels.'

'The jewels!' She laughed, such depths of bitterness in the sound that he wanted desperately to touch her again, and yet dreaded the agony that touching would release. 'I shall be rich,' she said with the same terrible gentleness. 'So rich.' And the tears spilled down her cheeks onto the silk of her dress, staining the yellow.

'Please!' he said desperately. 'Please don't!'

'I'm sorry,' she whispered. 'I'm not helping, am I?'

He tried to smile, actually did smile, and she said sadly, 'Did you know before you went? Is that why you left the pouch behind?'

'No,' he said. 'I only thought I might be put in prison – or held somewhere – '

'Surely that would have been enough?'

'You'd have thought so.'

They sat side by side on the window seat, as they had done long ago in the schoolroom at Tascombe, waiting for Parson Dagge to come and torment them about their faith, and to teach them the true way to love God – mostly with a cane. They sat for a long time like that. The maid brought them food, but the widow was not with her. Had she betrayed him, Ralph wondered. Was that why the commander had been so certain of the truth? But what did it matter? They tried to eat, and he even found that he was hungry. Yet after a mouthful the hunger was gone. They went on sitting there, holding hands in the small area of sunlight until it began to fade, grow grey. The room already dark. And in all that time they did not speak until at last she moved and said, 'I know. You could not have done it. I understand.'

He lifted her hand and kissed the fingers, one by one. The nails all broken, the hand scarred. He turned it over and kissed the roughened palm, the narrow, cold wrist.

'I love you,' she whispered. 'I will never love anyone else. Not all my life long.'

'Hush,' he breathed. The darkness crept onto their laps, covered them. Behind them the window was a black mirror. 'Don't think of anything but now.'

And in that instant he heard the rasp of the key in the lock and the door opened. The widow Koster was beckoning frantically and in the passageway the two soldiers lay sprawled, snoring heavily, an empty beer jug lying on its side at their feet.

'They are drugged,' the widow said urgently. 'Come!'

Catching up their cloaks, the pouch, running as silently as they could behind the billowing skirts of the Dutchwoman. Down passages, stumbling up and down unexpected steps until at last she was opening a side door onto a laneway. 'You have very little time,' she said. 'They will not sleep much longer. Go across to the canal. You will find a boat, a green boat, at the steps. Go south, through the town until you come to Schliedhoven – about two hours away. When you reach there look for Jan Voss the tailor. You will see the sign of the wooden scissors outside his shop. He will help you. But hurry!'

He wanted to thank her, to give her the chain, but she had shut the door behind them already, and they were standing outside it, the wall of the next house rearing high above them. He led the way, his shoulders brushing the two walls, until he could see the path, trees beyond and the gleam of water. He waited a moment, listening. No sound of people. Or not here. He stepped out quickly, drawing Una with him by the hand.

If they could get across to the shelter of the trees –

Away to their right, from the direction of the square and the town hall, there was movement, sound, too far away to identify.

'Not too fast,' he whispered. 'Try to look as if we are just taking the air.' How usual was it, he wondered, for a

255

Dutchman and his wife to stroll out at such an early hour? There was the sound of marching. A small group of soldiers was coming towards them from the direction of the square.

They were behind the tree trunk, almost but not quite hidden by it, and he was looking frantically for the green boat. He saw it, but it was yards away, bringing them much nearer those oncoming soldiers and out of the shelter of the trees.

He was untying the rope which held the boat when the first soldier reached the steps. Ralph turned as Una screamed, drove his clenched fist into the man's face, saw the body fall backwards and then the others were on him, three, four of them, dragging him up the steps, throwing him on the ground. There was a stabbing pain in his side as they kicked him, and then they hit him on the head and the faces above him grew enormous, like swollen bladders, became one huge obscenity which seemed to take him into itself.

And yet he did not lose consciousness completely for some time. He could hear Una calling his name. Knew that he was being dragged along the ground and then made to walk. He wanted to tell Una to go back to the inn, to the Dutchwoman, but he could not speak, could not see, and soon afterwards lost consciousness altogether.

When he did come to, he was alone in a cellar. There were bars to the narrow window set just under the vault of the ceiling through which he could see the yellow glimmer of a street lantern. His body felt stiff and sore and his sides ached where they had kicked him, but there seemed to be no bones broken and after a moment he rose shakily to his feet.

He went to the door and pushed against it. It was locked as he had known it would be, and yet he went through the motions of shouting, of banging on it, knowing that no one would come, no one would answer. After a few moments he gave up, and went to sit on the straw where he had been lying. How much longer did he have? 'The hanging will be tomorrow,' Geyl had told him on their way to the inn, and he had been too shocked to ask the captain anything else. But how long had he been in this cellar? He watched a beetle come out from between the stone flags of the floor and move slowly towards him. The beetle disappeared into a hiding place between the stone flags and he stood up abruptly, unable to bear his thoughts any longer, began to pace the length of the cellar, feeling his way in the darkness. After that he lay on the straw thinking of Una. Of what might happen to her. Trying not to think of tomorrow. Hours went by. Or were they only minutes? He heard the lock turning rustily. The door creaking open. Already? In the dark? Surely not yet? For a second the light of the candle in its tin holder blinded him.

She was wearing a long, dark cloak which hid everything but her face, and the door had been locked behind her before he was over the shock of seeing her.

'Una! UNA! Oh, my love!' Holding her. Tears on his face. Hers? His? 'Oh, my dearest, dearest love! I thought I would never see you again!' Then drawing back to look into her face. 'But how did you get in to me? Where – where is this?'

'The town hall.' She was loosening her hood.

A terrible thought suddenly struck him. 'You're not a prisoner too? They said – '

'No.' She threw back the hood and her hair fell to her shoulders, a shower of red gold in the candlelight. 'I'm not a prisoner. The Dutchwoman bribed one of the soldiers with a ring from the pouch to let me in. Are you not glad to see me?' She was smiling, but she was close to tears.

'Of course I am,' he said huskily. 'I – ' He could not go on and she looked round her at the walls, up at the tiny window, began to shiver. 'We tried to – get him – to let you escape – but it was no use. He will come back for me an hour – an hour before – ' She could not finish the sentence. Turned away and took off her cloak, laying it on the straw. He saw her hand go to the buttons at the neck of her gown and he put his own hand over hers to stop her, horrified at the thought of it. 'No! No!' Like blasphemy. And yet he found himself lying beside her, fumbling clumsily with the tiny buttons until they were all undone and her dress fell open. She was wearing nothing beneath it and he bent his head and kissed her, knowing that he mustn't, not for morality, not for Church laws, but for her. Not like this. On a pile of straw in a cellar. A man about to be hanged. But she herself was drawing down the edges of her opened gown, until only his own doublet was between them.

'Take me,' she breathed against his face. 'Now. Now.'

After a long time the narrow barred window was a grey shape in the darkness. The candle had guttered out long ago. They lay beside one another, not sleeping, not moving. Only her breath lifting her small breasts, very gently and evenly. His eyes were used to the dark, could see their shape. Her pale throat. Maybe – maybe we've made a child, he thought. What would that mean to her? To bear a dead man's child? His heart felt so heavy it was like a stone in his chest.

And yet he would not have undone what had been done. How swift is love in doing, and how long in desiring, he thought. And touched her bare shoulder, stroked it gently. Like ivory. Had she truly wanted him to take her? Or had it been a gift that hurt her? She had cried out as if she was being wounded, and he had wanted to stop there and then, in horror at the pain he saw in her eyes. But she had pulled him close again, whispering 'It is nothing, nothing, go on, I beg you.'

And now it was over, and he didn't know if it had been more joy than pain. Yet still he would not have undone it. Now she belonged to him and he to her, and she would have this night at least to remember – not the hanging alone. He prayed she would have the strength to stay away from that, so that this was all she would remember, this would be their goodbye.

'My love,' he whispered, not for her to answer but only to hear himself say the words, to know that he had the right to say them. But she did answer, whispering his name, turning on her side towards him. Her arm slid over his waist, her hand pressed against his back.

He did not mean to take her again, would have thought a moment before that it was impossible. And almost a sacrilege to think of, he was now so near death and she so near widowhood. But his body did not know that, and he felt a stirring, a longing, was pressed against her. Her lips opened and he felt her breath warm against his mouth. And then a soft gasp as they joined together, not this time with pain, but with welcome, with need of him. And for long, long moments there was no longer a prison cell and grey dawn, but only themselves enclosed in their own darkness, their own bodies. Until it came to an end in stillness as they lay side by side, their arms loosening their hold.

Minutes going by, the greyness of dawn growing not lighter but more distinct, a cold definition about their surroundings. Sounds in the street outside, passers-by in heavy clogs on the brick pavement, voices. Somewhere in the prison bolts drawing, a man cursing. The night was over. Love was over.

She stood, naked and beautiful against the grey stone wall. 'I must dress,' she said, her voice grown lifeless. 'He will be back soon.' She picked up the heap of yellow silk from the floor and he stood then himself, began to draw on his breeches, the ugly, grey doublet. Until they were dressed and facing each other, afraid to speak, as if whatever they said would be wrong. And he fumbled in the pouch until he found what he was looking for. A plain, gold ring. He slipped it on her marriage finger, held her hand in his.

'The ring is too big for you.'

'A little.'

'You must have it tightened.'

'I – I will.'

The key ground in the lock and a man stood in the open doorway beckoning her out. It seemed to have grown very cold. The man came forward and took her by the arm and she put up her hand and touched Ralph's face, his mouth. Then she turned away from him, walked slowly past the man, out of the cellar. The door closed and he was alone.

An hour later Captain Geyl and the soldiers came for him, a man in dark, clerical clothes following close behind. The captain's eyes met Ralph's with an obvious effort. 'It is time,' he said harshly. 'I have brought Pastor Gosson with me. He speaks some English.'

Ralph looked at the grey face behind Captain Geyl's, saw

259

the look of conscious piety that showed even in the hands holding the prayer book. 'You need not have bothered,' he said.

'You hardly expected a priest?'

'No. I did not expect that.'

The captain turned and led the way out of the cellar, and they brought Ralph up steps and along passages until at last they reached the courtyard where the gibbet waited.

Cold morning light, and another man standing beneath one of the nooses – MacFadden, his body propped on a wooden crutch under one armpit. He laughed as he saw Ralph. No pleasure in the laughter. Only hatred. And terror. Then he began to curse in Gaelic and Spanish, almost drowning out the voice of Pastor Gosson, intoning in Dutch from his black book.

The soldiers pushed Ralph up the wooden steps, onto the platform, to the second noose. He looked round the yard for the last time, feeling that sudden abject terror himself. He saw the handful of soldiers, Captain Geyl, and the stocky figure of the man who had passed sentence on him. The pastor. A small crowd of onlookers. MacFadden stopped shouting and turned his massive head to stare at Ralph. He no longer had his cap and sweat glistened on the smooth, hairless scalp. Horrifyingly, he began to cry. To cry and to pray, sometimes in Gaelic, sometimes in Spanish, while they tied his hands and blindfolded him and slipped the noose round his thick neck.

In another moment they had tied Ralph's hands too, and covered his face with the rough hood. He scarcely felt the harshness of the rope against his neck, nor heard the weeping of the terrified man beside him. I am not afraid, he whispered. All he wanted was for it to happen, be over.

God keep her safe. Please. Please, God.

He felt the rope tighten and waited for the jerk which would be the final, ultimate end of everything. And as the blood roared in his head he heard other sounds. Shouting. The thud of horses' hooves. Growing louder and yet remote, seeming to have nothing to do with him. Oh God, he prayed, let me die quickly. And the shouting was louder, and still they had not jerked the rope. He heard horses clattering inside the stone-flagged courtyard and the shouting voices seemed to be inside his head, swelling, threatening to burst it. Spanish voices. '*Á sangre! Á carne! Á fuego! Á sacco!*'

The noose round his neck slackening. Feet clattering down the steps of the gibbet. The shouting voices drowned by gunfire. Men screaming. Someone climbing the steps. Hands pulling off his hood. A man in armour staring at him, and below them both, a battlefield. Horses rearing and plunging, trampling the already dead. The air thick with gunsmoke, and on the bottom step of the gibbet Captain Geyl's body like a slaughtered animal's, his entrails fallen across his legs in a bloody, pulpy mess. Beside him Pastor Gasson, lying like a dead crow.

'Señor, what was your crime?' The man in armour had to shout his Spanish against the noise and Ralph found himself staring stupidly for a second or two at his own reflection in the highly polished, silver-fluted breastplate before he could croak his reply.

'I sailed with the Armada.'

His hands were cut free as MacFadden began to splutter, half-choking, through his hood. 'This man, he sailed also with the Armada?'

Before Ralph could say anything the galley master screamed again through the hood. 'I am a Catholic, señor! Save me, for the love of God!'

Ralph did not even bother to look as the Spaniard took off MacFadden's hood and cut his rope, did not bother to listen to what the galley master was saying as he stared down into the yard. The guns were falling silent, the bodies of the dead scattered about the courtyard, and near the entrance the Spanish soldiers were regrouping. Not more than a dozen or so, he saw now, all mounted, all carrying arquebuses. But the fighting was continuing out in the square, and even from where they were they could hear the agonized shriek of a woman.

'I must go to my wife,' Ralph shouted. 'She is at the inn, not far from here. Let me go to her!'

'I will come with you,' the Spaniard said quickly. 'It would

261

not be safe for you to go alone.'

Running across the courtyard, past the dead, following the mounted soldiers into the square. And for a second Ralph stopped, appalled. The Spanish had mown down the people as they stood round the stalls. Mostly women, but a few men. And children. A girl lay on her back across a pile of vegetables, half her head blown away. A woman who might have been her mother lay beside her, her basket still on her arm, a small river of blood flowing from her throat into the green of the vegetables. The few Dutch soldiers who had barricaded themselves behind an overturned stall lay in a heap, like carcases in a slaughter house.

They turned left out of the square, Ralph leading the way, running again, the officer beginning to pant under the weight of his armour. Behind them there was cheering, but here by the canal there was a terrible stillness reminding Ralph of the first evening he had ridden into Lemvan. Then, the town had been waiting for the Spanish to come. And now they had come. He did not dare let himself think of what might lie ahead. If Una was not in the inn. If he could not find her.

Near them the door of a house burst open and three or four Spanish soldiers came out, dragging a girl with them. She was already naked to the waist, too terrified even to cry out, and the man with Ralph stopped and roared an order to his men. They looked insolently back at him and for a moment Ralph thought they would defy him. They were older than their officer, as Geyl's men had been, hardened veterans, their clothes in rags. But they took their hands off the girl and she ran back into the house like a terrified animal, banging the door shut.

'My men have not been paid for months,' the officer said apologetically. 'No money. No proper food. No women. The best army in the world and we have come to this.'

'My wife,' Ralph said only. 'We must hurry.'

On the far side of the canal smoke plumed from the roof of a house, and within moments the whole house was on fire, turning the water of the canal blood-red. There were people running from the house carrying out their possessions. Or maybe they were soldiers, looting. Soon Ralph and his escort were within sight of the inn and for a moment he thought all was still safe there, until he saw a similar tell-tale plume of smoke. No flame but smoke billowing from the ground-floor windows and the open doorway.

Inside the door the servant girl lay on her back, spread-eagled, her skirts round her waist. Behind her the body of the widow Koster was propped against the wall. They were both dead.

'UNA! For God's sake! UNA! It's Ralph! WHERE ARE YOU?'

The flames licking at the wooden walls of the house and the crackling sound of them growing louder by the second. Trying to remember the way to their room and tripping over steps, calling her name.

Their room was empty, the smoke already oozing up through the floorboards. Where was she? And if she was not in the inn how could he ever find her? And the soldiers were searching for women even more greedily than for money or food, setting fire to the houses. Perhaps – perhaps she had left before the Spanish came. On a boat. Or a horse – but she wouldn't have. She would never have gone away before he was –

He turned to leave, and thought he heard a dull knocking that seemed to come from within the room. 'I imagined it,' he said aloud. 'It's only – ' And then he heard it again. Louder this time. Coming from the wooden chest.

Yellow silk. Terrified eyes looking up into his. And the terror changing to disbelieving joy. 'Ralph! RALPH! You're alive! Oh, thank God! I hid in the chest, and then I couldn't open it – '

She was on her feet and he was dragging her to the door when she held back. 'The pouch!' she gasped. He ran back to the chest for it and then they were through the doorway, out in the corridor. But it was full of smoke. He must find another way. Running. Stumbling. Past windows with shutters so tightly closed he could not open them. And just as he had given up all hope of finding it he saw the door.

It opened to his touch and they were through it, could hear

263

the terrified whinny of horses above the roar of the flames, and they found themselves in a small yard where several horses were tied and gone half mad with fear. There was an open archway behind the yard and Ralph cut the animals loose, all but two of them which he tried to soothe, gentling them with his hands and voice, Una doing the same, until they had quietened a little. He cut the ropes that tied them then, and led them away, still quivering but docile enough.

They found themselves now in a narrow laneway that ran behind the houses, parallel with the canal. The horses had bridles but no saddles and when they were quiet enough he helped Una to mount, and mounted himself, both of them riding astride, her cloak and yellow skirt pulled up about her. He led the way past silent houses, yards where nothing stirred, shuttered windows. The houses were smaller, meaner. Far behind them smoke and flames billowed towards the morning sky, but the Spanish had not come here as yet, with richer pickings to be found in the houses by the market square.

After a while they came to a turn in the lane and found themselves alongside the canal again which was full of boats heading south. The people of Lemvan were escaping – those who had boats and had lived long enough to get into them; men rowing, but women too, and children, the boats piled high with whatever they had managed to carry from their burning homes.

The south walls of the town were behind them and they rode on, not talking, not able to think of anything to say. After a while they stopped to rest the horses. The flat, ugly marshes were very quiet, very peaceful, as if peace was a usual thing.

They sat together, holding hands as they had done in the inn. After a while Ralph looked down at her hand in his and saw that the ring was still there. In spite of all that had happened, although it was so big, so loose on her finger that it could have fallen off at any moment, a hundred times in these last hours, when surely she had never stopped to think of it, it was still there. She looked down at it and up into his eyes.

264

'Yes,' she said. 'It will always be there.'

'And we'll find the tailor,' he said. 'He'll help us to sell the jewels. We'll be very rich.' He smiled, and she smiled in return. Not a brilliant smile, but at least a smile.

'Rich enough to buy the queen's pardon? Could one buy such a thing?'

'Yes,' he said, trying to sound confident. And then feeling confident. Had they survived so much to be stopped by that? He had heard people say that the queen would grant almost anything to a young man who offered her enough compliments and a handsome gift. 'Yes,' he said, no longer doubting it in the least. 'Enough for the queen's pardon, and to live in Bunsery besides.'

They mounted again and rode on, towards whatever the future held for them in Schliedhoven and beyond, riding slowly, as if the winds of God which had buffeted them so hard and long had sunk at last to a gentle breeze, which might even bring them home.